BABY JANE

a novel by

M. A. Demers

Egghead
Books

www.eggheadbooks.com
www.mademers.com

LIBRARY AND ARCHIVES CANADA CATALOGUING IN PUBLICATION
Demers, Michelle A, 1964—
Baby Jane / M.A. Demers—Trade Paperback, 1st ed.
ISBN 978-0-9868914-1-0

www.eggheadbooks.com

Cover photography and design by Michelle A. Demers

With thanks to:
Drs. Mark Skinner, John Butt, David Sweet, and Charles Lee;
Captain Chris Poulton, 39CBG;
Captain Chris Thomson, Vancouver Fire Investigations;
Squamish (Coast Salish) elder Eugene Harry;
Joyce Thierry-Llewellyn, Simone Demers-Collins, Andrea Gomez,
Emily Thierry Gray, Jacquie Wilson, and Evan Llewellyn;
and a very special thank you to Constable Lindsey Houghton, VPD.

ONE

The death of a child is never a good thing. A life taken before it had a chance to bloom: surely there could be no greater purpose, no divine rationale. Claire Dawson's child was dead, and nothing worthwhile could possibly arise from such a tragedy. Her child was *dead*. And it was her fault.

Yet here she was in a house paid for by that death, a house she could never have afforded otherwise, and she was perplexed and burdened by the paradox: her son was dead by the hammer of her stupidity yet that hammer would now build her a home. In what universe did that compute? "Where God closes a door, he opens a window," a well-intentioned friend had counselled, but as the friend had never suffered anything worse than disappointment the gesture had seemed hollow, a bone with all the marrow sucked out. So Claire had dismissed the advice, and despite the flutter of anticipation in her heart when she signed the purchase agreement, despite the tingling in her fingers when she began packing up her tiny, overpriced apartment, her ambivalence remained resolute. Every victory was followed by a robust certainty that she didn't deserve to be happy, that she should wear her culpability like mourning cloth, and thus she spent her days vacillating between waves of recrimination and trickles of tempered optimism.

Claire collapsed onto the sofa, kicked off her sneakers, bent one leg back and began kneading the swollen flesh beneath her toes. *The death of a child is never a good thing!* That she should consider the alternative, should let it sneak past her defences and pose itself, was troubling. Everything happens for a reason, Dr. Fitzsimmons had insisted, but while Claire had progressed sufficiently to entertain this pseudo-belief she wasn't able to wear it like her shrink did, like a second, thicker skin. Claire was still translucent, her fortifications an illusion: a heavy fog that dissipated with the mildest of winds.

She closed her eyes and wiped the sweat off her eyelids. The day had been hot for the start of summer, the movers' perspiration soaking through their thin T-shirts and onto the boxes, and she was glad she'd had the foresight to drape the sofa in plastic sheeting. The thought of rubbing against a man's scent didn't appeal to her: male company was not something Claire cared for these days, notwithstanding brief moments of carnal weakness that presented themselves as a vague discomfort along the inside of her thighs. Such moments passed quickly, and she imagined they simply moved on to a more receptive vehicle, as if thoughts could be passed on like fruit cake until they landed in the hands of the one foolish enough to take a bite. Passion: it was the candied cherries that made the messy pudding appear enticing, that suckered you in before your taste buds could register love's bitter aftertaste. No wonder it was the cake of choice for weddings.

The thought of the movers reminded Claire of her own unpleasant aroma so she pulled her unwilling carcass up off the couch with a groan and headed upstairs for a bath. She turned on the taps that curved over the end of the chipped claw foot tub, then wandered over to the window to survey the garden below. Its beauty tempered her ambivalence. Resplendent even in the shadows of a setting sun, the garden was awash in colour or the promise of it: giant hydrangea bushes waiting to flower, stunning red and purple rhododendrons already in bloom, roses and dahlias that were as yet just a promise, and a lilac tree that held court over them all. The garden had been the property's sole selling feature, beautifully maintained in stark contrast to the original 1930s condition of the house. It had been a shock to come inside, actually, the sad, faded wallpaper the first indication of a home unloved by time and ignored by its occupants. But the house had good bones, the inspector had assured Claire, and at the competitive price of $590,000 it left her money to renovate. She snickered at that last thought: "competitive" was a relative term in real estate and Vancouver had long ago dropped any pretence of affordability. For a middle-income earner—and Claire considered her teacher's salary barely even that—this was a two-wage town unless you got lucky enough to win the lottery or land an inheritance or, she thought cynically, to settle out of court.

And settled she had. Hush funds. Blood money. Seven hundred fifty thousand dollars in exchange for her silence. A silence that had proved deafening.

Claire stripped and sank into the tepid water, then leaned back to study the spider cracks that spun a haphazard web on the ceiling. *The death of a child is never a good thing.* The thought re-entered her mind again before she had the sense to stop it, and in her fatigue the tears welled up before she could stop them, too. She covered her eyes with one hand as the salty droplets trickled down her face and into the bathwater, her shoulders shaking from the small convulsions she tried to quell, and within seconds she forgot where she was, only why, and became lost in grief.

Claire's cries crept along the attic floor and echoed down the narrow stairwell, reverberating eerily in the darkening rooms below. At the back of the house a creature stirred in the gloom, its tiny ears trembling at the lamentations from above. The sound of a woman crying was frightening yet soothingly familiar, and the creature silently wondered if the house had reawakened after decades asleep. It listened, fearful yet strangely hopeful, until the sobbing slowly subsided and the house fell silent again.

TWO

Claire's eyes flickered behind their lids as sunlight poured through her bedroom window and penetrated the thin veil of skin. Without conscious thought she turned away, her soul still wandering in that indeterminate geography between sleep and wakefulness, the place where what is and what was and what might be collide in a kaleidoscope of cryptic narratives and archaic imagery. When she awoke she would remember the essence of her visions, could write it down for later scrutiny, but she didn't do that anymore, was weary of her dreams reduced to psychobabble and picked apart like scabs. She had chosen instead to put her dreams in what she believed is their rightful place: on a high shelf alongside blind hope and indiscriminate yearning.

The creature watched, curious but cautious, as the light slowly coaxed Claire awake. It had been hovering all night, slinking about at the edges of her bed, wondering if she might be its chance at freedom. But Claire seemed fragile, had whimpered often in her sleep, and the creature feared Claire might be as weak as the others whose spirits had already been broken in this house. To reveal itself would risk injury to Claire, perhaps even death; would she prove more resilient than she appeared? And even if she were, wasn't this too much to ask of a stranger who had merely wandered, unknowingly, into the den of a beast?

The creature retreated into the shadows as Claire opened her eyes and rolled out of the foetal position she'd curled herself into. She winced as sunlight burned into her retinas, a dull ache in her head. Her son had dominated her dreams as usual, though this time his face had been obscured, a curious change she would understand only later as events unfolded. But for the moment the change simply worried her: that the time was coming when she would no longer dream of him, would not be able to conjure up his face on demand, and while she knew this was progress it felt like abandonment. She fought the instinct to bury herself beneath the duvet, to indulge in a few more stolen moments with him, and after a few minutes weighing the advantages and perils of such indulgence she arrived at a verdict, throwing back the covers with a reluctant sweep of her hand and propelling herself out of bed. She stretched her back, shook the lethargy from her limbs, and headed for the bathroom.

In the tarnished mirror above the sink she scrutinized herself, a morning ritual that had begun in early adolescence when Claire had sprouted prematurely, quickly surpassing the boys who would take another three years to match her eventual five eight frame, and until they did taunted her with slurs and sexual innuendoes. She had grown up awkward in her skin, never truly believing that her gangly limbs had become shapely or that her face was worthy of lustful examination; and although she was aware men found her attractive she questioned their judgment. Admittedly, hers *was* an unorthodox beauty: ivory skin, narrow, almond-shaped eyes and dark hair that harkened back to her mix of Viking and Frankish blood, full but pale lips, a slightly upturned nose she believed made her unfairly appear standoffish, and a sprinkling of embarrassing freckles that Claire took pains to diminish with makeup and a compensatory rise of her chin. Her beauty attracted suitors, her insecurity predators, and to her shame she'd mistaken the latter for the former with tragic results.

She pushed that last thought away and forced a smile. "Today is a new day and every day is a new promise," Claire reminded the doppelganger in the mirror, the one who counted on these daily mantras to transform themselves into genuine confidence. It was a technique Dr. Fitzsimmons had taught Claire, had stressed repeatedly in their weekly sessions: the power of positive thinking. The phrase had irritated Claire at first, had sounded like one of the many late-night infomercials she'd come to depend upon when insomnia had been her only companion, but over time she'd come to accept there was truth to the idea. "Life is about attitude," she declared, mimicking Dr. Fitzsimmons' confident, authoritative tone. Besides, she reminded herself as she pressed a toothbrush into her molars, every cloud has a silver lining. Was it possible that the darker the cloud the shinier the lining?

She finished brushing her teeth, plunged her head beneath the bathtub tap and scrubbed herself awake, then dressed and grabbed her purse: nearby Commercial Drive was awash in coffee shops, and maybe if she also bought a bran muffin she could convince herself she'd eaten a legitimate breakfast. *You can't just drink coffee, Claire; now sit.* Her mother setting a plate of poached eggs and toast on the table then hovering about, cloaking her anguish in a stream of maternal nattering. *Come back to Calgary; your family is there. What's for you here? Nothing but trouble. Come home. We'll help you through this.* But Claire had refused, determined not to return to the bosom of a mother whom Claire adored but had struggled to separate from, and unwilling to submit herself to the disappointment of a father whose standards exceeded those of compassion and common sense. The move to Vancouver had been a deliberate accident: deliberate in that Claire had applied for the teaching position posted online, accidental because she never believed she would be chosen. But chosen she was, and she found in that affirmation an unexpected courage. It was that same courage that kept her here despite the fallout from her lapse in judgment, that persuaded her to stand her ground despite its ever-shifting sway.

She locked the door and headed west. Lakewood Road was quiet this late morning except for the *click-click* of hedge trimmers coming from behind a tall screen of green velvet boxwood four doors down, while across the street two older Italian women were in the midst of an animated conversation in their native tongue. Both women had thick ankles, dark moustaches and heavy breasts, with a cheap black handbag over one arm and the other dragging a metal shopping basket. One basket was full, the other empty. One finished, one not yet started, and neither going anywhere in a hurry.

It was this slower pace of life that attracted Claire to the neighbourhood. It possessed a tranquility that suggested peace lay behind closed doors, that no dark secrets lurked in shadows threatening to explode with an unexpected violence. It screamed, yes, but of barbecues and swing sets and a fierce competition for prize rose bushes. It was the classic suburban illusion, a brilliant visage that masked loneliness here, battery there, and neglect behind that green door of envy on the corner. Every street has it skeletons. Lakewood Road was no different.

The morning rush was over when Claire reached Audrey's Coffee House but most of the tables were still occupied. Commercial Drive was a hub for artists and film types mixed in with blue collar shift workers, and so The Drive (as the locals called it) seemed to follow a different schedule altogether from the rest of the city. It buzzed this day or that night without any apparent logic, the jumbled noise in perfect juxtaposition to the quiet streets it bordered. It was as if one minute you were in your garden and the next you were falling through the rabbit hole. And Claire loved it. She loved its beatnik flavour, its multiethnic hue, its cheap restaurants, artisan shops, and used furniture stores. It was vibrant and chaotic and schizophrenic and far removed from the posh private Eaton Academy where Claire had taught spoiled rich kids whose fathers thought nothing of seducing their sons' English teacher—

Stop it! Claire gave herself a mental kick in the shin. She had no one to blame but herself for that. Dr. Eric Mellor, esteemed cardiologist, devoted husband and father, had seduced her, but she had let him. She had let him ply her with flowers and champagne, with passionate, stolen nights, with diamond earrings on her birthday. Blinded by superb credentials, intoxicated by charm, Claire had willingly believed Eric's false professions of a future together, had been complicit in lust masquerading as love. She had no one to blame but herself, she confirmed. Still, her complicity had not prepared her for the brutality of his derision when she told him she was pregnant. "You stupid girl," he had sighed with exasperation, as if their baby had been conceived with no participation on his part. "I thought an English teacher would be smarter than that."

"Well," he'd added after his words were met with a stunned silence, "I assume you'll be discreet and get rid—"

A high-pitched wail broke Claire's reverie and sent a dose of adrenalin coursing through her nervous system. She jumped in her seat and spun around to find nothing more than a new mother settling in at the next table. Claire smiled awkwardly, trying to regain her composure, and hoped her face read surprise, not terror. "Somebody's hungry."

"No, not hungry," the woman replied with what Claire guessed was a Mexican accent, "just unhappy. He didn't sleep well last night." The woman looked to be about twenty-five years old, with a youthful if fatigued round face and large eyes. She wore casual grey slacks and a white cotton twinset with a small beige stain on one shoulder. At her knees was a baby stroller that seemed altogether too big for the tiny cherub nestled within. "He's teething. Hungry is a different sound altogether."

Her last comment intrigued Claire. "There's a difference?"

"Sí." The woman dipped the baby's soother in her coffee and put it back in his mouth. "At first I couldn't tell the difference, but I found if I listened closely enough I could hear a change in pitch." She paused, then shrugged. "Now it's automatic. You don't have children?"

"No," Claire said a little too abruptly, as if the question had been a judgment. She stood up, her faced taut with indignation. "I have to go. It was nice to meet you."

The woman smiled anxiously. "I'm sorry. Forgive me. I come looking for adult conversation and what do I do? I start talking about babies."

"It's okay. I understand. I'm just ..." Claire looked helplessly at the woman and her son. "I'm just late for a meeting with my contractor," Claire lied, and shot out of the café, leaving her muffin behind.

The walk home was riddled with self-reproach. It wasn't like Claire to be rude or unkind and yet in a single gesture she'd managed both. The journey back to herself seemed plagued with U-turns. She thought of the woman who had loved Eric, who witnessed a monster masquerading as a prince and looked the other way. She became adept at compensating, at leaving extra tips for mistreated wait staff or steering conversations toward the frivolous so as to avoid the inevitable verbal slaps Eric administered to dissenting opinions. She learned to feign pleasure, sold her self-respect for his approval, accommodated his caprice until she inevitably mistook the chameleon she became with the woman she had been. Friends who voiced their concerns had been vehemently repudiated until only the most loving and tolerant remained, and those she did not lose to her duplicity she later lost to despair.

It hadn't begun like that, of course; these things never do. It had begun with a need, hers to find an emotional anchor to replace the ones she'd left behind in Calgary, his to exercise a pathological narcissism. She would later discover how carefully he chose his victims: she needed to be vulnerable, so his attentions would feel extraordinary; kind and maternal, so she would pity his marital unhappiness and refuse to abandon him to his condition; incurably romantic, so she would naively believe the fairy tale he fabricated with every loving word and amorous gesture. He was a master storyteller, a skilled weaver of plausible fictions, so capable a manipulator that when he eventually dropped the pretense even that was expertly calculated, perfectly timed to coincide with the final surrender of her heart. Unable to free itself, the heart had remained committed while the mind adapted. It would take a year of therapy to untangle the mess.

Still, she reminded herself, something good *had* come of her stupidity and misfortune. The house on Lakewood Road was no Shangri-la but it was hers. She would make it a home, a sanctuary, a shelter from the storm. How it had come about was not important. The past was done and buried; all that remained was the future and the now, and the now was looking better every day.

She maintained that positive endnote until self-flagellation was replaced with optimism, and despite the latter's minor but perceptible false note Claire managed nonetheless to push the incident at Audrey's out of her mind as she organized her new space, and by late afternoon she was able to turn her attention to the start of renovations. She taped thick plastic sheets over the dining room floor and doorway then stood before the wall it shared with the kitchen, tapping her fingers on her arm as she contemplated the best approach to tearing it down. The heavy sledgehammer hanging from her hand felt surprisingly light, a contradiction she chalked up to excitement, and when she looked in the mirror after donning safety goggles and a dust mask she found herself giggling. Claire picked the best spot, she figured, for the first blow, took a fat felt pen from her pocket and drew a cartoon of Eric's face onto the pale beige wall, then swung the sledgehammer like a bat. It crashed into the wall with a leaden crack, thick veins snaking through Eric's cheek. A self-satisfied grin crept across Claire's lips as she paused to appreciate the moment, and remained there as she took another swing then another and another until Dr. Eric Mellor, esteemed cardiologist, devoted husband and father, was reduced to rubble at Claire's feet. This is better than therapy, she thought, laughing inside. Could have saved herself *a lot* of money had she simply crushed his head months ago.

The creature watched as Claire dismantled the wall with an intriguing ferocity. With each blow its own resolve was building, too, spurred on by an inexplicable sense of connection to this delicate yet curiously determined woman. But it didn't have a plan, only hope; would hope be enough to pierce the veil?

After about an hour of demolition Claire's euphoria gave way to pain from the shockwaves that reverberated through her body with each swing of the sledgehammer. She surveyed the pile of broken lathe and plaster and figured she was done for the day. A fine, silky dust hung everywhere, coating her hair and permeating every exposed pore, and when she pulled off her goggles the ring of clean skin around her eyes gave her a ghoulish appearance made all the scarier by its reflection in the small antique mirror that hung on the back of the closet door. Claire stripped down to her underwear, left her filthy jeans and T-shirt where they lay, and headed upstairs for a bath.

She sank her aching body in the steaming water then took a breath and submerged her head to loosen up her hair. One thorough shampoo and body scrub later, Claire was beginning to feel human again. An anti-inflammatory would sort out her muscles she reckoned as she stepped into her pyjamas and dried her hair with a towel. She took two ibuprofens then collapsed onto her bed, tired but pleased with her efforts.

She was just starting to drift off when she heard it. It was faint, muffled, like the sounds from the other side of an apartment wall. Claire's eyes opened wide with alarm and darted about the room. *No, it can't be. Not again!* A weight fell upon her chest; she could hear her pulse swishing against her eardrums. The corners of the room, slung low with shadows, began to fold in upon themselves, rapidly closing in and shrouding Claire in a claustrophobic caul. The sound slowly crawled up the stairs, becoming more and more audible until it became exactly what she feared most: the unmistakeable cry of a baby.

Claire's stomach did a somersault. She sprang from her bed and into the bathroom, heaving up the Chinese delivery she'd eaten earlier. *God damn it! Not again!* For months after her son's death Claire had suffered similar hallucinations, hallucinations she'd eventually eradicated with the dispassionate knife of analysis. Their return smothered her in a dark, cold panic—until something made her stop and sit at attention. There was something new, something odd about this now. *A different sound altogether.* A chill ran along Claire's spine as she leaned motionless against the toilet, straining to hear, trying to ascertain the nature of the change when—

BANG!

Claire screamed and bolted upright, her heart a bullet train. She pressed her back against the wall, frightened and alert, but everything had gone quiet again. And then she remembered she'd left a window open in the dining room to let out the dust from the demolition, and breathed a heavy, welcomed sigh of relief: the window had simply fallen shut, nothing more. And the baby must belong to a neighbour.

Her overreaction made her feel silly, and she quietly admonished herself as she padded down the stairs to reopen the window. She slipped into the shoes she'd left beside the doorway and entered the dining room, the air still heavy with dust that floated hazily in the waning shafts of light. She covered her mouth and nose with her hand as she crossed over to open the window—when the glass suddenly shattered! Claire gasped as an unseen force slammed into her back and hurled her toward the razor-sharp shards that clung to the window frame. A strangled cry escaped Claire's throat; her feet scraped helplessly against the plastic-covered floor as she tried to find her footing. She raised her arms in a desperate attempt to protect her body from the inevitable mutilation—when another unseen force spun her around and pulled her back to the center of the room. A dark shape appeared in the mirror but before Claire could see what it was the mirror shattered and fell to the floor, the shards exploding into a silver galaxy as they collided with the hardwood. And then it started again: the frightened, bewildered cry of a baby. And it was coming from the closet.

Claire stood paralyzed as the crying pounded in her ears and reverberated off the walls that closed in on her. The cries became momentarily muffled, as if someone were trying to smother them, before intensifying again and pressing down upon Claire. She could feel the tension of opposing forces, struggled to stay upright as the room spun around her. The caterwauling continued, incessant and demanding, bouncing off the walls and crashing into Claire in waves. "Stop ... this ... please," she stammered between waves of nausea. "I ... I'm sorry. I'm sorry. Isn't that enough?"

It wasn't. The wailing continued unabated. Claire sobbed as the wallpaper began to stretch then recede, stretch then recede, as if a heart were trapped behind it, pressing against the embossed roses. Claire began to hyperventilate at the same rapid rate as the wall—when a bear-like growl pierced the air and the closet doors began to vibrate! Claire screamed and backed away, beads of glass cracking beneath her shoes. The closet doors trembled violently as if someone were shaking them, demanding to be let out. The crying was eerily distant now, as if the closet were a door that led to other, far off rooms, rooms that Claire knew didn't exist. "What do you want from me?" she begged her tormentor. "I can't bring you back."

The closet didn't answer. The crying simply became louder and more insistent again, like a colicky baby who remains inconsolable no matter how long you rock it. The child's lament intensified until it filled every molecule of air in the room, until Claire could feel the tears filling her lungs, suffocating her. The doors were shaking violently, the hinges straining against the weight—then with an angry roar the doors flew open and an energy flooded the room that pushed Claire back and she fell, tripping over the sledgehammer and crashing down on her hip. She cried out as a sharp pain shot up through her spine and caused an explosion of fury within her!

11

She grabbed the sledgehammer and came up swinging, landing a heavy blow into the back of the closet. Bits of lathe and plaster sprayed out as she attacked the wall over and over and over again, tears of pain and anger mixing with the dust to form grey veins beneath her eyes. She lowered her head to shield her face from the flying debris—then stopped cold.

Two tiny eyes, frozen in time, peered out from between what appeared to be decaying strips of linen. Claire fell to her knees and feverishly began pulling away the wall with her bare hands, praying this were anything but what she imagined.

The crying had ceased. Claire, her hands raw and bleeding, pulled off the last bit of plaster. There was no mistaking it now. "Oh, God," she sobbed, then pulled herself up onto unsteady legs and staggered toward the phone.

THREE

Detective Dylan Lewis squatted down in front of the closet and stared at what appeared to be infant remains, then surveyed the room: wall debris and glass scattered about, the broken window, a large sledgehammer cast into the rubble. "Has anything been moved?"

"No sir," one of the responding officers replied. "As soon as we ascertained the situation we contained the complainant in the living room and called you. She's pretty shaken up but coherent."

"I'll need to talk to her. Keep her around and keep her calm. Anybody hear yet from Anil?"

"He's on his way. Was at the obstetrician's with the wife when we called. Hear she's expecting their third. So a dead baby should really complete his day."

Dylan shook his head and pinched the bridge of his nose. He'd been working Homicide for five years now, seen things most people would lose their lunch over without ever tossing his, but a dead child always gnawed away at his insides. And he knew it was the same for Anil. Dylan had seen the pathologist walk out of a field carrying the decapitated head of an accident victim then take a sip of coffee, all without missing a beat, but a child on his slab turned Anil's stomach into knots. For those who worked with the dead, for those whose job it was to apprehend criminals and comfort victims, emotional distance was a trick of the trade. There was a certain cynicism reserved for violence between adults but a child victim, especially a baby, changed all the rules: distance was impossible, cynicism unforgiveable. A dead child encapsulated everything that was wrong with the world, with the universe, with the idea of an omnipotent god. No one was in charge, it seemed, when something like this happened.

"Hey doc," the attending officer greeted Anil.

"Hey. You the one that called it in?"

"Yeah. Lewis is inside," the officer gestured over his shoulder. "There appears to be a baby in the wall."

Dylan looked up as Dr. Sanjit Anil, his clothes covered by a forensics suit, entered the room and carefully walked over the rubble to squat down beside Lewis. At five foot eleven the two men were equals but whereas Sanjit was slender with delicate features, Dylan was stocky and sturdier. It was the same with their personalities. Sanjit carried himself with an elegance that belied the gruesomeness of his profession while Dylan's composure said cop at first sight: purposeful, authoritative, intimidating. The men said nothing to each other, their relationship cemented by years working cases together; it was enough for Lewis to nod his head in the direction of the remains.

"Jesus," Sanjit whistled between his teeth when he caught site of the baby. "Mummified. That's unusual."

"Does it tell you anything?"

"Likely stillborn, I'd guess, then placed in the wall soon after. And probably in the heat of summer: the area would've had to be sufficiently hot and dry to allow for mummification. And there couldn't have been insect or rodent activity until after mummification took place. Other than that, not much until we get it to the lab."

"Why stillborn?"

"Babies are born without any bacteria in their gut and it's intestinal bacteria that triggers decomp. Without it the process is delayed until external bacteria can penetrate the body. So if the climate is right mummification can take place before the bacteria have a chance to do their thing."

"How long before you'll know for certain?"

"A day for the autopsy, but then tox and trace will take another few days. DNA is backed up something awful but I'll see what I can do. Dental's our best bet: the baby's teeth will tell us how long it lived, if at all."

"How long's it been in there, do you think?"

Sanjit shook his head. "No idea. I'll call the university first thing in the morning, get the bones dated. It might take awhile, though." Sanjit glanced over and saw the disappointment on Dylan's face. "I'll ask them to rush the results."

Dylan nodded his appreciation and rose to leave. He pulled back the plastic that sealed off the doorway and signalled to the forensics team the room was theirs. "So, where's the caller?" he asked the constable.

Claire was curled up on the couch, staring at the floor, a cup of tea held tightly between clenched fingers someone—she couldn't remember who exactly—had been kind enough to treat with antibiotic cream and bandages. A policewoman sat beside her making small talk. Lewis signalled from the doorway and the officer walked over to give a whispered account. "She's quite distraught. Just bought the house and moved in yesterday. Claims she was knocking out the wall for a kitchen renovation when she discovered the remains. Name's Claire Dawson. Teaches grade six at Eastside." The officer paused and raised a flirtatious eye at Dylan. "By the way, you going to Miller's retirement party Friday?"

Dylan recognized the invitation and chose to ignore it: Becky Wilson was a good cop and a good woman but Dylan didn't like to date within the force and he didn't like redheads. "Nah," he shrugged, "Miller's a prick," then pretended not to see the disappointment on Wilson's face as he left her to join Claire at the couch. "Ms. Dawson?"

She looked up, her face a roadmap of confusion and despair. Her hair, mousy brown from the dust, fell in clumps around her face, diminishing her prominent cheekbones; and red circles had formed around feline eyes the colour of seafoam. Beneath the dust Dylan could see Claire's face was well-proportioned, and she possessed a nose one might call regal if not for the smattering of freckles that reminded Dylan of Pippy Longstocking and made him nostalgic for a childhood when adults were, at their worst, clumsy fools easily outwitted by a precocious orphan. Dylan succeeded only partially to suppress a smile, an indiscretion he regretted immediately and which would later prove portentous. He straightened his mouth back into a grim line. "I'm Detective Dylan Lewis. Mind if I sit down? I'd like to ask you a few questions." Claire nodded but her eyes fell away as he sat down beside her and opened up his notebook. "Can you give me your full name and date of birth, please?"

"Claire Cynthia Dawson. July 8th, 1981." She kept her head lowered but raised her eyes over her teacup to watch him as he wrote down her details. He had clean, well-manicured hands and his fingers were long like a piano player's. Claire followed the lines of his hands to his wrists where fine black hairs peaked out from behind the cuffs of his black leather car coat. Underneath he wore a crisp sky blue shirt, a navy striped tie, black chinos and black leather shoes. His skin appeared lightly tanned, his hair jet black and cut short, and when he looked over at her again she noticed his eyes were so dark there was little distinction between iris and pupil. "Are you Native?" she asked impassively.

"Excuse me?" Dylan replied, his annoyance evident. What the hell did his heritage have to do with the situation? What the hell did it have to do with anything? No one was surprised that an East Indian was a pathologist, so why did everyone find it so damn interesting that a *Native* Indian was a cop?

"Your eyes, they're almost black," Claire explained, oblivious to his umbrage. "They remind me of the Native children I teach in East Van. They always have the darkest eyes." Her voice trailed off as she wandered into the black depths believing, perhaps, that she might find in his eyes answers to the mystery that now preoccupied her, answers that would free her mind from the morass of questions that sucked into its stranglehold all other thoughts—including the realization that the silence and intensity of her gaze had shrouded the two strangers in an ambiguity that was unnerving Dylan: she had breached his defences, and that she'd done so without apparent intent or even, he suspected, conscious thought made her doubly dangerous. His muscles contracted involuntarily in a primal fight-or-flight response, and he responded by mentally pushing her back so he could regroup.

"Ms. Dawson," he said, raising an eyebrow, "I understand this has been a traumatic discovery but I need you to stay focused."

The strategy worked, wrenching Claire out of her reverie with an embarrassing snap. "I-I'm sorry. I'll try to do better." She found a spot on the floor and stared at it, a flush of crimson in her cheeks.

Dylan kicked himself. He needed to keep Dawson on his side, to gain her trust, and he was letting personal issues mar his technique. *Focus!* he ordered himself as he reassured Claire with a smile. "No offence taken," he lied. "But perhaps we should stick to the matter at hand." He shifted back to his practiced, professional tone. "I understand you were taking out the wall to renovate the kitchen when you found the remains?"

"Yes."

"You hurt your hands," he said gently, eyeing the bandages.

Claire glanced down at her damaged fingers. The image of her frantic hands clawing at the wall came flooding back and she struggled to contain her despair. She nodded: yes.

"Did you tear out the closet wall?"

She nodded again.

"I'll have to ask you to provide fingerprints so we can separate you from possible suspects," he said in the same gentle voice. "Are you okay with this?" It was a courtesy question, really, since Dylan had a warrant, but it was always best to create the illusion of cooperation.

"Yes, I understand."

"I'll have Officer Wilson attend to that later." Dylan paused, then slyly shifted his approach. "I'm curious, why were you punching out the closet? It's not on the shared wall."

Dylan registered the startled look that swept across Claire's eyes and the paling of her skin. "Oh, um, well ..." Panic was paralyzing her tongue. What could she possibly say that wouldn't sound insane? She opted instead for evasion, staring into her teacup in the hope he'd forget the question and move on.

He didn't. "Ms. Dawson, there's a dead baby in your wall."

Claire scrambled for a plausible response. "There was a scratching noise. I thought maybe it was a rat's nest. I overreacted."

Dylan looked at her sharply. He'd been a cop long enough to know when he was being lied to but he couldn't pinpoint a reason why she was holding back. After all, it was Dawson who'd called police, who opened the door to the investigation. He chose another avenue. "Who did you buy the house from?"

"Whom" thought Claire to herself, and almost corrected him before remembering she wasn't talking to one of her students. The paralysis had ceased and she was able to look him in the eye again, his grammatical error having rendered him less threatening. It was petty, really, that an inconsequential error could make her feel stronger—a little superior even—and yet she didn't want to lose that feeling, didn't wish to cower again beneath his gaze. "It was a court ordered sale. Power of attorney or something like that. I never met the owners, or even the seller. Just their agent. He said his client was a lawyer. I can get the purchase agreement for you, if you like."

"Where is it?"

"Upstairs."

"I'll need to accompany you, if you don't mind."

The request caught Claire off guard and she became acutely aware she was losing ground again. "Is that really necessary?" she asked, uncomfortable. "My bedroom is upstairs."

"I understand," Dylan replied, and though his smile was meant to reassure she knew he was evaluating her. It was nothing more than a cop's professional mistrust and yet she felt crushed under the weight of suspicion. The sensation was so intense she wasn't even aware she had stopped breathing until Dylan glanced over her shoulder and hollered "Hey Wilson" and Claire's breath returned with a gasp. The female officer appeared in the doorway. "Could you please accompany Ms. Dawson upstairs. She needs to retrieve a document."

Claire smiled awkwardly at Officer Wilson as the two women headed upstairs. "I need to use the bathroom," Claire said to what felt like her captor. "May I have my privacy or do you need to accompany me there, too?"

"Relax, Ms. Dawson, it's just procedure. I'll wait outside the door."

Claire disappeared into the bathroom, sat down on the toilet and used the moment to collect herself. That Detective Lewis had, even fleetingly, considered her suspect rankled her: if he knew what she had suffered, if he saw her scarred body and wounded heart he would understand the crime he was investigating was beyond her comprehension, that she was incapable of anything so hideously inhuman. Did he know about her past? But even if he did, how could he equate carelessness with murder?! How could he be so quick to judge her?

She was shaking now, terrified to face him again yet knowing she had no choice. She flushed the toilet and washed her hands then splashed cold water on her face until she felt her calm return sufficiently, opened the bathroom door and addressed Wilson. "The document is over here," Claire gestured toward the second bedroom where she had dumped all her office boxes. She grabbed the purchase agreement then the two women headed back downstairs. Wilson gave Lewis a surreptitious "nothing unusual" signal as she and Claire re-entered the living room then Wilson disappeared back into the kitchen.

"The seller was Benjamin Keller," Claire read as she crossed back over to the couch. "The registered owners were Therese and Armin Keller."

Shit! thought Dylan, hoping it wasn't the Benjamin Keller he knew. "Was there anything in the property disclosure to indicate past renovations?"

"No," Claire answered, handing the agreement to Dylan and picking up her teacup. "The house is in original condition. That's why I was able to afford it." She watched him intently as his dark eyes skimmed over the purchase agreement and his slender fingers wrote down the particulars in his notebook. He was aware of her eyes on him but he didn't let on, reading through the document as if it might hold something of use beyond the names and addresses of the sellers. He knew it wouldn't, of course, but in the moments that elapsed he also knew Claire's anxiety was increasing again, ensuring he retained the upper hand he was certain he'd regained.

"Speaking of which, how does a single teacher afford her own home?" He asked the question as if he were simply curious, glancing up from the papers only briefly to register her reaction. In truth he *was* curious: he was always curious when single people bought property: had they resigned themselves to remaining that way? Houses were for families, in his book. A place to raise your kids, give them security and stability. Until he committed to that he'd never commit to a mortgage: he didn't see the point.

Claire's face paled at the question. That was twice now. "I bought it with the proceeds of a lawsuit," she replied, and in her voice Dylan detected a minute tremor, like the subtle shaking of the floor just before an earthquake hits. What was she hiding from him?

"May I ask the nature of the lawsuit?"

"I don't see how that's relevant," she replied cautiously, her fingers tightening around her teacup.

"*I* decide what's relevant, Ms. Dawson," Dylan snapped before he could catch himself. It was a substantial error: Claire's face was suddenly ablaze and she struggled to contain her indignation.

"I'm bound by a confidentiality agreement," she explained as evenly as she could manage, "so unless you get a court order I can't reveal the details."

"Fair enough," shrugged Dylan. And I just might do that, he added in his head.

"Do you have anything else for me, detective?" Claire asked, still clearly irritated.

"Not at the moment. But I may have to question you again as the investigation proceeds. I'd appreciate it if you stayed in town or provided me with notice if you go away." The moment he spoke Dylan regretted his tone: he'd been aiming for respectfully authoritative but what came out was surly and imperious.

Claire felt the hackles on her neck stand. "Fine," she lobbied back. "And how much longer will your investigators be in my house?"

"Until they're done," came the brusque reply. "It would be best if you stayed elsewhere tonight. Is there someone you can call?"

The question knocked the hauteur out of Claire. She looked stunned, as if she'd been slapped. She stared at the floor and bit her lip as the ground swallowed her whole. When she finally spoke again her voice was small and quiet. "No one I wish to impose upon."

Dylan's brow furrowed. The woman was all over the map; he couldn't keep up. One minute she was testing his patience and the next she was like an injured child he wanted to shield from harm. She had him off-kilter, shy of his game. And he didn't like it one bit. But what to do with her? He had the authority to kick her out of the house until Forensics were finished but he didn't want to create an adversary, especially so early in the game: he might need her later. And he had already antagonized her; any more and he might lose a potential asset. Dylan sized her up, calculated the risk and decided it would be advantageous not to burn any more bridges. Still, he would need to set firm boundaries. "I can allow you to stay here," he said with counterfeit contrition, "as long as you provide me with assurances you will not interfere with my team or attempt entry into the back room until I've released the scene." Claire nodded her agreement without looking at him. "And I need a number where you can be reached."

Her voice still a whisper, Claire gave him the number to the house and her cellphone. Finished for now, Dylan rose to leave. He called out again for Officer Wilson, who appeared so quickly Dylan wondered if she'd been lurking behind the doorway. "I need you to fingerprint Ms. Dawson for a comparison set and help her write up an official statement. And she'll require company until Forensics are done." Wilson nodded and Dylan turned his attention back to Claire. "Ms. Dawson?" Claire looked up and he saw in her eyes a sorrow he hadn't expected and which made him swallow his words. "We'll talk again," was all he managed to say. She nodded and went back to staring at the floor. Dylan felt like a bully.

He almost made it outside before a sense of shame stopped him just shy of the front door. He turned his head to face Claire. "I'm half," he offered, by way of apology.

She looked up, puzzled. "Half what?"

"Half Native," he admitted with a conciliatory gesture. "I'm half Native."

Claire smiled. "What's the other half?"

Dylan shrugged, "Dunno," then walked out the door.

Dylan got into his unmarked cruiser, put the key in the ignition then changed his mind. He leaned back in his seat, rested his elbow on the door and began an internal review. How could that have gone so awkwardly awry? He was trained to stay even-tempered, to keep his emotions in check, and yet the woman had managed to crawl under his skin without even trying, had upset his equilibrium and left him scrambling to maintain his artfully crafted composure. He felt outwitted, trumped. And it was pissing him off.

He tried to cast off the shackles of discomfort by forcing a shift in thought to more practical issues. The baby in the wall wasn't Dawson's— both experience and gut instinct told him so—and yet he couldn't officially rule that out until any connection between her and the previous owners had been disproved. And she was definitely hiding something.

But then aren't we all? he contemplated next. He hadn't lied when he said he didn't know his father's heritage but he did know his father had been white. White and drunk. His mother had been drunk, too, when Dylan had been conceived, had sobered up only long enough to have him before abandoning him to his grandmother. He'd been lucky in that respect, though, and he knew it: his *ta'ah* was a strong, proud and affectionate woman who raised him to respect himself, his elders, and the world around him. She never tired of telling him he could be whatever he wanted to be, never judged his dreams or squashed his imagination, not even when he was five and announced he wanted to grow up to be an eagle. Ta'ah had just smiled and said chances are he already was one, he just didn't know it yet.

Dylan smiled at the memory then made a promise to himself to visit her on Sunday, maybe take her out for lunch after church. That was another thing about his *ta'ah*: she was a woman who deeply loved the Creator. Her faith was an odd mix of Catholicism and traditional Coast Salish spirituality; and when he'd asked Ta'ah how could she still attend church after the horror of residential school, she had simply shrugged and said she thought Jesus would've made a good Indian.

Dylan started the car and headed for the station. He'd get his preliminary report written then head home. Tomorrow was going to be a long day.

FOUR

On the outskirts of a forest, at the edge of a river, a lioness gazed upon her reflection in the water but saw only a common domesticated tabby. The image troubled her for she recalled having been born a lioness, yet clearly the river did not lie. "You seem confused, my Lady," mused a large female bear as it ambled over to the riverbank and sat down beside the feline.

"What do you see, Bear, there, in the water?" asked the lioness.

"I see a lioness who thinks she's a cat," replied Bear.

"Hmmm, yes," murmured the lioness. "Most curious, don't you think?"

"Not curious," shrugged Bear. "Unfortunate. Your power, your pride: these were your birthright. You should reclaim them."

"But how does one reclaim what the king has taken?"

"The king's authority is not absolute," pronounced Bear. "And conditional love is not love."

"I was expected to do better," the lioness said sadly. "I failed. Should there not be a price for my shortcomings?"

"Perhaps it is the king who suffers shortcomings," Bear said dismissively. The lioness laughed lightly. "I envy your certainty, my friend."

"Reclaim your power, my Lady. You will need it." And with that Bear took her leave of the lioness. And Claire awoke from her dream.

Most curious, was her first semi-conscious thought, but the dream was quickly lost as the events of the night before slipped stealthily into her consciousness and pushed aside all images except those of the baby. In its mummified state it had looked almost simian, its skin blackened and shrunken tautly over its skull. From her perch on the sofa Claire had watched as the small body bag was carried out to the waiting van, and hours later, when the door had closed behind the last of the officers, Claire had sat in the dining room on the dusty pine chair and finally let flow the tears she had fearfully kept in check.

She glanced down at her bandaged fingers, the black ink on their tips still evident despite her best efforts with a fresh lemon and vigorous scrubbing. The act of being fingerprinted had felt invasive, the air thick with imagined accusation made all the more pervasive by Officer Wilson's barely concealed irritation, which Claire, not having witnessed the awkward exchange earlier between Wilson and Lewis, had interpreted as suspicion and contempt. The repressive atmosphere had made Claire nervous, and she had strained to hear the chatter of the police over the din of the television she'd pretended to watch, terrified they would find evidence of the guilt she carried about her person and believe it relevant to the case.

But now, as the morning light banished the shadows that had given form to her fears, the trauma of finding the baby was yielding to a curiosity that perplexed Claire: she felt oddly detached, and she wondered if her distance were a coping mechanism or something more disturbing, like relief. Relief that this hadn't been all in her mind; that she wasn't descending into madness or even over-imagination. That her house was haunted seemed strangely concrete, not preposterous as a sceptic would insist but a rational explanation, though one which now raised its own disturbing questions: Why now? Why Claire? Was there a relationship between her dead child and this one, some cosmic connection Claire didn't yet understand? Or was the relationship illusory, merely the kind of synchronicity that beguiles the gullible into seeing patterns in the universe where none exist?

And yet the former owners had lived here for decades, Claire reminded herself as she rolled out of bed and headed for the bathroom; surely they wouldn't have stayed had they suffered the same haunting on a daily basis. So then now what? What more did the spirit expect beyond discovery? What if it returned, demanding more?

And there had been something else in that room, something sinister. It had tried to maim Claire, had tried to smother the child's cries. What if it came back, too? The thought made the hair on Claire's arms rise, and her first instinct was to call back the movers and run; but something else was rising in her too, an unexpected fortitude that rapidly swelled while she scrubbed her hair and face, and by the time she rinsed out the last of her toothpaste she was in a fighting spirit: something had tried to harm her and something had caused a child to suffer, and damn it if Claire were not going to get to the bottom of both offenses!

But how? And where to begin?

Reclaim your power. What? thought Claire, and then fragments of her dream came floating back: a lioness gazing into the river, a bear, a conversation about ... what was it again?

Lost in thought, Claire tromped down the stairs only to be surprised by the smell of fresh coffee and cinnamon. Puzzled, she followed her nose to the living room and found a plump, grey-haired woman transferring a coffee pot and a Bundt cake from a tray to Claire's small pine table.

"Hello?" Claire asked.

The elderly woman spun around and clutched at her chest. "Oh, dear, you startled me," she gasped. Her accent was German, faded but still noticeable. She was wearing a lace-collared floral print dress, gathered at the waist, and flat, thick leather sandals over sagging stockings. Her face, wrinkled with age and framed by wispy grey hair pinned back in a bun, was bright and gentle.

Claire figured the surprise should be the other way around. "Who are you and what are you doing in my house?" she asked, polite but confused.

The woman chuckled and nodded earnestly. She struck Claire as the animated type, the kind who spoke with the grand gestures and exaggerated expressions of one who believes all of life is entitled to the exuberance of a thespian. "Of course, forgive me. I thought you might appreciate some sustenance after all the excitement of last night. I knocked on the back door but you mustn't have heard. It was unlocked so I thought I would just leave this for you with a note. Though I'd think you'd be more careful after a break-in."

"Break-in?"

"Yes, the police, they came and asked me questions. I asked them if the house had been burgled and they said"—she paused and raised a finger to pursed lips—"well, actually they didn't say anything, now that I think about it. But you really should lock your door."

"Thank you but who are you?"

"Oh, forgive me again," she said, clasping her hands together. "Yes, yes, of course you wouldn't remember me from a passing wave. I'm Frau Müller. I live next door."

The image of the elderly woman glancing up from her flowerbeds and waving as Claire had walked past with the home inspector came back to her. "Oh, yes, I remember now. You were gardening."

Frau Müller nodded enthusiastically. "Getting my spring bulbs in. A bit late this year, I'm afraid. My arthritis was acting up."

There was a moment of awkward silence before Claire remembered her manners, and sensed a possible opportunity. "I'm sorry. Would you like to join me for some of your cake and coffee? They both smell wonderful."

Frau Müller's face lit up at the invitation. She'd been hoping for just that: it's not often one sees so many police cars and men in funny white suits poking about and loading heavy black bags into a van. Her weekly ladies' Rumoli game had been abandoned for the window and they were all expecting an update at bridge on Friday. What would they think of her if she attended empty-handed?

Claire rummaged about in a box and pulled out two dessert plates and forks, coffee mugs, and a knife. "Would you like cream? I have some in the fridge. Sugar might be a tad more difficult. I haven't unpacked all my staples yet."

"Don't fret. Black is fine for me." Frau Müller cut two large slices of Bundt cake as Claire poured the coffee and set the cups down on the table.

"How long have you lived next door?" she asked, settling into a chair.

"Oh, a very long time. Since 1939. My parents fled Hitler's Germany. We were liberals, and," she added weightily, "we were Jews. In 1950 I became engaged and my parents gave me the house as a gift. They moved nearer to the university. My father was a professor."

Claire perked up. If Frau Müller has been living next door for seventy years she must know almost everything about this house. Maybe even something about the baby. "What can you tell me about this house?" Claire asked, managing to conceal her anticipation. "I'd love to know its history."

"Oh, let me see now. It was built in the early thirties, if I remember correctly. I was told there was a smaller house before, a shack really, and the owners tore it down when they started to do well. They were also German. Everybody stuck together in those days, Germans in these few blocks, Ukrainians over there, Russians a few blocks north. It wasn't until after the war that the Italians took over."

"The original owners, then, was that the Kellers?"

"No, that was the Zimmermanns. The Kellers moved in the year before I got married. Came after the war. Elsi and Franz Keller and their two boys, Armin and Randolf. Armin was the eldest, at twenty-two. Randolf was a year or two younger. They were only here for a few years when Armin got married. He bought the house from his parents. I don't know where they and Randolf went. Our two families didn't talk much." Her face puckered as if she'd bitten into a lemon. "Armin had been a member of *Hitler-Jurgend*, the youth wing of the party."

"Did Armin have any children?"

"Two. A boy and then a girl. The boy was the reason for the marriage, though it wasn't polite to talk about that in those days. Karl was born about five months after the wedding. Elisabeth came a few years later. Such a beautiful little girl. So different from her mother. At least at the beginning."

"What do you mean?"

"Oh," Frau Müller replied, lowering her voice and leaning across the table as if someone might be listening, "Therese was such a *Mauerblümchen*—"

"A what?"

"A wallflower. She always looked like she wanted to disappear. There was a brief period when I thought I should at least try to be friends but any time I said hello she would just tuck her head down and keep walking."

"And Elisabeth?"

"Oh, Elisabeth," Frau Müller sat back up and smiled, "she was such a charmer." The image of the little girl, her brown hair falling about her smiling face as she turned cartwheels on the grass, filled the elderly woman's memory. "So full of life and energy. She had a cousin—Benjamin was his name—they were about the same age and they would play for hours in the garden together, always laughing. So much laughter. I used to give them apples from my tree." Frau Müller paused, the smile fading from her lips. "It was so sad what happened to her." She shook her head and sipped her coffee.

Claire's curiosity piqued. "What happened?"

"She went crazy. I think the family was touched that way. Therese certainly wasn't right." Frau Müller feigned discomfort. "I don't wish to disparage them; it's just the truth."

"Of course," Claire said reassuringly. "When was this?"

"Well now, Elisabeth must have been about thirteen, I guess, when things went wrong." The sparkle of anticipation in Claire's eyes made Frau Müller smile inside: she loved a captive audience. She intentionally took a sip of her coffee to create more drama before continuing. "They had to take her out of school: she was becoming disruptive. Poor thing. Benjamin stopped coming to the house to play. The whole family stopped visiting, actually. Elisabeth never left the house again. Not until Armin had his stroke."

The wheels in Claire's head were turning. Was it possible Therese had had another baby, one she didn't want, one that also "wasn't right"? "Did Therese ever have any more children?" Claire asked.

"No, just the two."

"Are you *sure?*"

"Yes. Why?" Claire saw the expectant look in Frau Müller's eyes, knew she was hungry for some reciprocation, a little insider information about the "excitement of last night," the mention of which had not passed by Claire. She paused, debating in her head whether to tell Frau Müller about the infant remains, then concluded it would only be a matter of time before it reached the media, so why not?

"Last night I found the remains of a baby in the wall of the dining room." Frau Müller gasped and clutched at her chest. "Are you sure you never saw Therese pregnant again?"

Frau Müller nodded. "Yes, but I suppose I *could* have missed something." Her face was flushed with shock but it was shock tempered with a good dose of excitement. She couldn't wait for Friday's bridge game.

And Claire couldn't wait to talk to Detective Lewis again.

ভ

Dylan was contemplating a late lunch. He'd had a productive day so far but now he was on hold, waiting to hear from Anil and the university's Department of Forensic Anthropology. Anil had done as promised and by nine a.m. a section of the baby's femur was in an accelerator mass spectrometer. He'd already determined sex—a girl—but age was the domain of the forensic dental specialist and the man for the job was at a conference in Boston until Monday. There would be a DNA profile in a week but until Dylan found a relative to match it to the profile wouldn't be much help in identifying the remains. As for cause of death, Anil wouldn't even be able to guess until later in the day.

Dylan hated this part of investigating, this lull between questions and answers. He wasn't a particularly patient man, a fact obscured by what appeared to be a precise and methodical approach to solving whatever mystery was presented to him. He considered all angles, contemplated all motives, and even when he'd ruled out a possibility he kept his mind open to the unexpected twist that sometimes sprang from nowhere to land a swift uppercut to the jaw. Those were especially painful: the ones he didn't see coming just when he thought he had it all figured out.

Dylan drummed his fingers on his desk and glanced over the property search he had procured first thing that morning. Prior to Dawson the house had had only three owners, the Zimmermanns and then two generations of Kellers. This certainly narrowed the search for possible perpetrators or at least accomplices after the fact, assuming the house or its rooms had never been rented out. Dylan prayed this was the case: up until the war Commercial Drive had been a hub for migrant workers and if that house had known any of them it could make identifying Baby Jane essentially impossible. On the upside, Dylan considered, all the Zimmermanns who had lived there were deceased, as were Elsi and Franz Keller, so that narrowed the list a little bit more, though if the remains dated that far back Dylan would likely have nothing but dead suspects and a lot of unanswered questions.

The younger Kellers were a more interesting lot. Randolf was charming widows in a retirement community in Orlando. Therese and Armin were both in assisted living facilities, but not the same one Dylan had noted with curiosity, while daughter Elisabeth was in Bellevue Home for Psychiatric Care. Karl was dead: Bosnia, 1993. Then there was Benjamin Keller, star criminal defence attorney. Dylan bristled. He'd probably need a warrant just to *talk* to Ben. No, Dylan would start with the old folks first, he calculated, maybe get lucky and get some info before Benjamin got wind of the situation. The daughter was another story: Dylan would have to dance around hospital staff for her, and then it all depended on just how nuts she was.

As for Dawson, so far Dylan couldn't see any connection between her and the Kellers beyond buying their house. She hadn't even lived in Vancouver until four years ago when she'd left substitute teaching in Calgary for a part-time position at the private Eaton Academy over in Shaughnessy. She now taught full-time at the inner city Eastside Elementary—a demotion despite the pay raise, Dylan thought with a cynical chuckle. She was popular with the children, a "dynamic educator who inspired her students to dream big" the principal of Eastside proclaimed; they'd been fortunate to find her. Dylan had run Dawson's name through all the crime databases but none had spit out anything more interesting than a minor speeding ticket, which had been promptly paid he'd noted with a snort. His contact in Calgary had nothing to add on her. The only blotch on an otherwise immaculate sheet seemed to be "a personal indiscretion which had resolved itself" the headmaster at Eaton had volunteered before thinking otherwise and refusing to elaborate, citing privacy concerns.

Dylan put the property search aside and picked up the preliminary forensics report, hoping by some miracle something new had been added in the ten minutes since he last looked at it. There hadn't, of course, and so he dwelled instead on the one bit of good news the report contained: no evidence of further victims in the Dawson home or its grounds had been found: a cadaver dog had scoured the house from the attic eaves to the darkest recesses of the crawl space without pause, and the garden had yielded up nothing more than a few old chicken bones. So if Baby Jane had been murdered—and Dylan didn't know yet if she had—at least it seemed unlikely her death had been at the hands of a serial killer.

Dylan's musings were interrupted by the phone. He snapped up the receiver, hopeful for test results, and was disappointed when he heard the voice of the front desk clerk. "Detective Lewis, there's a Claire Dawson here to see you." There was a momentary pause for effect before she added, "She says it's about last night."

Dylan rolled his eyes at the accusation in the clerk's voice. Stupid old bat assumed this was a personal visit and was, as usual, jumping to conclusions. She was a constant irritation to everyone in the department but that didn't seem to be sufficient grounds for dismissal. There were some, Dylan knew, who secretly counted the days until her retirement, and when she'd had emergency gallbladder surgery last spring there had been a private betting pool on her prognosis. Dylan had put a fiver on fatal septicaemia.

"Tell her I'll be right down."

His mood soured by the clerk, Dylan found himself anticipating further irritation as the elevator descended to the main floor. The last thing he needed was Dawson poking her nose in his investigation so unless she had something pertinent to tell him this was going to be a short visit.

He found Claire pacing in the lobby under the accusing eye of the desk clerk. "Ms. Dawson?"

She turned around to face him and Dylan felt a rush of air hit his lungs like the sticky, portentous wind that heralds a storm. Her beauty was seductive in its simplicity: eyes that in the greyed light of trauma had been the colour of seafoam were a striking peridot in the sun; and her face, all dewy skin and rosé lips, was framed by cinnamon-sprinkled chestnut hair that shimmered and tumbled down onto the shoulders of a crisp white shirt opened to her breasts. His gaze fell to her cleavage then followed the lines of her body down, past the waist of low-rise jeans to curved hips and shapely legs until it came to rest on unpainted toenails that peeked out from a pair of strappy flats Dylan judged to be expensive. His eyes longed to make a slow assent but he corrected himself and quickly raised them to her face, which to their shared embarrassment had flushed beneath his unabashed inspection.

Claire swallowed nervously. "Detective Lewis, I'm sorry to come unannounced like this. You didn't leave me a number and I have some new information I thought you might find useful."

"Have a seat." Dylan gestured to the nearby deck of chairs and watched her as she moved ahead of him. Her hips swayed tantalizingly and the temptation to flirt caught him before he could smother it. "Where were you when I was in school? I would have paid more attention to Hemingway." Claire smiled uneasily as she sank into a chair, and Dylan immediately regretted his aloofness. "Sorry." He paused to underscore the sincerity of his apology, then pulled out his notebook. "You said you have new information?"

The question offered a hasty exit from the awkwardness that had developed between them, and Claire launched into a spirited recounting of her conversation with Frau Müller, eager to be helpful. Her information was nothing new, however: the canvass team had already blanketed the neighbourhood and the whole of the morning had been spent confirming facts and tossing out fictions. Still, Dylan didn't have the heart to tell Claire he was way ahead of her: he was enjoying the sparkle in her eyes and the way her breasts bulged slightly upwards when she clasped her hands in front of her for emphasis. So much so he was a little saddened when she reached her conclusion. "So you think Therese Keller had an unwanted child," Dylan said, more a statement than a question.

"It's a possibility, don't you think?"

"Anything's a possibility at this stage," Dylan shrugged, putting his notebook away.

"But it should be easy enough to prove," Claire replied with a wave of

30

her hand. "You just get Therese's DNA and compare it to the child's."

Dylan smiled privately at Claire's naïveté. "I wish it were that simple, Ms. Dawson. Unfortunately, I have to show a direct link between Therese and the baby before I can get a DNA warrant, and at this point we don't even have a timeframe for the remains. Also, Therese was neither the only female occupant of the home nor its only owner. I don't have grounds yet for a warrant."

"Why do you need a warrant? Can't you just take DNA off her juice box or something? You see it all the time on television."

This time the smile was public. Such misconceptions usually annoyed Dylan but in Claire Dawson he found them endearing. Had he paused to ask himself why he might have inwardly acknowledged the unflattering fact that his libido was making allowances for her, his tolerance exchanged for the opportunity to educate her, to appear erudite in her eyes. But he didn't ask, he simply indulged, leaning inward just a little when he answered her. "Well, yes, that's true. It's called castaway. But the police can only collect castaway in places where there isn't an expectation of privacy. Therese Keller is in a private hospital, which might be construed by the courts as no different than if she were in her own home. And she's mentally incompetent so I can't get a voluntary sample. I have to tread carefully here. As much as it might frustrate me to operate within the boundaries of the law, I have no choice if I want to secure a conviction. And it's also important not to get ahead of oneself. It's possible this may not even be a homicide."

"But even if it isn't a homicide, don't you want to *know* what happened to it?" Claire asked, her eyes suddenly ablaze. "Don't you care to give it a *name?*" She regretted the question even before she asked it but the words spilled forth anyway, unfettered and raw, the implied accusation hanging heavily in the silence that followed.

"*It* is a she, Ms. Dawson," Dylan declared, rising to leave, "but thank you for your information. It's interesting and may prove useful."

Claire felt a crimson flush in her cheeks. She kept her eyes on his face but struggled to hold his gaze, for it seemed as if he were growing taller or she smaller; and so she quickly rose in the hope of regaining some semblance of equality and salvaging what was left of her good intentions. "I'm sorry, I didn't mean—"

Dylan's cellphone rang. Saved by the bell, he thought as he fished the phone out of his pocket. He glanced at the text message from Anil: *Prelims in. Bad news.* Dylan tensed, and his annoyance at Claire's insult was pushed aside by expedience: he had bigger worries now. "I'm sorry, Ms. Dawson, but I have to address this. I appreciate you coming in. And please don't hesitate to call if you have anything further." He pulled out a card from his breast pocket. "This has my direct line and cellphone numbers."

Flustered by the abrupt dismissal, Claire nervously smoothed back her hair behind one ear. "Of course. I'm sorry to have bothered you."

"It was no bother," Dylan smiled, but the smile was tense. He held out his hand.

Claire shook his hand then raised her own to her chin. "There's just, um, one other thing."

"Yes?" he replied, impatient to move on to Anil.

"Shortly after I started at Eastside, a woman—a prostitute actually—died on the school steps one day. The children were traumatized and so a Native medicine man came in and cleansed the school. It seemed to work. The whole atmosphere changed for the better. I was thinking," she paused, anxious, "I was thinking it might be good to have my house cleansed the same way. I was hoping that since you're Native—"

"Half Native," he corrected her.

"Since you're half Native that you might know someone."

"I'm sorry, I don't," Dylan lied. "Have you thought to call your colleagues?"

Claire nodded. "I called this morning. The medicine man, he died six months ago and they don't know of anyone else."

"I'm sorry, I can't help you there."

Claire smiled but her disappointment was evident. "Right. Well, um, thank you anyway." She turned to walk away when an inexplicable urge made her stop. "Detective," she asked over her shoulder, "do you believe in ghosts?"

"Excuse me?"

"It wasn't a rat's nest. I heard the baby crying." She said this matter-of-factly, in a voice not entirely her own, and the confession caught them both by surprise. Her expression read shock then confusion, then she turned her face away and fled the station.

Through the lobby windows Dylan watched Claire sprint furtively up the street, then he dialled Anil. "Hey, it's me," Dylan said into the phone, too distracted by Claire's admission to pay attention to his tone. "Tell me something useful."

"I'm fine, thanks for asking," Sanjit answered with obvious sarcasm. "Been here since six dissecting a baby so I'm a bit wiped. And you?"

Dylan winced under the weight of the reproach. "Jesus, Sanjit" was all Dylan managed to say before Anil cut him short: "My first guess was wrong. The baby was full-term and born alive, at least in theory: lung floated, liver sank. Mind you, won't stop a good defence attorney claiming she was stillborn and there was an attempt to resuscitate but at least you'll have reasonable doubt."

"Anything on race?" Dylan asked, hoping for more.

"Caucasian, brown hair and green eyes. That's useful: the combination is statistically small. Most often found in North America in those of Icelandic or Germanic descent."

"Age?"

"Can't tell for certain without dental. There's no fat left on the body to give us an accurate weight but I can tell you the length: 19.5 inches. Statistically that puts her between newborn and one month old."

Dylan sighed and pinched the bridge of his nose. "Cause of death?"

"So far indeterminate. Tox and trace will tell me more. But there's no obvious physical trauma to the body, no hematomas or broken bones. Spinal cord and brain are intact. Babies are difficult, Dylan, you know that. All it takes is a light pillow over the face and even the gods couldn't prove murder, assuming it was murder. You might have to settle for concealment."

"Fuck that. A baby in the wall deserves more than two years."

"I hear ya," Anil agreed, then paused. "There's something else."

"Yeah?"

"It's off the record."

"Go on."

"Was having a chat with a friend over breakfast. Emergency room doc. Your homeowner was brought in about seven months ago hallucinating about a dead baby. Doc remembered her because she was ranting about a married colleague in cardiology. The guy claimed she was some nut job who'd been stalking him."

Dylan's head shot up. He bolted outside the entrance and surveyed the street but Claire was long gone. "Shit!" he muttered into the phone.

"I know. And you didn't hear it from me," Anil said, then hung up the phone.

FIVE

Dylan marched back to the squad room and ordered himself to calm down. He was rarely wrong about people and Claire Dawson did not strike him as a murderer. She was annoying but she wasn't homicidal. And she wasn't even really annoying so much as ... as ... disconcerting. Admit it, Dylan berated himself, the woman makes you stupid. I mean, what the hell were you doing sharing evidentiary facts with her? "*It* is a she" he had blurted out before his brain had caught up with his mouth. And to what end? To correct some perceived slight from a woman who knew nothing about him? What did he care what Claire Dawson thought of him?

You can't let her rattle you, he reminded himself; you have to remain objective. If Claire had truly been stalking a doctor, the hospital would have been obligated to report it, and Claire's sheet was clean. Anil's news was likely nothing more than gossip, and gossip was insufficient for an arrest. Still, what about the past hallucinations, and her strange confession just moments earlier?

Dylan noisily drummed his fingers on his desk. He knew exactly what his *ta'ah* would say if she heard this: that Baby Jane had reached out from the spirit world, had cried for help, and Claire Dawson's heart and mind had been open enough to hear those cries. She wasn't nuts; she was blessed. But then again his *ta'ah* wasn't charged with the task of finding out how Baby Jane had died in *this* world? Ta'ah wasn't saddled with the burden of sifting through the rubble of deceit and motive, of separating fact from innuendo, of proving what you already know in your gut but won't wash in court without supporting evidence. Claire Dawson was hiding something from him, that he knew. She'd been hospitalized in the past, hallucinating about a dead baby. And who other than Claire Dawson could place those remains in the wall? She'd been alone when she allegedly discovered them. Could she not have put them there then concocted this whole charade to cover up her crime?

And Claire Dawson had the same dark hair and green eyes of Baby Jane, a combination that was, as Anil had phrased it, statistically small.

Dylan mulled this over then realized what he needed to do. He grabbed his coat and keys and headed for the law courts.

CR

Claire threw her purse on the bed with a sigh of defeat, dismayed by her botched attempt to be helpful. *You can do better, Claire. I know you can.* She was suddenly eight again, awaiting approval of the bright red *A-* written across the top of the exam paper clutched in her excited hands, a mark she thought splendid until her father reminded her an A- meant there was still room for improvement. There was *always* room for improvement, unless you counted her father's perfect acts of subtle destruction.

"What else can I do for you?" Claire pleaded with the air as though the spirit might be hovering about and capable of answering. There was no reply, no sudden breezes or creaking doors, and Claire wondered if she'd let her enthusiasm run amok, had imagined a relationship between her dead child and this one simply because she *needed* to: to prove to the baby or herself or Detective Lewis that she was up to the task the universe had apparently bestowed upon her.

And what of Detective Lewis? she pondered next as she switched her new jeans and blouse for a stained pair of pants and T-shirt. His flirtations had been unwelcomed and inappropriate and yet he'd made her body throb with a nervous energy. She wasn't sure which had made her shake more, the way Detective Lewis' lips had curled ever so slightly when she'd turned to face him or the mischief she saw in his eyes. He'd caught himself, she'd noticed too, but that brief smile had aroused in her something she hadn't felt in a long time: her own presence. She had practiced being invisible for so long now she'd forgotten the effect she once had on men, had been running from it. But today? Did her reaction to Detective Lewis mean she was ready again for a man's attention? In the next breath she decided the why of it didn't really matter, only that she liked the rush of heat and the affirmation of his gaze. She liked his stocky frame, and the discreet hint of aftershave she'd detected when he sat down beside her. It was a warm, woodsy scent with subtle notes of musk and oak that reminded her of the rainforest where the smell of damp earth and new growth mingled in an invigorating blend of life and decay. It was a fitting scent, she thought, for a man who chased the secrets of the dead yet whose presence strongly suggested a potent virility.

She spoke his name aloud with a coquettish roll of her tongue, and felt the same rush of heat. She found him handsome, she admitted: he had a strong but kind face, and when he smiled fine lines formed around his eyes that had cocooned her within their folds—at least until she'd inadvertently accused him of indifference. Bright move, she scolded herself, and debated whether calling him to apologize would make things right between them or only draw further attention to the insult.

And then there was her confession. She cringed. What on earth had possessed her to tell him about that? The recollection made her uneasy. She tried to remember what she'd been thinking and feeling in the seconds before her confession, and recalled with a mixture of panic and curiosity that it had been the same internal voice that had made her stop and listen to the cries of a ghost. There had been a presence, Claire realised, something that had possessed her in the moment, had spoken to her in a voice similar to her own yet sufficiently different enough to catch her attention. Now it was gone again and she didn't know how to summon it at will, or even if she wanted to.

She laid back on the bed and stared at the ceiling, looking for clues. A baby had died in this house, most likely the offspring of Therese Keller, but how to prove it? Detective Lewis' hands were tied by legal technicalities and Claire's were ... not? *That's it!* What was to stop *her* from collecting Therese's DNA and having it tested, then handing the results over to Lewis for comparison? He'd been certain to approve, might even be grateful. And while it was definitely risky and possibly immoral, what other way would there be to prove maternity? The baby deserved a name, an identity; it was her *birthright*, Claire thought indignantly. The more she considered the end the more necessary became the means, and before Claire could talk herself out of it she was in Frau Müller's garden, staring down at the elder woman as she tended to the potted plants that rimmed the small stone

36

patio beneath her back deck. "Frau Müller, do you know where I might find Therese Keller?"

"I'm not sure," Frau Müller replied, slowly rising to her feet. "Why?"

"I want to ask her about the baby."

"Oh, dear," Frau Müller said, wiping her brow with the back of her forearm. "I'm not sure you'll get much out of her. I'm told her Alzheimer's is quite advanced. But let me make some calls. It shouldn't be too hard to find out which home she's in. Will you be staying for tea?"

"Thanks, but I can't. I have to finish tearing down the kitchen wall. Rain cheque?"

"Of course. I'll come by as soon as I hear from the ladies."

Claire nodded her appreciation then turned and smiled radiantly to herself. She was feeling gloriously devious: there *was* a part for her in this mystery; why else had she been led to this house? Everything happens for a reason, she reminded the forces of opposition; there's no such thing as coincidence. Okay, maybe she was still on the fence about that but now as before the theory provided a rationale for her good intentions, and she clung to this convenience with the earnestness of a child.

The glory faded, however, when she returned home and paused to reflect upon the gaping hole at the back of the dining room closet, the jagged edges of the plaster like the bared teeth of an angry animal. Claire closed her eyes to the offending beast and conjured up the contrasting image of a newborn baby girl, all pink skin and downy hair, one tiny fist raised in defiance. "We'll give you a name, I promise you," Claire assured the spectre, then turned and picked up the sledgehammer off the floor where the forensics team had left it. She narrowed her eyes at the wall, no longer seeing Eric within the crevices of the plaster but the shadow of a baby killer, and she imagined each blow as corporal punishment, an obligatory first response to an unspeakable crime.

ଔ

Dylan sat in his car in the law courts parkade mulling over what he'd just read. A photocopied Statement of Claim lay on the seat beside him: Claire Dawson, Plaintiff, versus Doctor Harold O'Conner and Saint Martin's Hospital, Co-Defendants. According to the document, Dawson had been twenty-one weeks pregnant when she suffered a miscarriage and was taken to St. Martin's where, it was alleged, Dr. O'Connor had botched the follow-up dilation and curettage. He'd left a sponge in her uterus that resulted in pelvic inflammatory disease; the infection had not only almost cost Dawson her life but had left her fallopian tubes scarred. Moreover, it was alleged, O'Connor had been high during the procedure: a known prescription addict the hospital had nevertheless allowed to retain privileges and operate.

Other than the Writ and Statement of Claim, the only other documents in the registry file were the Notice of Trial and a Notice of Discontinuance. Dylan snorted. Classic civil litigation ending in a pre-trial settlement: pay out, shut it down, no admission of liability, silence the vic. No further details made public for the next victim's benefit. Doctors and their slimy lawyers.

Still, the lawsuit raised troubling questions. Had it been a legitimate miscarriage or a self-induced abortion? Was it possible Claire Dawson had a history of unwanted pregnancies? Was this the "personal indiscretion" Eaton's headmaster had hinted at? If so, that seemed a bit old-fashioned. I mean, what century are we in? Dylan mused. Never mind that, he scolded himself in the next breath, the real question is whether Dawson was capable of concealing not only a pregnancy but a live birth as well. Was the woman he judged to be normal in truth something far, far darker? His instincts were good, better than most, and yet he was painfully aware he wasn't sure his instincts could be trusted just now: he found her intoxicating, and her inspired retelling of Frau Müller's recollections had left him wondering if Claire loved as passionately as she spoke, if her lips were as soft as he imagined them to be, if the breasts he had glimpsed were fuller still when swollen with desire. Even her insult had caused him an unexpected pleasure: the fire in her eyes had aroused him even as her words had fuelled his indignation, and he'd had to suppress the temptation to silence her criticisms with a penetrating kiss. If he were honest he would confess that he was as intrigued to find out about her as he was about the baby, but at this moment such a confession was an impossibility. At this moment he had no choice but to be Detective Dylan Lewis, with a job to do that could not, must not, be compromised by the woman with the fire in her eyes.

Dylan pulled himself together and started the car. There was only one way to find out what he needed to know. He'd have to question Dawson herself.

Claire stretched out her aching back and surveyed her handiwork. The wall was gone now, the rubble swept into heavy duty garbage bags that Claire had then dragged beneath the deck for disposal later, the studs cut and stored in the furnace room below for winter fires. The kitchen, open now and brighter from the light in the dining room, gave the room the expansive feel she had imagined. She stood where her island would be and pictured it there, its Blue Pearl granite gleaming beneath pendant track lighting. There were going to be Shaker style cabinets and stainless steel appliances: a gas stovetop in the island, two ovens in the wall to her right, with the sink and fridge against the wall behind her where they already stood. She'd add a dishwasher too, beside the sink.

Claire sighed with satisfaction and ran one hand through her hair, the tangle of dust and debris wrenching her back to the moment. Guilt over her flirtation with pleasure descended swiftly upon her, followed by an equally powerful rush of confusion: just what *was* she supposed to feel now? Her emotions were like notes in an asynchronous symphony, each moment dictating its own tone without regard for the whole. Hammering away at the wall she'd begun to feel a yearning that, like so much else in the past day, seemed not entirely her own: a wish to save the house from its sorrow, to raise it anew, to reclaim it from whomever had debased it with violence and used it as a tomb. Yet this brief, excited breeze that had swept in and lifted the gloom now seemed inappropriate, as if the house should be permanently shrouded and Claire its widow. Which was the more appropriate response? Or were they both equally valid? If the past year of therapy had taught Claire anything it's that you have to pick yourself up again no matter how brutal the blow; was this simply the universe's way of testing its student? Claire paused her thoughts to give the universe time to respond, but when the answer wasn't forthcoming she gave up philosophizing and headed for the ensuite.

By the time she'd filled the bath and stripped down, Claire had decided a positive response was the most productive, and so she allowed herself to appreciate her efforts regarding both the house and its victim. Frau Müller would find Therese soon enough, her DNA would be collected, the baby indentified and properly laid to rest, and Claire would renovate as planned: she would reclaim the house *and* her life from their twin tragic pasts.

Pleased with her conclusion, Claire smiled as she sank down in the steaming water and let the warmth engulf her. She closed her eyes, sighing softly as the heat seeped into her muscles, and was surprised when Detective Lewis emerged from the mist unannounced. The surprise was not so much his presence in her imagination as what he was doing to her there, and she realized with some trepidation that he had reached her in a place long neglected and now aching for attention. In that moment Claire knew she had to make a choice, to keep running from herself or embrace this reawakening. And so in the safety of her bathroom Claire took her first tentative steps, letting the fantasy go where it wanted until she felt the blissful shudder of new expectations.

CR

Dylan drove around the back of Claire's house, noted her car was there, then drove around front and parked his cruiser. He sat for a moment to compose himself and formulate his approach, an act he performed so often it was automatic; but it was an act reserved for suspects and obvious perpetrators, and this fact pulled Dylan's center of gravity downward, his feet heavily weighted by unwanted suspicions as he alighted from the car and trudged up Claire's front path.

Claire stepped out of the bath and was just reaching for a towel when the doorbell rang. She immediately thought of Frau Müller and assumed she had come with news of Therese Keller's whereabouts, so Claire quickly wrapped herself in her terry robe and headed for the front foyer, not bothering to check the peephole before swinging the door wide open with anticipation. She froze. There was a moment of awkward silence as Dylan eyed Claire's natty bathrobe and her wet hair dripping onto her shoulders. "Do you mind if I come in?" he finally asked.

Was this for real? Claire wondered. Because if it were this was *not* how she had imagined his arrival nor her method of welcome. In her reverie she'd been flawless and irresistible but right now she was about as enticing as a wet rat. "Ms. Dawson," Dylan asked, puzzled, "are you alright?"

Claire shook herself unfrozen then stepped back in a gesture of defeat. "Would you give me a moment to get dressed?" she asked wearily.

Dylan gave Claire that same reckless grin she'd seen earlier at the station. "Of course."

As soon as Claire disappeared up the stairs, Dylan seized the opportunity to scope out the main floor. The wall between the kitchen and dining room was now completely dismantled, he noted, though the closet with its gaping hole in the back was still intact. Other than the wall, nothing appeared to have changed: the main floor bath was still unused and there were no additions to the sparse furnishings in the living room: a flat panel TV perched on a moving box, a condo-sized sofa, and a cheap pine dining set. He flipped through the small stack of mail on the table. Most of it was addressed to the former occupants and Claire had written "Moved/Return to Sender" on the envelopes, no doubt intending to leave them in her mailbox for the letter carrier to take. Among the post addressed to Claire there was nothing unusual, just utility connection bills, a *House and Style* magazine, and a few items forwarded from her former apartment.

The banality soothed Dylan. He had investigated his share of psychopaths, many of whom possessed an extraordinary ability to blend in with the general populace, but each time there had been something not quite right about them or their environment, an intangible quality whose definition remained elusive but which always made the skin along his spine itch. He would fidget involuntarily as he walked through a suspect's home or workplace and know he had his killer, as if the stench of their crime clung to everything they touched. He had once asked his *ta'ah* about this sensation, hoping she could provide an answer to a question he had struggled to articulate, and her response became his private mantra: *to those who can hear, the spirits speak with clear voices; learn to trust your instincts for that is how they speak to you.*

But what if, as now, his instincts seemed clouded, obscured? Could he still hear the spirits through the fog? He was fidgeting here in Claire's living room, his spine was itching, but it wasn't the same feeling as when he was in the presence of a killer, just equally discomforting.

Claire returned dried and dressed and found Dylan sitting on her couch, picking at a loose thread on his jacket. She sat down beside him and eyed him warily. She had already wondered if her erotic musings had somehow made their way across the airwaves and into Detective Lewis' brain, had determined this was unlikely, and had concluded he was here to question her again. Moreover, he had wanted to catch her off guard, had not wanted to give her time to anticipate his intentions. He was no doubt here because of her odd confession, to determine whether she were homicidal or crazy or both. His suspicions made her nervous and embarrassed her even more.

Dylan turned his body to face hers and placed an arm on the sofa back, deliberately keeping his body language open, relaxed and unthreatening. The technique worked, he saw, as Claire leaned into the sofa, the defensive scowl on her face melting away. Another minute, he calculated, and she'd be putty in his hands. "Ms. Dawson—"

"Are you here about my confession?" she interrupted nervously.

"Do you wish to make one?" Dylan answered evenly.

"I'm sorry?" Dylan eyed Claire carefully as she slowly realized the ambiguity of her question. "What? No! What I meant was, is this about my hearing a ghost?"

"Not exactly," Dylan replied, maintaining his even tone. "Certain information has come to light that I need you to explain so I can proceed appropriately."

"Am I a suspect?" she asked, apprehensive.

"No, no, of course not," Dylan replied. He didn't like lying to her; but in all fairness, he told himself, he didn't *personally* consider her a suspect. There were just the uncomfortable matters of the hallucination and the lawsuit to sort out and then he could get back to the task of finding Baby Jane's real killer. "It's just routine. Whenever we investigate a crime we have to assume everyone might be involved until we can rule them out."

"Alright then," she said, relaxing a little. "What do you need to ask me?"

"I understand you had a medical emergency about seven months ago and were taken to hospital. You were hearing a baby crying. Can you tell me about it?"

Claire leapt from the couch, her face flush with embarrassment. "How do you know about that?" she gasped.

"I can't reveal my source. I'm sorry."

"You're *sorry*? You come here and tell me my privacy has been breached then have the gall not to tell me who did it?"

"Ms. Dawson, please, I'm not here to accuse you of anything. But you claim to have found the remains after hearing a baby crying, and seven months ago you were experiencing similar hallucinations. I need you to tell me why you think that is."

"I don't know why!" she cried. "You're the Indian. You tell me."

Dylan froze. He fought to contain the hot seed of anger slowly snaking through his belly. He couldn't afford to lose his temper: he needed information. He began to rise from the couch then stopped himself: the intimation of humility would benefit him. "Ms. Dawson," he asked as carefully as he could manage, "the baby you lost, was it your only pregnancy?"

Claire imploded, falling onto one of the pine chairs as if Dylan had punched her in the solar plexus. Her fingers were white around the edges of the seat, an anxious hold on her composure. "Who told you about that?" she whispered.

"No one. It's a matter of public record." Claire looked at him, uncomprehending. "Ms. Dawson, you settled before trial but your Statement of Claim is still in the court registry," Dylan explained.

Claire fought to keep down the bile rising in her throat. She felt violated, emotionally raped. "How dare you," she said, her voice shaking. "How dare you come here and throw that—"

"Ms. Dawson," Dylan interjected forcefully, "I'm not throwing anything at anyone. I just need you to tell me if Baby Jane was yours."

Claire burst into tears. "Get out," she cried.

"Ms. Dawson—"

"Please, just leave."

"Ms. Dawson—"

"I said GET OUT!" she screamed at him through her tears. When he didn't move Claire leapt from her chair and raced to open the door. "GET OUT OF MY HOUSE!" She was sobbing now, her breath laboured, holding onto the door for support. Dylan, his failure swallowing him like a giant black hole, said nothing in return, just walked past her and out the door as it slammed shut behind him.

SIX

Claire slid down the wall, dizzy and disorientated. Everything was flooding back, overwhelming her. She felt as if the whole of the past year had suddenly evaporated and she were back at the hospital staring at the ceiling in a morphine induced stupor, the loss of her child still incomprehensible to her. It was only a dream, a bad dream she had told herself. Everything was fine.

But when the morphine wore off and the midwife came to console Claire and to explain there was need for a D&C, the denial wore off, too. No, she had screamed in her head at God, this wasn't possible. She had given birth, had held her son despite the doctor's efforts to whisk him away. She'd seen his face, had willed him to breathe away the pallid blue of his skin. He wasn't dead. He *couldn't* be dead: just days before she'd seen him on the ultrasound monitor, his tiny fists raised in defiance. His was a life to be reckoned with, not cast out by the whims of fate.

Denial had been followed by excruciating pain, and pain by guilt: her body had failed her baby, had failed to sustain him before he was even born. She didn't deserve him, then, if her body were so selfish, so unloving. And then there was the manner in which her son had been conceived. What karmic vengeance had she wrought upon him for that? When the infection came it had seemed painfully appropriate, a fitting judgment upon her, the way plague victims used to think God spared only the righteous.

And so when Death had called for her she had welcomed it, had slipped into a coma with the passivity of one who expected to find neither heaven nor hell on the other side, only eternal nothingness. For three days she had straddled the frontier between worlds, her fractured soul torn between the promise of peace and the sound of her mother's voice. Claire remembered little of those days except that distant but alluring murmur and the fiercely determined way her mother had clutched onto her daughter's hand. In the end it was that which finally forced Claire to make a decision: each time she had tried to pull away she discovered she couldn't release her mother's grip, so Claire reluctantly opened her eyes again and faced her grief.

The anger came later. And the lawyer after that.

Dylan remained on the steps of the house, wanting desperately to open the door and beg forgiveness for his indiscretion. The conversation had been premature and he knew it: he had no idea of the date of the remains, no idea whether they were months or decades old. So why had he so foolishly rushed into this minefield?

He rested his head against the door, punishing himself with the muffled sounds of Claire's anguish. He was a better cop than this. It was a rookie mistake and he was too long on the force to argue inexperience. And he was smarter than this, much, much smarter. Why was it so damn important that he know—that he know *now*—that Baby Jane wasn't Claire's?

He tried to push the obvious from his brain but eventually gave in. The truth was that he wanted her to be innocent of this, he wanted her to be ruled out as a suspect, he just ... wanted her. And the sooner she was free of all this the sooner he could have her. But that was hardly going to happen now, was it? he chided himself. After his performance today he'd be lucky if she didn't file a formal complaint. Or another bloody lawsuit.

Resigned, Dylan walked to his car and slumped down in the driver's seat. He had messed up badly. There would be repercussions, of that he was sure. Maybe not immediately, maybe not as expected, but there would be payback. Ta'ah said everything you do can affect as many as seven generations to come, so somebody was going to suffer for his stupidity. Dylan wished the consequences upon himself. Failing that he hoped they weren't on anybody he liked.

He glanced wearily at the dashboard clock. It was getting on six; time to call it a day. He'd return the cruiser to the depot then drown his sorrows in a curry. Maybe Sanjit would join him. Dylan pulled out his cellphone and saw the text alert he'd missed while Claire was screaming at him. It was the university lab. "Shit!" he muttered as he quickly dialled the number on the screen, and was relieved when a voice answered.

"Sanders."

"This is Detective Lewis. You left a message earlier?"

"Detective, yes, this is Dr. Carl Sanders. I have your bomb carbon results. The remains date to mid-1971."

"How accurate?"

"Between you and me, six months. Infant remains are the most accurate due to the relatively inconsequential bone remodelling and the lack of external factors such as diet and medication. And the reason I'm a little late with the results is that I asked Dr. Anil to send me some brain tissue to do a comparison with since that tissue was intact and carbon-14 concentrations are highest there. But there can be regional atmospheric differences and of course the health of the mother, so to be safe I would testify to accuracy within one year."

"Thanks, doc. This is *very* helpful."

"I also found something else that might help, though it wouldn't be as definitive as the carbon results. Was the house air-conditioned?"

"Not that I'm aware of. Why?"

"Anil mentioned the remains were mummified. After I dated them I checked the historical climate data: we had a heat wave the last week of July '71 and again about a week later; recorded daily highs at the airport measured between 28.3 and 29.4 degrees centigrade. You'd then need to add about three to five degrees to approximate likely temperatures further inland, and in the confined space of a wall it could easily be two to three times the ambient temperature. It would have been enough to produce such remains."

"Well now, that is interesting. When will I receive your report?"

"I'll send it to your office tomorrow morning by courier, along with the climate data. And if you need any further tests call me directly. I'll see they get priority."

"Much appreciated."

"Good luck, detective. I don't envy you this one."

Dylan hit the end button then hit himself on the forehead with his phone. He wasn't sure what he felt more strongly, relief that Claire was in the clear or remorse that this proved his impatience all the more unforgiveable. He glanced over at the front door and wondered if he dared to knock. He didn't. He started the engine and drove off in defeat.

A hour later Dylan was huddled over a menu at Manfredo's on West Fourth: Sanjit had insisted on pizza in exchange for his company. Curry I can get at home, he had pronounced.

Dylan waved "over here" when he saw Sanjit enter the restaurant. He looked like hell. He had a day's growth of beard, and dark circles beneath his eyes spoke of a night without sleep. As Sanjit slipped into the booth Dylan eyed him sheepishly. "Damn it, Sanjit, I forgot you went in early. Why didn't you say something?"

Were Sanjit an uncharitable man he might have mentioned the sound in his friend's voice that spoke of a need for company, but instead he simply said, "Parvati's due in a week."

Dylan glanced over his menu and smirked. "So they've arrived then?"

Sanjit slumped down against the booth wall. "Last Sunday," he moaned. "I don't see why they couldn't have waited until *after* the baby was born. What if it's late? What if they're here for a *month*?"

"What does Parvati say?"

"She says if this baby is so much as an hour late she's having it induced."

Dylan laughed. Parvati's parents had flown over from Delhi to assist with the children after the birth but Parvati's mother was known to create more conflict than her help was worth. The day Dylan had met Sanjit's wife she had regaled her guest with a wickedly funny impersonation of her mother, a Bollywood addict who could imagine nothing greater for her daughter than an elaborate Hindu wedding. From the moment Parvati turned sixteen her mother had begun scheming and searching for the perfect husband, enlisting the help of every female relative no matter how distant. When Parvati graduated top of her senior class and announced her intention to pursue a career in biomedical engineering, her mother had replied by asking Parvati if she considered her cousin Rajdeep a suitable young man. Desperate times called for desperate measures, so Parvati appealed to her father's love with a thinly veiled threat to drown herself in the Yamuna. He had seen through the threat but elected anyway to became a co-conspirator in his daughter's escape. It was her father who signed Parvati's passport application, who drove her in secret to the Canadian High Commission, who paid for her first year of studies at the University of British Columbia, and who continued to pay for it with the loss of what little marital peace he'd had to begin with.

"How's her dad these days?" Dylan asked, remembering the elderly man's sacrifice.

"Going deaf and liking it. Her mom demanded money for a hearing aid; we sent over enough for two but her dad secretly gave the money to charity and claimed it never arrived. We're still hearing what ingrates we are but Parvati figures she owes him her silence."

"Conspirators for life?"

"I think so," Sanjit laughed. Then, changing channels, "Speaking of which, when's Tom back?" Tom was Detective Thomas Farrow, Dylan's partner, currently on holiday in the U.K. and itching to get back.

"Sunday. Can't wait apparently. Another man plagued by in-laws. Parents are fine but Jill's brothers are right snits. Oxford boys who fail to appreciate the empire's dead."

"Bet you'll be glad for his help on this one." Sanjit saw a flicker of pain cross Dylan's face and knew, instinctively, it wasn't about the baby. "What's going on, Dylan?"

Dylan rested his cheek in his palm and shook his head. "I screwed up with the Dawson woman. Big time."

"Anything you want to tell me?"

Dylan grimaced. "Not really."

"Then do you want pepperoni or spicy beef?"

"Both. I deserve to be punished."

✆

Claire awoke shivering in the darkness. She had cried herself to sleep on the foyer floor and now the cool of evening had awoken her. She groaned, her body stiff and sore and her mind fogged by fatigue and stress. She managed to pull herself up and amble up the stairs to her bedroom where she simply stripped off her clothes and buried herself beneath the covers. In minutes she was asleep again.

Dylan lay on the couch in his Kitsilano apartment watching a movie. The pizza was wrecking havoc in his stomach, a fine addition to the knot he'd had in his gut since six o'clock. He glanced at his watch. It was one a.m. He switched off the television, took another antacid tablet from the bottle on the coffee table and closed his eyes, hopeful for sleep. All he got instead was the image of Claire crying for him to get out. Dylan winced then forced the image to take a different turn. Claire wasn't crying anymore; she was back on the pine chair, looking down into his eyes. He asked if Baby Jane were hers. No, oh no, she replied, taking his face affectionately in her hands. Of course not. You mustn't worry. Relieved, he pulled her down to him and they kneeled together on the floor in a tight embrace that confirmed their mutual longing. He could smell the citrus in her hair, feel her breasts pressed against his ribs, her hands grasping his back.

He kissed the top of her head. She looked up at the touch of his lips and her eyes said it all: I'm yours. Take me.

So he did.

SEVEN

Claire walked back into her bedroom from the bathroom, her mood glum. Her attraction to Detective Lewis had taken an ugly turn, and Claire wondered if she were somehow cursed, that for her love would never be pure and beautiful and uncomplicated. Too depressed to make an effort, she threw on yesterday's clothes then grabbed her purse and headed for The Drive: she'd get a coffee, maybe read the paper and see if her head cleared sufficiently to figure out what all this insanity meant.

"Claire!" Frau Müller called out just as Claire reached the end of her walkway. She spun around to find Frau Müller standing beside her open screen door, waving for Claire to join her. "I found Therese," she said excitedly, and Claire suddenly remembered her earlier request. It had slipped her mind in all the drama, and now it seemed as if Frau Müller's timing was yet another example of cosmic intervention. Claire grinned and headed for the porch. "Come in. I have coffee for you."

Claire followed Frau Müller through a floral papered hallway and into her kitchen. It was dated but spanking clean, painted bright yellow with a floral border around the wall where it met the ceiling. Pictures of family graced the walls alongside needlepoint pictures of baskets of food, and knickknacks filled the space between the top of the kitchen cupboards and the ceiling. Sheer gathered curtains filtered the sunlight that streamed in through the south-facing patio doors, and the small corner kitchen table was covered with a lace cloth.

She sat Claire down at the table and poured out coffee, then sliced off a large chunk of carrot cake with cream cheese icing and set it on the table.

"Have you had breakfast, dear? I could make you some eggs."

"Thank you, this is fine." Claire peered upwards, perplexed, as Frau Müller hovered expectantly over her. "You said you know where Therese is?"

"She's at Twin Oaks. But I was thinking"—Frau Müller pulled out a chair and sat down across from Claire—"I was thinking it might be good if I came with you, what with me being her former neighbour and all."

"Oh, I don't know, Frau Müller. You see I—"

"I know you're up to something. I promise I won't tell. And I'd make a good decoy. If you go alone people will talk but it would be natural for *me* to visit."

"Natural, huh?"

Frau Müller fidgeted sheepishly with the buttons on her cardigan. "Well, more natural than *you*," she said with a coy glance upwards.

Though Claire detected a hint of blackmail in Frau Müller's tone she found no malice, and after a few moments more of Frau Müller's pleading Claire surrendered to the request despite her better judgment.

CR

Dylan rushed into the squad room twenty minutes late, a kink in his neck from the odd position he'd fallen asleep in on the couch. He grabbed a coffee from the small table set up at the back of the room, threw fifty cents into the pot fund, and asked if the pastry left behind from the day before had anybody's name on it. It didn't.

"Lewis." Dylan looked up at the sound of his sergeant's voice at the doorway. "A moment?" Dylan's heart sank. Jesus, that was fast. What did Dawson do, get up at six a.m. to write out her complaint? This was *not* going to be a good day. And he still had ten hours to go.

Sergeant James McTavish was a broad shouldered, no-nonsense Scot with a bald head and a bushy red moustache. He'd been head of Homicide's Team Two going on a decade now, with a fine track record and the confidence of his men and women. McTavish would go to the wall for anyone under him so long as they were deserving of his loyalty, but equally he was not a man to suffer fools or insubordinates or just plain cock-ups. Dylan sat down in the chair across from his boss and braced himself for the onslaught.

"I know it's early in the investigation, Dylan, but anything useful yet?"

The question caught Dylan by surprise: this was a friendly start to a flogging. "Sir?"

"No sleep last night, detective?"

"Not much. Sir."

"Well, wake up. There's been sniffs by the press on this and Media Relations wants to know if there's anything we can share before the rumour mill starts grinding out innuendo."

Bloody hell, thought Dylan. This is exactly what he didn't need, not yet anyway. The media could be useful on a case like this but only when the department could control the message, which would be hard to do this early on: infant remains would start a feeding frenzy. "The remains date to 1971 but I don't want that out until I've questioned the occupants of the home from that period."

"When will that be?"

"I hope to start today." Dylan paused, thinking. "Do you think an embargo is possible? The house was occupied by a relative of Benjamin Miller. I need some time before he gathers the family around and closes ranks."

"*Benjamin Miller* is involved with this?"

"I don't know. He was just a teenager in '71. Still, old enough to be a father and the neighbour said he and the female cousin who lived there were very close. Maybe too close. Either way, he knows all our tricks and I need to keep him ignorant as long as I can." Dylan scratched his chin. "Who's sniffing around?"

"Doolie from CKRW."

Dylan knew Chris Doolie. He'd been working the crime beat for the better part of twenty years and he played the game well. Dylan was confident he could get his embargo in exchange for prime info later. "Tell Doolie if he'll agree to hold off for now we'll give him an exclusive on available facts and also identity once we have one. If he can't or won't contain it, confirm remains were found but there are no visible signs of trauma to the body and we're awaiting further tests. Time of death is unknown. The homeowner is definitely not involved. Emphasize foul play is not suspected and that if anyone wishes to come forward and share information we will do everything we can to ensure privacy and protection of all possible witnesses."

"*Is* foul play suspected? What did Anil say?"

"Nothing conclusive yet. But you don't"—Dylan tapped the desk with an accusing finger—"stick a baby in the wall unless you meant to hide something. This isn't a case of a scared teenager who hid her pregnancy and made a mess of the birth. Girls like that always leave the baby somewhere it can be found, even if it's dead. There's guilt and remorse." He sat back in his chair and let the wave of anger subside. "Doolie will get it. Make him a deal."

"I'll do my best. But Dylan, these are old bones. No overtime on this, no unnecessary lab tests, no extra men unless you can give me a *very* compelling reason. Once the canvass team reports back you and Farrow are limited to the usual staff."

"Yes, sir." Dylan hesitated, not sure if he were dismissed.

"Well, get on with it then. There's a little girl in the morgue who deserves a better name than Baby Jane Doe."

"Yes, sir." Dylan exited McTavish's office and breathed a sigh of relief: he had lived to see another day.

Dylan entered the squad room and asked no one in particular if Wednesday had been even or odd shift. "Odd" came a response from behind a computer monitor. And today? Still odd. Excellent, thought Dylan, that meant Wilson was working the afternoon shift. He needed to get a message to Dawson not to talk to the media or anymore to Frau Müller about Baby Jane, and Becky would be familiar, female and, most importantly, not him. Dylan called dispatch and left a message for Wilson to call in. Moments later he had her on the line. "I need a favour."

"For you, anything," she replied, a courtesan's caress in her voice.

Great, thought Dylan, what's this going to cost me? "When you start shift this afternoon I need you to pay Claire Dawson a visit and ask her not to talk to the media about the case and especially not to mention infant remains. And ask her not to talk to her neighbours anymore about it either. In fact, she spoke to an Astrid Müller, lives next door in the white Victorian. Pay her a visit too." He paused, then remembered his manners. "Please."

"Will do."

"Thanks, Wilson, much appreciated."

"Just remember," she said, an obvious purr creeping back into her voice, "you owe me now."

Yeah, thought Dylan as he hung up the phone, and may I retire before you get a chance to collect.

Claire parked the car in the lot at Twin Oaks Assisted Living Villa and helped Frau Müller alight, her arms laden with flowers cut from their two gardens. The flowers had been Frau Müller's idea—Therese, she explained, had poured her heart into her garden so it would seem fitting to bring her a lovely reminder—a gesture Claire thought as clever as it was kind, and she tipped her hat to the elder woman's cunning.

"I must say," Frau Müller remarked as they walked toward the entrance, "that nephew of hers must make good money. Brigitte is in Clarence House and *that's* two grand a month." She said this in the assuming way that reminded Claire of her maternal grandmother, the way she too would talk of her friends as if Claire should know by some magic who the friend was and what the significance of the story was in relation to the conversation. Here she guessed that Clarence House was not nearly as expensive as Twin Oaks, which from their vantage point definitely looked upscale: the gardens were lush and immaculate, with benches and patio sets scattered throughout and a small area cordoned off for croquet and horseshoes. The air was still cool this morning but a handful of residents were already seated among the rhododendron bushes and four could be seen among the wickets. Through a wall of glass could be seen an indoor pool and exercise room, and another wall of glass revealed the common rooms with large patio doors opening onto the garden.

Inside, the dimly lit foyer suggested an atmosphere of calm and expected quiet: even the clerks in the charity gift shop beside the front door were conversing in low voices. The place had the air of a luxury hotel, the kind where staff learn to speak at just the right timbre so that one guest's business is never revealed to another; the place you choose when you want your privacy zealously guarded. They'd have to tread carefully.

They asked for Therese and were directed to the common room where those who were not bedridden had just finished a communal breakfast. The tables had been cleared and most of the residents were now gathered around in groups, engrossed in various activities. Some were playing cards or building puzzles, others were knitting, but most were gathered in front of a large television. Their expressions were glum despite the luxury and pretence, lost souls prematurely adrift on the river Styx. They had been abandoned, tossed aside by relatives too selfish or lazy or preoccupied to take on another burden despite their wealth providing no rational impediment to home care, who convinced themselves that a posh elder centre provided the companionship of peers and a better daily living experience. The truth was it didn't; it merely concealed the fact that their children were the kind who bristled at any intrusion into their privacy, who resented the presence of additional witnesses to their dysfunctional lives. Claire shuddered. Frau Müller crossed herself.

Therese was sitting in isolation by the window, staring into space and wiping her nose repeatedly on a tissue. "Therese?" Frau Müller said gently as they approached. "It's me, Astrid. From next door. Remember?"

Therese turned her head to scrutinize Frau Müller. "Can't say that I do," Therese snorted, suspicious of her guests. "And who the hell are you?" she added, glaring at Claire. The loud timber of Therese's voice was incongruous with her pale skin and frail, anorexic frame, though her wiry grey hair, pulled back into a severe bun, complemented the ferocity of her striking emerald eyes.

Claire felt a shiver ripple along her spine but she kept her unease in check, forcing the smile she'd plastered onto her face to remain fixed. "It's Claire, Therese. Look, we brought you flowers from your garden."

Therese looked quizzically at the flowers but then the light of recognition crept into her eyes and her face softened with nostalgia. "My garden," she whispered longingly. She looked out the window but what she saw confused her and she became distraught. "Where's my garden? Someone has stolen my garden!"

"It's okay, Therese," Frau Müller assured her. "It's okay. Your garden is still there. And it's well looked after. Don't you worry."

"Who *are* you?" she asked, her voice now tremulous.

"It's Astrid. Astrid Müller. From next door. Remember? I used to give Elisabeth apples from my tree."

The question sparked a memory but the sudden scowl on Therese's face indicated it was not a pleasant one. "Astrid Müller," Therese uttered with contempt, pointing a bony index finger like the declaration of the Reaper. "Think you're a better mother than me, you do. Always judging. Say I'm too skinny. 'Put some meat on your bones, Therese,' you say. 'What's Armin supposed to hold onto if you don't put some meat on your bones?' You and your fat ass always judging. Don't know the truth. Armin don't like fat girls. He likes his girls skinny. Have to stay skinny, he says. Or else."

Curious, Claire cocked her head toward Therese. "Or else what?"

But Therese wasn't talking to them anymore. "Have to stay skinny," she repeated and began rocking in her chair.

Claire laid a gentle hand on Therese's arm and coaxed her attention back. "But what about when you got pregnant, Therese? You didn't stay skinny then?"

Therese jerked her arm away. "No more babies!" Her eyes lost their focus again and she began to tremble, her head lowered and shoulders hunched like an obedient dog. "Yes, yes, I understand. No more babies. Have to stay skinny. Have to stay tight."

"Is that why you killed your baby?" asked Claire. Therese's eyes shot up in shock, fear sparking within them like the refractions of the sun. "Is that why you hid your baby in the wall?"

Therese reacted as if stunned by a violent backhand. She rocked back and forth in the chair until her breath came back, then swung up onto her feet, severely agitated. "I TOLD YOU NO MORE BABIES!" she screamed, then began pacing back and forth.

The room went quiet as all eyes turned on them. A nurse came running. She grabbed Therese by the arms and tried to calm her down. "Ladies, what are you doing upsetting her like this? Please, I have to ask you to leave." Claire and Frau Müller nodded apologetically, and as the nurse turned her attention back to Therese, Claire swooped down for the tissue that had fallen to the floor, slipped it into her pocket, then raced after Frau Müller who was already making a hasty exit.

EIGHT

"Well, that didn't go so well," Frau Müller admitted after they had put some distance between themselves and Twin Oaks. "I thought we'd be more Cagney and Lacey than Abbott and Costello. Oh, well, we'll do better next time."

"Next time?" Claire asked with a sideways glance. "I don't think we'd be wise to return."

"Oh, not at Twin Oaks," Frau Müller said matter-of-factly. "Bellevue hospital. That's where Elisabeth is, though I hear she's completely gone. Still, we can't rule her out as the mother so we'll need her DNA, too."

"Excuse me?" How did Frau Müller know Claire was collecting Therese's DNA?

"The tissue in your pocket. I watch television, you know." She paused to let Claire absorb that little nugget, then added, "Genesis Lab in Richmond. They can do it; they're private."

Claire tried to cover her tracks with a chuckle. "How do you even know stuff like that?"

"The news. It's very important to stay abreast of current affairs."

"That's all well and good, but I'm not collecting anyone's DNA and we won't be going to Bellevue. I'm dropping you off at home and then I have shopping to do. I need painting supplies."

Frau Müller pursed her lips in defiance. "You are too collecting DNA. And you'll need me even more at Bellevue. There'll be security and I know Elisabeth. You can't fake that. Besides, I have these." She pulled out two buccal swab pipettes from her purse.

57

Claire's jaw dropped. "How is it that you have buccal swabs?"

"They're from these child identification kits I bought a few years ago for each of my grandkids. Turned out my eldest had already bought two for her boys but I kept the kits just in case. I put the swabs in my purse on a hunch."

Claire let slide a sigh of exasperation. "Then why didn't you say something earlier?"

"Because I wasn't certain what you were up to," Frau Müller replied with a pout. "I was waiting for you to share."

"Oh, for God's sake. Okay, I admit it, I was collecting Therese's DNA. But it ends there."

"But why?" asked Frau Müller. "I never saw Therese pregnant again, and it *is* possible the baby belonged to Elisabeth. She was old enough. We need to be thorough if we're going to solve this case."

"You think I'm focussed on Therese because the alternative is too horrendous?"

"Yes, and you shouldn't assume the worst. Sometimes Ben and Elisabeth used to sneak off together into the garage. Maybe child's play went too far. Sometimes innocent acts can have unintended consequences."

Claire sighed. "Alright, alright, you win. But"—Claire pointed a warning finger at Frau Müller—"not a word of this to *anyone*."

"I promise," Frau Müller replied with a mental cross of her fingers.

"And I really do need to stop at the paint shop."

CR

It was nearing lunchtime when Dylan entered Bellevue Home for Psychiatric Care but the site and smell of it took away any appetite he might have entertained. Bellevue was a few steps up from a government facility but, Dylan thought, manicured gardens and indoor hydrotherapy pools hardly made up for the dire company and the smell of antiseptic. Not to mention the bars on the windows, decorative iron swirls or not.

He had thought much the same when he'd attended earlier at Twin Oaks in the hope of getting a feel for Therese Keller, but had been unable to do anything more than watch her rock herself in a chair—chanting "No more babies" in an eerily monotonous tone—until the mild sedative she'd been given began to take effect and she was led away to bed. She'd been upset by visitors, the nurse had explained, and her description of the offending parties had sounded suspiciously like Claire and perhaps her elderly neighbour. Dylan had tried calling Wilson to update his request for information but her phone went to voicemail, so Dylan had simply cursed to himself and left a message.

Things weren't looking any more hopeful at Bellevue when Dylan approached the nurses' station. The head nurse staring at him over the rim of her wire-framed glasses shrieked austerity and efficiency, her closely cropped hair and wool cardigan hurtling Dylan back to grade school where the sharp whack of Sister Henderson's ruler kept the unruly ones like him in line. May Scott, RN, looked at him dubiously when he claimed to be a family friend, then tapped something into the computer. "Lewis, you say? I don't see your name on the list of approved guests," she asserted almost mockingly, just the way Sister Henderson used to when she recognized deception.

"What," quipped Dylan, "no devil's roster of little boys who lie?"

"I'm sorry?"

Dylan pulled out his badge and came clean. "Detective Dylan Lewis. I need to ask Miss Keller a few questions if you think she might be up to it."

Scott didn't bother to hide her conceit for what she perceived as a win. "Well, detective," she stated haughtily, "I don't think your questions would elicit much of a response. Miss Keller, you see, is in a semi-catatonic state. *Non compos mentis* I believe is the term you people use. In any case, she's a ward of her cousin Benjamin Keller. I couldn't let you talk to her without him or a social worker present."

"Fair enough," shrugged Dylan, "but if you could be so kind as to point Elisabeth Keller out to me I would like to observe her. That"—he smiled with fake modesty—"I don't need permission for." He rocked back on his heels, hands in his pockets, and had to fight back an arrogant grin when he caught the amused eye of the junior nurse standing nearby: she'd been watching Dylan and Scott duel and was now trying to hide her amusement at her supervisor's rapid tumble off her pedestal.

"Very well." May Scott glanced down her nose at the nurse and gave a brief nod. "Vicky here will show you to the lunch room."

Once out of earshot of the iron lady, Dylan plied Vicky for information. Keller had been in the home since December when her father had had a stroke and Benjamin successfully petitioned the court for guardianship of his aunt and cousin. The cost of Elisabeth's care not covered by the government was funded by Benjamin who also visited twice weekly, every Wednesday evening and Saturday morning, like clockwork. Benjamin's love and affection for Elisabeth was "evident even to a blind man" and his hope for her recovery "sweet and endearing."

"What is the hope for her recovery?" asked Dylan.

Vicky frowned. "At the moment, not much. Part of the problem is that we don't know what caused the catatonia. It could be a genetic disorder like schizophrenia or it could be trauma-induced. She hasn't responded well to the usual medications. We're trying a new one now that's just been released for clinical studies. It's expensive but Benjamin is adamant we keep trying regardless of the cost."

"He sounds devoted."

"He's her lifeline," sighed Vicky. "He's the only one she has any emotional response to. When he visits he reads to her or takes her for a walk around the garden, always talking as if she were normal and one day might answer back. I never know whether to feel saddened or encouraged by his tenacity."

Dylan tried to reconcile the image of Benjamin Keller painted by Vicky with the one he'd formed from his vantage point on the other side of the courtroom. Dylan had to admit his was a limited viewpoint and one clouded by frustration whenever Keller won bail for some trigger-happy gangster or house arrest for a homicidal street racer. This new information had Dylan wondering if Keller ever contemplated the other side of Dylan, the one that wasn't a cop, the one that visited his *ta'ah* almost every weekend and planted flowers on his mother's grave every spring, but concluded Keller likely didn't. It was much simpler not knowing. It kept your eye on the target, kept you from fraternizing with the enemy and inadvertently spilling something you shouldn't. Dylan made a note to visit Benjamin Keller earlier than previously planned, not so much to discover the softer side of the man but in the hope of exploiting it. One of these Kellers put Baby Jane in a wall. One of them had to answer for it.

Once inside the common room Vicky pointed out Elisabeth Keller, sitting at the end of one of four white tables that spanned the length of the room. She was being fed the last of her dessert, ready-made chocolate pudding, and on the tray in front of her were the scraps of a lunch not fully eaten. She opened her mouth automatically with the touch of the spoon to her lips but registered neither disgust nor satisfaction with her dinner, simply failing to open her mouth again when she didn't want anymore, her face remaining void of expression.

Dylan sat down across from Elisabeth. In the middle-aged woman's face he immediately saw the resemblance to Therese: mother and daughter had the same sharp nose and angular jaw, the same wiry grey hair, the same anorexic frame. And when she looked up briefly he saw the same striking emerald eyes though hers, he noted, were much softer than her mother's.

"I'm curious," Dylan queried Elisabeth's minder, "how do you communicate with her?"

"One way," the nurse replied ruefully. "She seems to understand what we say to her and she responds to basic commands like sit, lie down, stand up"—she gestured with the spoon—"eat. But nothing more. We've been trying cognitive therapies similar to those used for the severely autistic. And of course medication. But until now she's never received any professional help so unlocking her mind will be a complex process."

"How long has she been like this?"

"Decades, according to her family." She wiped a bit of pudding off Elisabeth's mouth and tossed the napkin onto the tray, then removed the paper bib from around Elisabeth's neck. "Wait here for me, Elisabeth. I'm just going to get rid of your tray and then I'll help you to the couch. You can watch television until Dr. Mitchell sends for you." She was about to grab the tray when Dylan reached out.

"Allow me."

"Thank you; it goes onto the rack over there." Dylan took the tray and placed it in the rack as the nurse turned her attention back to Elisabeth. He watched as she allowed herself to be lead to the couch, shuffling her feet and holding her arms protectively high to her chest, her head down so she could suckle the tips of her thumbs. As soon as Elisabeth was seated in front of the television her eyes followed the screen but she didn't respond to the content; she was like a robot, absorbing everything but revealing nothing. It was sad and creepy.

But then, without prompting, Elisabeth rose and shuffled toward the open patio doors that led to the garden. Dylan wondered if anyone would stop her but the nurse only watched until Elisabeth sat down again in a chair in the shade, and, satisfied she were fine, turned her attention to a man who was undressing himself at the prompting of a trio of women.

Realizing there was nothing more he would get for now, Dylan headed for the front doors, mulling over the case as he strode past the nurses' station. As far as he knew, Therese and Elisabeth had been the only women living in the Keller home at the time of Baby Jane's death, both had been of reproductive age, both were Baby Jane's potential mother. Once Dylan knew which, if either, were the mother the case would become more focused. But there was only one way to get their DNA: he'd have to convince Benjamin Keller to allow a sample, and that would take either unbelievable luck or the diplomacy of a saint. "Charm's my only currency," Dylan mumbled to himself. "Guess I'd better work on it then." He stepped into the sunlight, momentarily blinded while he reached for his shades, just as Claire Dawson was parking her car not forty feet from his side.

NINE

"Get down!" Claire squealed as she dove beneath the dashboard, but Frau Müller, in mid-chatter about the high cost of psychiatric care, failed to grasp the urgency.

"What on earth are you doing, child?" she asked as Claire frantically waved her arms at Frau Müller's head.

"It's Detective Lewis! Get down before he sees you!"

"Whatever for? He doesn't know what I look like."

Claire pulled her arms in and cranked her head around to look up at her neighbour. "Oh. Good point."

"Besides, you can relax now; he's gone." Claire sat back up and smoothed her hair behind one ear. "But I must say, dear," Frau Müller continued, "if you're that easily spooked it might be better if I went in alone. This is clearly a job for a professional."

"Don't push it," Claire shot back as she opened the car door.

Seconds later they were inside the facility.

"This way, I think," whispered Claire, nodding her head in the direction of what sounded like a loud television. They scuttled past an unmanned nurses' station, grateful for the lucky break, and when they reached the common room Frau Müller poked her head through the doorway and quickly analysed the risk.

"She's just outside, in the garden," she whispered as she pulled her head back in. "But we can't go through here: there's too many people around." She paused, then her face brightened when she saw an exit sign in the near distance. "There," she pointed over Claire's shoulder. "That must lead outside."

They hastened toward the exit sign and found themselves standing on the patio about ten feet from Elisabeth. They approached slowly for fear of startling her, an unnecessary concern they quickly discovered: Elisabeth didn't seem to register their presence. Her head remained bowed though her hands were now resting limply in her lap. "Give me one of the swabs, please," Claire whispered, crouching down so she could look Elisabeth in the eye. "And keep a lookout for anyone watching."

Claire caught Elisabeth's eyes if not exactly her attention, smiled sweetly and whispered, "Elisabeth, watch me." Claire opened her mouth, hoping Elisabeth might mimic her, but failed to elicit any response despite repeated invitations.

"Let me try, dear," suggested Frau Müller. "She might respond to something familiar." She took an apple from her purse and held it in front of Elisabeth's eyes. "Would you like an apple from my tree, Elisabeth? And do you think Ben would like one, too? There's lots."

Elisabeth's eyes brightened. The change in expression was almost imperceptible but Frau Müller caught it. "Mmmm, apples for Elisabeth and Ben," Frau Müller murmured. Elisabeth opened her mouth to accept the offering, and Claire quickly reached up with the swab and swiped it across the corner of Elisabeth's lower lip.

"I've got it," Claire said, storing the swab in the sterile pipette. "Let's get out of here." She sprung to her feet and raced for the door, expecting Frau Müller to follow, but instead she remained a moment at Elisabeth's side, one hand on the younger woman's face in a grandmotherly caress. Frau Müller smiled melancholically and pressed the apple into Elisabeth's hands, then reluctantly joined Claire in their flight from the facility.

"You miss her, don't you?" Claire asked when they were safely back in the car.

"She was such a lovely child," Frau Müller replied, her face turned to the side window to hide her tears.

♋

It was after one o'clock by the time Dylan had downed a quick lunch of sushi then made his way through snarled traffic back to the station. The delay had given him time to think. Elisabeth was in a semi-catatonic state that could be trauma-induced, Therese was going on about no more babies, and Armin Keller was ... what? A control freak? An abuser? A possible Nazi? What little Dylan had gathered so far about the family dynamics told him Armin was not a kind man. How else to account for the lack of care provided to Elisabeth? It wasn't about money: her care would have been paid for by the state. No, Armin Keller didn't want his daughter talking to some shrink; her catatonic state was convenient. And he had kept her at home like that for decades, had kept her prisoner. But was he protecting himself or someone else?

And Therese, where was she in all this? Puttering about the house while her daughter wasted away? How fucked up was that?

Dylan walked into the squad room and found the canvass team's interim report sitting on his desk. Perfect, he thought, I'll pick this over while I wait for Wilson to call. He got himself a soft drink from the vending machine and settled in for a read. Nothing new since their initial canvass: most of the neighbours had moved to the area in the last decade; everyone knew the house was home to an elderly couple and their "crazy daughter" but nothing much more. There were never visitors, and the family rarely ventured out together. Therese spent a disproportionate amount of time tending to her garden yet never spoke to anyone. There were no police complaints, no ambulance calls except for Armin's stroke in December.

Then, finally, something worthy of a ticked box that signalled a need for follow-up: Karl Keller had left home, had "run away" an elderly neighbour had insisted, just days after his sixteenth birthday in September 1970. How could Mrs. Gambini be so specific? Karl had been dating her daughter, Bella, then also sixteen; three days after they had celebrated his birthday at the Gambini home he had stopped by late at night, duffel bag in hand, to say goodbye. Something terrible had clearly happened: Karl's face was bruised and he was severely agitated; a plea by her daughter for an explanation was met with an angry outburst. He left and was never seen again. A few years later he sent a letter to say he had joined the army and was sorry for the way he had left, requesting forgiveness. But Bella had moved on; she married a year later.

The story jigged. Dylan thumbed his way through the papers piling up in the file. There it was: Karl had a sheet for petty crimes commencing in late September 1971 and ending in October 1972 when he had joined the military. The crimes were consistent with a runaway—shoplifting, break and enter, vandalism, possession of stolen goods—and they probably started right after he left home, Dylan surmised, but there was nowhere to go looking for that: Karl's juvenile records would have been destroyed under the 1984 *Young Offenders Act* when a bar fight in 1990 had led to a public mischief charge and brought attention to his old file. "And now he's dead," muttered Dylan. "Damn!" Here's hoping Karl confided in somebody, thought Dylan as he placed a call to his contact at National Defence.

"Callaghan," answered a slight Irish lilt. Bob Callaghan was a career military man from a career military family whose father had defended everything British during World War II except the honour of one Bessie O'Brian, fathered Bob and brought both wife and child home to Canada to the surprise of relatives. That Bob had been the product of a wartime romance he wore with considerable pride, his very existence proof of the Callaghan clan's virility and sexual appeal. "Never met a woman we couldn't charm," he had declared, slapping Dylan on the back in the stands of the hockey game where they had met. Dylan had found the elder man's hearty laugh and *joie de vivre* irresistible and the two had become fast friends despite the demands of work and conflicting schedules. There were few opportunities to meet but when they did they behaved like father and son.

"Hey Bob, it's Dylan."

"Dylan, my boy," chimed Callaghan, "long time no hear. What's up?"

"I need some info on a deceased soldier. Name's Karl Keller. Born 10 September 1954. ID number sierra-nine-eight, echo-two-three, zero-eight-five."

Dylan could hear the tap-tapping of Callaghan's keyboard. "Twelve Service Battalion," he said after a few seconds. "Used to be at Jericho but now housed at the Sherman Armoury in Richmond. Reservist mechanic, Vehicle Technician Section. Career corporal. Died Bosnia, 1993, Operation Harmony. Buried at Mountain View on Fraser. Next of kin—oh, that's unusual."

"What's unusual?"

"No next of kin named. Final pay was directed to Children's Hospital as specified in Keller's will."

"Any idea who could give me more?"

"Yeah, his sergeant is now the deputy C.O. of 12. Major Gregory Williamson. I know him. He's a good man. Let me make a call first and I'll set you up."

While Dylan waited anxiously for the return call he calculated a new possibility. If the carbon test was off by six months to one year, Baby Jane may very well have died in 1970. Had Karl killed her then run for his freedom? Had the family covered up his crime? And yet Karl had no known history of violence save for that minor skirmish in a bar, and that only made him a drunken idiot, not a murderer. Still ...

The phone rang. "Homicide, Detective Lewis."

"Major Williamson here. Got a call from Bob Callaghan. Said you have some questions about a Corporal Karl Keller. Homicide, eh? Sounds ominous. Our boy didn't murder someone, did he?"

"Would it surprise you if he did?"

"Is this on the record?"

"Your call, major."

"There's a pub on Cambie called The Privateer. Meet me there in an hour."

CR

Claire nervously scanned the signs in a new industrial complex off Richmond's No. 3 Road, looking for the Genesis Lab. Frau Müller had written the address out for Claire but had declined to attend with her: the ladies were due for cards at two o'clock and Frau Müller needed to get the coffee percolating and last evening's baking set out.

Claire parked the car and drew several deep breaths to calm her nerves. Her earlier confidence had withered away during the drive south, and she'd had to remind herself repeatedly of the greater objective. When had she become such a coward, she wondered? She'd been so adventurous as a child. Was it just the socializing effect of growing up? Of learning respect for boundaries and rules? *I expect better of you, Claire. We all do.* Her father's stern disapproval when Claire had been suspended from school for hitting a boy who'd bullied one of the smaller kids in their class. She'd been defending the weak, Claire had argued indignantly, just like the U.N. Peacekeepers she'd just read about in her eighth-grade social studies; no one was suspending *them.* Her father didn't appreciate Claire's argument or her insolence, and grounded her for a week.

Reclaim your power, a voice in Claire's head rang through the detritus.

The thought emboldened her again, and she built upon that until she felt her earlier confidence return. Screw 'em, she concluded angrily: she was defending the weak, an innocent child. Her father was wrong then and he'd be wrong now. Claire threw off her seatbelt with a defiant flourish, opened the car door and marched into Genesis.

The transaction took only a few minutes. The lab asked no questions, an omission Claire attributed to her newly authoritative demeanour. She paid in advance, as required, and was promised results the following Friday morning.

With nothing to do now but wait, Claire headed for home, her mind awhirl. *I TOLD YOU NO MORE BABIES!* Someone—Armin Keller, no doubt—had screamed those words at Therese. Had she failed to obey and he killed the baby as punishment? Or was Claire's first thought correct: that the baby had shown signs of mental defect and its parents, anxious not to be saddled with a second disabled child, killed it? Or maybe Frau Müller was right, that Elisabeth was as likely to be the child's mother as Therese. Or was Detective Lewis correct, that Claire was jumping to conclusions and this wasn't a homicide at all? Might the baby have been stillborn? "But then why hide it?" Claire murmured to herself. Why hide a legitimate death? And why bury it in a wall? It doesn't make sense. None of it made sense. But then when does the death of a child ever make sense?

പ്ര

Constable Wilson knocked on Claire's door. No answer. Wilson went around back and noticed Claire's car was not in the driveway. On the back of one of her cards Wilson wrote a note for Claire to call in when she returned home and left it on the back door, then headed next door for a chat with Astrid Müller. Frau Müller answered the door promptly and when she saw who it was Wilson detected a fleeting look of panic on the elder woman's face.

"Yes, yes, come in," she replied a little too earnestly to Wilson's request for a chat. "And you're just in time. We haven't started our game yet." "We" Wilson thought grimly as she followed Frau Müller through the papered hallway and into the dining room: more wallpaper, striped this time, a faded wool area carpet in shades of peach and lime green, heavy lace curtains, and an antique sideboard covered with family photos. Around the oval teak table three other elderly women were seated, coffee and cake at their sides and a deck of cards between them.

"Afternoon, ladies."

"Is this about the dead baby?" one of the ladies eagerly asked.

Great, thought Wilson, might as well broadcast it on the news now.

"Annie, where's your manners?" admonished Frau Müller. Then to Wilson, "I must apologize. It's just it isn't very often such excitement comes our way. Though I suppose excitement isn't a good word for it. Poor thing. To have been murdered like that."

"Why do you say murdered?" asked Wilson, her antenna perking up.

"Well I don't suppose you end up in a wall if it's natural causes," Frau Müller replied tersely. "Besides, I wouldn't put it past that Nazi." Wilson's raised eyebrows intimidated Frau Müller. "Well, it's true," she responded indignantly. "Armin *was* a Nazi, just like his father. Tried to hide it when they came here but everybody knew. Armin's still a card-carrying member last I heard." The other women nodded solemnly in agreement.

"That's very interesting to know, thank you," smiled Wilson. "Though I should point out that we don't yet know how the baby died, when, or who put it in the wall, so it's probably best not to jump to conclusions." Frau Müller pursed her lips: she didn't like being scolded, even nicely.

"Now ladies," Wilson said, changing track, "I have to ask that you not discuss this further with anyone else. This is a very serious matter and we need to keep it under wraps for a little while longer to protect the integrity of our investigation. Can we be assured of your cooperation?" Wilson looked around at four disappointed faces. "Just a little while longer?" she stressed. The women begrudgingly nodded their heads.

"Great. Thank you. Now, before I go I need each of you to give me your name and date of birth, just for our records." The request made the women feel important and they all hoped they might be called upon as witnesses.

"Agnes Vreeland, May 9th, 1929."

"Annie Carter, December 16th, 1933."

"Abigail Manning, March 12th, 1935."

"Astrid Müller, July 24th, 1930."

"So that's Agnes, Annie, Abigail and Astrid?" Wilson confirmed, trying not to sound amused.

"Yes, we're the A-Team," laughed Agnes.

Wilson chuckled. "Well, ladies, thank you again. And remember," she said, putting a finger to her lips, "mom's the word."

"But officer," Abigail raised her hand for attention, "it *is* alright if we talk among ourselves, isn't it?"

"Sure." As if we could stop you, Wilson thought wryly, even if we surgically removed your tongues. She headed for the door with Frau Müller nipping at her heels. Just before Wilson made it out the door she turned and casually asked, "Mrs. Müller, by any chance were you and your new neighbour, Claire Dawson, at Twin Oaks Assisted Living Villa this morning?"

Frau Müller blanched but corrected herself. "Why, yes. I suggested to Claire that I take Therese some flowers from her garden; I thought it would cheer her up. She was an avid gardener, you see, like myself; we had that in common. And then Claire very kindly offered to drive me."

Wilson smiled. "What a lovely gesture. Do you know where I might find Claire now?"

"No idea. She said she had errands to run, but I don't know what."

"Well, thank you for your time." Wilson left Frau Müller's and walked around back to take one last look at Claire's driveway in case she had returned home, saw the still empty gravel patch, then headed back onto the road.

CR

Dylan entered the dimness of The Privateer pub and looked around. He wasn't sure if the major would be in uniform but that concern was quickly erased: Major Gregory Williamson was indeed wearing his stripes. He was a bear of a man, as thick as he was tall and still trim. Dylan had no doubt he'd probably lose a fight with the major despite the twenty years he had on him, and hoped Callaghan's recommendation had been glowing. Dylan walked over to the corner table and introduced himself.

"Detective, have a seat." Williamson reached out a hand and gave Dylan's a crushing shake. "Can I get you a beer?"

"Thanks, no, I'm still on duty. Soda water will do."

Williamson called out for the waitress by name. Clearly a regular. He waited for the soda to arrive and the waitress to move on before broaching the subject of Keller. "Can you tell me what he did?" asked the major.

"Truthfully, Major, nothing as yet. Remains were found in a house he grew up in. They date back around 1971, shortly after he left home. I'm still trying to fit the pieces together. What can you tell me about Karl Keller?"

The major blew out a heavy sigh. "Troubled boy. We joined at the same time, were bunk mates for awhile. He'd been in trouble with the law, just petty stuff really, but then you probably know that already. Joined the army to find a family, I think."

"How come he never made it past corporal in twenty-one years of service?"

"Had a short fuse, our Karl, what these days they call 'anger management issues.' He was a damn fine soldier and a brilliant mechanic—could fix an engine with duct tape and twist ties—but he wasn't leadership material. He knew that and he was okay with it."

"Sounds like there's a 'but' in there." Dylan looked hopefully at the major. Williamson took a long look at Dylan, sizing him up, then seemed to decide the detective was okay.

"There was an incident early on, not long past basic training. Some jerk called him a mother—well, you know, I don't like to say the word, it's offensive—and Karl just lost it. Broke the private's jaw in two places. But it was the seventies, attitudes were different then, and most figured the guy had it coming. Karl got off with a reprimand."

"You said he had a short fuse. How many other incidents like this were there?"

The major hesitated, his forehead furrowing into deep worry lines. "Understand, even though I moved up the ranks Karl was still my friend."

"I understand, Major," Dylan asserted. "But the remains, they're of a baby girl. I need to find out what went on in that house so if there's anything you can tell me, please do. Karl's dead, buried with full honours. Nothing you say today can hurt him."

Williamson's nostrils flared. "I can tell you for certain," he declared, rapping his middle finger on the table, "Karl was no baby killer. He was an angry man, no two ways about it, but he'd never hurt a child. Got himself killed trying to save one from a sniper."

Dylan backed off, opting for a different tactic. "Why do you think Karl never named his next of kin?"

The tactic worked: the major relaxed again. "I can't tell you for certain because Karl wouldn't talk about them. Said they were dead as far as he was concerned. Even considered legally changing his name until he found out he'd have to publish his intentions in the newspaper and he didn't want his parents to find out where he was. But there is someone who may be able to tell you. After Karl got into another altercation he was ordered into counselling. We sent him to the trauma centre at Vancouver General. Doc's name is Kerry Gladstone. She's now head of the Operational Stress Injury Clinic out at UBC. Must be near retirement now, though."

Dylan took that as an indication his time with the major was up. Dylan gave the man a solid look of respect. "Major, I thank you. And I promise you I'll be discreet. If Karl's innocent of this his secrets will be safe with me." The major nodded then looked down into his beer. He certainly hoped so.

TEN

Claire unloaded the painting supplies from her car and carried them inside. The cans were hot from the hours spent in the heat of her trunk, and when she opened the can of wallpaper remover the fumes practically steamed out. This turned Claire's mind to coffee, which she hadn't had since morning and was therefore long overdue. Thus, with the ease of a skilled procrastinator she delayed her plans to strip the living room walls and headed for Audrey's.

When she entered the coffee shop the Mexican mother from the other day was sitting in the corner nursing her son. Claire's instinct was to bolt but before she could the barista was asking for her order. Claire ordered a double latte and a bran muffin, then had a thought and ordered two.

She took her purchase and headed for the corner just as the baby was finished nursing, his mother removing the red embroidered shawl she had covered herself with. As Claire approached she smiled and the woman's face lit up in return.

"My name's Claire. May I join you?"

The woman gestured to the chair across from her. "I'm Maria," she replied with her unmistakable accent.

Claire sat down and pushed a muffin across the table. "A peace offering," she explained. "For lying to you. I didn't have a meeting with my contractor the other day. I just didn't"—she glanced down at the boy—"want to talk."

"I understand."

Claire raised her palms. "No you don't." She didn't wish to be snappy but it irritated her when other women, especially mothers, pretended they understood her pain. Besides, she didn't want to talk about it: she'd managed to push yesterday's incident with Detective Lewis out of her mind and this would only encourage the return of negative thoughts.

"I know that look. I had it once, too," Maria pressed on.

"What look?" Claire asked defensively, regretting that she hadn't chosen cowardice when she'd had the chance.

"Jealousy. Pain. Injustice. Because they have what you want, what you lost."

Claire looked at Maria in disbelief. Was it visible to *everyone*? Or was it a look only certain women shared? "You?"

Maria nodded. "Twice."

Claire's jaw fell. "I'm so sorry. When?"

"Many years ago. I married young, at twenty-two. At first I couldn't get pregnant. Finally it happened. We were so excited. But after three months it left us. Another came but also left us, this time at seven weeks. I felt so worthless. In my culture children are very important; a barren woman is less than nothing."

"And your husband?"

Maria smiled sadly. "My husband was perfect. He never blamed me, never made me feel ashamed. I did that all by myself." She paused, then lowered her voice. "After the second baby died I tried to kill myself. Carlos, my husband, he found me and took me to hospital. When I woke up he was crying. He said, 'Maria, why? Why would you leave me? Don't you know'"—Maria's eyes misted and her voiced trembled—"'don't you know I don't want children if I can't have them with you?'"

Claire listened, transfixed. Maria's openness was extraordinary. And to a stranger yet. Claire wondered if there were some secret society that only women of this identical wound were allowed to join. "And yet now you have a son?" The little boy smiled and gurgled and pulled at his mother's hair as if he knew he were the subject of the conversation.

Maria smiled. "Actually I have two. And also a daughter." She laughed at the surprise on Claire's face then turned serious again. "When I couldn't get pregnant I said, 'God is punishing me.' But I couldn't imagine what I had done to make God hate me so much. I was a good girl, I took care of my parents, I worked hard, I went to church. What had I done?

"And Carlos would say, 'Why do people think God only answers your prayers when you get what you want? God answers all prayers. But sometimes the answer is no, or maybe, or not yet. God is not giving us a child because He wants us to look outside our own hearts.'

"My husband was born in Tijuana. His family was very poor. He smuggled himself into the States and then Canada. He worked very hard and became an accountant. That is where we met, at college. Carlos thought maybe God wanted us to honour our new lives by helping other children. So we went to Tijuana. We found two children at an orphanage there, a brother and sister. Their mother was dead, from AIDS, and no one knew who the fathers were except that there had been two. So we adopted them. Juan is six now and in his first year of school. Bonita is five and in kindergarten."

"And this one?" Claire asked.

"This is Vicente. We named him after the president because he was a pleasant surprise too," she said with a laugh. Maria followed Claire's gaze down to Vicente's smiling face. "Would you like to hold him? I think he likes you."

Claire hesitated. She could feel her arms aching but her heart was pounding with trepidation. Did she dare? What would happen if she held him? Would she crumble right there in her seat? Or, worse still, instinctively run for the door while Maria screamed for her baby?

Claire nodded and Maria passed Vicente over the table. He smiled and put his fist in his mouth, then slobbered over Claire's blouse as she held him to her chest. "He's beautiful," she whispered as she inhaled his intoxicating baby scent.

Maria leaned across the table and laid her hand on Claire's arm. "You must have faith, Claire. It's hard to do when you're in pain but that is when your faith must be strongest. God has great plans for you. I can feel it."

Claire let her lips rest on the top of Vicente's head, closed her eyes tightly and let his presence permeate her senses. She drank in the smoothness of his skin, the smell of baby powder, the fine, wavy black hair that tickled her nose, the softness of his blue cotton knit sleeper. She sat like that for what seemed like minutes but in truth was only a few seconds, then raised her head and listened in amazement as her own story tumbled from her lips.

CR

Benjamin Keller returned to his office from court to missed messages from Twin Oaks and Bellevue. Two women had visited Therese and upset her; did Mr. Keller wish to impose any restrictions? Ben found the message odd, but the message from Bellevue was more disturbing still: a detective by the name of Dylan Lewis was there and had requested an interview with Elisabeth; he had been refused but then demanded to observe her, and was now in the common room. What did Benjamin want the hospital to do?

Benjamin tapped his forefinger on his desk. Dylan Lewis. The name was familiar but Ben couldn't quite place it. He typed the name in the firm's records search. "Ah, there you are," he murmured to himself, then, "Whoa! *Homicide?*" What the hell was a homicide detective doing visiting Elisabeth? Ben placed a call to the department. "Detective Dylan Lewis, please."

"I'll put you through."

"You've reached the direct line of Detective Dylan Lewis, Homicide Team Two," chirped Dylan's voicemail. "If this is an emergency please hang up and dial nine-one-one. Please note regular hours are Tuesday to Friday, eight a.m. to six p.m. Please leave your name and number and I will return your call during those times."

Benjamin tossed the phone down, annoyed, then thought better of it. If Lewis weren't back until Tuesday that gave Benjamin three days to ask questions of his own. And he knew just where to start.

Officer Wilson's cellphone rang as she sat in her cruiser typing up an incident report for the burglary call she'd just responded to. She had placed a call to Lewis earlier and, thinking it were him, didn't bother to check her call display. "Wilson."

"Hey gorgeous."

Wilson froze. She knew that voice, would recognize it a mile away, in the dark. And he was the last man she wanted to hear from right now.

"Rebecca, you're speechless. I'm flattered," the voice laughed.

"How can I help you, Ben?" Wilson asked, trying to sound all business.

"I want to know why one of your homicide detectives is visiting my cousin Elisabeth."

"How should I know? I don't work Homicide. I'm just a lowly constable."

"Because if there's a murder investigation *everyone* knows about it," Ben replied dryly. "And you shouldn't sell yourself short like that, Rebecca; there's nothing lowly about you. Quite the contrary."

"Flattery will get you nowhere, Ben," Wilson sniped at him.

"Worked in the past," he laughed.

Wilson's face went hard. She was starting to lose her patience. "I can't talk, Ben. I have to go."

"But Rebecca, haven't we always shared?"

"Look," she snapped at him, "just because you bedded me doesn't mean you own me! If you have a question for Lewis ask him yourself."

"How did you know I was referring to Dylan Lewis?"

"We're done, Ben." Wilson hit the end button and took a deep breath to stop her shaking. Damn it anyway! What was she going to do now? If she gave Lewis the heads up she'd have to explain why Keller was calling *her* for information. If she didn't give Lewis the heads up it could jeopardize his investigation, and with it any chance she had of capturing his affections. Either way she was screwed. Wilson felt a wave of nausea wash over her, then slowly dissipate. Okay, okay, yes she was thoroughly screwed right now but she was no fool. She knew who signed her paycheques and it wasn't Keller Jamieson Clark and Associates. She sucked in a deep breath and headed for the station.

℞

The after-work crowd was beginning to trickle in to Audrey's, punctuating the end of Claire's story. To her astonishment she had spared no embarrassing detail yet not once did Maria cast a disparaging look Claire's way. The affair with a married man, the pregnancy and miscarriage, the illness and scarring Claire interpreted as karmic retribution—Maria absorbed it all with no more than sympathetic nods and a comforting hand whenever Claire struggled to keep her composure in this public space. Maria's generosity touched Claire, and this time she was ready to receive it.

In return for her openness Claire learned more about Maria's life: that she was born in Mexico City and had immigrated to Canada with her family at the age of ten, that she was five years older than she looked, that she had waitressed at a local Spanish restaurant to put herself through college. Now she worked out of her home as a bookkeeper and accountant for a handful of clients, mostly self-employed small business owners and artists from the area. Maria liked the flexibility this afforded her, that it allowed her to take care of her children without entirely abandoning her career. Carlos worked for a large accounting firm, handling mostly corporate bankruptcies. Together they had built a solid life, one filled with family and friends. "I still have a few complaints," Maria had confided, laughing, "but I know they are petty."

The women had talked for the better part of two hours when Vicente woke up and made his displeasure known. "I must go," lamented Maria. "He needs his teething ointment and I left it at home."

Claire nodded and handed their coffee cups and muffin plates to the café's busboy as she and Maria prepared to leave. "I can't thank you enough, Maria, for all this. For sharing, for listening. I didn't realize how silenced I felt until now. You wouldn't think so after all the talking I did in therapy."

"It's not the same as finding others."

Claire nodded. "Yes, I think you're right." She gazed down at Vicente, sucking impatiently on his soother. "Do you ever think about them, the ones you lost?"

Maria shook her head lightly. "No. I think only about the pain I caused others by shutting them out. It reminds me to talk to Carlos, always."

Claire nodded her head, her thoughts drifting to the friends she had pushed away and lost. If only she had let them comfort her in whatever way they could; if only she'd been content with their willingness not to judge her, hadn't insisted upon their acceptance also. She wondered if she could win any of them back.

Maria reached out a hand to draw Claire's attention away from the floor and the dark clouds forming behind her eyes. "Listen, Carlos and I are having a barbecue on Sunday. You must come. There will be lots of people and"—she smiled playfully—"some nice single men."

Her grin was proving infectious. There was something about Maria's optimism that had Claire imagining herself drinking margaritas and charming roguish Mexican men. "Yes," she answered confidently, "I'd loved to." The women exchanged addresses and phone numbers then parted company.

There was a lightness in her walk as Claire made her way home, the burden of her shame cast off by exposure. It seemed paradoxical, this, and nothing she would have expected. Perhaps it was solely because Maria shared Claire's experience, knew intimately her pain, hadn't just offered empty platitudes about hope for the future; or perhaps, Claire contemplated, I'm just finally ready. Ready to face the world with whatever baggage I carry and not feel guilty or embarrassed. She thought again of Detective Lewis, how she had imploded when he asked what she now acknowledged was a valid question, and thought again about calling to apologize. The idea of doing so, of being able to do so, made her feel nervous and yet exhilarated. How amazing that a chance encounter could so radically alter one's earlier temperament, so radically change one's life.

But then maybe there were no such things as chance encounters, she pondered next. Maybe there really was something to this idea that everything happens for a reason. If Claire's morning had not been interrupted by espionage she would not have elected to visit Audrey's this late in the day, would not have discovered that the Mexican mother she had earlier ignored was a kindred spirit. And she certainly wouldn't be going to a party on Sunday. Perhaps, Claire concluded, serendipity was just the rational mind, unable as it is to see the whole picture, trying to account for its limited vision. Even though Maria's religious views weren't something Claire shared she was beginning to like this idea of a grand plan. It gave life meaning, gave it purpose.

When Claire reached her house she quickly changed clothes, eager again to push forward with the renovations. The thermal windows were coming Monday; she'd ask the installers to start with the living room and then she could paint while they finished the rest of the house. But first she needed to remove the wallpaper. It was going to be an ugly, tedious job but nothing could quell Claire's newfound optimism.

Ꮟ

Dylan slipped behind the wheel of his cruiser and glanced at his watch. It was four o'clock. Enough time to head back, dump the cruiser, finish reading the canvass team's report, then get his own in for the day. And then what? Most everyone would be going off to Miller's retirement party tonight. Dylan briefly toyed with the idea of attending just to take his mind off the case but the thought of Wilson cancelled those plans: when Wilson drank she became sexually aggressive and right now the last thing Dylan needed was to be chased around by a drunken redhead. Well, he thought next, at least it's the weekend. He could sleep in tomorrow. Maybe even put the case out of his mind for three days. Or if not out of his mind at least push it back a little bit. Oh, whom was he kidding? Baby Jane haunted him more than she haunted Claire's house.

Dawson came to mind just as Dylan was passing a florist. He stopped. Why not? He owed her an apology and nothing says sorry like flowers. But he'd have to choose carefully, no roses for love or anything like that. Simple, classy, professional, that was the ticket. He ignored the no stopping sign and parked: what was the point of being a cop if you couldn't park your cruiser anywhere you liked?

He explained his needs to the florist. Nothing romantic, nothing sexy, just simple, for a friend. She suggested calla lilies. "Really?" asked Dylan. "Don't you think they're kind of erotic?"

"How so?" she replied, sincerely clueless.

"Well, you know," he stumbled to explain, "the flower looks kind of like a, you know, and that thing in the middle—oh, never mind, I'll take three." He left a few minutes later, the lilies tied together with an elegant purple cloth ribbon.

Dylan headed into the squad room and found Wilson waiting for him at his desk. "Nice flowers," she smiled. "Are they for me?"

"No," he replied a little too abruptly. "They're for my grandmother."

"Kind of sexy for a grandmother, don't you think?"

Oh God damn it, he thought, he should have put more stock into his own opinion. "What did you find out, Wilson?"

"Dawson wasn't in but I spoke with the neighbour. She admitted she and Dawson visited Therese Keller this morning; claimed she wanted to take her some flowers from the garden—apparently Therese was an avid gardener—and Claire offered to drive. Anyhow, story's bunk. But I didn't want to press on in case I stepped on your toes."

"Thanks. And thanks for the favour. Much appreciated." He picked up the canvass team report so as to avoid any further conversation but Wilson didn't leave, instead loitering nervously in front of Dylan's desk. "Something else?"

She glanced anxiously around the squad room. "Walk with me?"

Dylan didn't like the sound of that: would she ask him again about Miller's retirement party? And what if she grew bolder and flat out asked him to join her? This was getting awkward: he was running out of excuses. "Give me a minute to check my messages and then I'll walk you out," he said, trying to contain the slight squeak in his voice. Wilson nodded and left the squad room. Dylan checked for messages, found nothing important, and begrudgingly rose from his desk and went after Wilson. She was waiting by the elevators. "What's up?"

Wilson looked uncomfortable and then relieved when the elevator door opened and it was empty. The two got in and she hit the main floor button. "I got a call from Benjamin Keller today wanting to know why you were visiting his cousin Elisabeth. Thought I should give you a heads up."

"Good to know, thanks. But why would Keller be calling you?" Wilson looked away in embarrassment. "No way," Dylan said, surprised. "You and *Keller* doing the dirty?"

Wilson could feel her cheeks starting to match her fiery hair. "It was a long time ago," she insisted, trying to make light of it. The elevator doors opened onto the main floor and the two headed for the front doors. "It was a brief fling; I don't think it lasted a month. We met at a party. He was charming; I was drunk."

"For the whole month?" Dylan mocked.

"Oh, shut up. Anyhow, I didn't give him any information. That's the important thing. Everything else is just—"

"Currency," Dylan interjected, laughing. "In fact, I think my silence makes us even." He slapped her on the back. "Enjoy the party tonight," he said as he turned and headed back toward the elevators, still laughing. "But if there's any lawyers in attendance you might want to lay off the booze." As Dylan walked away Wilson imagined crosshairs in the middle of his back and considered drawing her gun.

ᙉ

Dylan sat in his jeep on the street a little ways down from Claire's. From his vantage point he could see her up on a ladder scraping the paper off her living room walls. She was wearing cut-offs and a V-neck T-shirt, and the light from the window cast a striking highlight along the side of her shapely legs. He sat there watching her, entranced but apprehensive, the lilies on the seat beside him.

Claire stepped down off the ladder and put her scraper aside. She'd been at the wallpaper for almost two hours now and it was time for a break. The chemicals were giving her a headache and her neck was stiff from holding it slightly off to one side. More importantly, she was hungry. She grabbed the phone book, found a local pizza place and ordered delivery, then plopped down on the couch to watch the news—if only she could find the remote. She stood back up to search between the cushions when she saw out of her corner of her eye ... Detective Lewis? It was a different vehicle, a jeep instead of the usual Crown Victoria, and parked a few doors up, but Claire was pretty sure it was him. Was she under surveillance? She wondered how long he'd been sitting there, watching her. The idea shot a hot streak of acrimony along her spine. How dare he? She stomped over to the front door and flung it open but stopped in her tracks when she saw him get out of his vehicle and—were those flowers in his hand? She stood there, her mind awhirl, as Dylan walked to her door.

"Am I under surveillance?" she asked.

"Not officially," he smiled. "May I come in?" Claire nodded and stepped back. "These are for you," he said, handing her the lilies. "I owe you an apology," he explained a little too quickly. "For the other day. I was out of line. And I thought it would be bad form if I came empty-handed."

Claire felt embarrassed. Once again she'd jumped to conclusions, had been too quick to anger. There was just something about Dylan Lewis that made her too emotional. Claire smiled weakly. "Thank you, but I'm the one who should apologize. It was a valid question and I lost it. There's no excuse for flipping out on you like that. I'm really, really ashamed. Especially about the comment regarding your ethnicity. I didn't mean it the way it sounded and it mortifies me to know you believed otherwise. I have great respect for your culture and I'm profoundly sorry."

"I know," he replied with a shrug. "And for the record, it wasn't a valid question. The remains date to 1971. Ten years before you were even born. I jumped the gun. You're completely in the clear." He took a step towards her. "At least on that point."

"What do you mean?"

"Why were you and Astrid Müller visiting Therese Keller this morning?"

The question caught Claire completely unawares and she was momentarily seized by panic. Her perfect plan was in danger of unravelling, the grand unveiling of the test results at risk of premature revelation. She searched anxiously for a plausible excuse that would stave off disaster; what she came up with was, "Oh, just morbid curiosity, I suppose. After Frau Müller told me about Therese I wanted to see what she looked like, so we went to the home and she pointed her out to me." *Good grief, Claire, that was lame.*

"So it was your idea to go?"

"Yes. So if anyone is in trouble for this, it should be me."

"That's interesting. Because she says it was her idea to go—wanted to take Therese some flowers and you just so graciously offered to drive."

"Really?" Claire tried to sound genuinely surprised but she knew she was drowning.

"Here's a tip, Ms. Dawson," Dylan offered facetiously, "if you're going to do something you know you're not supposed to, do it alone or make sure you and your co-conspirators are on the same page. Otherwise you make my job way too easy." He paused to observe Claire's embarrassment then swooped in for the kill. "Now give me the claim ticket for Genesis Lab."

Claire's free hand flew up in frustration. "That blasted old woman! She *promised* not to tell anyone."

"She didn't. But thanks for the confirmation."

"What?" Claire asked in the second before she realised she'd been played. "Oh damn it! It was supposed to be a surprise."

"A surprise? For what, my birthday? This is a murder investigation, Ms. Dawson, not a party game. What were you thinking?"

"You said your hands were tied! And I thought since mine are not I'd have Therese's DNA profiled and give it to you to compare to the baby's. She deserves a *name*. I know it was wrong but it's not like it was *illegal*."

"True, unless you count the *Human Tissue Act*."

"Oh." Claire's face paled. "Am I under arrest?"

"You will be if you don't give me the claim ticket."

Claire looked suitably chastised as she fetched the claim ticket from her purse on the pine table, leaving the lilies behind. "Hold on, this is for two tests," Dylan said, glancing at the receipt. "Who's the second one? Elisabeth?"

Claire nodded. "I thought it was superfluous but Frau Müller argued we couldn't rule Elisabeth out. Easy for her to say; she didn't have to pay for it."

"And how did you pay?"

"With my credit card," Claire shrugged, as if it should be obvious.

Dylan shook his head again and laughed. "Here's another tip: when committing a criminal offence, pay cash."

Claire smiled despite her embarrassment. "Point taken. But to be fair I wasn't aware I was committing an offence." She paused. "Just out of curiosity, how did you find out about the lab?"

"Ms. Dawson, I've been a cop for fifteen years," Dylan answered with a grin. "You were so convinced Therese had an unwanted child that when I heard about your visit I put two and two together and called Genesis to see if anyone matching your description had been in today. And you used your real name. Duh."

Oh hell, thought Claire, he *is* good. "Are you angry with me?"

Dylan shrugged. "No. These tests may be inadmissible but they might prove useful. So I really should thank you, though if asked I'll deny it."

"You're welcome," Claire smiled back, her discomfort swept away by a wave of gratitude.

Dylan took an involuntary step toward her. "But you have to promise me, Ms. Dawson, no more playing detective. Are we agreed?"

"Yes," she replied humbly. "And you can call me Claire."

"Claire."

Dylan took another involuntary step toward her, his eyes never straying from her face. They stood there for what seemed like an eternity, just staring at each other, before Claire found her voice. "Kiss me." There was an explosion in Dylan's head and before he could weigh the consequences his mouth was on hers.

Her lips were soft and wet and hungry. He pressed Claire up against the wall, pressed his chest against her breasts; it was as if every inch of space between them had to be crossed, had to be eliminated so nothing stood between him and his desire. One hand held her waist, the other buried itself in her hair. All he could think, feel, breathe was the smell of her skin, the taste of her mouth. He wanted more. He wanted all of her. He wanted her naked.

Claire could feel her legs weakening under the weight of her hunger. She breathed in the scent of his cologne and pulled at his shirt, eager for the touch of flesh. His mouth was on her neck, his tongue licking the sweat forming at the base of her throat. "Touch me," she whispered.

He pulled back her T-shirt and the lace cup of her bra and engulfed her breast with his hand. He raised his lips to hers again, his mouth hard and demanding. "I want you. Say yes," he whispered as he deftly undid the button of her cut-offs—when the doorbell rang. Claire let out a scream and just about fainted from the sudden surge of adrenalin. Dylan let go and cursed the Fates. "God damn," he stammered, "who the hell is that?"

Claire caught her breath. "It must be the pizza."

"Mother Mary!" Dylan exclaimed and turned away from the foyer. He moved over to the couch and sat down while Claire straightened herself out and answered the door. As Claire handled the transaction Dylan struggled to get a hold of himself. This was stupid, dangerous, and he knew it. What the hell had he been thinking coming here, bearing flowers yet? You weren't thinking, he scolded himself, that's the problem. If McTavish found out about this there would be such hell to pay. An indiscretion like this could cost a man his place on the squad.

Dylan waited for the delivery boy to walk away then stood to go. Claire came into the room and started to laugh about the interruption when the look on Dylan's face told her something had changed. She put the pizza down on the pine table and braced herself. "Claire," he said quietly, "I can't do this. There are rules, my job."

Claire felt the colour drain from her face. "What? No. Stay."

Dylan shook his head. "I can't. I'm lead detective on a case that involves your home. I know you've been cleared but this is just the sort of thing some slimy defence attorney will use to discredit me." He took her face in his hands. "This will all be over soon," he whispered anxiously. "Wait for me. I will come for you. I promise." Claire's lungs deflated with a gasp. She couldn't breathe. She could only watch, helpless, as he fled.

Claire collapsed onto the couch. Her head was spinning, her body still trembling. What had just happened? One minute she and Dylan had been overcome by a tsunami of taste and touch and smell and the next he was fleeing like a wanted criminal. What was he playing at?

She tried to slow her heartbeat, tried to think calmly, tried to see things from Dylan's perspective. She understood his fears, understood the potential consequences of an affair, and yet he must have known this before he showed up at her door bearing lilies and a simmering passion. It had been so long since a man found her irresistible that it was difficult for Claire to imagine that anyone as assured as Dylan Lewis just couldn't keep away. Was his hunger fake, another investigative trick? Was he looking for a weakness he could exploit? Was he just another Eric?

Claire pushed that last thought away. No, she decided, it wasn't fake. His desire was as honest as her own, his lust as naked. He had come simply to apologize and to find out about Genesis; if she hadn't compelled him to kiss her they probably would have made it through the encounter unscathed. And then there was the baby, Claire thought remorsefully. Should a child killer remain free just so she and Dylan could give in to temptation?

She sat up, opened the pizza box and dug in, hoping to ease her misery with food. Dylan was forbidden fruit just like Eric had been. The men might be different but Claire's predicament was the same and she was not going to make that mistake twice, waiting on empty promises. The case could go on for months or even years. This was an impossible situation that at the moment had only one solution: on Sunday Claire was going to Maria's barbecue. On Sunday Claire would capture a dashing Latino for herself and push Dylan Lewis out of her mind.

Dylan raced home with the singular thought of relieving the throbbing in his groin. His mind was awash with the memory of Claire's face: the perfection of her porcelain skin, the smouldering intensity of her almond shaped green eyes, those charming freckles over the bridge of her nose. But what he recalled most vividly was the way her exquisite lips had parted and trembled when she spoke the words that had caused an eruption inside of him unmatched by past experience: "Kiss me."

At his apartment building he ignored his mailbox and the neighbour expecting acknowledgement and sprinted up the stairs to his third floor suite. Once inside he feverishly stripped on his way to the bathroom, turned on a hot shower and stepped in. As he lathered up he imagined her there, kissing him and stroking him. And then she slid down his body and held him prisoner there until finally, finally came sweet release.

℃

Claire readied herself for bed. The earlier sexual tension had proved useful in ridding the living room of the last of its wallpaper, her frustration eased with harsh scrapes that left nicks in the wall she was now going to have to fill and sand away. But no matter; at least the lousy job was done.

As the evening had turned into night Claire's annoyance with the situation had slowly turned into an appreciation for what the moment had brought. She'd spent the last year suppressing her desires, fearful of another predator, and now that Dylan had reawakened her she felt like Snow White lifted from a wicked spell. Claire decided Sunday was going to be her debut back into society and like any debutante she needed a new outfit. She'd spend tomorrow indulging in the shops on Commercial Drive and treating herself to a manicure and pedicure. The thought alone raised her confidence and as she snuggled down beneath the covers she imagined admirers gathered around her at the barbecue, soaking up her presence.

ELEVEN

Benjamin Keller took his cousin Elisabeth by the hand and lifted her off the garden bench. He had been reading to her for about an hour and his tongue had grown tired. They were now about halfway through *Pride and Prejudice* and on Wednesday he would pick up where he left off. "Come, Izzy," he coaxed. "Let's walk awhile. You need to stretch your legs."

He straightened out the cardigan he had wrapped around her shoulders when the crisp morning air had caused a shiver, then led her along the garden path toward the fountain. "Are you enjoying our book?" he asked. Elisabeth weakly pressed Benjamin's hand and the gesture encouraged him: today she was responding, if ever so subtly. He looked into her eyes and smiled. "I'm glad." She didn't smile back but he caught the slight lift in her eyes. It was negligible but it was progress.

He walked her back into the common room and sat her down in front of the television. It was time to go: his son had a soccer game and Benjamin was mindful not to let his devotion to Elisabeth encroach upon his other family responsibilities, especially as his ex-wife was always aching for an excuse to make him miserable. "I'll see you soon, Izzy," Ben promised as he kissed her lightly on the forehead.

"Mr. Keller?"

Benjamin turned at the sound of his name. It was Vicky. "How was your visit with her today?"

"A small improvement: she tried to squeeze my hand."

Vicky smiled, but it was a smile Ben had become all too painfully familiar with: encouragement tinged with pity. He knew what she was thinking: that Elisabeth had not tried to squeeze his hand, that his mind was playing tricks, anxious for a sign that the Izzy he had known was still in there somewhere. Izzy *was* in there, but whether she were imprisoned or cocooned he didn't know. And he didn't know which would be worse: to be trapped within her mind against her will or to have been so traumatized that she could find comfort only by shutting out the world, unburdened by the intrusions of well-meaning inquisitors. Izzy *was* in there; he knew it. And yet always that same condescending smile. Ben wanted to shake Vicky and scream *I'm not a foolish man* but instead he said, "May Scott left me a message about a Detective Lewis. What did he want with Elisabeth?"

"He wanted to ask her some questions; about what he didn't say. He asked me how long she'd been catatonic and whether we knew the cause. He wasn't here long; fifteen minutes maybe. What's this about?"

Benjamin shook his head: there was no need bringing these people into his business until necessary and right now he didn't really know what that business was. "I don't know," he replied. "But continue to observe protocol. And if he comes again call me immediately, please."

Benjamin sat in the Bellevue parking lot, tapping his forefingers on the steering wheel of his car. What the hell was going on? He pulled out his phone and called his contact at Crown Counsel. "David," Benjamin said when the cellphone was answered, "it's Ben Keller. Listen, sorry to bug you on a weekend but do you have any idea why a homicide detective is talking with my cousin Elisabeth Keller?"

"I dunno. Did she kill somebody?" David chuckled.

"Ha, ha, very funny. Of course not. She's in hospital."

"Can't help ya. Sorry. Nothing's come across our desk with the Keller name on it."

"You wouldn't bullshit me, would you?"

"Nope."

"Okay. Thanks anyway." Benjamin hung up the phone, unconvinced. He called another number.

The ringing of her cellphone made Rebecca Wilson's head throb. She winced and rolled over toward the sound of the ringer. She fumbled among her crumpled clothes on the floor at the side of her bed until she found the phone. The call display read "Ben." "Oh, bugger off," she groaned and hit the ignore button.

"Who's that?" a sleepy voice asked from the other side of the bed.

"Nobody important," Rebecca replied, praying the stars exploding behind her eyes would ease. "Go back to sleep."

"Too late," he murmured mischievously, caressing Rebecca's naked bottom. "I'm awake now."

She pushed his hand away. "Not now," she sighed wearily. "I've got a killer headache."

CB

By the time Dylan arose it was already noon. The night had been restless. He'd spent half of it memorizing every detail of his sexual encounter with Claire and the other half reminding himself of the risks. He tried to evaluate those risks fairly but realized he was too biased to be objective. Thank God Tom would be back at work on Tuesday; Dylan would put his dilemma past his partner and then decide from there if an honest talk with the brass would put the situation to rest. He hoped so. A woman as beautiful as Claire Dawson would not be alone for long and if he didn't step up to the plate someone else would. The thought tied his guts in a knot.

Dylan cleaned himself up and headed out. When his mind was troubled like this there was only one solution: he'd go chill out at Ta'ah's place.

It took about forty-five minutes in the Saturday traffic to reach his grandmother's home on the Capilano Reserve beneath the Lion's Gate Bridge. The recently elected band council's renovation projects were moving forward, with whole streets of new home construction slowly replacing the tear-downs, and ground had been broken for a new longhouse on the edge of the neighbourhood. Ta'ah's home reflected her status as a medicine woman and esteemed elder, not to mention mother of six children all of whom save one were now strong voices on council or in the community. The house was only a few years old and had four bedrooms and a large kitchen where on any given day some combination of children, grandchildren and great-grandchildren were gathered to cook, eat and share stories. At the rear of the house Dylan had built Ta'ah a medicine hut for women-only healing ceremonies and a small smokehouse for making her irresistible salmon candy.

Dylan arrived to the mouth-watering smell of rabbit stew. It was a dish Ta'ah had picked up from the wife of an anthropologist who had come years ago to study the rare creature that was a medicine woman in a traditionally patriarchal social structure. The anthropologist and his wife had since moved on to Alberta and the Plains Indians but the recipe for rabbit stew and the Yorkshire pudding Ta'ah liked to serve it with had remained behind.

"I see my timing is impeccable as always," Dylan joked as he squeezed Ta'ah's shoulders and gave the top of her head an affectionate peck. At barely five foot her small, plump frame and unassuming demeanour belied the powerhouse within and masked the sharp mind and eyes that saw both the visible and the hidden. She immediately saw the trouble behind Dylan's smile but knew from experience not to rush her boy. The words, she knew, would come soon but indirectly and she would decipher the code as she had always done. "Sit, my love," was all Ta'ah said as she pulled two muffin tins full of crisp Yorkshire pudding from the oven.

Dylan's cousin Kurtis and his wife, Denise, were already seated at the long wooden table that ran the length of the kitchen. Hellos were said all around then Kurtis went to the doorway to call his four children away from the television. "Lunch." There was a loud commotion as four hungry boys converged upon the table.

"Jeremiah," Ta'ah addressed the eldest as she put a pudding into a bowl and ladled a small amount of stew on top, "put this out for the spirits." Jeremiah did as told, taking the bowl out and placing in on the altar by the medicine hut before running back inside the house, fearful as only a sixteen-year-old can be that all the stew would be gone before he got his share.

"Working on anything interesting?" Kurtis asked Dylan as Ta'ah put the heavy pot of stew on a rack in the middle of the table.

"Yeah, but I can't talk about it," Dylan answered casually. "It's under an embargo at the moment." Beneath the official answer Ta'ah heard the voice that wanted to speak: something about the case was bothering him.

After lunch had been eaten and the dishes cleared and cleaned, after Dylan and Kurtis had talked fishing and politics and current affairs, after Kurtis and the boys had hit the home basketball court behind the garage and Denise had gone upstairs for a nap, Ta'ah sat down again at the table across from Dylan with two cups of tea. She pushed one cup across to him.

"Lunch was great, Ta'ah, thank you," Dylan said. "Just what I needed after a rough week." Ta'ah smiled and took a sip of tea. Dylan paused a moment then added, "Infant remains were found in a house in East Van.

Interesting thing is, the homeowner heard a baby crying *before* she found the remains. Sounds like the house is haunted." Dylan chuckled as if he were telling a ghost story handed down over the years. "And then the owner, she thinks just because I'm an Indian I could bring someone over to cleanse the house." He snorted sarcastically.

"Then we will go," said Ta'ah, and took another sip of tea.

"That wasn't a request," asserted Dylan. "I was just illustrating how annoying some people's assumptions can be."

"We will go," repeated Ta'ah.

"No, Ta'ah," Dylan insisted, "it would be inappropriate."

"Babies are easily lost when they're murdered. They don't know why they died."

"I never said she was murdered."

"She was murdered," Ta'ah declared, nodding her head solemnly. "We must go." She stood up from the table. "My bag is in the hall closet." She poured her tea in the sink and began a slow, arthritic waddle toward the kitchen door.

Dylan got up after her and poured his tea in the sink. "It's Saturday afternoon; she's probably not home," he protested.

"She'll be home," Ta'ah said and continued out the door.

"Don't you think I should at least phone first?" he called out after her.

"If you wish," she shrugged. Dylan rolled his eyes in exasperation, collected Ta'ah's hard leather case from the hall closet, and followed her to his jeep.

He helped her step up into his vehicle, then took the wheel and backed out of the driveway. "Stop at the George house," Ta'ah politely demanded. "Tell John to bring his drum."

"Anyone else?"

Ta'ah paused for a moment and Dylan knew she was conferring with her guardian spirits. "Jacob Joseph and Pete Williams. And call your uncle Stan. Tell him to meet us there."

"With his drum?"

"No. With his bag and some cedar branch."

The names made Dylan apprehensive. As elders go these were the heavy hitters; and Stan had been Ta'ah's apprentice and was now a full-fledged shaman himself though not yet as powerful as his mother. Dylan nevertheless did as instructed and twenty minutes later John George, Jacob Joseph, and Pete Williams were squeezed into the backseat of Dylan's jeep and three woollen drum bags were nestled in the hold beside Ta'ah's medicine bag. Stan was on his way to Claire's house and Dylan hoped his uncle would have the sense not to knock until they all arrived.

The approach to the Lion's Gate Bridge was chock-a-block and nothing appeared to be moving south. Moments later Dylan heard the sirens. "There's an accident on the bridge, Ta'ah. This may have to wait."

"It knows we're coming. Take the other bridge. Brothers?" The three men behind her murmured their assent.

"Won't it just create an accident there, too?" Dylan asked flippantly and immediately regretted his tone.

"We're sending guardians." Dylan looked in the rear view mirror and saw the concentration on the elder men's faces, their eyes closed tightly in prayer. Dear God, what have I started? thought Dylan as he forced his way into the far lane, pulled an illegal U-turn and headed east for the Second Narrows Bridge.

TWELVE

Claire stood in front of the mirror admiring her new outfit. At the boutiques on The Drive she had found a stunning jersey knit knee-length halter dress in swirling hues of teal and yellow that set off the reddish tones in her hair, teal-toned wedge shoes that lengthened her leg and wouldn't sink into the grass, and a yellow straw bag that was just the right balance between casual and fantastic. Her nails were French manicured and her toenails had been done in gold. All told the day had cost her over six hundred dollars after tax but she didn't care: she felt like a million bucks.

She was just about to change back into casual clothes when the doorbell rang. Frau Müller again? Claire wondered as she headed down the stairs to the door. She opened it to find Dylan, someone who looked like he could be Dylan's father, three elderly men and a tiny, elderly woman all standing at her door looking ... What was the look on their faces? Claire couldn't quite describe it. They stood there as if they knew her already, as if they weren't total strangers and unexpected ones at that.

"Wow," Dylan exclaimed before he remembered why he was there, "you look fantastic!"

"Detective?" was all Claire managed in return, glancing awkwardly at the crowd gathered around Dylan.

"Oh, right," Dylan twitched nervously. "This is my grandmother Sarah Lewis, my uncle Stan, and elders John George, Jacob Joseph, and Pete Williams." The men tipped their heads to Claire while Ta'ah just looked up and smiled. "You asked for someone to cleanse the house," Dylan reminded Claire. "My grandmother is a medicine woman."

Claire turned an accusing eye on Dylan. "But you said—"

"Yeah," he interjected, "can we talk about that later?" He tilted his head toward his grandmother and gave Claire a look that said *Can we get on with this?*

Claire looked down at the woman beaming up at her. Sarah Lewis' face was so deeply lined it seemed almost to fold in upon itself, framed by grey and white hair pulled back in a long braid and bobby pins securing the stray strands at her temples. Her eyes were heavily lidded behind large eighties' eyeglasses but even so Claire could see the kindness that shone from within. The old woman was simply enchanting and Claire found herself smiling back despite her annoyance with Dylan. "Mrs. Lewis, thank you for coming," Claire said as she stepped away from the door to welcome them in.

"You may call me Ta'ah," Ta'ah said as she walked past Claire and into the living room. "Everyone does." Ta'ah stood in the middle of the room and assessed the atmosphere. She nodded her head solemnly then walked toward the back rooms, Stan and the elders following at a respectful distance. Claire was about to follow them but Dylan held her back.

"Let's wait here," he suggested and walked her over to the couch.

"Why did you—" she began to ask but Dylan put a finger to his lips. Claire obeyed and sat down to listen.

When Ta'ah reached what had been the dining room she stopped and took in a sharp breath. "Here," she announced to the others. Stan put his and Ta'ah's bags down on the floor and opened hers. From its many compartments he took out a candle and matches, and from his own bag he carefully lifted out an eight-inch carved cedar bowl and a freshly cut cedar branch. He lit the candle and handed it to Ta'ah, then walked over to the kitchen sink to fill the bowl with water; in this he placed the cedar branch. When Stan was again by her side Ta'ah motioned for the elders to start drumming.

As the drumming began Claire's spine began to tense. Dylan saw her apprehension. "Come here," he whispered as he reached over and pulled her close to him. "Don't worry, you're in good hands." Claire curled herself tightly against him and laid her head on his chest. The strength of his arms around her made her feel safe and she relaxed a little. On his neck she discovered the same woodsy aftershave she'd smelled on him before, and she let the scent soothe her. She could hear his heart and as the drumming became louder it seemed as if it and Dylan's heartbeat became one sound that carried her into another world where her mind went completely liquid, a sea of colour and sound but no thought.

Ta'ah carried the candle around the room as Stan walked behind her carrying the water bowl in which he had placed the cedar branch. The light in the room had faded despite the bare window and the flame grew taller and brighter. But when she reached the closet where Baby Jane had been found the candle was suddenly extinguished. Ta'ah closed her eyes and saw in her mind's eye the hole in the wall and the world it opened into. Stan closed his eyes too and the two shamans communicated silently. "Shall I walk with you, mother?" his spirit voice asked.

"No," Ta'ah's spirit replied. "Wait here. It may try to escape."

Stan stood guard at the closet door: if the demon crossed the threshold into this world it would make itself vulnerable to capture.

Ta'ah left her earthly body behind and walked through the hole into the spirit world. She found herself at a forest's edge where the land turned to jagged rock that jutted out over a river. The sky above was dark and ominous. The demon stood before her, an amorphous cloud of swirling black insects, and she could feel its anger at the intrusion. "Your secret has been discovered," Ta'ah declared defiantly. "Let the child go."

The demon shape-shifted into a huge jackal and leered at Ta'ah. Its fangs oozed blood and saliva and its eyes were like molten glass. Behind Jackal Ta'ah could see the entrance to its den. "You cannot take what is mine," it snarled.

Ta'ah stood her ground, unafraid. "The baby wishes to be reborn," she commanded. "Release its soul."

"The baby?" Jackal laughed, incredulous. "What do I care for this defect?" Jackal relished the surprise and confusion on Ta'ah's face as it reached into its den then flung the baby toward Ta'ah. She caught it and wrapped it safely in her apron. Ta'ah eyed Jackal suspiciously. She knew it would not have given up the baby so easily unless it had something much more valuable hidden in its den. But until she knew what that was she couldn't risk setting it free. She stood down. The demon resumed its amorphous state, confident it had won.

For now.

Ta'ah traveled to a clearing in the forest where the sun shone high and hot. The child was crying. Ta'ah rocked Baby Jane from side to side and cooed soothing words while she waited for a guardian to arrive and claim the little girl. A few minutes later a large female brown bear left the woods and approached. Ta'ah's heart sang: the child's soul was in need of good medicine; she would get it now. Ta'ah and Bear acknowledged each other, one healer to another, and Ta'ah placed Baby Jane on the ground. She stopped crying when she saw Bear and instinctively reached out. Bear gave Ta'ah a look of gratitude, then gently picked up Baby Jane by the scruff of her neck and disappeared back among the trees.

Ta'ah spirit returned to her body, still standing in front of the closet. She raised her arm to signal the elders who slowed down the tempo of their drums then let them fall silent. Ta'ah and Stan opened their eyes. The light in the room had returned. Stan looked at his mother, a question in his eyes: *Why did you fail?* "I retrieved the child," she announced, correcting him. "But the demon is hiding something else. We must investigate before taking further action. Say nothing to Claire or it will feed off her fear."

Claire opened her eyes when the drumming stopped. She felt as if she'd been sleeping. She looked anxiously up at Dylan. "Is it over?"

"I'm not sure," he replied. "Wait here." He disentangled himself from Claire but before he could rise Ta'ah and the others entered the living room.

"Claire, do you have something for the men to drink?" asked Ta'ah.

Claire nodded. "There's iced tea in the fridge."

"Dylan, it's a lovely day. Iced tea on the deck would be good."

Dylan understood the command. "Stay here with Ta'ah," he said to Claire. "I'll serve the others." Though she didn't understand why, Claire nodded her assent.

Ta'ah gave Dylan a loving pat on his arm as he passed her, then addressed Claire. "The baby has been returned to her guardian. I will return soon to check on her. But for now I must tend to you."

Claire's eyes widened in surprise. "Me?"

"Yes. I must bathe you and give you medicine," Ta'ah answered as if this were a normal thing to say. "Is there a bathtub on this floor? My arthritis doesn't like the stairs."

Claire found herself nodding despite vague feelings of anxiety. She couldn't have explained her compliance, couldn't have described the quiet authority Ta'ah possessed so assuredly that robbed Claire of any objections. It seemed so simple, so natural that when Ta'ah requested something you just did it; you didn't argue or ask questions; you just obeyed. And Claire understood somewhere in her core that Ta'ah's was not a vain authority; it arose not from a love of power but the power of love. It was most extraordinary and Claire was mesmerized.

"Please fill a bath and remove your clothing. Do you have a robe?" asked Ta'ah. Claire nodded. "Go, then. While you prepare the bath I will prepare myself with prayer."

Claire went off as requested and when the bath was ready Ta'ah joined Claire in the small room, closed the door and motioned for Claire to enter the bath. Claire disrobed and slid down into the hot water. Ta'ah took a clean washcloth and some soap and began to wash Claire. Claire closed her eyes but had she not she would have seen Ta'ah's eyes become distant, ethereal.

Ta'ah found Claire at the side of the river, naked and sitting hunched over on a fallen tree, her eyes cast down and fixed upon a dead foetus at her feet, the umbilical cord still connecting mother and child. Ta'ah walked over to Claire, took out a knife and cut the cord. In her peripheral vision Ta'ah saw a coyote sneaking up on Claire, its eyes hungry and its tongue salivating from the smell of blood. Ta'ah pretended not to notice and sat down beside Claire again. Coyote inched his way toward them, belly to the ground. From his vantage point he saw two women, one young but despondent, the other too old to oppose him, and he smiled in premature victory. Coyote pounced but before he could react Ta'ah's arm shape-shifted into that of a grizzly bear and she swiped her mighty paw across Coyote's face. He yelped in pain and sprinted off back into the woods to lick his wounds as Ta'ah's arm took its human form again.

Dr. Eric Mellor, esteemed cardiologist, devoted husband and father, was shaving in anticipation of his evening's rendezvous. The wife and kids were off at the lakeside cottage celebrating the start of summer and Eric had the house all to himself. He had feigned disappointment when he claimed he was on call that weekend which, he smirked, wasn't entirely untruthful considering how demanding surgical nurse Katie Palmer could be. The woman had a voracious sexual appetite not to mention the skills of a porn queen. The thought made him grin.

Eric leaned toward the mirror to attend to the contours of his chin—then nearly jumped out of his skin when he saw a fleeting reflection of what appeared to be an old woman standing outside the bathroom door. His hand jerked involuntarily and the blade sliced into his flesh. "Ow! Fuck!" Eric grabbed a wet washcloth and pressed it to the wound as he dashed out of the ensuite and into his bedroom. He looked around but saw no one. He strode into the hallway, but still no one. He paused, straining to hear, yet heard nothing. As the adrenaline slowly subsided, Eric shrugged off the creepy feeling and walked back into the bathroom to tend to his chin. "You're getting old," he muttered to himself. "You're starting to see things."

He lifted the washcloth and surveyed the cut. It was still bleeding. He pressed the washcloth to the wound again as he fumbled around the vanity drawer for his shaving stick, something he didn't like using for the nasty sting it inflicted. He dabbed it on the cut. "God damn!" It stung for a moment more before the cut finally coagulated into an ugly red line on his chin. It throbbed annoyingly and, worse still, looked ridiculous. He could already hear the jokes about having the sure hands of a surgeon. "Great," he muttered angrily. "Just great."

Ta'ah smiled smugly as Coyote's haunches disappear into the underbrush, then she turned her attention back to Claire. Ta'ah removed her apron and used it to shroud the foetus, then set it upon the water to let the current take it home. "Come now, child," she said, coaxing Claire to the river. Claire silently obeyed, her shoulders still hunched and her head down. Ta'ah eased Claire into the water and washed the blood off her legs, then gently tugged at the remains of the umbilical cord. The afterbirth slid out and Ta'ah pushed it into the current.

Claire screamed and opened her eyes as a spasm rippled through her abdomen. She grabbed onto the side of the bathtub to keep from fainting. "Let it go," Ta'ah gently whispered as she stroked Claire's back. "Let it go." Claire collapsed into heavy sobs, at times gasping for air, until the pain slowly subsided and she felt herself break free. She caught her breath and when she raised her eyes to Ta'ah's Claire knew the invisible cord that had tethered her to her dead child was now finally and truly cut.

"Come out now, daughter." Claire was still trembling as she rose out of the bath and wrapped herself in her robe. Ta'ah took out a jar of medicine from her bag. "This is for your belly," she explained. Claire opened her robe and Ta'ah spread a clear oily salve across Claire's lower abdomen.

As Claire watched the soft, heavily lined hands rub across her stomach, she wanted desperately to ask why she had lost her child, if it had been punishment for her selfish disregard of another woman's misery and the sanctity of marriage, but Claire's timidity proved stronger. All she managed instead was to ask, "Ta'ah, what happened to my baby?"

Ta'ah sighed and put the medicine jar back in her bag. "The boy was afraid to be born. He had his father's cowardice. And he had his jealousy. He ran away but he didn't want anyone else to have you so he brought sickness to you." She shook her head in disgust.

Claire reeled from the revelation. "You mean it wasn't my fault?" she asked, and relief formed a lump in her throat.

"Men," replied Ta'ah, shaking her head again, "for some it starts before they're even born."

Claire laughed despite herself and her laughter caught her tears. "Thank you," she said, kneeling down to hug Ta'ah. "Thank you so very much."

Ta'ah patted Claire on the back then sat back on her haunches. "Sit," she gestured toward the toilet seat, "we must talk." Her words sounded ominous and Claire felt a sharp pang of anxiety. Ta'ah looked solemnly up at Claire. "There is tension between you and my grandson."

"It's this case," Claire replied lightly, hoping to God Ta'ah didn't know about the night before. "It's come between us."

Ta'ah nodded knowingly. "When I speak for the dead I tell people things they cannot see yet I am believed. When Dylan speaks for the dead he tells people things they can see and yet he is not believed. He must prove everything to everyone over and over again. His burden is great. It takes a special strength to be a policeman, or at least a good one. I'm proud of my grandson."

"You have every right to be," Claire affirmed sincerely.

"You have feelings for him?" Ta'ah asked without judgment.

"Yes," Claire admitted, looking down and twisting the tie of her robe between her fingers. "But he tells me because of the case he cannot reciprocate. He asked me to wait."

Ta'ah nodded knowingly again. "A proud woman waits for no one," she proclaimed. "If he wants your love he must earn it. Love given too easily has little value to a man." She patted Claire on the knee. "Don't wash the medicine off. It will turn dark and fall off on its own, taking the sickness with it. If you want to wash give yourself a sponge bath and take care around your belly. It will take a few days."

Ta'ah struggled to get up off the floor. "Let me help you," Claire offered, reaching out to lift Ta'ah onto her feet.

"Thank you, daughter. Old age is a curse. Now go rest, let the medicine work. We will let ourselves out."

"I should thank the others," Claire suggested, hoping for another moment with Dylan.

"No need," Ta'ah replied, ignoring Claire's disappointment. "I will thank them for you."

The jeep was silent all the way home. Dylan felt scattered, torn. One moment he was reliving the feel of Claire in his arms—the tension in her body that had melted beneath his touch and made him feel vital, the softness of her skin where he had stroked her arm, the smell of her hair— and the next he was staring into the haunted, vacant eyes of Baby Jane. He told himself she deserved his undivided attention only to have his mind wander back to each moment of interaction with Claire, her passions, her embarrassments, even her expressions of annoyance. Every moment made him long for another.

Dylan dropped the elders off at their respective houses, thanking each one in turn, then took Ta'ah home and escorted her into the kitchen. She told him then of her encounter with Jackal. "I must return to finish the cleansing," she concluded. "I will let you know when."

Her tone made Dylan uneasy; there was obviously more to this than he had expected. "What am I up against, Ta'ah?"

"A great evil is there," she said gravely, "but not a powerful one. He is vain; he thinks himself greater than he is. That is his weakness. We will beat him together. You in this world, me in the other."

THIRTEEN

Claire woke to a cool breeze from her window. The light in her bedroom had dimmed and she could hear in the distance the drone of a lawnmower. She rolled onto her back and stretched out languidly. She felt rejuvenated, her spirit bathed in contentment. She thought of Ta'ah and smiled, then thought of Dylan, how right it had felt to be in his arms, and her smile waned. *A proud woman waits for no man.* As much as Claire wanted Dylan, as much as he seemed to want her, the fact was his loyalties lay elsewhere and nothing was going to change that. There was no use pining or pouting, Claire reminded herself; the adult thing to do was accept things as they were, keep her chin up, and make a splash at the barbecue tomorrow.

She turned her head to check the time. The clock read eight. She put on her robe and headed downstairs to watch some television before calling it a night.

Something about the living room light struck her as odd. Claire stared out the window, eyeing the slant of shadows, then slowly realized it wasn't eight at night but Sunday morning. She'd slept for ... She did the math in her head and counted fourteen hours. She'd slept *fourteen* hours?! My God, what's in this stuff? she thought and opened her robe to check out her stomach. The salve had turned dark brown. It looked disgusting and Claire worried it might stain her new dress. She slumped back on the couch, not sure what to do with herself, then slowly realized she was hungry. Breakfast and a movie, she thought. A perfect Sunday morning. She got herself a bowl of cereal, popped in a DVD, then settled down to granola and a comedy.

Dylan woke to the smell of bacon and eggs. He followed his nose to the kitchen and found Ta'ah sitting down to a solo breakfast. "No one else around?" asked Dylan as he helped himself to a mound of bacon and scrambled eggs.

"Not yet," Ta'ah replied. "Did you sleep well, my love?"

Dylan shrugged and sat down to dig in. "Okay, I guess." He took a bite of eggs. "I'm worried about the Dawson woman. What if this demon wants her too."

"He doesn't," Ta'ah answered matter-of-factly. "Coyote wants her."

"Oh, she got rid of him already," Dylan smirked. "Some married doctor."

"Then he will come as another. The trickster has many faces."

Dylan looked up sharply. Was Ta'ah serious or just trying to get a rise out of him? Her expression gave nothing away and he was forced to play a card. "Why do you say that?"

"Because I saw him."

She eyed her grandson over the rim of her teacup. "The Dawson woman," she said after a moment, "is that the way to speak of one you desire?"

Dylan felt the heat rise in his cheeks. "Who said I desire her?" he asked, trying to sound nonchalant. Ta'ah didn't answer; she just smiled and took another sip of tea.

"It's complicated," Dylan said defensively. Ta'ah remained silent. "I can't pursue a complainant," he protested further. "It's conflict of interest; the defence would scream witness tampering. I wouldn't just get kicked off the case, I'd get kicked off the squad." He dug into his bacon, the tension building in his body.

"I understand."

"No," Dylan said angrily, "this time you don't." He rose from the table, his appetite gone. "You're an incurable romantic, Ta'ah; you think love conquers all. It's an admirable idea but it's not always the case. This is about more than just me and Claire. I have an obligation to that little girl"—he paused, embarrassed by his unsteady voice—"to that little baby girl whose life ended in a wall. In a *wall*." He strode out of the kitchen and into the yard looking for something, anything, to kick the crap out of, and found nothing. He sprinted off, frustrated, then broke into a run.

Claire's nerves were jangling as she approached Maria and Carlos' yard. She felt invigorated, back in the game. For the first time in what seemed like an eternity the dark cloud of loss had lifted, and she no longer felt the emotional pull of her dead son. Both their souls had been freed, it seemed to Claire, and she could finally move forward.

And Baby Jane? The child has been returned to her guardian, Ta'ah had proclaimed. The manner of her death, the solving of the mystery, seemed only an earthly concern now, of consequence perhaps to her killer but not to Baby Jane. Or was it? There was still an odd atmosphere in the dining room, the contrast of it to the rest of the house more pronounced now that everywhere else seemed lighter and brighter than before. Was that real or just my imagination? wondered Claire. No worry, she thought next as she opened Maria's front gate, Ta'ah said she would return soon to check on the baby, and Claire could ask questions then.

She could hear music coming from behind the house, a cacophony of voices in conversation, and children running about and laughing. She smoothed her dress and hair, adjusted the bouquet of rhododendrons she had cut from her garden, then walked around back. "Claire!" Maria called out and came bounding over. "I'm so glad you made it," she cooed as she hugged her new friend. "And you look stunning. *Where* did you find that dress? I'm going to have to put a blindfold on Carlos."

Claire laughed appreciatively. "These are for you," she said, handing Maria the flowers. "They're from my garden. Although I can't really take credit for them considering I just moved in."

"They're beautiful. But before I go find water I want to point out some people to you. See that handsome man in the red shirt by the barbecue? That's my Carlos. And the man beside him in the blue shirt is Rafael Morales. Very yummy and very single. And he's new to Canada so maybe you could offer to teach him English." She nudged Claire playfully. "And over there, the man in the striped shirt, is Lee Chang. He also works with Carlos. Comes from a wealthy Hong Kong family. Oh, and the blond by the fence, that's Dean Halloway. He works in technology. He's a little shy and boring but sweet and he has a nice bum." Claire thought she might avoid Dean: she needed a man capable of taking her mind off Dylan Lewis and boring was not going to do the trick.

"Carlos," Maria called out and gestured for him to join her and Claire. He came over and Maria introduced her husband. He was tall and elegant with thick, dark hair and a moustache, and modern metal-framed eyeglasses that set off the olive tones in his eyes and skin. "Now, Carlos, *mi querido*," Maria said, squeezing his arm, "I must find water for these flowers. Please introduce Claire around."

"My pleasure, *señora*," he said gallantly and lead Claire away by her arm. Carlos walked her around the garden, introducing her to friends and family, and many eyes followed her afterwards. Claire felt sexy and alive. So much so that when she was finally introduced to Rafael Morales her eyes were sparkling and her smile broad and relaxed. And it was a good thing, too, because Rafael was even better looking up close than from across the garden. He was only about five foot nine but he held himself tall and it was evident that beneath the blue shirt and black dress slacks his body was lean and toned. He had sensuous brown eyes with long, long eyelashes a woman could easily lose herself in, and a slender nose over a full mouth set in a closely cropped goatee.

The three made small talk until Carlos was called away to tend to the roasting chicken, his departure a welcomed opportunity to flirt. "What you pay for that dress," Rafael said, eyeing Claire shamelessly, "you double its value."

Claire giggled at the attempt at a compliment. "Rafael, are you flirting with me?"

"I hope," he smiled. "This is my intent."

Claire laughed and allowed Rafael to charm her with his awkward English and rakish smile. She learned he had come to Canada seven months previously, recruited by the accounting firm to handle Latino clients in the hope of expanding aggressively into the Americas. He loved baseball and was struggling to understand the rules of hockey. He hated the Vancouver rain but loved the fresh air, the sea, and the mountains. "In Mexico City the air is very bad!" Rafael exclaimed. "Many people die from, how you say, when you need help"—he made a gesture of an inhaler—"to breathe."

"Asthma."

"Yes, asthma. Very bad."

"Do you miss it anyway?" she asked.

"Mexico City, no. My family, yes. But," he flashed his most charming grin yet, "now I am more happy to be here."

While Claire was sunning herself in the warm glow of Rafael Morales,

104

Dylan was slowly burning as he applied white paint to Ta'ah's fence. He had returned from his run still frustrated and had tried to ease the tension with an electric sander. That impulse had led to another and now the last of the fence was glistening with a new coat of paint. He put the brush in a plastic bag so it wouldn't dry before he could clean it, closed the paint can and sat back to evaluate his work. From behind him a voice said, "Nice job. Can you do mine next?"

Dylan snickered as a middle-aged woman sat down beside him on the grass. "Nice try, auntie."

Dylan's aunt Sylvie was the second youngest of Ta'ah's children, born two years before Dylan's mother. Sylvie was a large woman with a heavy braid that fell down to her waist, a round face with deep laugh lines, and short, thick fingers on which she wore many rings. She patted Dylan on the leg. "What's her name this time?"

"What is whose name?"

"The girl you want but can't have?" Sylvie replied with a knowing smile.

"What makes you think there's a woman?" Dylan asked, wondering if his grandmother and aunt had been gossiping.

"Whenever you can't have a girl you want you build things," Sylvie explained. "Remember when you were nine and you kissed Stacey Williams but she laughed at you? You built a go-cart. When you were thirteen and had a crush on Beth George you built a fort. At sixteen you built the tree house when Mary James dumped you. Then—"

"Okay, I get your point," he said, rolling his eyes.

"You know, the tree house is still there. It's the meeting room for the boys' Secret Warrior Society, though it's not much of a secret," she laughed. "And teenagers make out in it. As if we don't know."

Dylan looked at his aunt sideways and smiled. Sylvie always had a way to lift his mood. On the days when she discovered Dylan pining over the few photographs of his mother that Ta'ah kept in an album beneath the coffee table, Sylvie never pried into his grief, always resisted the urge to replace the lost maternal voice with another. Instead she would regale her nephew with stories of her youngest sibling, of childhood pranks and conspiracies, of his mother's first crush on a boy. His aunt brought her sister back to life: she mimicked her voice and mannerisms, recited her words and guessed at her thoughts; and he would find in Sylvie's stories the mother he couldn't find in the pictures, the one who often turned her face away from the camera, perhaps convinced, as were her ancestors, that it would steal her soul.

"Her name is Claire," he confessed. "She's the complainant on a case I'm working on. Until it's over I can't see her socially. I asked her to wait but ..." He shrugged and picked at the grass in resignation.

Sylvie nodded her head in understanding. "Ta'ah always told me that a proud woman waits for no man and she's right."

"Liar! You waited for uncle Tim."

"No I didn't," she argued, shaking her head indignantly.

"Yes you did," Dylan protested. "When he went to Calgary to do his Master's he was gone for almost two years."

"There are many ways to court a woman," Sylvie declared enigmatically.

Dylan eyed her suspiciously. "I'm listening."

"When Tim went to Calgary he promised me his heart would not fail me, and that he would prove it every week with a letter. He kept his word. Every week until he came back he sent me a handwritten love letter." She sighed, remembering. "They were full of love and passion and—"

"Whoa. Stop," Dylan demanded. "Uncle *Tim* wrote love letters? Mister dinosaur bones, Mister I-get-all-embarrassed-at-a-dirty-joke uncle *Tim*?"

"Don't judge a book by its cover, Dylan," Sylvie replied, shrugging her eyebrows. "People are full of surprises. You should know that being a cop." She gave him a triumphant grin, patted him on the leg again and got up to return to the house. "And here's another tip. Put a drop of your cologne on the letters. Tim used to do that and every time I smelled that scent on a man I went crazy inside. By the time he got home I was—"

"Thanks, I get the picture." Dylan did indeed try to picture his uncle and aunt getting it on but the idea made him shudder. Some things were best left alone.

CR

It was early evening before the barbecue began to wind down. Rafael had kept Claire entertained to the exclusion of most others and in return she had rewarded him with a few snippets about herself, though she chose her stories carefully for fear he'd find her wanting if he knew too soon of

106

her faults and indiscretions. The strategy worked. "I walk you home?" he asked as she said her goodbyes to those still left behind.

"I'd like that," Claire said, and gave Maria a wink as Rafael said his goodbyes as well.

"Is it far?" he asked as he took Claire's arm and led her from the yard.

"No, just two blocks away," she replied, and assumed with satisfaction that he was eager to get her alone at her home.

"Then I am sad," he said, disappointed. "I will leave you too soon."

In what seemed like no time at all they were at her door. Rafael lifted her hand to his lips. "Beautiful Claire. I must see you more. Say yes."

His last words sent Claire's mind hurtling back to Dylan as his fingers undid the button—she flinched and hoped Rafael didn't see the loss that flashed briefly in her eyes. "Yes."

"Tomorrow? Will you eat with me?" Claire nodded and smiled. "Then I will come at six and one half. Yes?" Rafael asked expectantly.

"Yes."

"Tomorrow then." Rafael kissed her hand again and stepped down the stairs. Then, just as Claire was turning the key in the lock, he turned back and said, "I ask one thing only. Your dress. Wear it tomorrow?"

Claire laughed lightly. "I will," she promised, then opened the door and disappeared inside.

Claire bounded up the stairs and flung herself on her bed. Rafael Morales was just what she needed right now: smart, educated, handsome, sexy, charming. Not to mention unabashedly romantic. She began to fantasize about dinner with him in a restaurant as elegant as he, their eyes locked on each other, fingers intertwined—when her gaze fell on the calla lilies at her bedside. The fantasy came to an abrupt halt as her thoughts turned again to Dylan, and she found herself tabulating a mental comparison. She recalled Dylan's hunger the night they had kissed, their mutual impatience, his expression of unmitigated lust. It had been exhilarating but decidedly not romantic. In fact, so far the lilies were the only sign of a romantic side to Dylan. And yet ...

And yet the ease with which he'd forgiven her rudeness was a reflection of a generous heart, and his dedication to his job suggested a strong moral center. Both made her desire another look, and she wondered with regret what else she might have learned were circumstances not what they were. But they were. She turned her face away from the lilies and forced herself to focus again on Rafael. Tomorrow she would have dinner with him and if all went well then maybe she would let him do more than kiss her hand. But not much more. *Love given too easily has little value to a man.* Claire had given her love too easily to Eric and it was painfully obvious in the end it had no value to him. She would be more careful, more reserved in future. She owed that to herself.

FOURTEEN

The following evening found Dylan behind the wheel of his jeep, pondering the love letter on the seat beside him. It had taken the whole day and numerous drafts to write. Ta'ah had performed a healing ceremony earlier in the day for which Dylan had been railroaded into tending the fire, and as the patient had cried out her woes inside the hut Dylan had sat in the shade of the cedar trees trying to translate his longing into words. The first attempt had all the finesse of a police report, the second sounded like the confessions of a desperate man, while the third was more literary— but only if you counted juvenile literature, Dylan thought, frustrated, as he had tossed the letter into the fire beside the charred remains of the others. Several more attempts had taken their place in the flames until Sylvie emerged from the house and took pity on him, offering such simple and practical advice that Dylan wondered why he hadn't thought of it himself: "Don't use your head, Dylan, it will only find fault. Write from your heart and the words will write themselves."

So he had, and now the letter sat on the passenger seat finished, folded, sealed, waiting to be delivered. He had put a touch of his cologne on it as instructed, right beside his signature. All that remained of the task was to put it into Claire's hands. How hard could that be? All he had to do was drive up to her house and put it in the mailbox to surprise her with in the morning. So what's the holdup, Dylan? he asked himself. Don't tell me you're scared. That's ridiculous. You're a grown man, and a cop for God's sake. If you can face a hopped-up junkie with a knife in his hand, surely you can deliver a love letter. Just get on with it. What's the worse that can happen? She laughs and you build another fort.

Dylan handed his fate over to the gods, turned the key and drove off.

Claire put on the finishing touches of her makeup, dabbed perfume behind her ears and headed downstairs to await Rafael, ready to be pampered. Her day had started early with the arrival of the window installers and their carpenter, and as they had gone about their work Claire had filled and sanded the living room walls then washed the years of neglect off in preparation for tomorrow's painting. In between tasks she had cleaned the bits of wall plaster scattered on the floor in each room as the installers moved into the next. She'd hoped they would have finished in time for her to clean up the last of it but they'd left her only enough time to wash herself and change.

She had sponge bathed as instructed, careful not to touch her abdomen. The medicine was flaking off in large blackish-brown specks that looked like dark dandruff where it had fallen into her pubic hair. "Very attractive," Claire had muttered with disgust as she shook her hair out, and realized that even if Rafael chose not to remain chivalrous this evening there was no way she'd be getting naked for anybody.

Dylan came around the corner onto Lakewood Road just as a deluxe model BMW pulled up in front of Claire's house. He quickly slowed down and pulled over to watch. A Latino male alighted from the car and headed for Claire's front door. Dylan noted the license number and waited. Moments later the man escort Claire into the car. She was wearing the same stunning dress Dylan had seen her wearing on Saturday, his mind crashing into the image of her nestled in his arms while Ta'ah had cleansed the house. Dylan could feel the cold snake of jealousy slither its way into his gut and writhe about as the car drove off. How could she?! Just three days ago she was letting him touch her and now she was stepping out with some Don Juan in a sixty thousand dollar car and a silk suit. Okay, so it was Dylan who had snipped the bud off before it had a chance to flower, but wasn't this a bit quick? He had no right to be jealous and he knew it but somehow admitting it only made his jealousy grow. He opened up the glove compartment, tossed the letter inside and slammed the cover shut, then turned his jeep around and headed for home. Conveniently for Dylan, police headquarters lay between Commercial Drive and his Kitsilano apartment, making the idea forming in his head all the more irrepressible: he'd make a little detour into the office and run Don Juan's plate.

Rafael tossed the keys to his car to the valet at Pierre's and led Claire inside the restaurant. If he were trying to impress her he was doing an excellent job. The conversation in the car had been light and flirtatious and he had refused to tell her where they were headed for dinner except to say he hoped she liked French. Pierre's was the restaurant *de rigueur* at the moment and Claire was thrilled when the surprise was revealed. She'd read the reviews but at an average expense of over a hundred dollars a head it wasn't the type of restaurant she was used to, not even when she had been dating Eric. As they were led to their table in a quiet corner of the room, Claire wondered what other surprises Rafael Morales had in store for her.

Dylan plopped himself down at his desk and logged into his computer. He tapped in the license plate number of the BMW and leaned in to survey the details of his nemesis. Rafael Morales, age thirty-two, legally permitted, address a condo in Yaletown. And not just any condo, either. Twenty-fifth floor, Dylan noted with no amount of annoyance: big money. Dylan fished around a few moments more but nothing came up. Rafael Morales was clean, legal, and rich. "Bastard," Dylan muttered then shut the computer down and lumbered off.

He found himself fifteen minutes later at the Cop Shop, nursing a cola and a bruised ego. The Cop Shop was actually the Seafarer Pub, nicknamed for its popularity among police officers, themselves a target of the "blue bunnies" who frequented the place during happy hour and, if all went well, later into the evening. Dylan caught the eye of more than one eager bunny but his sour expression quickly doused any romantic notions they might have harboured, and they quickly if reluctantly moved on.

He wondered why he had come here if he were not in search of company. Claire Dawson wasn't the only fish in the sea, and it wasn't like he didn't have any luck with the ladies: he'd had several dates over the past year, followed on more than one occasion by a night of sex, but truth be told each encounter only left him feeling more hollow than the last. He knew what he truly craved was intimacy but he secretly wondered sometimes how capable he was of that. Intimacy required surrender, pushing aside fears of rejection and humiliation, and Dylan preferred to avoid all that. Still, he was confident he was no different than other men in this respect, so then why did they get a wife when he did not? Mind you, most of them were either miserable, divorced, or adulterers, so maybe they were just better at faking it; he, on the other hand, was too honest to be a successful con artist.

So then why not push this juvenile jealousy aside and accept you're not a player in a game that seems to benefit only the culpable? Because, he admitted to the universe, he wanted to surrender to Claire in a way he hadn't been able to do with other women, even if he didn't yet understand why or know with certainty if it were possible. He wondered what surrendering to her would feel like, whether it would be as terrifying as he imagined or a flight of ecstasy, and whether it would result in mind-blowing sex of the sort he'd heard other men boast of and which made him feel simultaneously jealous and sceptical, especially since their stories usually involved volumes of alcohol both in the alleged experience of and in the subsequent retelling. What he did know with certainty, however, was that he had taken one shaky, terrifying step in that direction, had strayed out of his comfort zone by writing Claire that letter, and that it remained in his glove compartment was not due to his cowardice but to Claire's infidelity of sorts.

Dylan sat like this for the better part of an hour, musing and sulking and watching from his perch the dance of men and women, some just there for the cheap beer, the rest willing participants in the hunt. He noted with some amusement a colleague from Homicide's Team One letting his hand wander unscrupulously under the expensive suit jacket of some corporate blonde, but the wan smile on Dylan's lips evaporated when he caught site of a leggy brunette getting dirty on the dance floor with Marco Esteban from Robbery. Dylan decided he'd had enough, paid his bill and slowly pushed his way through the crowd.

He was nearing the door when he saw her, leaning against the first of the room's two bars, flirting with a rookie who was buying her another drink despite Rebecca Wilson's obvious intoxication. She was clearly out of it, managing only a faint pout of disapproval when the rookie leaned against her and put his hand on her breast. He whispered something suggestive in her ear but Becky only laughed as she took a sip of her fresh gin and tonic.

Dylan approached and stepped in between Becky and her admirer. "Hey Wilson," Dylan greeted her with a voice he hoped didn't sound judgmental or condescending, "looks like you've had enough. Come on, I'll drive you home."

"Piss off, pal, she's with me," the rookie threatened.

Dylan glanced over his shoulder and stared down his nose at the shorter man. "That's 'piss off, *detective*,' to you," he admonished the rookie. "And if I'm not mistaken, Becky here is in no condition to give consent. So unless you want your career to start and end on a rape charge, I suggest you find someone else to play with."

Becky watched the rookie stomp off in a huff then fell laughing against Dylan. "You're funny, *detective*," she chirped. "Have a drink with me."

"Come on, Becky, let's go."

"Oooh," she cooed at him, "must be my lucky night."

Dylan took Becky by the arm and led her, stumbling and giggling, out of the bar and into his jeep. "You're such a gentleman," she gushed and caressed his arm when he leaned over to snap in her seat belt. He ignored the gesture, quickly closing the passenger door before she got her hands on anything else.

"Your place or mine?" she asked in a playful voice as Dylan slid in behind the wheel. She reached over to caress his arm again with the tips of her fingers.

"Where do you live, Becky?" Dylan asked in response, keeping his voice neutral.

"Mine it is," she laughed. "Corner of West Fourteenth and Beech."

He found her apartment easily enough, but getting her up the stairs and into her suite proved a greater challenge: Becky kept throwing her arms around Dylan's neck, trying to kiss him, making them both stumble whenever she lost her balance and he had to grab her before she hit the floor. Eventually Dylan succeeded in getting her inside her apartment and into her bedroom, where he laid her down and loosened her clothing. "Someone's in a hurry," she giggled, making a grab for Dylan's belt.

"Bad idea," he said as he evaded her hand with a deft retreat.

"I'm a bad girl," she purred, pushing out her breasts and licking her index finger in an attempt to arouse him. She slid her hand down her body and slipped it between her thighs. "Touch me," she whispered.

The words triggered a flood of emotion. Dylan could feel Claire again, smell her again, taste her again, but no sooner were they locked in a tight embrace than he imagined her in Rafael's car and now it was *his* mouth, *his* hands on Claire. Dylan felt a surge of jealousy and for a moment he was tempted to hurt Claire back even if she were unaware of his conquest.

He looked down at Becky. The bedside light was casting a warm glow on her ample cleavage as it heaved with anticipation. It would be so easy to lie down beside her, take her as he couldn't take Claire. It would be so easy and yet ... "I can't," Dylan whispered. "Get some rest, Becky." Then he left her apartment and headed home, a dull ache in his chest.

OR

After two hours of lobster bisque, succulent venison, a chocolate torte that almost gave Claire an orgasm, and the best shiraz she'd ever sipped, Rafael paid the hefty bill and escorted Claire outside. Over dinner he had behaved as imagined, slowly seducing her with gestures meant to arouse her while maintaining the appearance of chivalry: the sweep of a finger over her arm, a kiss on the back of her hand, a lean toward her to whisper compliments and profess his attraction. Rafael was a skilled paramour and he quickly had Claire wondering if his talents extended into the bedroom. In the next instant she thought of Dylan and felt a pang of regret, but forced her attentions back on Rafael with a silent scolding not to repeat past mistakes.

As they waited for the valet to retrieve Rafael's car, Claire caught sight of a dark Crown Victoria parked about half a block away, a man in the driver's seat. Claire strained to make out the face. Was Dylan following her in his police vehicle? Rafael saw the troubled look on her face and followed her eyes down the street. "What is wrong?"

She turned her face back to Rafael. "Nothing," she lied, pushing away the uneasy feeling that was threatening to blemish an otherwise perfect evening. "I thought I saw someone I know. I was mistaken."

The ride home was an exercise in self-control. Rafael's constant glances and subtle caresses convinced Claire she'd made the right decision to forget Dylan, and she briefly flirted with the idea of forcing the issue with a night of passion—were it not for the inconvenience of the stain on her stomach and that promise she'd made to herself that she was already regretting. By the time Rafael finally pulled up on Lakewood Road, Claire was tingling from head to toe. He saw her safely inside her door then deftly placed his hand around her waist and pulled her to him. His mouth was *fantastic*. He possessed the most astonishing kiss and Claire's knees weakened. When he pulled back he had to keep his hand on her waist for fear she'd fall down, and when she slowly awakened from her reverie he was smiling victoriously. "May I see you more?" he asked. Claire nodded, speechless: if she had any objections they were lost somewhere between his kiss and "more."

"Tomorrow I go to Mexico. For business. I come back Friday. Dinner?"

"I'd like that, yes."

"Same time?" Claire nodded and smiled weakly: he could have asked her anything at that moment and she would have agreed. Rafael leaned in and kissed her again, lightly this time, and took his leave of her.

Claire leaned against the door frame for support as she watched Rafael stroll back to his car and drive away. When he was no longer in her sights she reluctantly accepted his departure, went upstairs, laid down on her bed, and began to relive every delicious moment of the evening.

CR

Coyote looked up from his feast of rabbit and licked his chops, a satisfied grin on his face. The wound across his snout was scabbed over but still evident, and he had to lick his nose again to wipe away the last bits of rabbit blood and flesh that clung to the scab. And then he caught on the wind the scent of another, and the hackles along his back stood up. He spun around sharply, growling and standing over the rabbit carcass in a defiant refusal to share. Jackal backed away a little, keeping a respectful distance from the meal. "I have no interest in your supper," he called out to Coyote. "I have come only to warn you that the one you desire is also desired by another, and his influence will make her wise to your charms. You need to act quickly to secure your mate."

Coyote eyed the intruder. "Since when is Jackal a friend of Coyote?" he asked, suspicious.

"Since her distraction is of mutual benefit to us." Jackal laughed and turned to leave. "Enjoy your feast," he called out over his shoulder. "But don't take your eyes off your prize or it will be snatched from beneath your nose."

Ta'ah watched in silence as Jackal sauntered back into the woods. She was crouched down low in the tall grass, downwind from Coyote so he wouldn't detect her presence. The exchange between the two disturbed her, and she pondered the consequences of a united front. She thought she had scared Coyote off Claire but he had simply licked his wounds and now he knew to double his efforts. She needed to protect Claire, but how best to do so? If Ta'ah warned Claire her fear would return and Jackal would feed off it, would become stronger and more difficult to oppose, and whatever he were holding hostage in his den might never be freed. But if Coyote succeeded in ensnaring Claire's heart, one captive would simply be freed in exchange for another.

Ta'ah sighed heavily and returned to her body, then pulled her old bones off her bed. She needed to act quickly, before it was too late.

FIFTEEN

When Dylan dragged his weary body into work the next morning he found his partner, Tom Farrow, already at his desk, reading over case files from the past three weeks he'd been away. Tom was of average height and build but hidden beneath the dark trousers and white polo shirt was a deadly body toned by years of judo. His blond hair, cropped short and combed back from his forehead, was gelled in spiky shards that gave his angular face a chiselled appearance. But one only had to look closer at his sky blue eyes to know the hardness was reserved for the riff-raff for whom Tom had little patience. Dylan had seen more than one female witness fall under the spell of those blue eyes, and when Tom smiled and called a woman "luv" it was hardly even a contest anymore.

Tom glanced up as Dylan lumbered in. "Mornin', mate." Tom's English accent was back in full form now that he'd been back to the "Motherland" as he called it. He had joined the force five years earlier when the department, unable to keep up with attrition, had begun recruiting from the U.K. and Australia. Tom had been a homicide detective with Scotland Yard and, after a few years learning the local ropes and Canadian ways, had joined the squad six months ago. He was an irreverent man who often used British slang when interrogating suspects just to screw with their heads: "You're a right scary pillock, aren't you, mate? I'm bricking it, I am. Got the collywobbles in my John Thomas. Now why don't you stop this shite before I give you a right good bollicking." It cracked Dylan up every time.

Dylan plopped down at this desk to log in. He was looking a bit rough, his night interrupted on several occasions by anxious dreams about

Claire. "What's up, Dyl?" Tom quipped. "You look like shite."

"Glad to have you back, Tom," Dylan mocked in return. "But I recall flagging you as a high security risk." He rolled his eyes with disdain. "Can't trust Border Services to do anything right."

"Thanks. And I found the drugs you planted in my suitcase."

"Oh, good. The evidence room will be needing those back. See they get 'em."

Tom laughed then leaned in to Dylan and asked in a lower, genuinely concerned voice, "Seriously, mate, what's going on?"

Dylan's eyes glanced around the bustling squad room. "Over lunch."

Tom nodded and sat back. "So what's on the agenda then?"

"The Baby Jane case is our priority today," Dylan replied, piling the appropriate files into a zippered, soft leather file case. "I want to interview both Armin and Benjamin Keller. And the military shrink is making time at ten o'clock. You want to tag along or stay here and go over updates?"

"Tag along. You can bring me up to date as we ride."

"Okay, just remember which side of the road we drive on."

"Surely you jest. When do I ever give you cause to worry?"

"Every time I let you drive," Dylan said, smacking Tom on the arm with the leather file case as the two men rose to leave.

"Hey Lewis, hold up," demanded a voice from the doorway. Dylan turned to see Detective Gordie Bullen from the drug squad approaching and he didn't look happy. "Give me a minute?"

Dylan shrugged. Tom shot him a look that asked *Should I stay?* Dylan motioned *Why not?* He had no idea what Bullen wanted. "What's up, Gordie?"

"I got a hit on Rafael Morales when you ran him. Why's he of interest to you guys in Homicide?" Bullen asked, making only a vain effort to sound polite. The question troubled Dylan: if Bullen knew about the plate inquiry it meant he had placed an invisible flag on Morales, which meant Morales was the target of a highly sensitive investigation the drug squad didn't want anyone else to know about.

"Want to tell me why you flagged this individual?" Dylan asked in the same tone.

"No," Bullen shrugged, and judging by the look on his face he was prepared for a pissing match. But then Gordie Bullen was always prepared for a pissing match.

Dylan tried to diffuse Bullen's perpetual hostility with a smile. "Come on, Gordie. You show me yours I'll show you mine."

Bullen weighed his options. "Fine. But this is strictly confidential, you two. We've had Morales under surveillance for the past three weeks. We got word from Mexico's Federal Investigations Agency that Morales had been recruited to launder money for the Baja Cartel, using the Canadian accounting firm to bypass Mexican and US scrutiny. But the FIA is so freaking corrupt we don't know for certain if this is meant to throw us off another scent or if Morales really is crooked. What we do know is that he seems to spend way beyond his means—fancy condo, expensive car, three hundred dollar dinner last night—yet he supposedly earns seventy-five grand a year? Unless he's got some stellar investments we haven't found yet, our Rafael is riding someone else's gravy train." Bullen crossed his arms and pushed out his chin. "Okay, your turn."

Damn, thought Dylan, this is awkward. "Morales was seen in the company of a complainant on a murder investigation. It was a routine check. Nothing more," he shrugged.

"Routine, huh? You weren't on the clock last night, Lewis. But you were here looking for info on Morales."

"It was a chance observation," Dylan lied, hoping the sweat forming beneath his arms wasn't noticeable in the light. "And I was nearby. So I stopped and ran it."

"This complainant, by any chance would this be the looker he was wining and dining at Pierre's last night?"

Bullen snickered knowingly when Dylan's eyes twitched. "Okay listen up, Lewis. I don't know why this woman's got you all in a sweat, but"—he threw a warning glance at both men—"if you fuck up our investigation I'll have you eating each other's balls."

"Would that be fried or poached?" Tom joked. Bullen didn't laugh. "Bloody hell, Gordie, lighten up."

"Morales is just one possible player," Bullen hissed. "We've been watching the cartel's movements here for eleven months. A lot of time and money has gone into this investigation and if you screw it up over some broad, I'll shoot you myself." He tossed one last warning glance their way and left.

Dylan drew in a deep breath. What was he going to do now? If Morales were in with the Baja Cartel that put him and anyone with him in the line of fire from rival cartels, none of whom were above killing a woman.

Tom eyed Dylan with concern. "Jesus, mate, what *have* you gotten yourself into?"

When Claire awoke Tuesday morning she was still floating from her dinner the evening before. She was feeling vivacious and sexual, and couldn't wait for Rafael to return and continue his dance of seduction.

She twisted to stretch her body out, and the site of Dylan's lilies momentarily distracted her and filled her with a sense of loss. She wondered why this were still so when in truth she had experienced so little of him— but before she could ruin her mood with melancholic regrets she jumped to her own defence, lifting the vase off the bedside table and taking it with her to the bathroom so she could put the flowers on the window sill where they'd be less intrusive. She had to keep her sights on Rafael, she reminded herself, on a man who wasn't just interested but *available*. She would learn from her mistakes. What good would it serve to keep torturing herself over the unattainable Detective Lewis?

She had a quick bath—the medicine had all flaked off now, Claire noticed with pleasure—then dressed to start painting the living room. In her kitchen she made herself a light breakfast, hurriedly chomping on toast and eggs while standing at the counter: she had less than four hours to get things done before Maria was due for lunch and all the juicy details of Claire's date with Rafael. Claire smiled with anticipation, but the smile faded as her eyes fell upon the open dining room closet door. She crossed over to close it, to shut out the memory, but the hole inside, still awaiting repair, refused to be ignored. Claire stared at the wall's gaping wound, and the image of the mummified baby in her cramped, dusty grave came flooding back along with a surge of grief. Claire kneeled down and ran her fingers along the jagged edges of the broken plaster, then stared into the wall as if by some magic she could see what lay beyond it the way Ta'ah could. Claire pressed the palm of her hand against the rough wood of the interior wall, closed her eyes and tried to focus her mind. *Can you talk to me, Baby Jane? Do you still need my help? I'll do anything you need. All you have to do is give me a sign.*

Claire felt the floor beneath her soften as if she were now standing on sandy ground, and the smell of pine trees and damp slowly filled her nostrils. She opened her eyes to discover she was at the edge of a forest where the trees gave way to jagged rock that led to a river below. She was kneeling in front of what appeared to be an animal's den, the small opening dark and uninviting. Curious, she leaned down for a closer look—when like a flash of lightening Jackal pounced from within, snarling and lunging at Claire with his teeth bared and ready to strike. Claire screamed, found her feet and ran as fast as she could toward the forest but Jackal circled round and threatened again, sending a panicked Claire scrambling backwards. She lost her balance and went tumbling down the slippery, mossy slope toward the precipice, frantically grabbing at boulders and bushes in a vain attempt to stop her descent. It was no use: Claire went over the edge—and fell back hard onto the dining room floor, her mind back in this world and her heart pounding like a freight train. What the hell had just happened?

"You shouldn't go places you're not prepared for, Claire," a soft voice whispered. Claire gasped and spun her head toward the voice, and found Ta'ah and Stan standing beside the kitchen counter, looking down at her.

"Dear God, Ta'ah, you scared me!"

"Not nearly as much as Jackal."

"Is that what that was?" Claire asked, still shaking as she climbed onto her feet.

"It's a demon," Stan explained. "Evil has many disguises."

Claire's face blanched. "Is my house some kind of doorway into hell?"

"No more than any other," Ta'ah shrugged. "And an open door can always be closed."

Claire glanced down at the hole. "How do I close it, Ta'ah?"

"I saw paint cans in the front room," Ta'ah answered, smiling.

"Paint cans?" Claire asked, incredulous. "I'm supposed to cover up this horror with a coat of paint?"

"Not cover it up," Stan assured Claire, "take away its power. Evil feeds on fear, despair, hatred. Fill this house with love, happiness, hope and you starve the beast."

"You make it sound so simple."

"The concept is simple," Stan replied, smiling, "it's the execution that's difficult. Life's hard. It takes effort to be happy."

Ta'ah and Stan gave Claire a moment to digest that thought, then Ta'ah turned her attention to business. "Now, Claire," Ta'ah said as she leaned down to open her medicine bag, "we came to give this room another cleansing. Go, start your painting, and leave us to our task."

Claire nodded her assent, but Ta'ah saw the tension that remained in Claire's hunched shoulders and the arms folded in an unconscious gesture of protection. "Don't fret, daughter," Ta'ah reassured her with a matronly caress. "Great things await you. But you must do your part." She indicated toward the closet. "Leave these other matters to us."

Claire reluctantly did as she was told, and when she had left the room Ta'ah let down her positive façade. "What have you seen, mother?" whispered Stan.

"It's not what I've seen but what I haven't," Ta'ah answered cryptically, her brow furrowed. "Jackal wishes for Claire to remain distracted by Coyote. Why?"

"Perhaps it knows Coyote will disappoint her and her pain will feed him again."

"No," Ta'ah replied, eyeing the closet door suspiciously, "there's something else, something more it's hiding, something it fears Claire will find."

"How shall we proceed?"

"We must end the distraction."

SIXTEEN

Dylan and Tom signed out their cruiser and hit the road. "Where to first?" asked Tom.

"Georgia and Burrard," Dylan replied. "Let's start with Benjamin Keller before court opens."

The law offices of Keller Jamieson Clark and Associates were situated on the twentieth floor of the posh Grosvenor Building with a stellar view of the North Shore mountains and, if you perched yourself at any one of the floor-to-ceiling windows, of the city teaming below. The offices were expansive: the lobby alone was the size of a typical Vancouver apartment. "Blimey," cracked Tom as the elevator opened, "we're working the wrong side of the street."

They strolled up to reception. "Can I help you?" the petite blonde behind the counter asked.

"We're here to see Mr. Keller, please," Dylan answered, matching her polite and professional tone.

"Do you have an appointment?"

Tom held up his badge and smiled. "Do we need one?"

The receptionist didn't flinch but simply smiled back and picked up the phone. "Mr. Keller, there are two police officers here to see you. Would you like me to send them in?" She listened a moment then put down the phone. "If you could wait a moment Mr. Keller's assistant will be right with you."

Dylan and Tom sat down on one of two large leather couches in the reception and began contemplating a large abstract painting on the wall.

"What do you think that's worth?" Tom asked.

"Half our pay for the year, I'd guess," snorted Dylan.

"Before or after taxes?"

Dylan chuckled. "Definitely before."

An attractive blonde in a black pencil skirt and white blouse approached, her stiletto heels clicking on the marble tiles. "Officers? If you could follow me, please, Mr. Keller will see you in the boardroom."

She turned and they followed. She had a nicely shaped bum that didn't go unnoticed by her guests and Tom couldn't help cranking his neck in exaggerated appreciation. Dylan cast him a sideways glance and mouthed "Behave," but Tom just grinned impishly and added a little more swagger to his walk.

Benjamin Keller was waiting for them in the boardroom. "Gentlemen," he welcomed them with a friendly tone—though he didn't cross the room to shake their hands, the detectives noted—"please sit down. Can Linda get you anything? Coffee, tea, spring water?"

"No thanks," Tom and Dylan answered in unison.

Linda nodded to her boss and left, closing the door behind her.

Nobody sat down.

"So which one of you is Detective Lewis?" asked Keller with a sly smile on his face.

"That would be me," Dylan answered, unfazed. "And this is my partner, Tom Farrow."

"I understand you've been observing my cousin Elisabeth. Were you the same officer talking to my aunt Therese?" Keller asked, fishing for a point of leverage. "If so, it seems an odd use of your time, talking to an old woman with dementia."

Dylan nodded as if in agreement then said, "Interesting thing, dementia. It attacks recent memory but often leaves long-term memory intact. So if, for example, I wanted to know about the death of a baby some forty years ago, I might still get a response."

Keller's eyes went dark. "What baby?"

"The one found buried in the wall of your aunt's former home," Dylan said matter-of-factly. "Know anything about that?"

All the arrogance drained from Benjamin Keller's face. He sat down at the conference table, stunned, at first unable to speak. Tom and Dylan kept their eyes on him, observing every minute detail of his reaction.

"Have the remains been dated?" Benjamin asked weakly when he finally found his voice again.

"Circa mid-'71," Dylan replied.

Benjamin raised a hand to support his forehead as he stared down at the table. He looked ... confused? Shocked? Horrified? His face was a kaleidoscope of emotions yet none of them revealed knowledge. At least not definitively. Dylan made a move. "Is it yours?"

Benjamin looked up and his face read disgust. "I hardly think so."

"Then would you mind submitting a DNA sample?" Dylan asked as if this were a simple request. "Just to rule you out."

Benjamin's face said it well enough that his words were redundant: "I hardly think so."

"Would you consent to DNA samples from Therese and Elisabeth?" Dylan pressed on.

"Not at this moment."

"Then I'll get a court order."

Benjamin snorted. "If you had grounds for a court order, detective, you wouldn't be here requesting permission."

"Or perhaps I'm trying to protect their privacy," Dylan lobbied back. He paused to contain his irritation and to relax his tone again. "I don't think I have to remind you an order would be accessible by the public"—he paused to let that sink in before throwing his curve ball—"and the press."

"I'll get a publication ban."

"Sure, if that's your only concern," Tom joined in with a disapproving shrug. "But if either sample shares DNA from the baby you won't be able to stop what's going to happen next."

"My aunt Therese has advanced Alzheimer's," Benjamin retorted dismissively. "If she's the mother Crown Counsel will do absolutely nothing. And if Elisabeth"—his voice caught in his throat for a fraction of a second before Benjamin got it under control again—"if Elisabeth is the mother then somebody did that *to* her."

"Any idea who?" Tom asked.

"No. I wasn't allowed to visit after her thirteenth birthday. I never saw her again until my uncle had his stroke last December."

"Speaking of which, I understand from the hospital Elisabeth has been ill for decades," Dylan continued digging. "Why did she never receive proper medical care?"

Benjamin sighed angrily. "Her parents refused. And unfortunately, gentleman, the law is clear on the matter: the court cannot impose psychiatric care unless the patient is a danger to themselves or others. You should know that."

"But she was a minor at the onset of illness," Tom said, acting confused. "Didn't anybody think to challenge the parents?"

"Yes!" Benjamin snapped. "Me! But by the time I was old enough to do something about it, Elisabeth was also no longer a minor."

"How hard could you have tried, mate?" asked Tom, shrugging off Benjamin's response. It was a ploy to illicit a strong response and it worked. Benjamin jumped to his feet, eyes blazing.

"Fucking hard, that's how!" he spit at Tom. "I tried the moment I passed the bar. I tried again when my aunt was first diagnosed with Alzheimer's. And I didn't waste a *fraction of one minute* after my uncle had his stroke."

"Hey, whoa, sorry," Dylan apologized. "I'm sure my partner meant no disrespect."

"Oh, cut the crap, detective," retorted Benjamin. "Are you forgetting whom you're talking to? The good cop-bad cop formula doesn't work in this office."

"Then what does work?" Dylan asked sincerely.

Benjamin looked taken aback. He hadn't expected that one. He walked over to the window and looked out to the mountains, to the last bit of snow that still clung to the peak of Mount Seymour, and quietly replied, "I don't know what went on in that house after Elisabeth became ill. I don't know why she became ill. I'm told she might be schizophrenic and apparently there's a history of it on my aunt's side. A brother and her grandfather. Both were euthanized under Hitler's T4 program."

"I was told it could also be trauma-induced," Dylan said, digging again but more gently this time.

Benjamin nodded in agreement. "Yes. And I have my suspicions. But if somebody hurt her she never told me; she never called me for help."

"Is it possible," Dylan asked, "that this baby might prove some of your suspicions?"

"Perhaps."

"Then help us."

"How, detective?" Benjamin raised his hands at the futility of the request. "Even if I were to consent to you interviewing Elisabeth, you've seen her. She's locked in her own mind. It could take years, decades, to unlock it."

"Then let us talk to her doctor," Tom suggested.

126

Benjamin carefully considered the request. "No," he finally decided. "*I'll* discuss this with Dr. Mitchell. Then depending on what he has to say we'll take it from there."

Dylan and Tom recognized they were being asked to leave. They glanced at each other and their expressions said they were in agreement: there was nothing more they were going to get here today.

"We'll see ourselves out," said Dylan. Tom opened the door to leave but as Dylan followed he stopped as if suddenly remembering something. "Oh, one last thing," he asked, his hand on the door, "whose idea was it to sell the house?"

"Mine. Money was needed for Therese and Elisabeth's care and I didn't see the point in leaving an asset empty and its value unrealized. The judge agreed."

"So Armin opposed the sale?"

Benjamin snorted. "Yes. And now we both know why." The adversaries sealed their pact in silence, then Dylan left.

Benjamin collapsed into a chair. His mind raced back to Elisabeth as a child, when she was his best friend and the love of his life. He saw her as vividly as if it were yesterday: her goofy smile, her singsong voice calling to him from the other side of the garden—*Watch me, Ben, watch me*—her brown hair dancing in the sunlight as she twirled a hula-hoop or turned a cartwheel on the grass.

"I'm watching, Izzy, I'm watching," Benjamin whispered, then hung his head and wept.

☙

Dr. Kerry Gladstone's offices were decidedly less plush than Benjamin Keller's. The Operational Stress Injury Clinic out at the university, created to deal specifically with military and police officers in need of psychological assistance, was tucked away in a quiet corner of the hospital, a fitting spot considering the stigma many soldiers and cops still felt when required to see a shrink. Dylan wondered if the day would come when the Baby Janes of this world would have him crying on the couch, and counted his blessings he wasn't there yet. When he had first joined the force he imagined himself stronger than most, twenty-odd years on the rez having desensitized him to violence and despair. His fortitude had been a source of pride until the day Ta'ah lovingly warned him not to confuse cynicism with emotional strength. He vehemently denied he'd ever done so but that was a lie: he had already been missing a small fraction of his humanity when he became a cop, and fifteen years of dealing with the dregs of society hadn't improved that figure. Still, he was saner and kinder than most cops, he believed—hell, he was saner and kinder than most *people*—and he was right. For that he thanked Ta'ah.

Dr. Gladstone's receptionist was considerably older and much less perky than the petite blonde at Keller Jamieson Clark and Associates, but her welcome was definitely warmer. The men waited in the uncomfortable chairs hospitals are notorious for, anxious that someone they knew might chance by and misconstrue their attendance here as personal business or, worse still, ordered by the department. So it was with much relief that the wait wasn't long before Dr. Gladstone emerged from her office and introduced herself. "Come inside my office," she said after handshakes all around, "and we'll chat."

She was a plump woman in her early sixties, Dylan guessed, with a thick head of dyed silver hair around a pleasant if average face lightly dressed with blush and lipstick. She was clothed in a simple navy linen suit and pink silk blouse that tied in a bow at the front, and sensible but well-made leather pumps. Her demeanour was kind but straightforward, a quality Dylan imagined was appreciated by her brand of clients.

"Just so we're clear up front," she said as she took her seat behind a large hospital-issue desk, "Major Williamson has spoken to me about the situation and it's the military's position to encourage interagency cooperation." Her tone was professional but friendly. "Nevertheless I'm required by the rules of my profession to insist upon a court order for my file on Karl Keller."

"Would there be any objection to the warrant?" Dylan asked casually, the implication clear.

Dr. Gladstone gave them a sly, conspiratorial smile and replied, "Normally the military contacts the family for approval but as Karl never named his next of kin we have no reason to make such a request. In fact, Major Williamson and I took it upon ourselves to write a joint letter containing this fact." She slid a letter across the desk. "You can attach it to your application. And I've already had the file retrieved from the archives."

"And if I were to take the time to write up such an order," Tom joined in the game, picking up the letter, "would it be worth our while?"

"Very much so."

"And when we get Karl's file," Dylan added, "what might we find?"

"That you need to take a close look at the father."

"It just so happens we're on our way to have a chat with Armin Keller," Tom said. "Is there anything in particular you think we should ask him?"

Dr. Gladstone sat back and considered the question. What *could* she tell them now that wouldn't breach ethics? "Ask him why Karl left home. And then don't believe whatever trite answer he gives you. It was a *significant* event."

"Thanks, doc," Dylan reached out to shake her hand goodbye. "We appreciate the cooperation."

"My pleasure," she smiled back. As the men turned to leave she added, "By the way, Karl Keller was a decent man. And no decent man should've gone through what he did."

Dylan nodded his head in understanding. "We'll do what we can to keep the details closed from public view."

"I appreciate that, officer, for Karl's sake."

Dylan and Tom hurried back to their cruiser. They both had the same thought: they wanted that file and they wanted it yesterday. If they hurried back to the office they could have the ITO written up and on a JP's desk before lunch. Their impatience was palpable, and when Tom found himself stuck behind a line of cars waiting to turn left, he muttered "screw this" and used a few bursts of the siren to clear a path. He was never one for rules.

When Dylan and Tom returned to the squad room there was a report from the forensic dental specialist waiting on Dylan's desk. Upon his return from Boston on Monday, Dr. Matthew Jones had received the baby's deciduous teeth from Anil and had done an immediate analysis. So while Tom wrote up the Information To Obtain warrant, Dylan went over the dental findings. He glossed over the scientific details and zoomed in on the conclusion: "The thickness of the neonatal line in the Striae of Retzius is 10.33 microns, consistent with normal vaginal birth history. Fatality due to birthing complications is not indicated. There is some though not significant post-natal growth of the deciduous enamel, indicating the infant was not stillborn and death occurred within a few weeks after birth at maximum. Final matrix on the leading edge of forming enamel is not well mineralized, indicating poor or absent nutrition in final days of life."

Dylan phoned Anil. "Hey Sanjit, it's me. Have you read the dental report?"

"Yeah. I was just about to call you." He paused, and his voice became sombre. "It gets worse."

"Worse?" asked Dylan. *How could it possibly get worse?*

"I got the tox and tissue tests back a half hour ago. Tox was negative, but Dylan," Anil hesitated, "there were microscopic linen fibres and plaster dust found in Baby Jane's lungs."

There was silence as Dylan processed this new information. Finally he asked, "Sanjit, are you saying she was wrapped in the cloth and put in the wall *alive*?"

"Alive and left to die."

Dylan's voice went quiet as he tried to control the rage threatening to push its way past a decade and a half of law enforcement. "How long would it have taken for her to die?"

"Dehydration in a baby will start to kill within forty-eight hours. She would have suffered organ failure and likely slipped into a coma. But actual death could have taken up to two weeks depending on her body mass at birth."

"Thanks, Sanjit," Dylan said as calmly as he could manage. "When will I have your final report?"

"Thursday. And Dylan, if the bastard who did this is still alive, make sure he doesn't remain that way when you find him."

"I won't." Dylan put the phone down and rose from his desk. Tom watched, concerned, as Dylan strode angrily out of the squad room. Tom waited a moment so as not to attract attention from the other detectives then walked out into the hallway and into the men's washroom where he knew he'd find his partner. "What's going on, Dyl?"

Dylan continued running cold water over his face until the urge to scream obscenities at the Great Spirit subsided. Tom handed Dylan a towel when he finally stood back up. "She was buried alive, Tom," Dylan said as he mopped his face. "Some son of a bitch buried a newborn baby girl alive in a wall."

"Man that's sick."

"Sick doesn't even come close to describing it." Dylan grabbed onto the edges of the basin, trying to find his equilibrium, trying to make sense of something that one just couldn't make sense of. He pushed back from the sink and headed for the door. "Come on, Tom, let's nail the garbage who did this." Tom nodded sympathetically and patted his partner on the back.

"Do you want to go to the range on Saturday?" Dylan asked as they walked back to the squad room. "I need to put a bullet in something."

☙

Rebecca left Dr. Gladstone's office a half-hour after Dylan and Tom had attended, oblivious to the fact that the man she was talking about was just outside the door executing a warrant. Dr. Gladstone had given nothing away to either party, no hint to Dylan that she knew he was an object of desire, no hint to Rebecca that he'd been there earlier. Instead the doctor simply put a face to the name now when Rebecca spoke of him, and encouraged her as she always did to pursue more meaningful relationships whether with Dylan or someone else. "How much longer are you going to punish yourself for something that was not your fault, Rebecca?" Dr. Gladstone asked for the umpteenth time. "How long before you recognize your right to be respected—as a woman, not as a cop?"

It was a question Rebecca still didn't have an answer for, and she wondered if she ever would.

SEVENTEEN

Claire put the finishing touches on lunch. She'd spent the morning painting as she had originally planned and Ta'ah had suggested, but the cheerfulness Claire had awoken with had refused to return. The smell of burnt cedar hung in the air long after Ta'ah and Stan had left, leaving behind an aromatic reminder of Claire's brush with danger. She couldn't get the image of Jackal out of her mind, and though she understood Ta'ah's directive to leave such matters to the experts, it nevertheless felt condescending. Claire was strong now, the fight in her had returned, and she wanted to fight for Baby Jane. It wasn't enough for Claire to be happy again, to starve the demon as Stan suggested; that wasn't going to solve the case. New paint on the walls and dinner with Raphael wasn't going to bring a killer to justice. She needed to do more. But what?

The strike of the doorbell forced Claire to push her ruminations aside. Maria was dying to hear about the success of her matchmaking, and Claire didn't wish to disappoint. She concealed her gloominess behind a perky façade and answered the door. "Come in, come in," she chimed as Maria crossed the threshold and embraced her. "And Vicente, how are you?" Claire cooed, leaning down to tickle him in his stroller. He gurgled and laughed and squeezed Claire's finger.

Maria looked into the living room from the foyer. "I love this colour!" she exclaimed, eyeing the terracotta walls. "It's beautiful. It reminds me of Mexico."

"Careful, it's still wet," warned Claire. "I just finished the first coat. We can have lunch on the deck to escape the smell. I hope you like egg salad sandwiches and mixed greens."

"Sounds wonderful."

Claire led the way through the kitchen to the back deck where a cheap beach umbrella was serving as temporary shade from the sun. The patio furniture had been left by the Kellers and, while it was dated and falling apart, it was proving just fine in the interim. "New furniture," Claire explained, "it's on the list."

Maria laughed. "What does the furniture matter? It's the company that counts." She gave Vicente a toy to keep him amused while the women ate, then leaned in for the goods, her eyes sparkling with anticipation. "Well, tell me all about it."

Claire recounted her date with Rafael and found her mood lifted by the recollection. If happiness were going to banish the evil lurking about the place, perhaps Rafael Morales *was* just the ticket; and dating him, Claire decided, didn't preclude helping Baby Jane.

"Wow," Maria said, grinning with admiration, "he must be smitten. The last woman I set him up with he took to dinner at a tapas bar."

"I like him," Claire admitted. "And he has the most *amazing* kiss. What can you tell me about him?"

"Carlos tells me Rafael was hand-picked for the job here by a few of the firm's big Mexican clients who do business with Canada. They wanted someone who understood the language and Mexican business practices. Which is a polite way of saying someone who understands how to pay and account for bribes."

Claire laughed. "Is it really that bad?"

"Oh," said Maria, shaking her head, "I love my country but it is very corrupt. Everything—police, business, politics—suffers from corruption. You can't even get your phone hooked up without paying a little extra. And now the drug wars have become very, very dangerous. So many people killed every day. It's madness. But there is no one to protect the people because so many police are involved with the cartels. In Tijuana it became so bad the president sent in the army to protect the city because the police could not be trusted." She looked down at Vicente and sighed. "I'm glad to be a Canadian now, and to have hope for my children."

"Do you know anything about Rafael's family?" asked Claire. "He told me only that he is from Mexico City, has two sisters, both married with children, and that his parents run a successful grocery store."

Maria laughed as she took another bite of her salad. "He's being modest. The successful grocery store is really ten large stores around the capital." She leaned in conspiratorially. "I don't know if this is true, but Carlos suspects Rafael will inherit most of the shares and run the company some day. That is why his father insisted Rafael become an accountant." She gave Claire a look of satisfaction. "Don't let this fish go, my new friend, now that you have hooked him."

Claire sat back and smiled, took a sip of lemonade, and thought about Rafael's remarkable kiss. But then Rafael's face blurred with Eric's and Claire's anticipation faded. "We'll see," she said cautiously. "Money and charm are nice but they're not the measure of a man. But,"—she then added with a twinkle back in her eye—"if he has integrity to match I'll not be tossing him back into the sea, *that's* for certain."

03

Coyote was sunning himself on a slate ledge, the river below cooling the breeze that blew his fur lazily to and fro. Another, slightly older and stockier coyote limped down to the ledge, a dead gopher in his jaws. Coyote jumped to his feet and for a moment it appeared as if he would challenge the older animal, yet despite Coyote's obvious physical supremacy he kept his head low in deference, and when the gopher was dropped at his feet Coyote demonstrated his gratitude with a sycophantic squeak. The older coyote looked satisfied, almost smug, as it hobbled back up the ledge and trotted off toward the forest, leaving Coyote to feast alone.

03

Tom and Dylan were pacing impatiently in front of the court clerk's counter, waiting for a justice of the peace. There was a small line and Tom's orations on the urgency of the matter were falling on deaf ears. "Let me see that," the clerk had demanded, looking sceptical. "Medical records? Hardly an emergency. Wait your turn."

"You know," Tom leaned in to the desk clerk and whispered, "my partner was remarking as we came in how gorgeous he thinks you are."

"Too bad for him, then," she replied, leaning in to match Tom's stance, "that I'm married."

"How unfortunate," Tom smiled in defeat and, turning to join Dylan who had settled into a chair, added under his breath, "for your husband."

It was a good hour before they got their signed warrant and both were feeling hungry. "Lunch?" asked Dylan. "Or should we suffer until we get the records?"

"Lunch. My earlier excitement has been tempered by time."

"Lunch it is."

Dylan hadn't realized how little he'd eaten since the afternoon before until they walked into Best Burgers and the smell of broiled beef hit his nostrils. His stomach began growling its displeasure, lengthening the time it took for their beefsteak sandwiches and potato salad to be finally plopped down on their table.

"So," asked Tom as he wiped the grease from the first bite off his chin, "what's this trouble you're in?"

Though reticent, Dylan revealed the whole of his interaction with Claire, right down to the sexual encounter though minus the intimate details. "Huh," was all Tom said at first. He considered the information for a moment more then asked, "So, mate, on a scale of one to ten, how badly do you fancy this bird?"

"Twelve."

"Then go for it."

"Are you insane?"

"Look," Tom gestured dismissively with his burger, "her testimony on this case is going to be confined to 'Did you find this baby in your wall?' It's going to be forensics that will make or break this one, not eyewitness accounts. And the remains date to well before she was even born. So how much damage can some skanky lawyer do? It's only useful for blackmail if you keep it a dirty secret. So go out with her, in public, don't be shy, and let the cards fall where they may."

"I'm glad you can be so phlegmatic about it," Dylan replied dryly. "It's not your career on the line."

"Dylan, the brass is hardly going to fire you. And I sincerely doubt you're the first cop to find love at the other end of an emergency call."

"They could take me off the squad."

"True. But I hear they're recruiting in Vice."

"Very funny."

135

"If she's a twelve, Dylan, would Vice be so bad?" Tom looked Dylan squarely in the eye. It was a good point.

"What if she's not a twelve?"

"You just said she was."

"No, you asked me how badly I wanted her."

"Semantics, mate. If you want her that badly there must be a reason. Or is this just your dick talking?"

"It's not my dick, though it certainly has an opinion." Dylan paused. "Maybe I should talk to McTavish, see what he thinks. Maybe get permission."

"Baaaaaad idea," Tom disagreed, shaking his head and rolling his eyes for effect. "He says no and you're doubly screwed. Best to act first, apologize later. That's always been my motto."

"Yeah, how's that working out for you?" Dylan asked sarcastically.

Tom laughed at the inside joke. Just prior to going on vacation with his wife to England, Tom had drank a wee bit too much at a party and was caught by his wife flirting with the barely legal daughter of their host when the girl had returned home from a date. "Judas."

"Although," Tom added momentarily, "I did appreciate your attempt to save my balls with your useful and well considered advice. It was most helpful."

Dylan grinned. "All I said to Jill was, 'Who cares where he gets his appetite as long as he only eats at home?' How unhelpful could that have been?"

"Profoundly. Still, heart was in the right place, mate, so all's forgiven." He sat back and eyed his partner. "But seriously, Dyl, if she's worth it go get her."

Dylan mulled over Tom's advice as they drove back to the hospital. His points were fair and, were Dylan honest with himself, Tom was right about not talking to McTavish. Still, Dylan wasn't quite ready to abolish his place on the squad. There had to be a way to salvage both, he figured, and he knew just whom to ask. At day's end he'd go have a chat with his *ta'ah*.

Dr. Gladstone was occupied when they arrived but her receptionist had been instructed to copy the file and it was waiting for pickup. One hand-delivered warrant later and the men were in possession of Karl Keller's psychological treatment file.

It was several pages of this and that, of anger issues and probable causes before Tom hit the jackpot. "Mother of God," Tom's jaw dropped as he read the section. "Are we bleedin' *serious*?"

"What?" Dylan asked impatiently, momentarily taking his eyes off the road.

"It says that when Karl turned sixteen, his father told him that in order to become a man Karl had to perform a rite of passage which involved sexual intercourse with his mother. When Karl refused he was severely beaten by his father who berated Karl with each blow, calling him pathetic, a disappointment, and that he had failed the 'Party' and the 'Motherland.' When queried as to the effectiveness of the beating, Karl became too distraught to reply."

The men looked at each other, incredulous. There wasn't much they hadn't heard in their time on the force but this was a new one. "No wonder he buggered off," said Tom. "But I would have fixed the old man first myself."

"You know what this means, of course?" Dylan said unhappily.

"Yup. Baby Jane might be Karl's daughter *and* his sister. How sick is that?"

ভ

After Maria left with Vicente, Claire painted the small living room ceiling then tackled the unpleasant task of hauling to the trash one of the heavy bags of construction debris she had stored beneath the deck; she'd only be able to put out one bag per week to comply with city bylaws unless she could find someone with a truck or a sport utility vehicle to help her haul it all to the dump. She remembered Dylan's jeep but pushed that idea away; she had to stay focused on Rafael.

As Claire walked back to the house Frau Müller came out into her yard and raced toward the fence. "Claire," she whispered, looking anxiously about for eavesdroppers, "have you got the results yet?"

Claire frowned. "Oh, I'm sorry, Frau Müller, I meant to tell you: Detective Lewis discovered our plan and demanded the claim tickets. And we've been warned to stay away from the investigation."

"Oh." Frau Müller's disappointment was swift and palpable. "Right, then," she stammered. "Well, um ... Well, I, I just put the kettle on, and there's leftover pie from yesterday's canasta. Would you like Earl Gray or that new-fangled green tea?"

"Green," Claire responded kindly. "Just let me get out of these filthy clothes and I'll be right over."

Claire changed into a clean pair of jeans over which she threw a light sweater and headed next door. She found Frau Müller in the kitchen steeping the tea and doling out generous slices of apple pie.

"Frau Müller," joked Claire, trying to lighten the mood, "if you keep feeding me your wonderful baking I'm going to look like the Dillberry Dough girl soon."

"Dillberry Dough," replied Frau Müller with disgust, "pah. Cheap imitation. Now sit and enjoy the real thing." She set the plates of pie on the kitchen table then poured two cups of tea and sat down. There followed a moment of awkward silence as both women pretended to be occupied with their tea. "It's my fault, isn't it?" Frau Müller finally said, averting her gaze to the garden below. "I wasn't clever enough when that police lady came around asking questions."

"I'm afraid neither of us was clever enough," Claire chuckled. "It didn't take much effort to pry it out me. He's a tricky one, that Detective Lewis."

Claire's levity had the desired effect. "And I suppose we weren't very subtle with Therese," Frau Müller laughed back.

"I don't think CSIS will be recruiting us any time soon."

"Get down, get down," Frau Müller laughed, flailing her arms about over her head, mimicking Claire.

"Oh, be quiet," Claire retorted, grabbing Frau Müller's arms, and the two women fell together in a fit of laughter.

"Oh, dear," Frau Müller said when they managed to compose themselves, "what next then?"

Claire blew out a sigh. "I don't honestly know. I've been wracking my brain, trying to think of something, but I have no idea what. I don't really know enough about the Kellers, I guess is the problem, so I don't know where to start."

"And regrettably I know almost as little," Frau Müller admitted. "We may have been neighbours but we were worlds apart. It was ironic that Armin moved here, next door to my father."

"Because you're Jewish?"

"Yes, but that was only part of it. My father used to be a renowned geneticist at the University of Heidelberg. In the early thirties Hitler passed a law that forced doctors to report patients with illnesses the government believed were hereditary, and then they were sterilized against their will.

The Nazis tried to recruit my father to defend the law but instead he and six other doctors and scientists openly opposed it. They were all fired from their positions and one was arrested. My father applied to other universities but many countries—even Canada back then—believed in eugenics and were sterilizing people. So his opinion wasn't very popular, not with anyone, including many at temple. Perhaps they would have been more supportive had they known where it was headed."

"So how did you manage?" Claire asked as she took another bite of pie. "By the way, this pie is fantastic."

"Oh thank you, dear," Frau Müller beamed at the compliment, then continued on. "My mother found a job in a factory and I worked as a cleaner. Eventually the insult was forgotten and my father managed to get a position at a small university in Wittenberg. But he already knew he wanted to leave Germany. He said the law would only lead to worse and he was right. One prejudice leads to another. At first it was the sterilization of the lame and ill, then the killing of the children started—"

"What?! Wait, stop," Claire demanded, shocked by the revelation. "What do you mean, the killing of the children?"

"Early in 1939, Hitler secretly authorized the killing of all children under the age of three with severe disabilities, to begin the purification of the German race."

Claire was dumbstruck. She had no idea. She knew about the attempted extermination of the Jews but not this. "But how could their parents let this happen?!"

"They didn't. They were lied to. They were told their children were going to a hospital for special treatment, then they were killed and the parents were told the reason was pneumonia or some such rubbish. Thousands of children were murdered." She shook her head: it was an unspeakable cruelty.

"My father found out about the program," she continued after a pause to collect her thoughts, "and he wrote to the newspapers about it. That's when they came for him. Luckily for us my father was warned by a friend and we were able to escape to France. Then the war began. We lived off our wits for six months and then we were lucky again when my father was given a job here at the university. We were also lucky my father had the foresight to send most of his money to a relative in New York after his first brush with Hitler's henchmen."

"It's a terrible story," Claire said sympathetically. "But how do you know Armin supported such things? He was just a boy during the war. He wasn't responsible for such atrocities."

"Shortly after they moved here," Frau Müller responded somewhat indignantly, "my parents went next door to welcome our new neighbours. Franz Keller and my father got into an argument about the war. Armin joined in, calling my father *Lebensunwertes Leben*. It means 'life unworthy of life.' That's what the Nazis called those they killed with their so-called euthanasia program. Which of course eventually extended to us Jews."

"And you think Armin never changed his ideas, even after all these years in Canada?"

"No," Frau Müller adamantly shook her head. "The Nazi party was outlawed after the war but they've resurfaced over the years under many new names. There were always rumours that Armin kept a membership in one party or another, both here and in Germany. And he often went back there. At least once a year."

Party, thought Claire. Party. There had been a letter addressed to Armin from Germany, something official looking, something *Partei*. "You know, something came in the mail last week. I think I still have it. Wait here. I'll be right back." Claire sprinted back to her place, to the stack of mail on the pine table. Near the bottom of the pile was an envelope addressed to Armin Keller from the *Volkssozialistiche Partei Deutschlands* and postmarked Berlin. "There it is," she murmured to herself and headed back next door.

"Does this mean anything to you?" asked Claire as she settled back down at Frau Müller's table.

"See," said Frau Müller, tapping the envelope. "See. *Volkssozialistiche Partei Deutschlands*, German People's Socialist Party. New Nazis. A leopard doesn't change his spots." She sat back and took a self-satisfied sip of her tea, justified in her dislike of Armin Keller.

Claire weighed the envelope in her hands. Was this the secret to Baby Jane's death? Or just the wayward politics of a pitiful old man? She had no idea which but she did know one thing: she had to tell Detective Lewis. But first ... Claire sat back and considered the implications of opening the letter: on the one hand mail tampering was a criminal offence, but on the other hand the letter might contain a clue into the death of an innocent child. Claire looked at Frau Müller for a moment then spoke carefully. "I think you should put the kettle back on. I'm going to need a translator."

EIGHTEEN

Frau Müller smiled excitedly and put a fresh kettle of water on the stove, then reached under the sink and pulled out an unused pair of rubber cleaning gloves. Claire stood to take them but Frau Müller shook her head and put the gloves on herself. "What can they possibly do to a silly old woman?" she smiled. "Give it to me." Claire handed over the letter. Frau Müller wiped Claire's fingerprints off the envelope with a towel and the two women waited in silence for the water to boil.

When the whistle finally blew Frau Müller held the letter over the steam and slowly pried the envelope open with a butter knife. Inside was a newsletter. She slid it out and unfolded it, and from within its pages a handwritten note fell out. Frau Müller scanned the newsletter first. "Anything important?" Claire asked expectantly.

"Just the usual neo-Nazi garbage: Jews are taking over the world, the government is weak, we must prepare to defend our beliefs. The true Aryan state is threatened by racial pollution. Nothing particularly original."

"What does the note say?"

"Dear Armin: Am saddened to hear of your loss. Your nephew is a traitor and a thief. Our hearts go out to you and your family. In solidarity, Frederick."

"Is there an administrative list in the newsletter? Check if there's a Frederick on it."

Frau Müller flipped the newsletter over and found the list of board members on back. "Yes. Frederick Brandt. Chairman."

Claire's eyes narrowed. "Do you have a small plastic bag?"

Frau Müller nodded, opened a drawer and pulled out a clean sandwich bag. "Put the note in there," Claire said. Frau Müller did as directed, then pulled out a larger resealable bag from the drawer and put the newsletter and envelope in that: she was quickly getting the hang of this espionage thing again. Maybe CSIS would come calling after all.

"What now?" she asked.

"Now," said Claire as she popped the last bite of her apple pie into her mouth, "I'm going to show this to Detective Lewis." She bid Frau Müller a sincere thank you then sprinted home again in search of Dylan's card, the ill-gotten treasure in hand.

CR

Dylan's phone rang as he and Tom pulled up to Westview Elder Centre in south Vancouver. "Hey, Sanjit," Dylan answered, having checked the call display first. "What's up?"

"My report's going to be a few days late. Parvati's gone into labour."

"Fantastic!" exclaimed Dylan. "Keep me posted. And don't worry about the report; a few days isn't going to make a difference."

"I know. But just in case you need details call my grad student, Tina Edmonds. She'll be holding down the fort until I get back."

"Will do." In the background Dylan heard Parvati screaming something in Hindi. He had no idea what but Dylan guessed it wasn't polite. "And give my love to Parvati."

"I will. But I think she'd rather have an epidural."

Dylan laughed as Anil hung up the phone. "Parvati's gone into labour," Dylan explained to Tom as they alighted from the car. "Report on Baby Jane's going to be a few days late."

They headed for the entrance. "Brave man, that Anil," said Tom. "Don't know how he manages to do what he does and still have kids."

"How do any of us manage to have kids? You just gotta trust in the universe, I guess."

"Yeah, well, you trust in the universe. Me, I'm keeping my faith in a vasectomy."

Dylan was surprised by the admission; Tom hadn't told him this before. Was Baby Jane already getting to him, too? "Seriously, pal, you cut

142

the tie that binds?"

"Ages ago."

"What about Jill?"

"It was her idea."

"Any regrets?"

Tom opened the door to Westview and shrugged. "Not really. Some days I wonder what it would be like and then some pervert rapes a six year old and I realize if I had any wee ones I'd become a self-appointed executioner. I'd round up all the molesters and child traffickers, take them somewhere quiet and empty my gun. So it's probably best I stay childless," he snorted, "cause God forbid should vigilantism erupt on our democratic soil."

"I hear ya," Dylan said as they approached the nurses' station. He pulled out his badge. "Detective Dylan Lewis, ma'am. Where might we find Armin Keller?"

"In a coma?" the nurse answered dryly.

"Seriously?" asked Tom, genuinely concerned their suspect might be incommunicado.

"Sorry, occupational humour. Room 1215. That way," she pointed over her shoulder to the hallway behind her.

They found him sitting in a wheelchair at his window, staring into the gardens. Armin Keller was partially paralyzed on his left side: his shoulder sunk down over a useless arm and his mouth drooped slightly, giving his face the appearance of a permanent scowl. He struck his visitors as cranky and impotent except for the hardness in his eyes, his glassy stare still formidable. Both men offered up their badges. "What do you want?" Armin grunted, his voice edged with loathing. The stroke had left him with a slight lisp and he compensated by enunciating each syllable.

"We've come to ask you a few questions," answered Dylan in his polite, professional voice, "about infant remains found in the wall of your former home."

Armin Keller's eyes flashed with indignation. "What nonsense is this?"

"Oh," said Tom, leaning against the window, "I think you know too well what nonsense this is, don't you old man?"

Armin smiled feebly. "Then you are mistaken."

Dylan stood, back straight and arms folded across his chest, and looked down his nose at Keller. "We don't think so. You see, we know all about Karl. About your little Oedipus fetish."

The comment brought a sarcastic sneer onto Keller's face. "He was such a disappointment, our Karl. A man puts his future in the hands of his son, he expects loyalty and fidelity. Not a coward who runs away from his responsibilities."

"Is that what you call banging one's mum?" Tom retorted. "A responsibility? Pretty sick idea there, mate. What next,"—he leaned down to look Keller eye to eye—"sticking a helpless baby in a wall to die? Is that what came next?"

An expression of mild amusement crept across Keller's face and his eyes followed Tom's as the detective stood back up. "I have no idea what you fools are going on about. Perhaps you could be more specific."

"Okay," shrugged Dylan, "how's this? Sometime around 1971 you wrapped a newborn baby girl in linen, put her in a wall alive, and then plastered over the hole. Is that specific enough?"

"Those are serious accusations, detective," Keller responded, his face unchanged. "And yet you ask such silly questions."

"The only question left for you, you old wanker," Tom spat at Keller, "is whose baby was she? Karl and Therese's? Elisabeth's? Whose baby did you kill, Armin?"

"If you thought I killed some baby, you wouldn't be asking questions; you'd be arresting me. Which I see you are not. So unless you have something more substantial, I must insist that you leave."

"Fair enough," said Dylan, rocking back on his heels. "But we both know what you did, and we both know you thought you'd die in that house and your secret would die with you. But"—he leaned down for his own look at Armin Keller eye to eye—"that little girl proved stronger than you expected. Reached out from the grave and demanded to be heard. We found your dirty secret, Armin Keller. And we will find out who she was and why you killed her. And then stroke or no stroke you're going to prison. You can die there instead."

Dylan stood back up, threw a glance Tom's way, and the two walked out of Keller's room. Once out of earshot, Tom scowled with irritation. "Right cheeky bastard, isn't he? Not an ounce of shock or remorse. In fact, I'd say he just looked miffed. He did it. I know it."

"I think so too. Still, we can't rule out Therese or Karl or even Elisabeth. Maybe they were all in it together. Maybe Baby Jane is everybody's dirty secret."

"We need his DNA."

"I know, but that would only prove if he's the father or not. Can't nail him for the murder unless he left something behind on Baby Jane and Anil didn't mention trace coming up with anything useful. And there's the small matter of actually getting Armin's DNA. It doesn't look like he leaves that room much."

Tom eyed the nurse at the station as they approached. "Let's see what the Good Humor lady has to say about that."

Tom sidled up to the nurses' station and flashed his baby blues at "Barbra" as her nametag revealed. "Barbra, luv, I was wondering if you could help me with a little problem?"

Barbra looked down at Tom leaning on the counter and grinning shamelessly up at her. "Would this be about our resident Nazi?" she asked. Both men flinched: that was direct. And easy.

"I take it he's not shy about his views?" Dylan asked. It was a rhetorical question.

"His first week here, I go to give him his bath and he spits at me. *Spits* at me. Says no Jew lady is allowed to touch him, that he'd rather 'sit in his own shit' than have me bathe him. So I said fine and left him to sit in it as desired. Other nurses handle him now. Except for Carol 'cause she's black and you can imagine what he says to *her*."

"Charming," quipped Tom. "Tell me, does he ever leave his room?"

"Nope. Nobody will talk to him in the common rooms. Doesn't seem to realize his ideas are a bit outdated, to say the least."

"Absolutely never?" Tom asked.

"The only way Armin Keller will leave that room is if he has another stroke. Or God willing something worse. But whatever it is, I'm hoping the end is slow and painful."

Tom and Dylan looked at each other. This was not good news. There would be no castaway from Armin Keller. They'd need a warrant. Disappointed, the men said their thank-yous and left Barbra jabbing her clipboard with her pen.

Dylan unlocked the car doors and the two got in. As they put on their seatbelts and Dylan started the engine, he glanced back at the care home doors. "Whatever happened in that house, Tom, we're going to find out why and who. I don't care what somebody's political beliefs are, I don't care about their religion or their culture or whatever else they invent to justify their crimes, nobody, *nobody* gets to put a baby in a wall and not answer for it."

"Perhaps we're jumping to conclusions," Tom suggested with obvious sarcasm, "but Armin Keller is a sick, wicked fuck with an overinflated sense of self-importance. Something tells me Baby Jane isn't his only vic."

℘

Claire was surfing the web on her laptop in the living room. She had left a message for Dylan on his voicemail and figured while she waited for his response she'd find out all she could about the Nazi eugenics program Frau Müller had spoken of. The information was both frightening and repugnant. Just as Frau Müller had said, it had started with a program to sterilize the mentally and physically disabled but the definition of "disabled" quickly expanded to include criminals, chronic alcoholics, homosexuals, the weak or idle, gypsies and Jews—pretty much anyone the Nazis considered inferior. Sterilization had led to infanticide, then the mass murder of adults began when the war broke out and public preoccupation was on the enemy without instead of the enemy within. There had been opposition, of course, but there had also been a strong campaign of deceit, with the families of the victims given false death certificates and an urn of ashes to create the appearance of legitimacy. But the ashes were as false as the death certificates, a random selection from mass cremations.

Claire marked the Internet pages and put her computer aside. Was it possible that her first idea had been right, that Armin and Therese had another child who wasn't "right" somehow and they killed her for it? Claire tried to get her head around that idea. She would have loved her son no matter how he had turned out, whether healthy as an ox or challenged in any way. Where would a parent have to go inside their head to kill their own child? To kill any child? Claire felt the sudden need for comfort. She pulled her knees up to her chest and wrapped her arms around her legs. There was something seriously wrong with the universe if it gave such a precious gift to someone so deranged yet left someone like her painfully barren.

The voicemail alert sounded in Dylan's cellphone. He checked in and heard Claire's voice. She had new information and some possible evidence. Could he come by at the end of his day? He erased the message and turned off his phone. "Damn."

146

"What's up?" asked Tom.

"That was Claire Dawson. She's got possible new evidence. Wants me to pick it up."

"No problem," Tom said with a sly smile. "Just drop me off and I'll do the day's reports while you take a little drive east."

"It might be best if we had a chaperone," Dylan suggested, hopeful for Tom's company. "Besides, you'd get to meet her."

"On the contrary, mate, three's a crowd. I'll meet her at the wedding."

Dylan resisted the urge to punch his partner. "You're really enjoying this, aren't you?"

"You have no idea," Tom laughed. "There's going to be significant mileage in this one, I figure."

"Now who's Judas?" Dylan chortled. Then, switching back to the task at hand, he said, "Not to change the topic or anything, but I still want Armin Keller's DNA."

"Yeah, I know. I'll write up the ITO and we'll take it to a JP first thing in the morning."

"It's going to be a long shot," Dylan said, shaking his head with regret.

"We'll ask for the justice in a good mood. Maybe if a JP gets lucky tonight we'll get lucky tomorrow."

Dylan chuckled. "Let's hope."

He dropped both Tom and the cruiser off at the station. It was already after four o'clock and Dylan figured he'd take his jeep and not have to worry about returning the cruiser on time. Besides, he had already calculated that if he hurried he could make a quick trip across the bridge to his *ta'ah* and have the conversation he needed before he risked another rendezvous with Claire. Then maybe if he got the answer he wanted, Dylan smiled playfully to himself, he wouldn't be in a hurry to leave her this time around.

Dylan found Ta'ah in the garden tending to her medicinal herbs. She glanced up when he approached, unsurprised by the visit: she'd been sending out messages all day, subtly invading his thoughts, calling him to her. She didn't like manipulating him this way but the situation demanded it: she had to end Claire's growing interest in Coyote, had to break the developing bond between it and Jackal. The spirits were in agreement, had even hinted at their own plans for Claire and Dylan, and Ta'ah hoped their hearts were not to be sacrificed for the greater good. As for the risk to Dylan's job, Ta'ah would handle that. At least she hoped she could.

"He sends doubts your way," she said when he reached her side.

"Who does, Ta'ah?" Dylan asked, unsurprised. When he was younger Dylan had found it aggravating that Ta'ah could see what others couldn't, mostly because he'd been up to no good and having a seer for a parent was not conducive to getting away with mischief; but now he accepted her vision for what it was, a gift to be respected.

"The trickster Coyote."

"Why, Ta'ah? What does he have to gain?"

"The heart of one who should rightfully belong to you." She picked up her basket of herbs and offered her hand to Dylan. He helped Ta'ah to her feet and together they walked slowly toward the house.

"Ta'ah, how can I beat him and not betray my responsibility to Baby Jane? How can I do both without one messing up the other? I've searched for a solution and I can't find one."

"You did find a solution, my love. But you let jealousy and anger kill your resolve."

"What do you mean?" He suspected she was talking about the love letter but ...

"The glove compartment is no place to keep your heart."

Dylan dropped his head and nodded: busted. Then anxiety took hold again. "If I give her the letter do you think it will be enough for now? Will she wait until I solve this case?"

"A woman who waits for a man is a fool," Ta'ah answered sharply. "But," she added, affectionately rubbing Dylan's arm, "a man who rushes a woman is equally foolish. Open your heart, be respectful at all times, and your heart will earn its reward."

"And the case?"

"Don't worry about divided loyalties. They will sort themselves out. But Dylan," she warned, stopping to look up at him, "that is not a license to be careless. The spirits have cleared a path for you but there is much opposition."

Dylan nodded his understanding and agreement. He gave Ta'ah a long, warm hug and kissed the top of her head. "Thank you."

"You're welcome, my love. Now go."

Dylan took the letter from the glove compartment and tucked it into his breast pocket, then headed for Claire's. Ta'ah's message from the spirits had him singing to himself and oblivious to the rising tensions of rush hour traffic. Dylan would still play things cautiously, as warned, but knowing he no longer had to choose between obligation and desire, between his

148

competing personal and professional agendas, had lifted a significant burden off his shoulders. Being the grandson of a seer had its perks, too.

When he pulled up in front of Claire's house Dylan could see her through the window, sitting on her couch and looking down, at what he couldn't see. As he approached the door she caught sight of him and he saw her face light up with genuine joy. He hoped it was for him.

Claire answered the door smiling excitedly. "Dylan, please come in." She led him into the living room. "And thank you for responding so quickly. Can I get you anything to drink?"

"No thanks." He surveyed the room. "Nice colour. And I like the ceiling. Me, I would have just left it white. White and boring. You've got a real talent for this. I should get you to do my place."

Dylan brought his gaze down from the ceiling and back to Claire. She was glowing from the compliment and by God she looked mesmerizing. Dylan found himself staring—then rushed to collect himself before he went astray. "You called about new evidence?"

Claire gestured to the couch. "Please sit down," she said as she took a seat herself. Dylan sat down beside her and noticed her mood had changed: she was a little uneasy now. "There's just one thing. This evidence, it was collected somewhat illegally."

Dylan groaned, annoyed. "Oh no, not again. I thought we had an agreement?"

"I know, I know," Claire pleaded, "but I think I'm on to something."

"Uh-huh. Would this be a misdemeanour or another indictable offense?"

"Um, not sure," Claire replied slowly. "Hypothetically speaking, what would mail tampering be?"

"Hypothetically? Up to ten years."

Claire's face dropped. "Oh."

Dylan laughed and shook his head. "Oh no, what have you done now?"

Claire reached into a pile of papers on the floor and sheepishly pulled out the plastic bags with Armin's newsletter and the note. "This came in the post for Armin," she said, handing the bags to Dylan. "Frau Müller told me it's from a neo-Nazi group. And Dylan,"—Claire grabbed her laptop off the floor—"I've been doing some research. Frau Müller told me how the Nazis had a eugenics program that led to state-executed infanticide, and then I found this." She pulled up a page on the Internet. "Look, it says here that

Hitler wrote a book where he expressed his admiration for the Spartans because they used to leave deformed children out in the fields to die of exposure or for the animals to kill. He wrote: 'Sparta must be regarded as the first Völkisch State. The exposure of the sick, weak, deformed children, in short, their destruction, was more decent and in truth a thousand times more humane than the wretched insanity of our day which preserves the most pathological subject, and indeed at any price, and yet takes the life of a hundred thousand healthy children in consequence of birth control or through abortions, in order subsequently to breed a race of degenerates burdened with illnesses.'"

Dylan eyed the contents of the bags. "So you and Frau Müller did this together again?"

"Well, technically," Claire answered carefully, "I gave it to Frau Müller and she opened it."

"So then that's up to ten for her and a few for you for conspiracy." Claire's face went white and Dylan burst out laughing. "Well, it's all in German. Any idea what it says?"

Claire blushed. His laughter made her feel silly and self-conscious and yet she found herself smiling back. "The newsletter is just the usual neo-Nazi garbage but the note is interesting. It says, 'Dear Armin: Am saddened to hear of your loss. Your nephew is a traitor and a thief. Our hearts go out to you and your family. In solidarity, Frederick.' We think Frederick is Frederick Brandt, the chairman of this group."

Dylan eyed the note with interest. "Now that *is* interesting." He eyed it a moment more then gave Claire a sideways glance. "Okay, this is how it's going to go down. I'm going to take these and it's going to be our little secret. You never saw this letter, you never opened it, you never gave it to me. Understand?"

Claire nodded happily. "Understood."

"Same goes for Frau Müller."

"I'll pass that along. But Dylan," she asked earnestly, "did Baby Jane have any deformities?"

"Not that I'm aware of. But then I haven't received the pathologist's full report yet." He paused, eyeing her. "Why? You think Armin killed Baby Jane because he's a Nazi and she was deformed?"

"It's a possibility, isn't it?"

"It's one, yes."

"Then why are you looking at me like that?"

150

"Like how?"

"Bemused," Claire answered, annoyed by the perceived affront. "You have the same bemused look on your face that you had when I suggested Therese Keller may have had another child."

"I'm not bemused," Dylan objected sincerely. "I think your passion for this case is commendable. And I appreciate you giving me this information. You may very well be right. But there are other possible scenarios and one thing you learn as a detective is not to let your enthusiasm for one scenario blind you to others. You miss stuff that way."

"Then why are you staring at me like that?"

"Because I think you're beautiful."

Claire felt her face go blank—and then flush as Dylan leaned over, took her face in his hands and kissed her. She felt a surge of energy course through her body that made her dizzy and desirous and she didn't try to stop her mouth when it sought out more from him. Instead, he did it for her. "Don't st—"

"No," Dylan whispered as he placed a thumb over her lips. He stroked her face with his fingers and gazed at her as if he were trying to record every detail for later recollection. "Don't say anything or I'll forget myself and my manners and Baby Jane and all I'll think about is how beautiful you are and how much I want to taste you. So help me here. Don't let me take you, Claire; make me earn you." Dylan pulled out the letter from his pocket. "This is for you. Wait till I'm gone to read it. And then know I'll be back for you." He gave her another long, sensuous kiss then rose to leave. He picked up the bags with Armin Keller's papers in it, gave Claire's chin an affectionate caress with the back of his forefinger, then walked backwards to the door, his eyes never leaving hers, until he reached the foyer, turned and was gone.

NINETEEN

Claire remained on the couch, clutching the letter and watching through the window as Dylan sprinted to his jeep and drove away. She was vibrating, breathless. His kiss had been extraordinary. His kiss had been ... How could she describe it? It had depth, she thought, if a kiss could be described as such. It was authentic, sincere. Rafael's kiss, on the other hand, had been astonishing in its ... technique? Yes, that was the word. He had amazing technique. His lips knew exactly how to move, how to apply just the right amount of pressure to her lips to achieve his objective. She remembered his expression of satisfaction, like a conquering hero. She had been happy to be conquered then but now she wasn't so sure.

"Don't let me take you, Claire; make me earn you." It was only one sentence but it spoke paragraphs. She wouldn't be war booty to Dylan: her heart wouldn't be looted, her body plundered. It wasn't going to be a contest or a battle of wills where she was the trophy when he won the game and she lost. That's where she had gone wrong with Eric and had fate not intervened this night she might have made the same foolish mistake with Rafael. Claire felt that rush of relief one feels after narrowly escaping a traffic accident. And she felt a huge awakening. To think like this was new to her. She had always accepted the idea of romance as a game, had accepted the status quo of man as hunter and her the hunted. But Dylan was challenging her to reject that idea, to see her love as a reward for his affections and honest conduct, for genuine chivalry and not just the pretence of it. And not just chivalry toward her but also to Baby Jane, to his responsibility to find her killer even if meant personal sacrifice. Ta'ah had said a proud woman waits for no man but Dylan wasn't asking Claire to wait anymore; he was asking her to bide their time. There was a difference and both of them understood that now.

She looked down at the card-sized letter in her hands and ran her fingers over the textured envelope. She opened it gingerly, not wanting to risk any damage, and gently pulled out the blue sheets of stationary. As soon as she unfolded the pages she could smell his fragrance. She held the letter to her face and took in a long, slow breath that brought him momentarily back to her side, then opened her eyes again and began to read.

"Dear Claire," it started simply enough, but what came after was anything but simple. His prose was poetic in some places, awkward in others, but to Claire every last word was utterly divine. He was sweet here, overtly sexual there, and always breathtakingly honest. He spelled out his affections, confessed his desires, admitted his jealousies. He melted her heart and made her hunger for him. She read the letter several times, savouring each word, then laid back to indulge in the craving it created. Her body tingled and moistened, the subtle throbbing of desire winding its way through her nervous system. Claire wanted nothing else except for Dylan to come back and make love to her. She held the letter to her face, taking in his scent, and willed herself back to the night when Dylan had ravaged her with his mouth, had proclaimed his lust. *I want you. Say yes.* "Yes," she murmured and let the memory carry her away.

The drive home was full of anxiety. Dylan wondered if Claire were reading the letter, wondered what she was thinking. Had he been too direct, too forthcoming? Was it too much too soon? He kept glancing down at his cellphone, wondering if it would ring, wondering if he should call her tonight. The silence was torture.

He poured himself a bowl of cereal when he got home: he could barely eat, never mind prepare himself anything of greater substance. He tried watching television but couldn't follow the plot even though it was a rerun. And then he had the most delicious idea.

Claire's phone rang and lifted her out of her dream. "Hello," she answered throatily, as if just awakening.

"Claire?"

She smiled at the sound of his voice. "Yes?" she said, curling onto her side and cradling the phone.

"Did you read my letter?" His heart was pounding, fearful for the telltale discomfort in her voice that would tell him he had gone about this all wrong.

"I did. It's beautiful, Dylan. It's the most beautiful gift anyone has ever given me."

"Really?" He smiled into the receiver, happy and relieved.

"I would gladly trade every gift every other man has given me for this one letter, although I'll appreciate it if you won't make me." She laughed and her laugh was exquisite to him.

"Claire, can I take you to dinner tomorrow evening?"

"Yes."

"I'll be finished my day around six. If I pick you up at six thirty would that be okay?"

"Yes."

"I'll see you then."

"Dylan, just one thing. What's the dress code so I know what to wear?"

"Um, casual, elegant?" he guessed, as if he'd know.

"Then casually elegant I shall be."

"I think you'd be elegant in rags, but that's just my opinion."

"I think you'd be elegant naked," she laughed and hung up the phone.

Dylan stared at the phone for a few minutes, grinning, enveloped by euphoria. And then he shook himself into action. He had work to do. He scrolled through his cellphone directory and, still grinning madly, hit the talk key.

CR

Jackal squirmed uncomfortably in the grass beside his den, anxious about the turn of events. He needed Claire's solitude, her periods of despair. He'd been furious with the change of ownership of the house but Claire had at least appeared promising: he had drank her tears, feasted on her anguish. Even the discovery of the remains had initially proved unexpectedly fortunate: Claire's nascent anticipation of a new life had been replaced by confusion and more grief. That vile detective's lust had been a cause for concern, but introducing Claire to the gleefully insincere Coyote had successfully thwarted that. But where was Coyote now? On his master's leash, that's where, like the dog he is. Ineffectual little shit.

154

And why wouldn't that meddlesome old woman leave him be? He'd given her the child; what right did she have demanding more, demanding his prize?

Jackal turned and disappeared inside his den. His anger had made him randy and he needed release.

CR

Rebecca took her place at the bar and ordered a gin and tonic. She downed it quickly and ordered another, and when Constable Richards from Traffic sidled up beside her and offered her another, she gladly took him up on the suggestion. "Tell me something," she asked when he proposed they go someplace quieter, "do you respect me?"

"Of course," he lied, and she saw both the sarcasm in his eyes and his own self-loathing.

"Good," she said, sliding off her stool to leave. "That's good enough for me."

CR

Dylan had just arisen to get ready for work when his cellphone rang. It was Anil. "Hey, Sanjit," Dylan answered with a cheerfulness one usually reserves for the expectation of good news. "Boy or girl?"

"She gave me a little girl this time," Sanjit replied, his emotions raw. "She beautiful, Dyl. She's just so beautiful. What am I going to do?"

"What do you mean?" Dylan asked gently, concerned with Sanjit's obvious distress.

"How am I going to keep her safe, Dylan? What am I going to do if someday we get that call and it's her in a wall?"

"You can't think like that, my friend. We're all going to keep her safe. No one's going to hurt your beautiful little girl. No one. Not on our watch. I promise."

"Thanks," sniffled Sanjit.

"How's Parvati?" Dylan asked, deliberately changing the subject.

"Good. Good. She's sleeping now. She had a rough night."

"Have you picked out a gift for her yet?"

"Yeah. It's a heart-shaped pendant of pink diamonds set in platinum. It was going to be sapphires if it were another boy."

"She'll love it. Now get some sleep, Sanjit. I'll try to stop by the hospital today to see Parvati and—what did you name her?"

"Dalaja. It means honey."

"It's perfect. I'll see you later."

Anil put down his cellphone and cradled his daughter close. In the hour after Dalaja had been born Sanjit had floated in that intoxicating mix of adrenalin and sleep deprivation that is a long and arduous birth. He had watched Dalaja nurse, had praised and kissed his wife and stroked her to sleep, had stared endlessly at his new beauty. But when the room was finally empty of everyone except himself and his sleeping wife and daughter, the weight of the Baby Jane case had come crashing down on him. It had taken a good half hour before he could stop weeping and make the call to Dylan. And while Sanjit appreciated his friend's promises, he knew they were ultimately empty. They could all watch and worry every second of every minute but every day Dalaja's world would get bigger, would grow to encompass people Sanjit didn't know or didn't trust, and all he'd have to fall back on was his own assurances he'd done everything he could to teach her self-respect and good judgment. Other than that she was in God's hands, and so far Sanjit's job had shown him God was often absent from creation.

And yet the alternative was unthinkable. To not know Dalaja or his sons, to be too frightened to have children, was not an option for Anil. They were a beacon of light and life at the end of every day of death; he only had to glance in their direction to feel joy and pride and an indescribable sense of completeness. They made his love for Parvati more intense, his admiration for her deeper. Whatever complaints he had about parenthood they were nothing more than momentary lapses in appreciation, the ramblings of fatigue or stress, or gestures of charity towards those who had no children. But he never fooled anyone with his grumblings, least of all himself.

Sanjit put his daughter back in her basinet, laid down carefully beside Parvati so as not to disturb her, and finally let himself fall asleep.

CR

Despite the good news of Dalaja's healthy arrival, the rest of Dylan's morning didn't follow suit. The warrant for Armin Keller's DNA was rejected by the JP. There wasn't a straight line, the justice had pointed out, from the presence of infant remains in Armin Keller's former residence to his being either its father or its killer. Anybody could be the father, and there were other potential murder suspects, namely Karl Keller and the two Keller women. The evidence collected thus far at most pointed to a failure to intervene if, in fact, Armin had even known about the baby. JP Hugh Kingsley also pulled it out of the detectives that Armin Keller was known to have traveled back to Germany on many occasions; could the child not have been conceived, born or killed during any one of these many journeys? Unable to offer a good argument to the contrary, Dylan and Tom admitted temporary defeat and retreated to their cruiser.

"Well, no surprise there," Dylan sighed. "We knew we didn't have a hope in hell."

"Never hurts to ask, though," Tom chuckled, leaning back in his seat. "Okay, now what?"

Dylan drummed his fingers on the steering wheel. "We wait. We wait until Friday when we find out who the mother is. Well hopefully, anyway. Then we reassess. It's our only sensible option."

"And until then?"

"We work on the Benson case."

Tom slumped down in his seat, disappointed by the choice. "Oh, who the hell cares who killed a low-level pimp?"

"We do," answered Dylan in mock chastisement.

"Oh, right, my mistake."

Dylan glanced at his watch. "Are you up for a detour? Parvati had a daughter this morning."

"Yeah, sure. And let's get some flowers on the way."

Parvati was asleep when they arrived so Dylan and Tom left the flowers with the station nurse, took a quick look at Dalaja through the nursery glass, then headed back to the office. They piled the Benson case boxes on the floor beside their desks then settled down to the arduous task of wading through several lengthy forensic reports, dozens of crime scene and autopsy photographs, surveillance reports on three key suspects, and a mountain of witness statements—such as they were—from the multitude of street people who had seen the shooting but whose recollections were skewed by either alcohol, drugs, mental illness, fear, loathing, general indifference, or some combination thereof. It was going to be a bitch of a day.

Two miles away it was an altogether different story. Claire was in the shops pulling together her living room and riding a wave of sheer bliss. It was as if everything were suddenly coming together in perfect harmony. She had a date with Dylan that evening, the anticipation of which had her checking herself in every mirror she happened upon, and her earlier retail research was now paying dividends. She found everything she needed exactly where she expected to and by five o'clock her car was laden down with purchases, and larger items were scheduled for delivery. It was a joyous day about to be topped off by an even better evening.

From five o'clock onwards Dylan was checking his watch every ten minutes and it was starting to drive Tom nuts. "Hot date tonight, Dyl?"

Dylan looked up from the barely coherent witness statement he was reading and feigned incomprehension. "Why do you ask?"

"Because all day you've been smiling to yourself and I don't think it's the reading material that has you chuffed. And now you're looking at the clock like a man on death row. Fear mixed with pleasure always equals a bird."

Dylan looked around the room to make sure no one else was listening. "I took your advice. I asked her out."

Tom grinned like a schoolboy who'd just convinced his best friend to join in an act of criminal rebellion. "You asked the twelve out? Good on ya, mate. And don't worry, when they come for you I'll throw in a helpful word."

"Yeah, thanks for that. Though something tells me if they do come for me, you're not going to be my first phone call."

Tom leaned back in his chair and linked his fingers behind his head. "Well, just remember then," he retorted with a laugh, "Vice is nice."

Dylan straightened himself out in the mirror of the men's washroom. He had worn dress pants that morning instead of his usual dark chinos, and had brought a clean shirt and tie with him to change into for his date with Claire. He'd also had the foresight to give himself time to shave away his five o'clock shadow—an act that warranted a sly remark from every colleague who wandered into the men's room—then slapped on a bit of his cologne. Dylan gave himself the thumbs up and headed back to the squad room to log out. He briefly considered wearing the blazer hanging over the back of his desk chair, decided it was warm enough to do without, left it there and headed out.

Claire answered the door wearing a black silk pencil skirt, a white pleated silk halter top, and black strappy heels. Her hair was pulled back in a loose chignon, setting off the diamond stud earrings Dylan had seen on her the day they had met, and a narrow bangle of white gold encased her wrist. "You look stunning," he smiled at her as he leaned down to give her a kiss hello. "Oh," he added when he smelled her perfume, "and you smell just as good." When he stood back again he noticed her lips had curved into a radiant smile.

Claire reached out a hand to caress Dylan's face then gave him a long, sensuous kiss. "What was that for?" he asked when he got his breath back.

"Thank you for my lovely gift. You now have my undivided attention."

"Good," was all Dylan said in reply, then took her hand and led her to his jeep. He opened the door for her then walked around and jumped into the driver's seat.

"Are you going to tell me where we're going?" Claire asked as they headed east.

"Nope. It's a surprise."

"You're just full of surprises, aren't you?"

"Not normally," he shrugged and smiled at her. "But I'm trying."

"The effort has not gone unnoticed."

"Good."

She asked him about his day and discovered the case of Baby Jane was on hold pending the DNA results, for which he reiterated his unofficial thanks. "And then what?"

"Depending upon the results, and how they compare to the baby's, we re-evaluate. And then if it's useful news I have to find a way to make what you did admissible so I can use the results in court. Or at least as leverage. But I'll be honest with you, we've hit a huge roadblock."

"How tedious," she offered in sympathy.

"A lot of police work is tedious," he volunteered. "It's not at all like it is on TV."

"So I guess you won't be solving this case in an hour less commercial time?"

Dylan chuckled. "I wish."

"I wish there were something more *I* could do. I feel compelled, I feel obligated, but I don't know where to start. Ta'ah and Stan told me to decorate the house, and I'm doing that, but it just seems so facile in relation to what everyone else is doing."

159

"If there is one thing I've learned as Ta'ah's grandson *and* as a cop," Dylan said with a reassuring squeeze of Claire's hand, "is that things are rarely what they seem. Sometimes the most innocuous, most mundane acts can have extraordinary consequences."

Hmmm, thought Claire, unconvinced.

Her attention was brought back to the road when Dylan turned off the freeway and headed east toward the inlet of Deep Cove. "Are we going to Deep Cove?" she asked.

"Uh-huh," answered Dylan and gave her a sly, sideways look. "I'm taking you to its best kept secret."

Ten minutes later the jeep was parked and Dylan was leading Claire to The Cove Bistro at the end of Gallant Street, overlooking the marina. The view was spectacular from the bistro's large patio and Claire hoped for a table outside so she could enjoy the smell of the water and soak up the landscape. She was disappointed when they were led inside, and then disappointment turned to confusion when they were led through a back door to the condo above the restaurant and out onto a private patio. At the edge a table had been set up and dressed in the restaurant's linens and candlelight, with two chairs side by side so both diners could enjoy the view. Claire's face was a question mark as they were seated, then completely baffled when the waiter took their drinks order but failed to leave any menus. Dylan grinned and put an arm around her shoulders but said nothing. "Are you going to tell me what's going on?" she asked.

"This place belongs to a school buddy of mine," Dylan finally revealed. "A guy named Lawrence Metscalin. He bought this condo and opened the restaurant about four years ago. He's a fantastic chef and a good guy all around."

"Well if the menu is even half as wonderful as the view, I'm going to be in heaven."

"We're not eating off the menu. Lawrence has designed a special dinner just for us." Dylan saw Claire's surprise and revelled in it. He kissed her lightly on the nose. "I hope you like it."

How could she not? For starters they had seared giant scallops with grapefruit and radicchio followed by field greens drizzled with a balsamic vinaigrette that contained a twist of something spectacular Claire couldn't quite place; a mains of wild west coast salmon on mango risotto; then a light-as-air white chocolate crème brûlée with local blackberries. In the lull between courses she nestled against Dylan and soaked up the view of the inlet, and listened to his stories about Lawrence and their unexpected friendship. They had gone to the same high school together in North Vancouver, but while Dylan was large and athletic and popular, Lawrence was slight and effeminate and the target of homophobic teenage boys too uncomfortable with their own sexuality to tolerate a "fag" among them. Dylan had tried to convince his peers that differences should be respected— there was Ta'ah's influence again, Dylan explained—but to no end. And when Dylan intervened in a beating of Larry the Fairy, as Lawrence was labelled, the lines were drawn.

The act had cost Dylan a great deal of his earlier popularity but there had been an upside, he confessed: Lawrence had always loved to cook, had been in the kitchen since he was nine, and he tested his recipes on Dylan. "I ate *very* well in high school," Dylan laughed. "While those homophobes were eating greasy hamburgers and fries, I was feasting on braised ribs and lamb ragout. It was almost better than sex."

"Almost?" Claire asked mischievously.

"Believe me when I tell you nothing is better to a teenage boy than sex. Except maybe beer. But," he winked at Claire, "I was never a drinker."

"I noticed. How come?"

The light in Dylan's eyes went out as if he had been suddenly broadsided. "I'm sorry. Was that too personal a question?" Claire anxiously asked. The date had been going so well and she was terrified she had just inadvertently destroyed it.

"No, it's not too personal. It's just ... my mom was an alcoholic. So was my dad, as far as anyone can tell me. He was a ship in the night, if you know what I mean. When my mom got pregnant she came home to my grandmother. Cleaned up long enough to have me but the call of the bottle was just too strong. I was only five days old when she left."

Claire eyes swept over Dylan's face. "I'm sorry."

"I'm not," he shrugged. "It would've been worse if she'd kept me. Instead," he squeezed Claire's shoulders, "I was raised by the most amazing woman I've ever known. Present company excluded, of course."

"I adore Ta'ah. She has such a wonderful face, and so much kindness. Why is she called Ta'ah?"

"It means grandmother. Everyone calls her that, even her own kids, which tends to cause much confusion amongst outsiders. The only person who called her Sarah was my grandfather and he's been dead for over a decade."

Claire kissed Dylan on his cheek, holding her lips there for a moment before whispering, "Thank you."

"For what?"

"For everything. For the letter, for this dinner, for telling me about your mom. These last twenty-four hours have been amazing."

"You're welcome," he said with a broad smile, but then he saw the pensive turn of her expression and his smile faded. "What is it, Claire?"

She bowed her head, afraid to see in his eyes the rejection she would risk by her confession. But if he were going to reject her she wanted him to do it now, before she made any further emotional investment, before she was too far in to get out unscathed, just as she had been with Eric. "When I," Claire began slowly, "when I was at Eaton I had an affair with the father of one of my students. He was a surgeon—mature, successful, generous, and … married. I got pregnant and Eric—that was his name— he demanded I have an abortion but I refused. So he had me fired; said a unwed mother was a poor role model for the students. Of course he never mentioned his part. Anyhow, first I lost my job and then I lost the baby. And, well, you know the rest." Claire gathered what little courage she had left and looked up again at Dylan. "And I'm afraid I don't deserve you."

Dylan's eyes swept over her face, at the apprehension in her peridot eyes, the flush of red in her cheeks, the slight quiver at the corners of her mouth, and wished he could arrest her anxiety the way he could arrest a criminal. Her crimes were insignificant to the ones he investigates, he wanted to tell her, her punishment too harsh. But instead he simply shrugged and said, "We all make mistakes, Claire. I've yet to meet a blameless person, myself included. And the fact that you don't think you deserve love is precisely why you do." He gazed into her eyes and the gratitude he saw there made him want her more. He kissed her, gingerly at first and then more passionately, letting his fingers slide down her arm and the palm of his hand lightly graze her breast. The gesture aroused them both, and for a moment Dylan was tempted to forget his honourable intentions. But only for a moment. He drew back from her. "I'm going to make you mine, Claire Dawson. Just so you know."

She grinned at the shameless, flirtatious presumption and knew it wasn't anywhere as impudent as it seemed. She was going to make him hers, too, just so he knew.

Eventually it came time to go. They reluctantly made their way off the balcony and into Lawrence's condo. "You know," Claire said as they walked through the immaculate interior, "I should have known he's gay. This place is spotless."

"Great," quipped Dylan, "now I can never take you home to my place. You'll only be disappointed *I'm* not gay."

When they reached the restaurant Lawrence came out from the kitchen to greet them. Dylan gave his buddy an affectionate hug. "Thanks, pal, it was fantastic."

"Oh my God, yes," Claire sincerely added. "The food was divine. Thank you *very* much."

They proceeded to leave the restaurant and as soon as Claire's head was turned Dylan gave Lawrence another friendly pat on the arm and leaned in to whisper, "I left an envelope with the hostess."

Lawrence nodded. "By the way," he said, looking at Claire's shapely legs, "very nice. If I ever change sides I hope you'll share."

"Not on your life."

Arms entwined, Claire and Dylan walked slowly to his jeep, neither wanting the evening to end. The drive home was equally slow, with Dylan obeying the speed limit despite the lack of traffic. Claire's eyes tried to watch the landscape but continually wandered back to study Dylan's face, his body, his hands on the wheel; and when he caught her staring he smiled and caressed her with his eyes in return. By the time they reached her home she was shaking.

He walked her to her door. Both knew what they wanted but both knew their unspoken agreement precluded further intimacy. And when she stood on the bottom step to match his height so she could look him squarely in the eye, he found himself chuckling. "What's so funny?" she asked as she wrapped her arms around his neck.

"I feel like I'm six years old again and it's the week before Christmas. All I want is to open my presents but everyone keeps telling me I have to wait."

"I know what you mean," she said and gave him a long, impatient kiss.

"I think I'm going to disappoint Santa," he admitted between the light kisses that followed, "if I stay another minute." He pulled back from Claire. "Besides, I think we're being watched." He nodded in the direction of Frau Müller's house.

Claire burst out laughing. "Looks like I'll be invited for tea again tomorrow."

"Is she always so nosy?"

"Yup. Eyes like a hawk. But she has a good heart so I don't mind so much."

"That's good. 'Cause now you two are forever bound by your criminal secrets."

Claire laughed at the reference to the DNA collection and mail tampering. "They're your secrets now, too. Does that mean *we're* also bound forever?"

"I hope so. But in the meantime when can I see you again?"

"Tomorrow?"

Dylan frowned with disappointment. "I can't do tomorrow. I promised to meet up with a friend. He—" Dylan stopped himself before he told her of Sanjit's new baby; he didn't want to see Claire's iridescence fade. "Some family event at his house. How about Friday?"

She was about to commit to Friday when she remembered her date with Rafael. Claire squirmed with discomfort. "There's, um, a small problem with Friday."

"What kind of problem?"

She groaned and shifted from foot to foot. "I have—oh God this is awkward—a date."

Dylan absorbed the unwelcomed information. "Would this be with a one Rafael Morales?" he asked with a twinge of jealousy.

Claire's jaw dropped. "Have you been spying on me?" she asked, incredulous, though her smile indicated more curiosity than displeasure.

"Well, you see," Dylan looked sheepishly away, "I came to deliver my letter on Monday and I saw you get into his car and I, um, ran his plate."

Claire laughed. "You're terrible."

"Guilty as charged. And not to deflect attention away from my crimes or anything, but any chance you can cancel?"

"That's the problem. He's out of the country right now and I have no way to reach him. I don't even have a cellphone number. And I can't just not be here when he comes for me. That would be really rude and I'm not like that. Besides, wouldn't you rather be told to your face that you can't see someone again? It's only fair."

Dylan nodded reluctantly. "I see your point. And though it pains me to say this, I agree."

"I'm sorry," she said, genuinely uncomfortable with the unintended conflict of interest.

"No need to be sorry," Dylan said lightly. "It's my fault. I should have stepped up to the plate sooner. I'll take it on the chin like a man. So, go on your date and,"—he added with a grin—"dump the guy and then call me."

"I will. I promise." She kissed him again and her kiss said it all.

Dylan could feel his desire rising and knew he had to leave—now! He removed Claire's arms from around his neck, kissed her hands and said goodnight. "Could I ask just one thing?"

"Of course."

"Please don't let him, you know, touch you."

"I won't."

He nodded his gratitude. "Now go on then. I'll wait until you're safely inside before I leave."

Claire unlocked her door and blew Dylan a kiss before she closed the door and let him walk away. Inside she wrapped her arms around herself and leaned against the door for a few minutes to absorb the reality of what felt like a miraculous turn of events. When she heard the door slam and his jeep drive away, she blew him another farewell kiss, then went upstairs to finish their date.

◌3

Claire woke up the next morning to a bright sun and thoughts of Dylan but there was no time to indulge in memories: deliveries were due today and she needed to finish painting the window trim before the furniture began arriving. There was also a plasterer coming to smooth out the gap between the kitchen and dining room left behind by the knocked out wall, and to repair the hole at the back of the closet. This last task Claire was most eager to have completed, as if mending the hole might mend that last part of her heart that remained wounded, that bled whenever she looked at the gaping mouth of the beast and saw a child's tomb.

The tradesmen arrived at nine o'clock sharp and everyone set to their respective tasks, chatting only briefly during breaks or to ask Claire for direction. She was grateful for their professionalism for it afforded her the luxury of her own thoughts, which consisted mostly of imagined conversations and intimate moments with Dylan.

Dylan's day was another slog through the Benson file, of more inch-thick forensics reports and unintelligible witness statements, punctuated with short walks to stretch his legs or get a coffee or veer off into imaginative detours. He tried to stay focused on work but the Benson file was so badly handicapped and its victim so repugnant it was hard to cultivate any enthusiasm, and so Dylan's mind continually strayed, and mostly into forbidden territory. And it didn't help that Tom demanded a recap over lunch, eager to learn if the date had been worth the hell his partner would likely incur if the liaison caused the Baby Jane case to go pear-shaped in ways they hadn't anticipated.

After lunch Dylan allowed himself the pleasure of calling Claire under the pretext of thanking her for a lovely evening, when what he really wanted was to be reminded of the silkiness of her voice so his imagination could accurately reproduce it later that evening during what he expected would be some serious fantasy time.

But first he had to attend Dalaja's homecoming. Dylan arrived shortly after six to a small gathering of friends and family helping themselves to a lavish Indian buffet and doting on Parvati, enthroned on an overstuffed chair and holding Dalaja. She was as beautiful as Sanjit had claimed, with a thick head of wispy black hair, her mother's nose, and Sanjit's delicate mouth. Dalaja weighed in at a respectable seven pounds six ounces, and was not one minute in this world when she had loudly vocalized her opposition to the idea. First pictures were of a very annoyed baby girl staring at her mother with an expression of abject displeasure. "She'll get over the betrayal," Dylan quipped.

"But then she'll punish you when she becomes a woman," Parvati's mother added but without Dylan's humour. "She'll run off and marry a foreigner and never come home to visit her poor mother." Sanjit's eyes rolled back into his head and Parvati made faces behind her mother's back that made their two boys giggle and her father hide a smile in his chai tea.

Dylan ran interference before anything unpleasant erupted. "Are you going to hog her all evening, Parvati, or do I get to hold her?" The diversion worked: everyone ignored Parvati's mother again as Dalaja was placed in Dylan's arms. He sat down on the sofa with her cradled in one arm while the other reached a hand up to caress her sweet face. "She really is beautiful, Parvati. You did good. And you too, Sanjit."

They both saw the glimmer of longing that swept briefly across Dylan's face. "You're next, my friend," declared Sanjit. "Just get yourself the right girl, Dylan, and then Bob's your uncle."

"Hmmh," was all Dylan said in reply. He was falling in love with

Claire, with a woman who would likely never give him a child. Did he care? Yes, a little, if he were honest. But then parenthood can come in many forms, he reminded himself, as his own upbringing proved. And then there was the disproportionate number of Native children in foster care waiting for someone like him to come to the rescue. They could always consider that.

Dylan handed Dalaja back to her mother and called it a night. He hadn't been sleeping much lately and it was starting to have an effect. He said his goodbyes all around, wrestled Sanjit's boys to the door, then headed home to bed.

CR

Claire collapsed onto her new chocolate leather sofa and admired her efforts. It had been a long day but the results were fantastic: at her feet a plush wool area rug now graced her hardwood floors, and on the rug an Art Deco-inspired walnut and glass coffee table now sat, flanked by the couch and two modern cream leather accent chairs with sloping arms; and behind her a sofa table in a dark olive colour matched the side table now to her left. An armoire hid her flat panel TV, a small stereo, and Claire's modest collection of music and DVDs; while an Art Deco sideboard now housed her late grandmother's wedding china. All that remained to do were the blinds and drapes; these would be ready and installed in a week and then, she thought playfully, she could have Dylan on the couch without worrying about putting on a show for the neighbours.

The thought made her grin, and she became acutely aware of a change in the atmosphere of her home, though she wasn't certain if it were only a reflection of her buoyant mood or something more substantial. She wanted to believe it were the latter, that her efforts were indeed intrinsic to the defeat of the dark forces that had consumed this house, but she wasn't particularly successful at convincing herself of this: interior decoration seemed trite, almost ridiculous when one considered the stakes and the enemy. It made *her* feel trite and ridiculous, relegated to the sidelines with a pat on the head while the experts went about their serious business; and her burgeoning joy began to dissipate. Ta'ah, Stan, Dylan, they were all keeping something from her: Ta'ah said Baby Jane had been returned to her guardian, so what was it that had etched the worry on Ta'ah's face that she had tried, in vain, to hide from Claire? What, exactly, was it that still needed to be banished, that needed to be cleansed from the essence of this house?

Claire squished her toes into the rug and pushed herself up onto her feet, then walked over to squat in front of the dining room closet. The hole was repaired now, the new plaster still wet beneath her touch. She closed her eyes as she had done before and stilled her mind until she reached that place between sleep and wakefulness, until the floor beneath her feet changed to soft sand and she found herself at the edge of a river. She was squatting on all fours, and when she looked down she saw not her hands but thick, furry paws. Curious, Claire approached the water's edge and peered into a shallow pool where the current didn't flow, and saw her head on the body of a lioness, sphinx-like and regal. She slapped the water with her paw and her reflection disappeared in the concentric ripples, and when the water stilled Claire looked and saw she was no longer a sphinx but merely a woman again. Perplexed, she rose to her feet and went in search of answers to this riddle.

℘

Jackal emerged from his den and sniffed the air. A strong, sweet scent burned his nostrils and made him nervous, and he crouched low in defence. His stomach growled, and for the first time he became aware of hunger. Jackal sniffed the air again, hoping to catch the scent of prey, but found only that same sweet stench. He considered hunting further afield but then disregarded this, not wanting to leave his den unattended and his prize vulnerable to theft or escape. Jackal hissed with annoyance, then lay down in wait: Coyote was due soon; and while Jackal doubted Coyote's cleverness, he still had hopes for his success.

TWENTY

Friday morning Tom and Dylan headed down to Richmond for the results from Claire's illicit sleuthing, and as they battled the traffic back into the city the call came they'd been waiting for: DNA results on Baby Jane were in. Tom pulled an illegal left turn and they headed for the government lab. Forty minutes later they were exchanging hellos with the DNA lab technician.

"I need a favour," Dylan said, pulling out the profiles on Therese and Elisabeth as the lab tech handed him the results on Baby Jane. "Do you see any relationship between Baby Jane's results and these?"

The lab tech looked askance at first then decided not to ask questions. She took the Genesis Lab results and placed them on the counter beside Baby Jane's. "Well, the first thing I can tell you is that these two are also females, and as the mitochondrial genome is identical for all samples, these females are directly related." She pointed to another graph. "The nuclear DNA of your two samples suggests the relationship is maternal, not fraternal, meaning they're mother and daughter, not sisters. I would think this sample here is the mother of this sample, and that sample belongs to Baby Jane's mother." She arranged the pages in chronological order. "So there you go: Baby Jane, her mother, and her maternal grandmother." The lab tech's brow furrowed. "Which reminds me, there's something in the report on Baby Jane I need to call to your attention."

"Go on," Dylan said, though it sounded like bad news.

"Well, normally there are two homogenous alleles on a locus that indicate relations, but on four loci in Baby Jane's DNA we found *three*

169

homogenous alleles and an indication of autozygosity."

"In English, please," Dylan deadpanned.

"Inbreeding. Baby Jane's father is also a relation of her mother."

Dylan and Tom looked at each other, the wheels in their heads doing a collective somersault. "Can you tell us *which* relation?" Tom asked.

"Not without their DNA to compare it to. But I can tell you it's most likely a close male relative: father, brother, son, maybe an uncle or cousin. But not any further removed than that."

"Thank you and"—Dylan gestured with the Genesis reports as he gathered everything up—"thanks again." The lab tech nodded solemnly in reply.

Dylan and Tom walked briskly back to the cruiser, excited by what seemed to be progress. "Hot damn, Tom! Hot damn! We knew it! Now we just have to find out which S.O.B. is the father and we'll close this up."

"Okay," Tom replied, tapping a finger on the dashboard, "possible scenarios. One: Elisabeth and Karl Keller. Maybe mommy wasn't the only one he was made to kneel in front of. He leaves home, never knows about the baby, and Elisabeth or her parents or some combination of Kellers kills Baby Jane. Two: Elisabeth and Armin. Daddy's little girl and then some. Same outcome. Three: Elisabeth and Benjamin. Case of the kissing cousins. They get caught and that's the real reason Benjamin is banned. Same outcome. Four: Elisabeth and Randolf. The funny uncle but nobody's laughing. He's the reason his family is never allowed to visit again. But—"

"Same outcome," Dylan finished the sentence as the soft hiss of their rapidly deflating balloon whistled between them. "That's our problem. Paternity only determines who gets done for incest or statutory rape or both. It doesn't tell us who killed Baby Jane. Only three people really know what happened to her. One isn't talking and two can't."

"Then we go back to Benjamin Keller and on Tuesday we go back to the JP."

Dylan rocked back on his heels and pondered strategies. "I have an idea," he said, pulling out his cellphone and note pad. He looked up a number in his notes then dialled.

"Keller Jamieson Clark and Associates," answered a chirpy voice.

"Detective Dylan Lewis for Mr. Keller, please. Tell him it's urgent."

A few seconds later Keller answered. "Hello, detective," Benjamin said into the phone, surprisingly pleasant.

"Listen, Ben, we got DNA results back from the lab. Don't ask how;

170

you won't like it. Suffice it to say Elisabeth is the infant's mother."

On the other end of the phone Benjamin covered the mouthpiece so Dylan wouldn't hear the obscenity that escaped from Ben's throat. His knuckles were white around the receiver and it took every ounce of self-restraint not to smash the phone against his desk. When he finally contained himself enough to respond, all he said was, "I see."

"Something else came up in the results. The father is a close male relative."

Benjamin's voice turned to steel. "Which one?"

"They can't tell us that until we get comparison samples." Dylan paused to let that sink in then zeroed in on his target. "Benjamin, look, I know the baby isn't yours. But no judge is going to give me a warrant for every male relative's DNA just so I can prove who raped Elisabeth. He's going to want more. If we can at least eliminate as many male relatives as we can, I might get the warrant for Armin. So if you could give us a voluntary sample, and if you could convince your father to give us one, that would narrow things considerably. And if I have to exhume Karl's corpse I'll bloody well do it. But I need your help."

Benjamin thought it over. "Alright," he said after a moment. "Send Ident over for a swab. I'll be here until five. But I have conditions, Lewis: my identity remains confidential from the lab and the sample is never stored or databased. Are we in agreement?"

"Deal."

"I'll see what I can do about my father."

"Thanks, Keller."

"One more thing. I don't know how you got Elisabeth's DNA, but I know it wasn't legit. Have Ident bring me a consent form for her. Backdate it. I'll sign it."

"Thanks," Dylan said, his voice subdued: he was feeling a newfound respect for his former adversary. He ended the call then hit the speed dial button for the Forensics Ident squad. A few minutes later two officers were on their way to Keller Jamieson Clark and Associates with strict instructions.

"Slick, Dylan, very slick," said Tom when Dylan put his phone away. "I wouldn't have thought he'd give it up so easily."

"You saw his face when he talked about Elisabeth. He loves her. And now he wants to know who the father is just as badly as we do. If we're lucky he may blow this case wide open for us."

CR

Benjamin Keller said goodbye to the Ident officers then left his office early. He spoke to no one except Linda, concerned someone would detect the fury that clenched his fists around his car keys and the handle of his briefcase, and disappeared down a private elevator. If he chanced the common areas there would be glances between colleagues and queries laced with false concern, his failure to answer grist for the rumour mill that swirled interminably around the water coolers and photocopiers. Ben had always had a particular dislike for office politics, a necessary evil he endured only because he could play them better than anyone else, but one should not confuse skill with fondness or approval.

His face was expressionless, his mouth a hard line sculpted into his jaw. He possessed the singular objective to learn the truth about Elisabeth and her dead baby if he had to beat it out of his uncle. Benjamin cared little for consequences at the moment and was frightfully grateful for his choice of practice: he had more than enough clients who owed him their freedom, who owed him a favour or two. It would only take a phone call.

When Ben arrived Armin was eating his afternoon snack. He didn't look surprised by the visit; on the contrary, his eyes sparkled with a peculiar satisfaction as they followed Ben's purposeful strides across the room. "Glad you've come, Ben," said Armin. "I may need a lawyer soon."

"Don't be a flippant prick." Benjamin backhanded Armin's water cup across the room to keep from hitting his uncle. The cup crashed against a pine bureau, spraying its contents against the cheaply finished wood and the floor beneath. Armin's face registered neither fear nor anger, just the same peculiar satisfaction. Benjamin began to pace, trying desperately to contain his fury. He could envision his hands around his uncle's neck, could feel the satisfaction as Armin's life force drained away. It frightened Ben how little it would take to make the vision a reality so he squeezed the bed rail instead. "I know what you did to Izzy, you filthy Nazi pig. And I will see you rot in hell for it if I have to cross to the other side of the courtroom to do it."

"You are so sure of my guilt," Armin said arrogantly. "How easily the mind tricks itself."

"What the hell are you talking about?"

"Did you never wonder why your family was banished from my house?

172

It was to protect my daughter."

"From whom."

"From you, of course. Do you think we didn't notice the way you looked at your cousin? That we didn't know about your escapades in the garage?"

Benjamin's face went red, first with embarrassment then incredulity. "We were eight years old! We were just children! Exploring. It was natural."

"And when we caught you in her bedroom on her thirteenth birthday, was that natural too? When she stopped bleeding, we knew what you had done."

Benjamin shook his head with indignation and denial. "I did no such thing!"

"Hmmm." Armin shrugged his good side. "Are you sure? Or have you blocked it from your mind? Perhaps you should ask your father. The apple rarely falls far from the tree."

Benjamin kicked Armin's wheelchair back, sending it crashing into the wall behind him. Armin grabbed onto the chair's side rail with his one good hand to keep himself seated, and a flicker of fear swept across his face. "My father never touched Izzy and neither did I," Benjamin growled and bared his teeth.

Armin cowered in his chair but remained determined. "And yet you fought me three times for custody. Why else would you want her so badly unless you think I stole what was yours?"

Benjamin walked menacingly toward his uncle. "You sick bastard. You think you can mess with my head but you can't. And what you fail to appreciate is that technology has caught up with your kind. You may have gotten away with this forty years ago but not today." He grabbed the sides of Armin's wheelchair and leaned down to look his uncle in the eye. "They know Izzy had a baby by a close male relative and one by one we will prove our innocence until the only one left is *you*."

"Better get on with it then," Armin said defiantly. "I'm an old man."

Benjamin's rage exploded. He grabbed Armin by the throat and began to squeeze. Armin grabbed Benjamin's arm and tried to pull it down but it was futile. Images of Elisabeth flooded Ben's mind and erased all cognizance of what he was doing. Armin gasped for air but Ben's hands remained around his uncle's neck. The room receded from view as if Benjamin's peripheral vision were stripped away and all he could see was his uncle's distorted expression of fear, and he Benjamin's revulsion. Their faces were but inches apart and the proximity distorted the image further still. It was as if Benjamin were looking at Armin through a fisheye lens, Armin's heavily lined eyes bulging, his damaged facial muscles slackening ... "Go ahead, kill me," he whispered hoarsely. "But you can't kill what you did."

The warning snapped Ben back to consciousness. His hands went limp and he fell away from his uncle. With his one good hand Armin rubbed his throat, trying to coax himself back to life. He wiped away the mucus that had pooled on his upper lip and glared at Ben. "Go ask your father," Armin hissed. "Then ask yourself again, Who raped Izzy?"

Ben imploded. *No, no, no,* a voice screamed in his head. *No.* He stumbled backwards out of Armin's room and crashed into the hallway wall. *No.* Ben looked up and saw Barbra staring at him, confused, and when she began walking toward him he bolted out of the care centre and into the blinding sunlight.

Ben covered his eyes from the glare as he raced for his Mercedes. He collapsed into the car, shaking uncontrollably. *It's not true, it's not true,* he repeated over and over in his head. *When you spied on her dressing for her birthday, was that natural too?* He saw her there, standing by her bed, looking down at her new birthday dress draped over the quilt. Elisabeth was wearing only her panties, her emerging breasts small and round, the areole like pale pink flowers. She looked up and saw him watching her, and smiled. He moved toward her, hand outstretched, his heart pounding. She let him touch her, let him put his lips to her own—and suddenly so much commotion! His aunt's shrill voice, the sting of a hand on his face, the twisting of his arm as he was dragged away by his father, away from Izzy, who sobbed and screamed for Ben as her half-naked body was wrapped in a blanket.

Ben fought back the nausea that threatened to overpower him. No, no, it wasn't true. He would know if he had ever touched his Izzy like that. He would know. He wasn't suppressing anything. Yes, he had spied on her that day. He had wanted to see her budding womanhood before she was gone from him for good, before he would have to share her love with other boys, but that's all. He had never touched her, not in that way. He had never hurt her. He wouldn't have done that and erased it from memory. He would have killed himself first.

Or would he? Had he buried something within his subconscious, if not the act itself then perhaps some unfulfilled desire? There had been that fateful night when he'd accidentally whispered Izzy's name while making love to his wife, an accident he'd assured her had been nothing more than his preoccupation with the application for Izzy's guardianship due to his aunt's diagnosis. Samantha claimed to forgive him but months later filed for divorce, and to this day remained suspicious of his motives for guardianship. Had she seen something in him he couldn't bear to see himself?

Ben pushed open the car door and vomited onto the asphalt. When he had emptied himself of his shame he sat back up and reached for his cellphone. "Linda," he said to his assistant, trying to steady the quiver in his voice, "I need you to book me on the first flight to Orlando. I'm on my way home to pack. Call me with the flight details." Benjamin started his car and pulled out of the lot, his head full of questions for his father.

∞

Jackal laboured beneath the weight of unwarranted accusations. Did no one understand how *necessary* had been his actions? How perfect had been his plan? Did no one see how precious was his Izzy, how inconceivable it would have been for her to mate with others? He recalled the softness of her lips, her dewy skin, the small breasts that shuddered with apprehension as he mounted her. He had seen his future in her eyes, and the future was immense.

TWENTY-ONE

Claire glanced at the clock on the DVD player. She had spent the day searching for window treatments, eventually settling upon a sheer blind bookended with Dupioni drapes, and now it was time to get ready for Rafael. The thought made her fidget with the silk pillows that accented her couch. It was going to be an awkward evening. She never enjoyed hurting others, and to be dumped was always humiliating no matter how early in a relationship. She tried to think of kind words to use and began working on their delivery as she trudged up the stairs to get ready.

As Claire brushed her teeth and put on her makeup, she thought of her date with Dylan and how radically different it had been from her date with Rafael. Both had been dinner dates in lovely restaurants but that's where the similarity ended. While Rafael had sought solely to impress with his choice of establishment, Dylan had chosen a place that for him had meaning. It had been an invitation into his private world, another way in which he had opened himself to her, something she now realized he'd been doing from the moment they met: he had divulged his heritage, brought his grandmother to Claire, confessed the contents of his heart, told her about Lawrence, and even about his mother when Claire had inadvertently pried. And what had Rafael told her? Nothing. His answers to her questions had been short, often evasive, though so skilled was he at deflecting attention back on her that at the time she hadn't noticed his reticence. Maria had suggested it was humility but Claire now suspected it was really about leverage, about maintaining the upper hand: he would know everything about her but she'd know next to nothing about him. It had all been so perfectly scripted.

She dressed in black silk trousers paired with a simple knitted twinset and lower heels: she didn't want to encourage any further attraction.

Claire's heart sank when the doorbell rang. As she descended the stairs she wished that by some miracle it would not be Rafael but another surprise visit from Dylan, a wish she admitted next was thoroughly in vain. She was just going to have to suffer through this discomfort whether she liked it or not. She opened the door and hoped her smile didn't look as forced as it felt.

"Claire, *mi querida*," Rafael said as he swooped in for a kiss. He was expensively dressed as usual, and when he stood back to take her all in she noticed his puzzlement at her less formal attire.

"Forgive me, Rafael," she said, "but I've had a long day and I would prefer something more casual tonight. Are you okay with this?" It was a lie, of course; the truth was that Claire didn't want him spending another three hundred dollars on a dinner she planned on making their last.

"Of course," he smiled and took her hand. Rafael made a call on his phone to cancel their dinner reservation then made another call to someplace else, speaking this time in Spanish. When they reached the car he held the door for her, and when he walked around to his side he took off his suit jacket and hung it on the hook in the back seat. "Now," he said, smiling at her when he was seated, "we are the same."

He took her to a lively Spanish restaurant where, the sign said, there would be a salsa band at eight o'clock. "We dance tonight," Rafael said, gesturing toward the sign. "I teach you how." When they entered the restaurant the maître d' fawned over Rafael, speaking effeminately in Spanish as he led the couple to a table near the dance floor. The room was packed and it didn't take a genius to figure out their choice table had come at the expense of someone who had made a reservation sooner than twenty minutes ago; such, apparently, was Rafael's pull here.

Claire and Rafael were munching on spicy prawns and making light conversation when an older well-dressed man approached the table. From a distance he looked like any other respectable businessman but up close Claire saw in his eyes a savagery that chilled her. She shivered beneath her twinset as if the dampness of night had already descended despite the early hour. The man gave a concerned glance in Claire's direction but Rafael gestured leisurely and said, "*No te preocupes, ella no entiende.*" Actually Claire did understand, at least that much: she had studied Spanish at university as her foreign language requirement, though she'd forgotten most of it through disuse. She was about to confess as much when her eye caught sight of the holstered gun beneath the man's suit jacket when he leaned down to give Rafael an affectionate pat on the back. Her lungs constricted involuntarily and a quiet gasp escaped her throat before she could suppress her fear, and was relieved when neither Rafael nor his visitor noticed.

As the men conversed in rapid Spanish, Claire sat quietly and sipped her wine as if politely waiting for the return of Rafael's attention, but in truth she was trying desperately to comprehend the conversation. She picked out a few, easily remembered words—*mucho dinero, precio alto, la semana próxima*—but the rest was a blur of complex conjugations and unfamiliar nouns. The conversation appeared convivial though Claire thought Rafael's expression obsequious, his gestures false, and she wondered now if his flattery of her had been equally sycophantic.

The conversation ended abruptly with another slap on Rafael's back, and the man limped back to his table where three others like him were seated. Claire's mind was whirring but she managed to fake only a passing interest. "Who was that?" she asked casually.

"Client. Big client. So I have to be like friends."

Claire smiled weakly and was grateful their entrees arrived and diverted attention away from the men. She kept up pretences through the main course and dessert, even allowed Rafael to teach her the samba before feigning fatigue and asking to end the evening. He smiled sympathetically and called for the cheque. "Next time I teach you meringue."

The bill came and Claire reached for her wallet. Rafael looked at first confused then insulted at the gesture. "What is this?" he asked, suspecting something was amiss.

"I would like to pay half, if that's alright."

"Why you insult me like this?" He looked nervously over at the table where his clients sat.

Claire squirmed uncomfortably in her chair and avoided his eyes. She was panicking inside: insulting Rafael was exactly what she had meant to avoid and now she was hurtling headlong into disaster with no obvious escape. How stupid could she be, risking his wrath just so she could assuage her own guilt for being here in the first place? "I don't mean to offend you, Rafael; I just don't think a man should always have to pay," she lied, as if the gesture had been nothing more than feminist pride.

"Put it away!" he snapped at her in a low voice. Claire acquiesced and put her wallet back in her purse. The situation was quickly disintegrating and she was beginning to feel nauseous. Rafael paid the bill and escorted Claire swiftly out of the restaurant. "Why you do that?" he demanded. "I no understand."

"I told you, I just don't think a man should always pay. A woman—"

"You lying!" he said, raising his voice. "All night you lying. Why?"

"I can't see you anymore," she blurted out, unable to conjure up a more diplomatic delivery.

He looked stunned, broadsided by the announcement. "I no understand," he repeated.

"Things changed while you were away," Claire tried to explain without bringing Dylan into the conversation. "I'm sorry. It's not you. You've been wonderful and generous and kind but things have changed. I can't tell you any more than that. I hope you'll just respect my decision."

"What changed?" he demanded to know.

"Things."

His eyes flashed with anger. "What things?" Claire shifted from foot to foot and Rafael saw in her eyes the ghost of competition. "Ah, I see. Someone else."

"Yes," she admitted.

"No problem," he said and smiled, though his eyes remained cold. He seemed relieved that this was the obstacle, as if another man were no more than a pesky insect Rafael could swat away. "I make you forget this man. It will be simple."

"No," Claire said, shaking her head, "it won't."

"Yes, simple. Now get in the car."

There was something about the way he said it that made Claire recoil with fear and she backed away. "I think I should just get a taxi."

He grabbed her by the wrist and jerked her forward. "Don't embarrass me more. Get in the car." The violence and unpredictability of the gesture frightened Claire. He suddenly struck her as impulsive and erratic, the veneer of chivalry wiped away by an alarming machismo. The situation was escalating and Claire feared it would quickly spiral beyond her control if she didn't extricate herself quickly.

"Please let me go," she quietly insisted, believing if she maintained an even temperament it would calm Rafael. "You're hurting my arm."

But he didn't let go. Instead he maintained a firm grasp on her wrist as he opened the passenger door and tried to push her inside. A rage was building in his eyes that terrified her. "Rafael," she raised her voice at him, "let go of my arm or I'll scream. I swear it. And everyone in the restaurant will hear." She stared him down and finally he let go, pushing her away from him in disgust.

"*Puta*," he spat at her. He strode around to the driver's side and drove off, tires burning and showering Claire with gravel.

She leaned against a tree to keep herself upright and placed a shaky hand over her stomach that was threatening to reject the last of her dinner. She closed her eyes to stop the dizziness, and when she opened them again the man with the gun was staring at her as he led his party out of the restaurant. He took a step in her direction, perplexed that she were alone and unwell, but what might have been concern Claire interpreted as menace and she fled in the direction of Robson street, hoping to lose herself in the crowd. She was almost there when she saw a dark Cadillac driving slowly beside her. She glanced over and saw the man with the gun eyeing her intently through the open passenger window. He raised his hand in a gesture of invitation but Claire mistook his extended forefinger for a gun. She stifled a scream and bolted the last thirty feet to Robson Street, her spine jarred by the slamming of her heels against the concrete. She slipped in behind a group of teenagers who continued laughing and talking among themselves, oblivious to her distress, her head down and shoulders hunched over her purse clutched between taut fingers. She scanned the street for the Cadillac and when she caught a glimpse of it she took refuge in a busy coffee shop. Her heart was throbbing against her ribs, her eyes locked on the car as it passed her and continue down Robson. A couple bustled against her in the doorway, casting disparaging glances as they cursed "excuse me" at her, and Claire stumbled back onto the sidewalk, cast out and exposed. She caught sight of the car turning right at the corner and her fear immediately assumed it was circling round for her. She jaywalked across Robson, dodging the slow moving traffic, and raced up Burrard Street to the safety of the Hotel Vancouver. They wouldn't dare shoot her there, she told herself: there would be security guards and cameras and too many witnesses.

Claire made her way to the lobby and dialled a panicked call to Dylan from her cellphone. He saw the name on his call display and grinned. "Hello beautiful," he sang into the phone. "Shall I come whisk you away now?" He was expecting an equally flirtatious response so when Claire instead collapsed into tears and didn't answer, Dylan's descent into anxiety was doubly jarring, jolting him out of his seat on the couch. "Claire, what's wrong?" The hairs on the back of his neck rose and his imagination was quickly racing down a dark road. "Claire, talk to me. Tell me what's wrong."

"He's r-really angry," she stuttered, shielding her eyes from curious onlookers. "They had guns. They're looking for me. Dylan, I'm frightened."

"Where are you?" he asked, already out the door and headed for his jeep.

"At the Hotel Van, in the lobby."

"Stay there; don't move. I'm on my way. Warn security and if you see these men again, *hide*. And I'm going to call for some officers. But Claire, say nothing to them. Just wait for me. Do you understand?"

"Yes."

"Say *nothing*."

"Yes, yes, I understand. Nothing."

Dylan hung up the phone then called central dispatch. "This is Detective Lewis, 1638. I need a unit sent to the Hotel Vancouver. A woman is being followed by armed assailants. Complainant is Claire Dawson, five eight, slim build, shoulder-length auburn hair, thirty years old. Waiting in lobby for assistance." He jumped into his jeep and sped out of the parking lot, tires squealing.

Dylan had no idea how many traffic laws he violated en route to the hotel and neither did he care. Instead he cursed the lack of a siren when he narrowly missed a car turning left as he ran a red light, his determination to reach Claire in time etched deeply across his face. And as he sped across the Burrard Street Bridge he found himself in conversation with the Creator: *please, God, don't let it happen.* And though Dylan had no idea who Claire's guardians were or how to reach them like his grandmother could, he put a request out to the universe anyway.

It took only ten minutes to reach the hotel but Dylan knew it would have taken less time than that to fire a fatal shot. Without a radio he had no idea what might have transpired in the lapse between his call and his arrival, and his nerves were on edge as he pulled up in the hotel's driveway. The valet approached, his hand out for the keys, but Dylan just flashed his badge and barked, "Leave it."

He almost collapsed with relief when he saw Claire seated on one of the paisley couches in the lobby, two uniforms at her side and hotel security loitering nearby. She saw him striding toward her and, not thinking, jumped up to embrace him. The two constables gave each other a sideways glance as Dylan comforted Claire. He hugged her tightly for a moment then whispered, "I need to deal with these officers. I'm going to sit you down for a moment, okay?" Claire nodded and allowed Dylan to lower her back onto the sofa.

He showed the two uniforms his badge and motioned for them to walk with him out of earshot of Claire. "Hey guys, listen, thanks for attending. I appreciate it. I'm just gonna take her home now. She'll be alright."

"What's this about, detective?" asked one of the officers. "She wouldn't tell us anything. What are we supposed to write in our report?"

"Suspect didn't return. I came and escorted the victim. The rest is Code 12." Code 12: police lingo for private, top secret, none of your business, move on. The officers looked irritated by the command.

"Not good enough," the other uniform said. "Our sergeant is already aware of this call. We're not taking this on the chin for you."

"Look, this is part of an ongoing investigation I cannot discuss. Write an intelligence file and route it to me. I'll see that it gets where it's supposed to go. If your sergeant wants more he can call me."

The two uniforms eyed Dylan, not entirely buying it. "Seriously, guys," warned Dylan, "you push this you'll find nothing but grief. Just write up the intel file and send it to me." The two men conceded defeat and marched off with the intention of calling their sergeant: whatever was going down was not taking them with it.

Dylan walked back to Claire and took her hand. "Come on, I need to get you out of here." He quickly led her to his jeep, and under the curious eye of the valet helped Claire sit down and buckle up. He drove off, unsure as to the best place to take her. She was still shaking, and the adrenalin in his own veins was pooling in his groin, aching to prove to himself with a hard, anxious screw that she were still alive, still flesh and bone and sweat. He drove around aimlessly until his anxiety subsided then said, "Tell me what happened."

She related as best she could the evening's events, hoping she hadn't forgotten any important details. He asked her how she met Rafael, about Maria and Carlos, and what Rafael had told her about himself.

"The conversation between Rafael and the armed man, did you understand any of it?" asked Dylan.

"Not much. Almost nothing, really. Something about lots of money and high value, and something next week, but Rafael's an accountant so maybe it's not significant to be talking about money."

"It is if your clients are packing. This man with the gun, what did he look like?"

"Um," she answered, scanning her memory, "early fifties, your build but not as tall; Latino, with short dark hair, a moustache and sideburns; and lots of hair on the back of his hands. He was dressed in a suit, expensive looking, white shirt and gold cufflinks." She paused, remembering his face. "He had cold eyes. And a scar on his right temple. Not ugly but noticeable. You know, those thin white scars you often get from a superficial injury."

"Which side did he carry his gun on?"

"Left. Oh," she said, suddenly remembering, "and he limped. It wasn't pronounced, but he had an awkward gait."

"And this Rafael, he didn't actually threaten you, correct?"

"No. He just called me a whore and took off in a rage." The question made her feel foolish. "Did I overreact?"

"Maybe," he shrugged, "but I'd prefer you overreact than risk serious injury." He gave her a reassuring smile. "I'd rather have a hundred false alarms than one real tragedy."

She smiled her gratitude. "Thank you."

He squeezed her hand and gave it a kiss. "Any time."

"Where are we going?" she asked after a moment.

"Not sure yet. I need to think some more." Claire nodded and went quiet. Dylan mulled over his options and tried to calculate the risks potentially inherent in each. Rafael was currently under surveillance so if he came anywhere near Claire's house Gordie's team would know, and yet they had obviously seen the earlier altercation and done nothing. Dylan wondered how far they would let Rafael or his cohorts go before they would risk blowing their cover, and concluded if the case were as big as Gordie Bullen suggested they'd probably let them go very far indeed— and that, Dylan thought determinedly, he was *not* going to let happen. He could take Claire home with him until he could sort things out with Gordie, but would Dylan be able to remain a gentleman with her in such close proximity overnight? And what if they did become intimate? Could the repercussions be any greater than if they remained just dating? And would he tell himself no just so he could justify his actions? He wasn't sure how far he trusted himself right now but decided he was still the safer of the two bets.

"Claire, listen, I think you shouldn't stay at your place tonight. This Rafael knows where you live and I'm not allowed to carry my service piece off duty. So until I can ascertain exactly what the risk, if any, to you is, I'd like you either to stay with a friend or with me."

Claire looked at him and said, "I choose you," and Dylan felt his foundation sway.

He flashed her a shaky smile. "Okay. We can stop by a drugstore so you can get whatever toiletries you need." Claire nodded and Dylan turned the corner, headed for home.

TWENTY-TWO

While Claire perused the aisles in the drugstore for the bare essentials, Dylan hung back and called central dispatch again with an urgent message to Gordie Bullen to call in. Five minutes later, as Claire and Dylan stood in line at the checkout, Dylan's cellphone rang. "Claire, I have to take this privately. I'll meet you outside." She looked worried. Have I gotten you into trouble? her face queried him. He gave her a comforting shake of his head and a wink and walked outside. "Gordie, it's Dylan. There was a situation this evening—"

"So I heard. What the hell are you playing at, Lewis?" Dylan's back went up: was there ever a day Gordie Bullen wasn't looking for a fight?

"I'm not playing at anything, you prick," Dylan lobbied back. "In fact, my intervention saved your ass. If Dawson had called it in your surveillance might have been compromised by a couple of uniforms. As it is, I've come to the rescue—hers *and* yours—and she has no idea Rafael is under suspicion. So back off and try a little appreciation for once."

"Fair enough. But what's she doing with this guy? I need to know."

"Nothing. She met him at a barbecue last weekend, had a couple of dates and blew him off. He didn't take it well. But then you already know all that 'cause you've been watching."

"If you're intimating that we failed to intervene, I resent that. She handled herself alright. She's not in any danger."

"Sure she isn't—until Rafael or one of his coked-up chihuahuas puts a bullet in her."

"Rafael isn't packing."

185

"His friends are."

"Which ones?" Gordie asked, suddenly sounding interested. Dylan relayed the description Claire had given him earlier as well as the man's interaction with Rafael. "Scar beside the right eye, eh? Sounds like Felix Hernandes," Gordie said, his tone becoming more conciliatory. "Hmmh, that's useful to know."

"And it sounds like something's going down next week."

"Again, also useful." He paused. "I suppose you'll be wanting something in return for this information?"

"I want your boys to call me if Rafael or his cartel friends go anywhere near Claire Dawson's house again. I'm taking her someplace safe for the night but she'll want to go home soon enough."

"Okay, we can live with that. You keep your Cinderella safe and we'll let you know if Rafael or any of the wicked stepsisters tries for a visit."

"And not *after* the fact—" Gordie hung up before Dylan could finish his demands. He kicked at the wall, frustrated: Gordie Bullen just didn't know when to stop.

"Dylan, is everything alright?" Claire asked from behind him. Dylan spun around, surprised—she was not supposed to see that—but regained his composure in a heartbeat. He shrugged and put his arm around her shoulders.

"It's just politics," he sighed as he walked her back to his jeep.

"I'm sorry I've caused you trouble."

"You haven't caused me any trouble," he assured her, squeezing her shoulders and kissing her on the forehead. "And even if you have, you're worth it."

The conversation was light during the last of the ride to Dylan's apartment, but the deliberate simplicity did little to ease the sexual tension between them. Each also fought with themselves, Dylan wishing to preserve his chivalry for fear of offending whatever spirits had warned him not to rush things, Claire wondering what defined love given "too easily." When at last Dylan parked the jeep in the building's lot, each was firmly resolved to keep their hands to themselves.

Dylan led Claire around to the entrance. He was so focused on her presence that his usually keen antennae failed to pick up the woman sitting in her car some fifty feet away, trying to find the courage to walk to the front door and buzz his suite. Becky watched with dismay as Dylan led a tall brunette to the door and disappeared inside, a woman Wilson could

186

have sworn was Claire Dawson, the complainant on the Baby Jane case. *What the hell was Dylan doing? He could hang for this!* And what the hell made *Claire Dawson* worth the risk? What did she have that Becky didn't? *Value, that's what! You're worthless, Becky, damaged goods! No man will ever want you. But I do, don't I, Becky? I want you. Hush now. Stop your crying. I do this because I love you.*

Shut up! You're a liar! Shut up! Men want me. They do. I've proved that over and over again. Dylan wanted me. He just hadn't wished to take advantage, that's all; he's an honourable man. But he had *wanted me. He had wanted* me! Becky's tears began to flow. "Fuck you," she yelled, pounding her fist on the steering wheel. "Fuck you, fuck you, fuck you," she screamed through clenched teeth, then lost the last of her control: she grabbed her hair and thrashed her head from side to side until she almost passed out from the pressure.

Becky collapsed against the window, her frustration spent. She breathed in deeply until she regained her equilibrium, then straightened herself out in the rear view mirror and drove off, headed for the Cop Shop.

Dylan opened the door to his small but neatly kept apartment and led Claire inside. She looked around at the sparsely furnished living room dominated by a large, flat panel TV and entertainment system, and a comfy looking overstuffed beige couch, and bit her lip to suppress a smile. "What's so funny?" Dylan demanded to know.

"Nothing."

"Liar."

"Your place, it's just so masculine," Claire teased. "By any chance have you ever lived with a woman, well other than your grandmother?"

"For your information," Dylan pretended offence, "it just so happens I once lived with a woman for a whole year."

Claire dismissed him with a shake of her head. "A year is insufficient time to make an imprint on a man."

"And yet I've only known you a few weeks and look what an imprint you've made."

"That's very flattering but I was talking interior decoration."

"Now, Claire, an intelligent man knows there's no point in learning interior decoration because the minute he moves in with a woman she's going to decorate their space whatever way she likes. He'll have no say whatsoever and all his stuff will be relegated to the basement. So why bother? Better just to focus on sports."

"Hence the humungous television."

"Exactly. And I have surround sound, too. Just wait till you hear it." He walked over to turn on the TV: they needed a distraction. "How about a movie?"

"What have you got?"

"No chick flicks, if that's what you're asking." He opened up a cabinet with about fifty movies in it. "You can choose from here or we can check the movie channels." Claire perused the selection which, except for the lack of romantic comedies, was otherwise surprisingly diverse: classics, epics, suspense, action, comedies, caper films. She chose one from the last category. "Do you want popcorn?" he asked.

"No, I ate enough earlier. But you go ahead."

"Naw, on second thought it's too late to eat. It'll just keep me up." Now there's an idea, Claire thought before reminding herself of necessary boundaries.

They curled up on the couch together and watched Michael Cain and cohorts steal four million dollars in gold, and by the time the closing credits ran Claire was happy to fall asleep where she lay, entwined in Dylan's arms. He turned off the television and whispered in her ear, "It's time for bed, Claire. Do you want to wash up?" She nodded sleepily. Dylan rose from the couch and lifted Claire up by her arms. "Come on, I'll show you to the washroom."

While Claire washed her face and brushed her teeth, Dylan tossed the couch cushions aside and pulled out the sofa bed. When Claire returned from the bathroom she found him tucking in fresh sheets and spreading a summer weight blanket on top. "Would you like to sleep here or do you want my bed?" he asked before he realized that was ambiguous. "I mean, you can have my bed and I'll sleep here or you can sleep here on fresh sheets. Whichever you prefer."

"I'll sleep here. I'd hate to kick a man out of his own bed."

"In that case I'll get you some pyjamas." He disappeared into his bedroom then returned moments later with a pair of cotton striped pyjamas, still with their original creases in them and the tags attached. "Ta'ah," he explained. "She hasn't figured out yet I no longer wear pyjamas and I don't have the heart to tell her."

"Normally I don't wear pyjamas either," Claire responded with a glint in her eye. "But I'll make an exception, just for you." Dylan grinned and shook his head with mild disapproval then headed for the bathroom.

While Dylan took his turn getting ready for bed, Claire changed into his pyjamas. They were several sizes too large and were it not for their drawstring waist they would have fallen around her ankles, but they were soft and comfortable. She slipped beneath the covers and listened for Dylan. When finally the bathroom door opened she wished more than anything for him to slip beneath the covers beside her, and when he came back into the living room she thought perhaps he'd decided the same. But he only leaned down to kiss her and whisper goodnight, then he turned out the light and retired to his room.

Sleep proved elusive. In their separate rooms they stared into the darkness, each thinking of the other yet not wanting to be the one to break their promise. It was a battle of mind over matter, of self-control, of the will to tame primal instincts whose pleasures were nearly impossible to resist, especially now when the heart hungered as much as the body. But resist they did until fatigue finally overwhelmed desire and they both fell into dream.

ભ

Benjamin Keller hailed a cab at Orlando International Airport and collapsed into the back seat. He was exhausted. Ever since that first visit from Lewis and his smart-ass partner, Ben had felt his energy draining away, as if someone had covered him with leeches that were slowing bleeding him out. Fear, anxiety, guilt—they were taking their collective toll. He gave the cabbie the address for Evergreen Trailer Park, then closed his eyes for the thirty minute drive.

Evergreen Trailer Park was comprised of about sixty mobile homes set on permanent foundations, and most homes featured either an attached wooden deck or an expansive awning opening out over an extended concrete pad. You could easily tell the gender of most home owners: the men accented their patio furniture with large barbecues while the women created little garden oases with hanging baskets and large potted tropical plants. There was an exception to this trend in the manner of one Edward Kempler, a former professional gardener whose lush patio had spread into the surrounding gardens now resplendent with exotic species blooming beneath the palms. Kempler was a spritely man who tended to his plants and the park's women with equal religiosity, and had been known in his youth to have fertilized more than a few clients' wives.

The mobile homes were arranged around a small community centre where weekly dances were held for the residents and nearby locals, bingo on Saturdays during the winter months, and even the occasional wedding when a romance turned serious. At the edge of the park was a hook-up area—the double entendre not lost on its users—for transitory residents who drove the retirement circuit in their bus-sized mobile homes, staying a week or two before heading on to the next town. And like all retirement communities, Evergreen was a subculture of its own with unwritten but fiercely enforced rules and expectations, and a *fin de siècle* undercurrent made possible by medical marvels and interventions. Such hedonism wasn't for everyone but it suited Randolf just fine.

Evergreen in particular was popular with the expat community, which explained the unusual quiet this day: most of its residents were snowbirds who traveled back to Canada for the summer months, leaving only the diehard sun worshippers like Randolf to mind the ship year round. This he did with military precision, following his own strict schedule for watering neighbours' plants and feeding their fish; and he kept an eye out for troublemakers and thieves. All this he did with a mind to reward, and as he was still relatively fit for his age the late autumn return of the many female residents meant a particularly hectic time in his social life, which was finally in full swing again after an unfortunate incident two years back when he had contracted chlamydia from a woman from New Brunswick and infected three others before the onset of symptoms shut him down for the season. The temporary removal of Randolf had meant a boom in popularity for Edward, their friendship built upon a fierce rivalry that logically should have made them dislike each other yet surprisingly had the opposite effect.

Benjamin found his father lounging beneath a large palm tree, reading the weekend papers and drinking a beer, the first to keep his mind sharp and the second, he claimed, to maintain his vigour. "Benjamin, my boy, how was your flight?" Randolf called out when he saw Ben alight from the taxi. Randolf rose from his chair and, beer still in hand, walked over to hug his son. He embraced him tightly, noting with concern the rigidity in Ben's body and interpreting his wan smile and dark eye circles as professional stress; and was grateful his boy was here where the Florida sun might add some colour to an otherwise pasty complexion.

"Long. I had to go through Dallas." Benjamin headed inside Randolf's luxury double-wide trailer and put his luggage down in the kitchen. It was much cooler here where the air conditioning hummed low and the windows were closed against the stifling heat. "How are things with you?"

"Not bad. Bit slow this time of year, of course. If it weren't for Jean Witlow staying put I wouldn't be getting any at all!"

Benjamin shook his head with mild exasperation. His mother had been dead five years now and yet the idea of his father as a resident gigolo was still a difficult one for Ben to get his head around. He moved into the sitting area and plopped down on the couch. "Can I get you a beer?" asked Randolf from the kitchen, eyeing his son with concern.

"I don't know why you stay here all year," Ben said as he opened his collar to the air conditioning. "The heat's unbearable. Why don't you come home for the summers?"

Randolf dismissed the idea with a shake of his head. "Naw, too many memories." His face went dark for a moment and Ben realized the wife and mother he thought forgotten was anything but.

"Speaking of which, I didn't come for a visit, Dad," Ben waded straight in. "I need to talk to you about a very serious matter and I need you to be brutally honest with me."

Randolf's forehead furrowed. "You in some kind of trouble?"

"No. Well, maybe. I don't know." Benjamin hesitated for a moment then blew out the last of his reservations. "I don't know how else to say this except just to say it. Forty years ago Elisabeth had a baby. Somebody killed it and stuffed it into the wall. Do you know anything about this?"

Randolf sank into the sofa's matching chair, a mixture of shock and revulsion etched into his face. "I don't know nothing about any baby ..."

"But?"

"It was always a strange house. Armin was always a strange fellow, right from when we were boys. Always killing things. Insects, frogs, mice. Even killed a cat once. And he never just killed them, either. He'd torture them first. And he was always so mean to Therese."

"Why didn't you do anything about it?" Benjamin asked in earnest.

"We tried, in our own way. I tried talking to Armin but he'd tell me to mind my own business. Your mother defended Therese once when Armin was nasty but we later found out it only made things worse for her. So we didn't do that again."

"Why didn't you intervene when Elisabeth took ill? Why didn't you make somebody take her to a doctor?" Benjamin tried to restrain the tone of accusation in his voice but the sense of injustice was building.

"Son, times were different then," Randolf shrugged. "A man's home was his castle. You didn't interfere in another family's business."

The nonchalance of Randolf's answer sent a shot of adrenalin through Ben's system. "Elisabeth wasn't another family's business!" he bellowed as he bolted from his seat. He began pacing furiously, punctuating each sentence with a fist to his chest. "She was *our* family. She was *our* Izzy. And she was *my best friend!*" He turned his back to his father, the fury threatening to erupt into another act of violence. Benjamin wanted to destroy everything within reach, as if trashing the trailer would somehow erase the past, erase the guilt, erase forty years of failing to act. Had he become so used to defending criminals that he no longer saw the victims even when it were someone he loved? Was believing that Izzy had a genetic illness the machinations of a guilty conscience? Why had he never aggressively pursued his suspicions? *How hard could you have tried, mate?* The detective's words echoed through Benjamin's brain, torturing him, taunting him. Ben had exploded in righteous indignation but that was just pretence. How hard, really, truly, had he tried? What was the true extent of his own culpability?

And how much of his rage was not for Izzy's benefit but his own? He'd always been the one in control—of the courtroom, the office, of his women and children—always the one on top, always the winner in life's endless contests, but now failure had descended upon him with a vengeance. It was crawling through him like a swarm of insects, eating away at his fortitude, devouring his certainty, threatening him with collapse. And he was discovering to his shame that he had little rectitude with which to counter the attack, few saving graces willing to build him a defence. For the first time in his adult life Ben felt utterly alone and outgunned.

Randolf sat in his chair and stared guiltily at the floor while Benjamin continued to pace, confused, agitated. He needed desperately to escape but there was nowhere to go. There was nowhere to go that Izzy wouldn't haunt him, that his uncle's arrogance wouldn't mock him, where Ben's conscience wouldn't plague him with its constant questions and accusations. There was nowhere to go so he broke down instead, crying silent, internal tears of helplessness.

When his fury finally subsided, Benjamin steadied himself then turned to face his father again. "Why were we banned from the house? Armin said we were expelled because he saw me spying on Elisabeth when she was dressing. He said the apple doesn't fall far from the tree. What did he mean by that?" Randolf's jaw dropped open and were it not for his pacemaker his heart would have stopped. His eyes implored his son not to ask again but Benjamin hadn't traveled across an entire continent to leave empty-handed. "What was he talking about?" he repeated firmly.

Randolf took a sip of his beer. "My beer's getting warm," he said and headed for the fridge.

"Don't avoid the question, Dad. I *need* to know."

Randolf opened a fresh bottle of beer from the fridge and sat down at the kitchen table, putting some distance between him and Ben. Randolf nervously rubbed his hands together to remove the condensation that now coated his fingers, then pressed them into the table. "Please understand, the war made people do strange things."

"I'm not here to judge you," Benjamin implored his father. "I'm here because I need to know the truth. I need to help Izzy."

Randolf nodded his head in quiet resignation. The mind was a complex organ, he thought philosophically, so adept at burying memories never intended to be recalled, so skilled at protecting the heart and ego that the story Benjamin was now demanding the retelling of had long been dead and buried. Anytime the image of Gertrude had invaded Randolf's mind it had flexed its muscles, quickly replacing the thought with something less painful, some mundane reminder of a task to do or perhaps yesterday's conversation with a neighbour. It was only now, forced by circumstances to relive the past, that Randolf became cognizant of how determined his mind had been to erase Gertrude from his awareness until she barely existed, then and now. And yet here she was again, reasserting herself through his son and the horrific crime that had brought Ben to Orlando on a hot day in June.

Randolf stuttered his way through a few false starts before managing, finally, to recount the past. "When I was young I had a cousin I loved very much," he began slowly, "just like you and Izzy. Her name was Gertrude. Gertrude was a year younger than me and I was very protective of her—had to beat off more than one unsuitable cad." The recollection made him smile momentarily, but only just: Gertrude was a wound in an otherwise stoic heart. "Anyhow, when the war broke out and all the propaganda started, Gertrude became very patriotic. She volunteered at a hospital for returning injured soldiers. Early in '45, when things weren't going well for us—the Allied forces had crossed the Rhine—Gertrude was terrified we'd all be killed or captured." Randolf took a long sip of his beer, the bottle shaking a little from the tremor in his hands. "So she came to me with a request." The last word arrived with another stutter, a sudden flood of anguish threatening to conquer the courage Randolf had summoned on behalf of his son. Ben waited patiently while his father pushed through his remorse, and when Randolf finally continued he spoke with the determination of one trying to justify his actions as much to himself as to his audience. "She wanted me to deflower her so that she wouldn't die a virgin, or if she were raped then her first time would not have been at the violent hands of a foreigner; she wanted it to be with someone she loved and trusted, with somebody German."

"And did you?" asked Ben. "Did you honour her request?"

Randolf felt the trailer closing in. The room grew warmer, the heat seeping in through the cracks in his resilience. "We knew it was taboo, knew our parents would kill us if they found out. But she was so scared of the invaders. And so determined. So, yes, I honoured her request. Because I loved her and I would have done anything for her. Even that."

"How did Armin find out?"

Randolf's face flushed. "My mother caught us as we were getting dressed. My uncle was furious; called Gertrude a whore and a disgrace to the family. She ran away with a soldier she met at the hospital and I never heard from her again. A letter came for me a year later apparently but my father burned it without opening it. He didn't confess to that until we moved to Canada."

Benjamin collapsed onto the couch, another wave of guilt washing over him. "Then this *is* my fault. He was just protecting Izzy. If I hadn't—"

"Nonsense!" Randolf barked, his embarrassment replaced by indignation. "He was not protecting Izzy from you. He was keeping her for *himself.*"

Benjamin looked like he was about to be sick. "How do you know that? How do you know that ... that he raped Izzy? How do you know that *I* didn't?"

"Don't you think you'd remember?" Randolf answered with a dismissive snort.

"I would think so but ... what if I've suppressed it? What if I did something so horrible that I had to forget it?"

"You didn't rape Izzy!" Randolf barked. "No son of mine would do that!"

194

"How do you *know*?" Ben implored.

Randolf didn't. But he felt he had to, for Ben's sake, for his own, maybe even for Izzy's. "There was a day that still sticks in my mind. Izzy was about eleven, I guess. She was turning cartwheels on the lawn—she was always doing that, remember?—and wearing a blue summer dress. With each turn of a cartwheel her dress fell and revealed white cotton panties. She was oblivious to the indiscretion, as was I until I saw a peculiar look on my brother's face that made me turn around to see what he was looking at. I saw her turn a cartwheel, her dress fall, and that peculiar look in Armin's eyes staring at her panties. It sent chills down my spine." At least he thought it had, now that it counted. The mind was a complex organ.

Randolf looked over and saw the horror on Ben's face, not only at what the story implied but at the complicity inherent in Randolf's inaction. He looked away, unable to bear the glare of Ben's silent indictment. "I'm sorry, son. I'm really sorry. Please tell Izzy I'm sorry, too."

"You can tell her yourself," Benjamin proclaimed, snapping out of his grief. He jumped up from the couch with defiant determination and pulled out his cellphone. "You're coming home with me."

Randolf's eyes widened with fear. "What for? What can *I* do?"

"They know from DNA tests the father of the baby is a close male relative but not which one. You can help me prove that Armin is the culprit by submitting a voluntary tissue sample to rule you out, just as I've done."

Why would you do that, son? Why? "But I can do that here, can't I? I have plants to water."

"Screw the plants and whatever you get in return for it," Ben demanded. "Using a lab here means more paperwork and a hole for a defence attorney. I *know*. So pack a bag. I'm calling a taxi."

TWENTY-THREE

Claire arose quietly so as not to disturb Dylan, washed up, then headed to the kitchen to make some breakfast she could surprise him with when he awoke. She rummaged through the cupboards, fridge and freezer but the pickings were slim: Dylan was a man who clearly didn't eat at home much. Nevertheless, she managed to find a coffee pot and coffee, oranges and a small electric juicer, some frozen whole grain bread, milk, and a half dozen eggs. "Well, it's scrambled eggs and toast, I guess," she murmured to herself and went to work.

She was just setting the table when she heard Dylan in the bathroom. He'd been awakened by the smell of the coffee and, hearing Claire clattering about the kitchen, realized with embarrassment she'd seen the sorry state of his pantry. He had planned to avoid that by taking her to breakfast then suggesting a trip to the market, and would now need to fabricate a plausible rationale for his meagre offerings. Dylan had never thought of himself as a pathetic bachelor before but Claire's barely suppressed ridicule of his décor and now her discovery of his poorly equipped kitchen was making him rethink his position on domestic indifference. He stepped into the tub intent on formulating good excuses while he showered and shaved.

He had just come out of the shower when Claire knocked on the door. Dylan wrapped a towel around his abdomen and opened the door to find her looking waifish in his pyjamas and holding a cup of hot coffee. She glanced coyly up at him, the sly smile on her lips juxtaposed with a freshly scrubbed face that otherwise appeared deceptively innocent. "I brought you some coffee. And there's eggs, toast and juice when you're ready." She put the cup on the counter. "I hope you don't mind my taking the initiative." Her eyes never left him as she spoke, her gaze roaming over muscled arms and shoulders and nicely toned abs. His chest was bare save for a scattering of straight black hairs on his breast bone, and a "treasure trail" of fine hairs down the center of his belly disappeared beneath the thick towel that bulged slightly between his thighs.

"Not at all," he said and took a sip of the coffee. She didn't respond further, her eyes fixed wistfully on the rim of the towel. "Claire?"

"What?"

"I think this is the equivalent of my talking to your breasts."

She looked up quickly, embarrassed. "Sorry. But in my defence, you are *spectacular*."

"So are most breasts but we get smacked for it anyway."

She laughed and mischief replaced the embarrassment on her face. "Can I see what's behind door number one?"

"No."

"Come on, I dare you to drop the towel."

Dylan chuckled. "You *dare* me? What am I, twelve?"

"Of course not," she smiled. "No twelve year old I know looks like *that*."

Dylan grinned and stepped forward to give Claire an appreciative peck. It was a mistake but in truth a conscious one: the peck turned into a kiss and the kiss into a deluge of lips on flesh and before they knew what or where they were headed the towel had fallen to the floor and they were stumbling into the living room and onto the sofa bed. Dylan pulled Claire's pyjama top over her head and feasted on her breasts while one hand undid the drawstring waist and slipped beneath the bottoms, lifting her up and pulling them down with one movement. Claire wrapped a leg around Dylan's hips and pulled him to her, impatient to consummate her desire. He let her hurry him, sliding into her as a sigh floated up from her throat. His breath was warm and heavy on her neck as he thrust rapidly, passionately, her moans of pleasure urging him on until he had no other option but to let himself go, neither of them mindful of possible consequences.

He fell beside her and pulled her close, holding her tightly for a few moments before speaking, his voice quiet with regret. "I'm sorry."

She looked up into his eyes, alarm on her face. "You're sorry? Why?"

"That was too fast," he said, unhappy with himself. "I didn't take the time to please you."

"That did please me. Dylan, I've been dying to have you inside me from the moment I laid eyes on you. Waiting was *torture*."

He smiled, relieved. "Next time, then."

"I'll hold you to it."

He kissed her and then looked sheepishly away. "One other thing. I realize this is a bit after the fact but ... shouldn't we have used a condom?"

Chastened, she had to agree. "Yes, we should have. So, um, I'm healthy and, well, you've read my Statement of Claim so no worries there."

"Good, good," Dylan replied, equally subdued. "Me too. Well, the healthy part, that is; I can't really speak for the boys. I had my annual physical a month ago; there were no infectious diseases you'd rather I didn't bestow upon you."

"Are there infectious diseases I *would* want you to bestow upon me?" she asked playfully, lightening the mood.

"No," he laughed. "I guess that is redundant. I'm going to have to be more careful dating a teacher." He paused, then added, "At least my reports will improve."

She laughed lightly but then it was her turn to feel apprehensive. She propped herself up on one elbow and looked intently down at him. "Dylan, does it bother you that I can't ... that I can't have children?"

"Why do you say 'can't', Claire? You're scarred but you're not infertile." He shrugged and brushed a wisp of hair off her forehead. "There are ways and means."

"But if I can't, would you rather be with someone else?"

He thought about that for a second. "No," he replied honestly. "There's alternatives. Adoption, fostering. And I think sometimes the Creator makes those with the bigger hearts look elsewhere 'cause not everyone has the capacity to love somebody else's kid. But I think you do, Claire. I think you have a really big heart. So don't look at it as some sort of punishment or a judgment on your character. The idea of fecundity as a reflection of a woman's value is so medieval. And I don't subscribe to that."

She snuggled back down beside him and held him tightly. "Thank you," she whispered.

"You're welcome. Besides, we don't have to think about this right now. Children and stuff like that is a ways away. We've only started dating. First we have to determine if you can put up with me and my domestic failings, and then there's a few oddballs in my family that might make you wary of any permanent attachment. Oh, and did I mention my sixth toe?"

She smiled. "I see only five."

"I had it surgically removed," he lied, straight-faced.

"Well, in the interests of full disclosure then, I had a third breast but it was also surgically removed."

"Whatever for? It would have been useful if you'd had triplets."

"And an overbite. I wore braces."

"Well, now *that* I understand. But a third breast would have been extraordinary." He leaned in for a kiss. "Most extraordinary." He was ready to go again and so he let his mouth begin wandering over and down her body, slowly this time, as promised. And, true to his word, she was mightily pleased.

CR

The weekend was a blur of sensations. Each moment was part pleasure, part discovery, and all theirs. The new lovers shopped at the markets, cooked and feasted upon simple meals, watched movies and debated their merits, took long walks along Kits beach, ate ice cream and played in the sand: mundane activities that suddenly became vibrant and significant for no other reason than they were shared. In between their excursions into the world were lengthy, exquisite bouts of lovemaking whose rhythm and intensity varied—at times passionate, at times playful, with moments of heartbreaking tenderness that had them shaking from the avalanche of emotions. And though each had no doubt where their heart was, where it was headed and where it would end up, neither confessed the inevitable for fear of intimidating the other. Their hearts said "I love you" but their mouths simplified things: "I adore you." "You're beautiful." "I love ... it when you do that."

Monday morning brought with it more sunshine and pleasure. Claire woke up aroused but Dylan looked so heavenly lying there naked on his stomach beside her, the covers pushed away in the heat of the night, that she didn't have the selfish heart to wake him. Instead she let her eyes wander over his magnificent body: smooth, light brown skin, taut buttocks and thighs, toned arms. She took in the details and committed them to memory: a small mole on his right shoulder blade, a vaccination scar on the outside of his left bicep, a thin white scar on the side of one ankle, a tattoo of an eagle whose wings spanned across the small of Dylan's back. Her fingers traced the lines of the tattoo—gently, so as not to disturb him—but the caress woke Dylan anyway. He opened his eyes to find her staring down at him. "Good morning," he sighed.

"I'm sorry. I didn't mean to wake you."

"That's okay. You can wake me any time you want."

She smiled then continued tracing the eagle's wings with her fingers. "Tell me about this," she requested.

"If I tell you, you have to promise not to laugh."

"I won't laugh," she said sincerely.

He turned languidly onto his back and propped his head up on one arm. "When I was a kid I wanted to be an eagle," he said, grinning and rolling his eyes in embarrassment: he imagined it sounded silly to her. "I guess I was about seven when I finally realized that was never going to happen. So, when I was old enough not to need Ta'ah's permission, I had the tattoo done. I found out later the eagle is my power animal, so it made sense in retrospect."

"What's a power animal?" Claire asked, intrigued.

"It's an animal spirit that protects you. We all have one. We're given one when we're born. That's why children often have a special love or affinity for a particular animal. Your power animal can change depending on where your life takes you, and many of us are blessed with more than one. My grandmother has several. It's one of the reasons she's such a formidable medicine woman."

"That might explain my love of dolphins," Claire replied thoughtfully. "When I was a kid I had everything dolphin: dolphin posters all over my bedroom walls, dolphin stuffed toys, dolphin picture books; I even had a tape of dolphins singing. My brother used to tease me mercilessly about my obsession and to this day he still gives me little gifts like a dolphin keychain or fridge magnet. When I graduated from university he gave me a gold necklace with a dolphin pendant." She paused, smiling at the memory. "He's a bit of a prat, actually," she added, laughing.

"Where's he now, your brother? In Calgary?"

"No," Claire frowned, "he ran away down east."

"Ran away from what?"

"The same thing I did: our father."

"Do you want to tell me about him?" Dylan asked cautiously.

Claire shrugged. "My dad was what you call a control freak. He used his affections as a weapon: approval was the carrot, disappointment the stick. We spent our whole childhoods trying desperately to meet his expectations. Still are, I suppose. Distance is our only refuge."

"And your mom?"

"What my father tore down she rebuilt. She was very loving, very accepting. But the downside was we became overly reliant on her love; it was hard to find our independence. So my brother ran away, first to Carleton University in Ottawa then to a finance job in Toronto. He's married now; has a kid, a dog, a mortgage, and uses all three as excuses to return only for weddings and funerals."

"Do you miss him?"

"Very much." Her voice fell to a whisper so Dylan let his next question fall away unasked and pulled her close instead. She imagined what he wanted to ask: whether her father's emotional games had made her vulnerable to Eric, had kept her tethered to him even as he tore her heart asunder, had made her beg for his approval even though he was unworthy of hers. They had, of course, but Dylan remained silent, didn't express any need to query or analyze her; and she found in his silence the acceptance she'd always sought but never found. And so, her movements barely a whisper, Claire reached down and stroked Dylan while she kissed his shoulders and chest. He responded by slipping his hand between her thighs but she gently lifted his hand away and whispered, "No. This time the pleasure's all mine," then let her mouth follow his treasure trail south.

ᕲ

Randolf Keller was sitting in his son's office at Keller Jamieson Clark and Associates, staring nervously at the Forensic Ident officer as he scraped the inside of Randolf's mouth with a buccal swab. Arrangements had been made that Dylan and Tom would become aware of soon enough, and while the clout Benjamin Keller seemed to have with the police brass would raise a few eyebrows among sceptics, Inspector Ken Chow, head of the Major Crimes Section, followed the adage that it was best to keep your friends close and your enemies closer.

A few uncomfortable minutes later the officers were gone. "How long do I have to stay in Vancouver?" Randolf asked Benjamin.

"Until the test results are confirmed. I want to make sure there are no complications before I put you back on a plane."

Randolf looked uneasy. "Are you sure this is a good idea?" *All that commotion. And Izzy's naked body.* He too remembered that day, even if he didn't admit it. He couldn't lose his son. Ben was all Randolf had. "Even if Armin did do this, what's the point? He's a sick old man. What can they do now? I don't want to know what he did. It makes me feel dirty."

Benjamin eyed his father with suspicion. He'd been adamant about Ben's innocence, had offered repeated assurances Ben's memory was intact, that nothing more sinister than a boy's curiosity had transpired that day. Armin was the culprit, the beast who had raped an innocent girl. He had to be. And yet Randolf was obviously nervous about Ben's DNA sample, which made Ben nervous, too, made him wonder if he'd been duped by his own mind and what the consequences would be if he had. And then he wondered if he cared anymore about his freedom. If he had locked Izzy in a cage, should he not be in one, too? His mind whirled about with questions and possibilities but he chose instead to perpetuate their shared denial. "I know. Me too. But Izzy is entitled to justice, even if she may not comprehend it."

Randolf looked away, his mind wandering aimlessly down a dark alleyway full of sinister shadows and terrifying threats. He needed a distraction, Ben saw, so he offered up one. "Listen, Dad, why don't you take the kids and go to the house in Whistler. You can go hiking or just hang around the Village, whatever, just get away from this ugly business and indulge your grandkids. I'll call you when you can go home."

Randolf nodded submissively. The last two days had sucker-punched the fight out of him. "You're right. A few days with the kids might help me forget this sorry affair." It was a lie of course—nothing was going to erase this from Randolf's conscience, not for a very long while—but at least he might be able to assuage his guilt with some distance even if that distance were only a two-hour drive away.

"Go on, then," Benjamin said, tossing his car keys across his desk. "You can take my car. I'll call Sam and let her know you're taking the kids."

Randolf stared pensively at the keys then slowly rose. "Do you think Elisabeth will ever be able to tell anyone what happened to her?"

"I don't know. But as long as she can't speak for herself we're going to have to speak for her." He paused. "Whatever the consequences," he added, in brief violation of their conspiracy of silence.

Dylan and Claire finished washing up the breakfast dishes then pondered what to do with their day. "Dylan," asked Claire as she folded the dish towel and hung it on the rack, "could we visit Ta'ah? I'd really like to see her again. Or do you think it's too soon to be presenting ourselves as a couple to her?"

"Oh, I think you'll find she's way ahead of us on that front. Besides, there's something on the reserve I'd like to show you. But don't ask me what; it's a secret."

The drive to Ta'ah's was quick and painless. When they arrived Ta'ah was sitting at the altar near the medicine hut, communing with the spirits. Ta'ah had made several attempts over the past week to learn more about the demon and whatever or whomever it was holding hostage in its den, but so far her efforts had achieved little. She had tried twice as well to speak with Baby Jane but Bear had refused access to her, citing Baby Jane's trauma and need to heal. This Ta'ah respected but the more Ta'ah was thwarted in her quest for information the more she was convinced the child was the key. So she was trying once again, standing at the edge of the forest where she had handed Baby Jane over to her guardian.

Ta'ah called out with her spirit mind and moments later Bear appeared and sat down on her haunches opposite Ta'ah. "Medicine woman," Bear said respectfully, "you are persistent."

"Justice must be done. Baby Jane has been released but another remains enslaved. Has the child told you anything?"

"Only that the walls hold further secrets."

"Will you not let me speak with her?"

"I can not. And I beg you, do not ask again. I am trying to prepare her for rebirth but her fears are many. She has already suffered greatly in this matter. Let her be." Above them the cry of an eagle was heard, sending their eyes skyward. "Eagle is hunting," observed Bear.

"He seeks as I do."

Bear nodded her head in sympathy. "There has been talk on the wind, but I cannot confirm whether these whisperings are from friend or foe. You must decide for yourself."

Ta'ah nodded her assent. "Tell me what the wind has whispered."

"Lure Coyote and he will fall, and Jackal will fall behind him."

"How might Coyote be lured?"

"By the very wind that whispers his name." And with that Bear took her leave of Ta'ah.

Ta'ah opened her eyes and saw Dylan sitting near her in silence. He jumped to his feet and helped Ta'ah onto hers, then offered his arm as they walked. She looked up and saw Claire sitting on the porch watching and waiting. "I see you've brought my daughter to visit."

"I wish you wouldn't say stuff like that, Ta'ah; it freaks me out."

"Why? You must already know this in your heart."

"Yes, but what about all that no rushing things, blah, blah?"

"Just because you can see the target doesn't mean you have to run to it. You know that as a policeman. It's no different in love." They reached the porch and Ta'ah opened her arms to Claire. "Welcome, daughter." The women hugged and then Ta'ah slowly lowered herself into a chair. "Tell me, has my medicine brought you relief?"

"I'm not entirely sure," Claire answered honestly.

"What colour did it turn?"

"A rather gross shade of blackish brown. Reminded me of sludge."

Ta'ah smiled and nodded her head. "Good, good. It took much sickness with it then."

The three talked of this and that until Ta'ah dozed off in her chair. Dylan gestured to Claire for her to walk with him. "Come on, I'll show you my secret," he whispered with a mischievous grin. He led her out of the yard, down the street and into the grove of trees that separated the reserve from the rail yard that ran along the inlet. They walking purposefully on the sun-dappled path until they arrived beneath a large, ancient oak with a cedar tree house nestled in its branches. Dylan grabbed onto the rope ladder and held it steady for Claire. "Go on. Up you go." Claire grinned and climbed up the rope and into the tree house, Dylan right behind her.

The structure was about six feet square and roughly as tall, with a pitched roof and a window cut out on one side with a sheet for a curtain. The exterior wood, left unfinished, had turned dark grey but the inside, where the cedar had been sanded and sealed, retained its warm orange glow. On the floor was a stash of blankets, girlie magazines poorly hidden beneath a stack of comic books, a wind-up LED lamp, and a can of mosquito repellent. "Clearly the hideout of adolescent boys," Claire surmised as Dylan pulled the ladder up and closed the hatch.

"And a love nest for teenagers, or so I'm told."

"And was it your love nest?"

"I built it."

"Really?!"

"Uh-huh. When I was sixteen and a girl named Mary James dumped me. Apparently—and this was just recently brought to my attention—I build things whenever I'm sexually frustrated."

"Well now that's good to know. If I frustrate you sufficiently will you build me a new bathroom?"

"I think you're more likely to get a new bathroom out of me," he said, nuzzling her neck, "if you performed certain sexual favours instead."

"Hmmm," she murmured in anticipation. "What did you have in mind?"

"Take off your clothes," he playfully ordered her as he laid out some blankets across the floor, then sat cross-legged in the middle of the space and watched her undress. When she was fully naked he ordered her to sit in his lap facing him and he began examining her body like one might scrutinize a painting. "Do you know how beautiful you are?" he asked as he ran his fingers along her shoulder blades.

"Beauty is in the eye of the beholder," she answered noncommittally.

"In that case you're more than beautiful; you're resplendent."

"Don't be silly," Claire answered shyly. "I have uneven breasts."

"I love your breasts."

"And freckles on my nose."

"I love your freckles."

"And dimples in my bum."

"I love your bum."

Claire relented with a sigh and fell quiet, watching Dylan as he examined her intently. He wanted to tell her that beneath his lust he felt a stillness: that whereas other women made him feel claustrophobic and his feet itch, Claire made him feel cocooned and grounded. He wanted to confess there were also moments when he awoke in a cold sweat, terrified of the recognition that in her eyes he saw not the mother who abandoned him but a woman who would walk beside him into the future. But most of all he wanted to admit how often he'd wondered what it would feel like not to want to ravage or consume but to surrender, and that he had done so with her, and it had been glorious.

But he didn't know how to say these things so instead he continued to wander with his eyes and hands for a considerable length of time, and when at last it seemed he had taken his fill of her, he laid her down on the blankets, removed his clothes, and loved her until they were spent.

TWENTY-FOUR

The lovers lay together a little while afterwards then dressed and opened the curtains to let in the cooler air. Dylan sat back against the wall and pulled Claire close. "You like being a teacher, don't you?" he asked, in the mood now to talk.

"Yes, very much," she smiled. "The pay's terrible and the workload's obscene, but the rewards can be profound. All it takes is that one kid whose heart and mind you touched who goes on to excel or to overcome adversity and you know you've made a difference. What about you? Do you like being a cop?"

"Yes. I don't think we're appreciated enough by the public—I don't think they really comprehend the chaos and violence that would land on their doorsteps if we didn't exist—but most days it's enough for me to be appreciated by the victims or, in my case, their families. I'm glad to be done with regular patrol, though. That's no more rewarding than housework: you clean up the mess and it just gets dirty again. When I became a cop I finally understood why all those housewives in the fifties became addicted to Valium."

"Why did you become a cop?"

"Because I wanted to make a difference, if you'll pardon the cliché. I thought I could as a cop. There's a disproportionate number of Native people in trouble and in jail. I wanted to be a good role model for others and I wanted to be sure those Natives who ended up in my custody were treated fairly. And I believe in law and order. I believe in justice. I think criminals should be punished and victims defended. That the system often fails them and me is not my fault. I do my job and if the courts drop the ball, it's on their heads, not mine."

"Was it difficult to get onto the force?"

"In general or because I'm an Indian?"

"Both," she answered hesitantly, concerned that might appear a wee bit racist.

Dylan shrugged. "It was rigorous but I didn't find it difficult. What I find more difficult is putting up with systemic prejudice: a lot of people assume I got onto the force because of affirmative action but that's nonsense. I have all the same credentials as a white cop and a few more. I have a degree in criminology—with honours, I might add—a bit of martial arts training, and I didn't need a sensitivity course to understand that battered wives and rape victims aren't asking for it. I learned *that* just from watching Ta'ah treat the women here. And I understand racial conflict but that *doesn't* mean I excuse anyone's bad behaviour. Addiction isn't an excuse to hurt others, and prejudice or poverty isn't an excuse to become a criminal."

Claire was intrigued. The subject was clearly an issue for Dylan, and in his words and gestures he was revealing an interesting part of his character, the part that was both proud of and burdened by his heritage. She secretly wondered how much of it had to do with his mother but didn't dare pry for fear of seeing the same dark cloud that passed over his eyes the last time Claire had asked. She chose instead another avenue of debate.

"But what about those victimized as children? The cycle of violence is an obvious one."

"Yes, but whatever happened to you, once you're an adult how you respond is a *choice*," Dylan enunciated, punctuating the last word with a definitive nod of his head. "Failing to seek help or refusing it is a *choice*."

"Fair enough, but prejudice is very real—"

"Claire," Dylan interjected impatiently, "prejudice is everywhere! We live in a multicultural society and not everyone is keen to assimilate. They gravitate toward the comfort of their own. Then their kids try to straddle two worlds, and then *their* kids wonder what all the fuss is about, and maybe by the third or fourth generation there's true assimilation. But like anything else you have to want it. Don't forget, prejudice runs in all directions. It's been my experience that those who scream discrimination the loudest are usually themselves the biggest bigots." He paused for air. "Do you know what some Natives will call me because I've fallen for a white woman?" Claire shook her head. "An apple: red on the outside, white

208

on the inside. Which is not only an insult to me but to you! As if you have nothing more to offer me than the colour of your skin, a status symbol I can parade before my peers. It's *bullshit!*"

Claire considered all this and agreed but it still seemed too black and white for her tastes. "Look," she said, sitting up to square off with Dylan, "this is all true but there are still huge social impediments that can't just be willed away because you want them to be. You've just said so yourself how annoying the assumptions made about you are."

"Yes, they *annoy* me. But I don't let them *stop* me."

"Great. That's you. You with your innate courage and intelligence and your wonderful grandmother and your successful aunts and uncles. But not everyone has that. What about the ones with foetal alcohol syndrome or some other learning disability, or who try to find a job but can't?"

"Claire," Dylan said with a finality that indicated he was keen to end the debate, "look at my family. Me and all my uncles and aunts were raised on this reserve, surrounded by drugs and alcohol and gangsters promising easy riches. But we *chose* not to pursue any of that. We *chose* to remain in school, to go to university, to get a job. Ta'ah made sure of that. She gave us total freedom but she always emphasized personal responsibility. She never accepted our excuses, never once just shrugged her shoulders and said, 'Kids will be kids.' She disciplined as passionately as she loved. She never hit, she never hurt, but she punished. And with one exception we turned out great."

"You mean your mom," Claire said gently.

"Yes," Dylan answered and she heard the cry he caught in his throat. He didn't offer anything further and Claire wondered how he would react if she asked more questions. He looked away from her inquisitive eyes. "You want to know about her, don't you?"

"Only if you're okay with telling me."

"I suppose it's only fair," he answered, turning to face her again. "What would you like to know?"

"Where is she now?"

"In Capilano View Cemetery," he replied unemotionally. "She died in an alley on the Downtown Eastside when I was eight."

"I'm sorry."

Dylan sighed and shrugged his shoulders. "Like I said, Claire, life is about choices. My mom had all the same opportunities as her sisters and brothers. She just didn't want to work for anything. It was more fun to hang around with dropouts and get drunk. It was easier to accept society's assumptions about her than challenge them. That was her choice. And it was my choice not to grow up all bitter and twisted over her. I'm not saying I don't have issues. It bothers me that I wasn't"—he paused to steady his voice—"that I wasn't worth sticking around for, and that other people, *lesser* people, knew her while I didn't, but I choose to count my blessings. Of which you are the latest." He pulled Claire close and kissed the top of her head. "I'm so very grateful for you, Claire."

"And I, you. And if it's any consolation," she said, giving him a squeeze, "*I* think you're worth sticking around for."

"Thanks," he said quietly. "And I have another confession."

"What's that?"

"Debating with you turns me on. But I'm too hungry to manage another round. Let's go," he added, patting her on the bum, "and find something to eat."

Claire agreed and they left the tree house in search of nourishment. Dylan descended first, holding the ladder steady for Claire when he reached bottom. As Dylan led her back along the path through the trees he fell quiet and she wondered if his mother were on his mind again. "What are you thinking?" she asked gently.

"I'm thinking how I don't want this day to end. These past few days have been unbelievable and yet tomorrow I have to return to work and try to prove who killed a baby. It's just the incongruity of that with this and you. I can't get my head around it."

"Have you made any progress on the case?"

"Well, thanks to your efforts we know who the mother is and that the father is a close male relative, and we're slowly testing suspects, but that's all." He offered nothing further, for as much as he wanted to share the details with Claire he couldn't; he needed to protect the integrity of the case.

"So Armin fathered a child with Elisabeth then killed it to hide the rape?" Claire asked, more condemnation than question.

"I didn't say that."

"You didn't have to."

"I can't prove it," he admitted, giving in a little.

"But you know it in your gut."

"I know he's guilty of something. But even if he raped Elisabeth it doesn't mean he killed the baby. Elisabeth could have done it. Or her mother. Her brother. There are two crimes here, and proof of one is not proof of the other."

"But if he did rape her then he set into motion the events that led to the murder. So maybe you settle for half-justice."

"Maybe. But you know what really bugs me? Right now I can't even get the bastard for the rape. The JP wouldn't give us a warrant for Armin's DNA because God forbid should we violate that Nazi's human rights. How's that for ironic? So unless we can find some compelling evidence that points *specifically* at Armin we have to eliminate every other bloody suspect before we'll get what we need. We may even have to exhume Elisabeth's brother. Do you have any idea what that costs? We'll have to dance like circus bears for that."

"But why won't they give you a warrant? Isn't it *obvious* that he's a suspect?"

"Have you forgotten our earlier conversation?" he snapped at her, failing to control his frustration. The sting was biting. Claire turned her face away and walked on.

"Claire, I'm sorry." Dylan sprinted to catch up with her. "I'm sorry. It's just too hard sometimes. We can't get a DNA warrant on suspicion; we have to have compelling evidence. Right now all we have is human remains, the identity of the mother and some idea of paternity. There's no actual evidence Armin raped his daughter, no evidence he killed the baby, no evidence he was even aware of it. His proximity to the crime, his relation to the baby, his Nazi connections—it's all circumstantial. I need reasonable and probable grounds; what I *have* is dick all," he said, kicking at the dirt.

"How frustrating."

"It's *very* frustrating. All we need is just one piece of evidence that implicates Armin Keller and then we'll get all the warrants we need. But without a warrant it's unlikely we'll find that evidence. It's a classic Catch-22."

"Too bad you can't just shoot him and be done with it."

"I would except ..."

"Except what?"

"Except what if I'm wrong? What if I'm letting my *own* prejudice cloud my judgment? Armin is definitely an abuser, but ..."

"But what?"

Dylan stopped and looked sternly down at Claire. "If I share something with you, you mustn't tell anyone. No one, Claire. I'm serious." She knew he was referring to Frau Müller.

"I promise."

"We know Armin forced his son to have sex with his mother. What else did he force him to do? What did he force others to do? Or convince them to do? Some predators prefer to watch so they indoctrinate others into the cause. They groom them. Brothers. Sons. Nephews. Neighbourhood boys. They twist their heads so tightly around that the victims start to believe the lie. That's the thing about pedophilia: it can be next to impossible to differentiate between victim and abuser."

"But this would still leave Armin guilty."

"Of course it would. But what if Armin didn't rape Elisabeth? What if it were Karl? He's dead so he can't testify. And if it were Randolf or Benjamin Keller, will they give Armin up or protect him? How deeply were they indoctrinated? Ben has volunteered a DNA sample but I've had rapists volunteer before only to discover it's because they're nuts or they're so wracked with guilt they want to get caught, or—and these are the scary ones—they're so sure of the righteousness of their actions that they can't comprehend society punishing them for it. They live in some weird moral bubble and truly can't see how twisted their values are." He paused to quell his anger, and when he spoke again his voice was subdued. "And what if it were someone outside the home, someone Armin knew and perhaps shared Elisabeth with?"

"Frau Müller said Elisabeth never left the house."

"Frau Müller's nosy but she's not omniscient. And forty years ago she was a busy mother of three children: there would've been soccer games and school recitals and scheduled trips to the grocery store. There would've been family holidays. And if she were watching the Kellers that closely, what's to say they weren't watching her? All Armin had to do was pick the right moments to sneak someone in or Elisabeth out."

"I guess things aren't always what they seem," Claire admitted ruefully.

"Exactly. That's why I mustn't assume the obvious. I can't"—the words caught in his throat and he turned his face away—"I can't make a mistake, Claire, not on this one. And I fear I may already have."

"You mean me?" Claire asked quietly.

"Yes."

They walked the rest of the way home in silence, Dylan kicking at anything that had the misfortune to be in his path while Claire watched him with a mixture of sympathy and fear. She felt him slipping away from her, and she worried Dylan were contemplating ending their relationship. The idea of letting him go, even for the greater good, terrified her. The past few days were *not* a mistake, but what argument could she proffer that wasn't as selfish as it would sound?

They reached the porch expecting to find Ta'ah still asleep in her chair but found her instead in the kitchen cooking up a late lunch of fried chicken and potato salad. She looked pensive, and the room was quiet as Claire and Dylan set the table. When the three were finally seated and their plates filled, Ta'ah spoke. "Dylan, the media embargo on the Baby Jane case, how long must you enforce it?"

"I don't have to enforce it. The embargo was at my request. But I don't think it will hold much longer: there's already a reporter onto the story. Chris Doolie from CKRW. We made a deal with him and he's going to want to be fed soon."

"Feed him," Ta'ah said decisively.

"Why?"

"They said to lure him with the wind."

"Who said?" Claire asked, trying to follow the conversation.

Ta'ah smiled and patted Claire's arm. "The spirits, dear," Ta'ah said matter-of-factly. She left out the part about Coyote, for what his role would be in the case Ta'ah didn't know and she didn't want the matter confused with more questions; her instinct told her this was enough.

"How do you feel about that, Claire?" Dylan asked.

"What do you mean?"

"As soon as Doolie airs his story the press are going to be swarming like flies around your place."

Claire thought about this a moment, tried to imagine how bad it might be, and concluded no matter how invasive the situation became it would pale in comparison to being murdered and stuffed in a wall. "I'll be okay," she nodded her consent. "If it will help with the case then it's the right thing to do. Baby Jane deserves a voice."

"Okay then," Dylan said and pulled out his phone to call Tom. He found him at home, watching English soccer on satellite and drinking a beer. "Hey Tom, it's me. Been thinking it might be time to make good on our deal with Chris Doolie. We need something to shake this up and maybe a public finger pointing is in order. You good?" Tom was good so Dylan placed a call to Media Relations: he needed to discuss what to tell

213

Doolie and to get input on how the department wanted the inevitable media storm to be controlled.

Constable Charles Brown, Media Liaison Officer, was standing in front of a luxury home in Fraserview preparing to explain to the handful of reporters gathered why the home was cordoned off and its owners en route to jail, while in the background drug squad detectives and colleagues from the tactical unit were hauling out weapons, boxes of illegal drugs, and suitcases of cash from the house. Brown was a subversive choice for police spokesperson: he held himself straight and spoke with authority yet possessed a baby face that inspired trust even as he was spinning the facts. He'd been in the position only for eight months but his popularity with the media—especially female journalists—had quickly rivalled his popularity on the force, and those who knew him well knew someday he'd likely take the podium as chief.

"Brown," he said into his phone.

"Charlie, it's Dylan Lewis from Homicide. Listen, that deal we made with Chris Doolie regarding the Baby Jane case, I need to make good on it as soon as possible. Can we meet first thing tomorrow and go over the details?"

"Yeah, sure. Does McTavish know?"

"Not yet. I figure I can bring you both up to speed at the same time. Can we aim for eight thirty?"

"Should be okay."

In the background Dylan heard shouting. "Are you on the street?" he asked.

"Yeah. Major drug bust in Fraserview with simultaneous arrests in Yaletown and Coal Harbour. Check it out tonight; it'll probably lead."

"Would this be Bullen's crew?" Dylan asked, curious.

"Uh-huh. The Baja boys are going to be unhappy campers when the news hits their hacienda. We just confiscated *a lot* of their money and product."

"The Yaletown arrest, who was that?"

"Some high-flying accountant named Rafael Morales. Looks like the Baja are going to have to find someone else to clean their dirty money. Poor things. And it was going so well until now," Brown chuckled cynically, then Dylan heard someone calling. "Sorry, gotta go," Charlie said. "Tomorrow, eight-thirty."

"Tomorrow it is." Dylan put his phone away. "Well, now that's interesting."

214

"What is?" asked Claire.

"Rafael Morales has been arrested along with several others in a drug sweep. It'll be on the evening news." Dylan studied Claire carefully as her face went blank.

"The men at the restaurant? The ones who were following me?" she asked.

"I believe so, yes."

"Does this mean I can go home again?"

"I think you should." The statement dripped with double meaning and Claire felt a cold wind momentarily freeze her lungs.

Dylan glanced over and saw that Ta'ah's eyes were closed and she appeared to be nodding off again. "Come on," he whispered to Claire, gesturing in Ta'ah's direction, "let's clear the table and head out." Claire nodded then began quietly clearing the dishes while Dylan wrapped the remains of lunch and put them in the fridge.

They left Ta'ah in her chair, her head to her chest, her breath deep and even. But Ta'ah wasn't asleep. She had heard the spirits whispering and, concerned with what she'd heard, had gone to query them. But instead of finding allies Ta'ah found herself confronted again by the demon, his amorphous shape swirling about in anger, whipping dust up into her face, trying to blind her.

Ta'ah called upon the wind spirits who swept the dust from her eyes and pushed the demon back. He changed into Jackal and threatened Ta'ah with a low growl, his teeth bared and dripping saliva. "You are playing a dangerous game, old woman," he snarled. "Take what is mine and I will take what is yours."

Ta'ah took a threatening step forward. "You cannot and you will not. I will chase you into the depths of hell before I let you harm a single hair on his head, or hers. Quit while you still have form, demon, for when we are done with you, you will be reduced to nothing." The two adversaries stared each other down, Jackal pacing and snarling in an attempt to frighten Ta'ah into submission, Ta'ah standing silent but firm.

"Blood shall be spilled," Jackal sneered ominously, "but it will not be mine." He then shape-shifted back into his black insect cloud form and disappeared into the ether.

TWENTY-FIVE

When Claire and Dylan arrived at her home Claire's answering machine was flashing with messages from Maria that became more urgent as they progressed: "Claire, it's Maria. Rafael is here. He's very distraught. Call me." "Claire, it's Maria again. I came by but you don't seem to be home. Are you okay? Call me." "Claire, why don't you call? I'm very worried. You mustn't think I'm angry because of Rafael. I still want us to be friends. He'll get over it. Call me, please." "Claire, have you heard? Rafael has been arrested. The police came to ask Carlos questions. We had no idea about any of this. I'm so sorry. Please call me."

Claire hit the erase button and sat down. "Are you going to call her?" asked Dylan.

"Yes, but not tonight. It can wait until morning. I just want to be with you right now." *Because I'm terrified if you leave you won't come back.* Claire curled up beside Dylan on the couch and turned on the news. The sight of Rafael and the man with the gun being led away in handcuffs was reassuring yet also disconcerting, for it raised a troubling question. "Did you know?" she asked Dylan.

"Know what?"

"That Rafael was under suspicion?"

Dylan winced. He knew that question might come up and if it did it would tear a hole in the trust they'd spent the weekend building. "Yes. I found out the day after I ran his license plate. And I know what you're going to ask next: Why didn't I tell you? Because I couldn't, Claire. It would have jeopardized a major investigation."

She rose from the couch and stepped away from him, creating a distance she needed him to cross to prove his fidelity. "But you let me go out with him again. Knowing what you knew." Her eyes implored him for an explanation she could understand.

"I know. But I also knew he was being watched. I assumed they wouldn't let anything happen to you. And when I wasn't sure of that any longer I took you home with me. I kept you safe, Claire. I did my best to serve both masters." He stared at her, anxious. "Do you want me to go?"

"No. Do you want to leave?"

"I can't."

"What about earlier? About this being a mistake?"

"I know, but I can't." Dylan rose up, emotional but determined. "Right or wrong, I just can't." He strode toward her and pulled her to him, burying his face in her hair as his hands pressed her to him. "I just can't." Dylan lifted Claire up and carried her, straddling him, up the stairs to her bed. He undressed her slowly, then himself, then made love to her with such tenderness and longing she almost cried. There was anxiety in his touch and afterwards, as he held her in a tight embrace that spoke of a complex combination of affection, need and desire, he whispered, "You've changed everything, Claire. Everything."

This time the tears broke through. Claire wept into Dylan's chest and witnessed the departure of all her pain and anger at God and the universe and fate and Eric. When she finally opened her eyes again she saw he was crying, too. Dylan kissed her, his mouth gentle but hungry. And then without warning he entered her again, pushing in deeper and deeper as if by some magic the whole of him could be inside her, cocooned in her softness and warmth. Claire wrapped her legs around him and held him tight against her, urging him on, crying out his name between gasps of pleasure until she shuddered beneath his weight and he let himself go, secretly hoping for a miracle.

The next few hours were a heady mix of declarations and confessions, words that escaped from the heart and tumbled from the lips, that mixed with sweat and the scent of lust to coat the lovers' skin and mark each as belonging to the other. Walls collapsed, defences broke, boundaries were crossed. The onslaught left Dylan and Claire dazed and disorientated yet paradoxically more aware: each caress, each gesture, each murmur was imbued with meaning, saturated with significance. Their senses were heightened, their touch electric. Their bodies pulsed and throbbed and shook, each climax a milestone on a one-way road that both knew had no off-ramps or escape routes. There was no turning back now and, even if there were, neither of them wanted to.

They remained in her bed, oblivious to everything but each other, until the shadows fell long in the garden and Claire, exhausted and sated, fell fast asleep beside Dylan, a smile on her face. He watched her sleeping for a little while then carefully disentangled himself and ascended from the bed. His nerves were still raw, his hands shaking as he quietly dressed. And though Dylan didn't possess Ta'ah's intimacy with the spirit world, he could have sworn he felt the wings of the eagle on his back lift a little beneath the breeze that wafted in through the open window. He bent down and gently kissed Claire goodnight then silently descended the staircase and let himself out.

Frau Müller entered her living room to watch the late news when she saw a man leave Claire's house and drive away in a jeep. He looked to be the same man she'd seen kissing Claire last Wednesday evening, and the lateness of the hour could only mean one thing, at least so Frau Müller imagined. Moreover, she was also sure this was the same man who'd been there the day the infant remains were discovered, and wondered if he were the detective Claire had mentioned when the two women had opened Armin Keller's letter. Yes, Frau Müller thought to herself, this would be a good time to invite Claire over for more tea. Frau Müller went through a mental recollection of the contents of her pantry and decided she'd bake a plum cake to compliment the tea.

She turned on the news and was shocked when another of Claire's acquaintances featured in the lead story. Frau Müller was quite certain that the Rafael Morales being led away in handcuffs in front of his Yaletown condo was indeed the dashing Latino who had driven Claire off in his car on not one but two occasions. What was going on? Maybe a plum cake *and* banana bread were in order. And two types of tea.

ᘓ

Jackal lay at the foot of his den, his breath laboured. The melancholy of his captive was his only nourishment now, and he knew it wouldn't be enough to sustain him much longer. He blamed his misery on Coyote, on the lesser beast's vanity and weak-mindedness, and his resultant failure to lure Claire into heartbreak. But most of all he blamed that pathetic detective with his lame romantic tears and insatiable appetite, and Jackal decided he had only one option left. He let his anger swell, gripped it tightly in his jaws to quell the pain in his belly, then set out into the forest, angry and determined, in search of a kill.

CB

When Dylan arrived at work early Tuesday morning Tom was waiting for him on the front steps. "Dyl, Chow's called us to McTavish's office this morning. Something go down over the weekend I need to know about?" Dylan nodded, and as the men made their way up to McTavish's office across the hall from the squad room, Dylan brought Tom up to speed on the Morales drug affair and Claire's brush with danger. "Lucky for you, then, that Morales has been arrested," Tom decided. "Good cover story."

"Yeah, I know," Dylan smirked. "I'd send Gordie a thank you note but he'd only use it against me."

"Just one thing, mate. Did she live up to her rating?"

"Naw," Dylan shrugged, then gave Tom a sly smile. "She exceeded it."

"Blimey, mate, spare no details!"

"Can't do that, partner. You know I never kiss and tell."

"Since when?" Tom asked, his scepticism valid.

"Since now."

Tom clutched at his chest—"Dyl, you're breaking my heart"—but his laugh abruptly vanished when they reached McTavish's office door. Tom knocked and a gruff "Come in" was heard from the other side. Dylan and Tom threw each other a look of support then Tom opened the door.

"Have a seat you two," McTavish ordered from his spot behind his desk. Dylan and Tom sat down and cast wary eyes at Inspector Ken Chow, standing beside McTavish and holding a file folder in his hands.

"Two bits of business, gentlemen," said Chow. "First up, the Baby Jane case. Yesterday Randolf Keller attended at the offices of his son, Benjamin Keller, to volunteer a DNA sample. The sample has been sent to Genesis Labs in Richmond. I've also taken the liberty to transfer Benjamin Keller's sample from the government lab to Genesis. You'll have the results on Monday."

"A private lab, sir?" asked Dylan, confused. "I was under the impression there were to be no perks on this one."

"Randolf Keller attended at his own expense," McTavish cut in. "We saw no need to keep him here any longer than is necessary. The government lab will take weeks." Tom and Dylan looked askance at each other but said nothing: Benjamin clearly had some pull with the brass but why look a gift horse in the mouth?

"Now," Chow moved on in a measured tone, "to our second order of business. Detective Lewis, there was a possible gun incident Friday evening in which you attended and removed the complainant. Uniforms were told it was Code 12. Can you explain?"

"The complainant on that call is also the complainant on the Baby Jane murder case. She had a date on Friday with Rafael Morales, the suspected money launderer for the Baja Cartel. During dinner she observed an acquaintance of Morales carrying a gun. The date ended badly and she feared for her life. She called me and I agreed to attend as I was aware of the drug investigation and knew Bullen's efforts might be compromised by lower level involvement."

Chow wasn't buying it. "But why did she call you? Why not just call the emergency line?"

Dylan shrugged. "She knows me from the murder case. She had my card. She trusts me. And a good thing, too, as evidenced by this weekend's arrests."

"Is she involved in this drug business?"

"No sir."

"You're certain?"

"Yes sir."

"Hmmm," Chow answered. He paused to weigh the pros and cons of pushing further and concluded it was in the best interests of the department and their case against Morales to let sleeping dogs lie. "Fair enough. Good work, detective. I'm sure Bullen and his team appreciated your intervention." He looked down at McTavish who was tapping his pen on his desk and eyeing Dylan suspiciously. "Anything you wish to add, sergeant?" Chow asked, his tone and expression suggesting the matter were closed to his satisfaction.

"Yes," McTavish replied, ignoring the hint. "You banging this woman, detective?" Chow closed his eyes in silent dread: this was about to get ugly.

"If what you mean by that, sir," Dylan responded evenly, "is am I in an intimate relationship with Ms. Dawson, then yes." Tom saw McTavish's eyes narrow at the perceived affront and leaned back in his seat to watch the fireworks.

"Don't be insolent!" barked McTavish.

"I mean no disrespect, sir," Dylan replied tersely. "But I will not allow her to be spoken of in that way."

McTavish felt his blood begin to boil. He turned his wrath on Tom. "You aware of this?"

"Could you define 'this' please, sir?" Tom asked, straight-faced.

"Whose side on you on, Farrow? And I suggest you choose carefully."

"With all due respect, sir, you're not the one watching my back out there. And you Canadians carry *guns*."

McTavish's nostrils flared as Chow unsuccessfully suppressed a laugh. Aware he was losing ground, McTavish brandished his sword. "Ms. Dawson is a complainant in a murder investigation," he snapped at Dylan. "You will end this relationship immediately."

"No, sir," Dylan shook his head.

"That wasn't a request; it's an order."

Dylan kept his calm but held his ground. "No can do, sir."

McTavish stood up and leaned over his desk to stare Dylan down. "There's no room on my squad for insubordinates," he threatened, his moustache twitching like the tail on a squirrel.

Dylan stood to face McTavish nose to nose. "I'm a bloody good detective. My record speaks for itself. If you want to toss me off your squad, I'll go elsewhere."

"Are you *seriously* going to jeopardize your career over some roll in the hay?"

Dylan exploded inside but outwardly he remained calm. "I've given fifteen years of my life to this department. I've never disobeyed an order, never cocked up an investigation, never given any of you cause for concern. I've been an exemplary officer, so if you're foolish enough to think I'd jeopardize my career over 'some roll in the hay,' as you put it, then I'd like to know what *exactly* earned you those chevrons on your arm."

McTavish's eyes bulged with disbelief. "You are OFF this squad, detective!"

"Suit yourself. I hear Vice is recruiting."

"Stop it, the both of you!" Chow intervened. Neither man moved. "I said, stand down *now* before you both regret where this is going," he ordered. "Sergeant, I've read the Baby Jane file. It's a forensics case. Ms. Dawson's role is insubstantial. Nevertheless, in the interests of optics you two are formally removed from this matter. You will focus your efforts on the Benson case. The Baby Jane investigation will be reassigned. And, Lewis, if this comes round to bite us we *will* reconsider your place on this squad, perhaps the force. Are we clear?"

"Yes, sir."

"And as for you, Farrow, mind that tongue of yours. This isn't *Monty Python*."

"Yes sir," Tom replied, choking back his next quip.

"Alright," Chow gestured toward the door, "Lewis, Farrow, back to work."

With the two subordinates gone, McTavish cast an angry gaze on Chow. "I don't appreciate you siding with a subordinate. It undermines my authority."

Chow sighed. "Let this one go, Jim. Love makes men do stupid things and quite frankly we can't afford to lose a good officer. Give it a few days to settle down then make your peace with Lewis."

McTavish fell back down in his seat, sullen but acquiescent. "This is bullshit," he grumbled.

"Look, I agree he was insolent and insubordinate. But he's been put on notice. It's an appropriate and sufficient response for the time being. Don't let your ego run away with your judgment, Jim; you didn't get this far because you're a man who loses his cool." Chow patted McTavish on the shoulder. "Who's available to take over?"

"Duncan and Lu just wrapped the McGinty file. They're with Crown Counsel all day but I can hand it to them tomorrow."

"Good, then that's done." Chow left the office, hoping that would be the last of this mess. Both Lewis and McTavish were good men and Chow didn't want to lose either of them. Especially not over something as silly as a woman, he thought wearily to himself, then pressed the elevator button.

Jackal sniffed the air and growled. He could smell her, that pernicious crone. She was hiding nearby, had no doubt been responsible for Chow's irrational benevolence. Her constant obstructions had surpassed mere annoyance, had become dangerous, and Jackal vowed he would tear her to shreds when he regained his strength. He should have killed her when she'd first dared to intrude upon his domain. She might fool others with her humble demeanour but he saw her for the blood-thirsty bitch she was. She was leading everyone down a precarious path and all because of a worthless subhuman whose existence had been a disgrace. Why did everyone care so much about that defective bit of flesh?

A few seconds later the elevator doors opened and Constable Brown alighted. "Morning, Inspector."

"Morning, Charlie. What brings you up here?"

"Lewis and Farrow want me to meet with them and Sergeant McTavish about releasing some of the Baby Jane details to the media."

"Oh," Chow said awkwardly. "Thank you, Charlie, but that'll need to be postponed. The case is on hold pending reassignment."

Brown looked perplexed but figured it best to stay out of somebody else's business. "Yes, sir." Chow said nothing further, just entered the elevator and closed the door. Curious, Brown made his way to Homicide where he found Farrow pretending to read a file and Lewis stewing over a cup of coffee, his feet on his desk. He looked surprised when he saw Brown. "Shit!" Dylan said, quickly sitting up. "Sorry, Charlie, I forgot I asked you to join us."

"Just saw Inspector Chow. Said this meeting's on hold pending reassignment. Something going on with you guys and McTavish?"

Farrow looked up from the file in his lap. "Lover's spat."

"Right. Got it. Okay then, later."

"Hey, Charlie," Dylan said, "before you go, hypothetically speaking what would've been your approach?"

"Hypothetically speaking?" answered Brown, settling in to a chair. "Do I understand correctly that you think Armin Keller's your guy and you need to apply some pressure, see if he'll crack?" Dylan and Tom nodded. "But you wouldn't want to humiliate Elisabeth Keller, even if she is catatonic?" They nodded again. "Well, we couldn't release her name anyway because she's a victim and, on the outside chance she's also responsible for the death, she was a minor at the time. Hmm, tricky one."

Brown rocked his chair back onto its rear legs and tapped his fingers on the armrests. After several moments pondering the facts and thinking up a strategy, he offered this: "Well, what I'd do—hypothetically speaking again, of course—is tell Doolie that newborn remains dating to approximately 1971 were found in the house. Definitely a homicide, but I'd keep the buried alive in a wall part in reserve; it's potentially a fact only the killer would know. I'd tell him the baby's mother has been identified but we can't release that information due to her age at the time of the homicide, and the father has not been identified but significant leads are being looked at. I'd mention the home owner is not involved and clearly distraught at the discovery. Then—and this is where it would get clever—I'd tell Doolie that the previous owner's Nazi past may be connected to the crime but I can't say that officially, then sit back and let the media with their penchant for innuendo connect the dots. They'd head straight for the owner and that elderly neighbour of hers who'd most likely yak with delight for the attention, then they'd dig up Keller's Nazi connections and go to town. It wouldn't have come from us, not officially anyhow, and the media would get to pretend *they* discovered Keller's dirty secrets. It'd be a win-win."

"Thanks, Charlie, much appreciated," said Dylan with a sly smile. "And don't worry, we never had this conversation."

Brown got up. "I know. I just came up to let you know the Centurions are playing a charity game next month. Tickets are twenty-five dollars. Shall I put you guys down for two or will you be bringing dates?"

Tom laughed. *Touché.* "Two will be sufficient, thanks," Dylan grumbled.

After Brown left, the squad room secretary approached with a large manila envelope. "Pathologist's report on Baby Jane," she said and handed it to Tom, then turned on her worn down heels and walked back to her desk.

The two eyed the report then each other. Tom glanced over his shoulder, saw everyone else engrossed in their own business, then opened Anil's report and scanned it for anything they didn't already know. "Poor thing," Tom whispered after a few moments. "As if being the product of a rape wasn't enough to bear."

"What?" Dylan whispered back, intrigued.

"Kid had a cleft palate. I had a cousin with that. Baby Jane would've needed surgery if she'd lived." Dylan's mouth opened as if to speak and his face had the look of one contemplating a possibility. He grabbed the phone.

"What?" asked Tom.

"Do you remember Benjamin Keller telling us about Hitler's T4 program, the one that euthanized Therese Keller's brother and grandfather?" Dylan asked as he dialled Claire's number. "When Claire found out about Armin's Nazi connections she went online, did some research." Claire's phone rang a few minutes before she answered with a throaty hello. "Hey, it's me," Dylan said, switching his attention to Claire. "Sorry to wake you."

"That's okay. You can wake me anytime."

"Very original."

"What's up? Or need I ask?" she laughed seductively and rolled over onto her back.

"Behave yourself; this is an official call."

"Then why are you whispering?"

"Never mind. Claire, listen, remember that research you did into the Nazi eugenics program? What criteria did they use to decide which children to exterminate?"

Claire sat up in bed, jarred awake by the question. "Uh, give me a minute. I have to get my laptop." Claire put on her robe and headed downstairs. She booted up her computer and logged onto the site she'd bookmarked earlier, then picked up the living room phone. "Okay, here it is. All children under three who were known to have, or suspected of having, any of the following serious hereditary diseases: idiocy and mongolism; microcephaly; hydrocephaly; deformities of all kinds, especially of limbs, head, and spinal column; and paralysis, including spastic conditions."

"Thanks. Can you email me the link? And the one about Hitler and the Spartans too."

"Sure. I'm doing that as we speak. And Dylan, are you coming over for dinner after work?"

"If I'm invited," he smiled into the phone.

"Of course you are. I'll see you then." Claire hung up the phone then went back upstairs to put her bedroom phone back in its cradle. She sat on the bed for a moment, contemplating whether or not to get up now that she was awake, and decided she might as well. She plodded to the washroom and ran herself a bath.

"So," asked Tom, "you think Keller killed Baby Jane because she didn't turn out all Nazi picture perfect?"

"Yup. I don't think Keller considers the rape of his daughter a crime or even immoral. He thought he was contributing to the creation of a master race by inbreeding."

"Or eugenics was just a convenient cover for a pedophile," Tom said through a sneer.

"Or that. But either way, the plan went awry: Baby Jane was born deformed. She had an obvious physical deformity that devalued her in Armin's eyes." Dylan opened his email and clicked on the website link Claire had provided, then scanned the overview of the Nazi eugenics program. "Listen. According to this, in Hitler's *Second Book* he wrote about his admiration for the Spartans because they allegedly kept their race stronger by leaving their deformed offspring in the fields to die. Which is bloody cowardly, if you ask me. I mean, even if you believe in eugenics why not at least kill the babies directly and give them a proper burial?"

"I agree. But what's your point, Dyl?"

"My point is that Baby Jane wasn't smothered. She wasn't strangled or shaken—the usual ways people kill infants—but she also couldn't just be left out in a field where she might be found. So he, or they, put her in the wall to die of starvation and figured no one would ever find her."

Tom considered Dylan's theory. "But the Nazis did kill directly. So why wouldn't Keller do the same?"

"Because Hitler came under fire from his own people over the program. So Keller went back to the source. He went back to the Spartans. In fact, let's contact the Germans, see if they've had any similar cases connected to this *Volkssozialistiche Partei Deutschlands*."

"It'll all still be circumstantial. And we can't contact the Germans: we're off the case."

"Oh yeah, fuck." Dylan tapped his fingers on his desk and weighed options. "In that case," he said, opening up his desk drawer and pulling out the plastic bags with the newsletter and note addressed to Armin Keller, "we'll be needing these."

"What's that?"

"It's a newsletter and note from Armin's Nazi pals in Germany. Acquired unofficially." Dylan slipped them into his breast pocket and stood to leave. "I think we need to revisit the Benson scene."

"Gotcha."

$\wp$

Claire sat on the couch munching yoghurt and granola and contemplating the Baby Jane case. That Dylan had asked about Claire's research suggested something new had arisen this morning, and she was impatient for his day to end so she could badger him for details. Had he found evidence that pointed the finger at Armin? If so, what? Had Elisabeth or Therese kept a diary? Or maybe Dylan had found something of Armin's. Psychopaths often keep mementoes—pictures, clothing, a piece of the victim's jewellery perhaps—tucked away in boxes, hidden beneath a false drawer bottom or closet wall—

"Damn it!" Claire exclaimed, bolting upright from the couch. *Why had she not thought of this before?!* She set her breakfast aside and ran up to her bedroom, opened the end closet and urgently began pulling out its contents. She tossed her clothes on top of the bed then ran downstairs to grab her tool box from the kitchen, returned to her bedroom and quickly began disassembling the custom shelving she'd installed, casting the pieces aside with the same disregard she'd shown her clothing.

There it was. About ten inches above the floor, embedded in the side wall the closet shared with the bathroom, was a large plastic plate that Claire had assumed was the access panel for the bathtub taps. She hadn't removed it before painting, and some paint had seeped into the space between the wall and the panel, but she determined that if she cut carefully around it she could remove it without significant damage. She took a sharp utility knife from her toolbox, freed the panel, then popped it out. She shone a small flashlight into the wall and found the shut off valves to the tub as expected, then her eye caught sight of something shiny further into the wall. She reached in but the object lay just at the tips of her fingers. "Damn," she muttered then bounded down the stairs again and into the kitchen where she began opening boxes until she found what she needed: barbecue tongs. She raced back upstairs and seconds later the tongs were clutching a large resealable plastic bag containing a bulging manila envelope. She debated whether to open it herself or call Dylan, and decided it would be silly to call him without knowing the contents, though as Dylan would later point out her decision was less a gesture of consideration and more an act of impatient curiosity. She opened the plastic bag, withdrew the envelope and spilled its contents onto the floor.

What greeted her eyes Claire was unprepared for. Scattered at her knees were dozens of Polaroid photographs that made Claire's stomach tighten involuntarily and her hand jerk up to quiet her revulsion. "Oh my God," she whispered through her fingers. She sat there for several minutes, transfixed by the horrific images, unable to look away despite the sharp contractions in her gut, the way one stops to view a car wreck despite feeling sick from the sight of blood on a windshield or pooled on the road. "Oh my God," she whispered again to herself. "That poor little girl."

TWENTY-SIX

A few moments later Claire finally shook herself free of the photographs and reached for the phone. Dylan's cellphone rang. He checked the call display, smiled and said, "Doolie, give me a minute. I have to take this."

"Oh, blimey," quipped Tom when he saw Dylan's grin, "please tell me she's not one of those call-you-every-hour type."

"Who's that?" asked Doolie, his reporter's antenna perking up.

"Nobody," Tom warned.

"What's up, gorgeous?" Dylan asked after he put sufficient distance between himself and Doolie.

"Dylan, you need to come right away," Claire replied. "They're awful."

"What's awful, Claire?" he asked, perturbed by the trembling in her voice. Tom caught the look on his partner's face and walked over.

"I found pictures, Dylan. Horrible pictures. In an envelope."

"We're on our way," Dylan said and motioned to Tom they were leaving. "Claire, don't do anything more, okay? Don't touch or move anything anymore than you already have. We'll be there in a few minutes. Promise me you won't touch anything."

"I promise."

Dylan hung up the phone. "Doolie," said Dylan, gesturing toward the newsletter in the reporter's hands, "get to work on that angle. And stay by the phone." Dylan opened up the car door and got in behind the wheel, Tom already beside him in the passenger seat.

"What's going on, Dyl?"

"I think we've got him, Tom. We've got the son of a bitch."

Twenty minutes later Claire, Dylan and Tom were gathered in her bedroom scrutinizing the photographs. They were of a fortyish man with a young girl, then the same figures but older, and then older still, spanning over several decades. Some of the pictures had dates written on the bottom; the earliest was marked November 1969. "Is that Armin Keller?" asked Claire.

"Yes," Dylan replied quietly.

The three fell again into silence, their eyes darkened by the photographs. The pictures were profoundly disturbing, even for the two men whose work brought them in daily contact with the shadow side of the human heart. Elisabeth's pubescent face, though faded in the earliest of the pictures, was clearly traumatized, her eyes imploring whomever was behind the camera to help her. Armin's face was buried in his daughter's hair, his fingers pressed into the mattress, his body obscuring hers save for a thin white leg splayed out and dangling over the edge of the bed. Other pictures were more graphic: fellatio, painful anal sex that twisted Elisabeth's face into a gross caricature of adolescent innocence. There were photos, dated May 1971, in which Elisabeth was clearly pregnant, her belly hanging low over the bed as she was raped from behind. Yet it wasn't the acts themselves that haunted Claire the most but rather the rapid transformation of Elisabeth's expression from pained to resigned to vacant. Her eyes no longer implored the camera or the person operating it, they no longer fixed themselves on a point on the ceiling, they simply stared into space. "It's as if her soul had abandoned her," Claire whispered.

"It did," Dylan whispered back.

"Who do you think took these awful pictures, Dylan? One of Armin's Nazi friends?"

"Maybe. Maybe not. There were three people living here and only two of them are in the pictures."

"That's sick," Tom chimed in. "What kind of a woman would let this happen to her daughter and then not only fail to stop it but photograph it?"

"I guess that depends on what he did to her, too." Dylan blew out a sigh. His earlier excitement at the news of photographic evidence had been tempered by the sickening realization that the pictures would nail Armin for rape and incest but they still wouldn't prove murder. "Fuck," Dylan swore, pinching the bridge of his nose. What was it going to take to get justice for Baby Jane? Especially now since they were off the case? His eyes zeroed in on Elisabeth's ghostly image. *If only you could talk, Elisabeth. If only you could talk.*

"Claire, honey, can you give us a moment, please?" Dylan said, breaking the silence.

Claire looked confused but the look on Dylan's face told her not to pry. She nodded and left the room, and when the soft thump of her feet against the stairs receded, Tom said in a low voice, "What are you thinking?"

"I'm thinking these belong to Sex Crimes, not Homicide."

"Who do you have in mind?"

"Farak and Bennett," Dylan replied as he dialled the squad. Tom laughed: Farak was an inspired choice: he was a huge man that scared the hell out of suspects but possessed a soft voice and gentle demeanour that soothed their prey; but it was not so much Farak's gentle giant ways that made Tom laugh but that the man was both black and Muslim, and for Armin to be arrested by him would be sweet justice indeed.

"Sex Crimes," a voice answered.

"It's Dylan Lewis from Homicide. Is Jamal Farak around?"

"Yeah. Hold on."

"Farak, here. What's up, Lewis?"

"I need you and a forensics team asap at 1834 Lakewood Road, off Commercial."

"What have you got?"

"Incest and rape of a minor."

"We're on our way."

The two men left the pictures where they lay and headed downstairs. "Claire," said Dylan when he found her waiting anxiously on the couch, "I've called Sex Crimes to take possession of the photos, interview you about the discovery and process the scene. They'll be here soon."

Claire looked perplexed. "Sex Crimes? I don't understand."

"The photos don't implicate Armin for murder," explained Tom, "they only indicate incest and rape. So we have to hand it off to Sex Crimes for now and then the cases will be connected later if appropriate."

Claire looked accusingly at the two men. "What aren't you telling me?"

"I'll be in the car writing our report," Tom said evasively then made a beeline for the door.

"What's going on, Dylan?" Claire asked as the door closed behind Tom.

Dylan looked skyward for assistance then confessed. "The brass found out about us. Ordered me to stop seeing you. I refused. They weren't very happy about it. It's no big deal. They'll get over it."

Claire shot up from the couch. "No big deal?! Dylan, I can't let you lose your job over me!"

"I haven't lost my job. I'm still here, aren't I?" he said, trying to make light of the situation.

"But what *exactly* did they say?" Claire demanded.

Dylan paused a moment with a mind to lying, then decided that would be disrespectful not to mention potentially costly if Claire later found out the truth. "If our relationship compromises a conviction, I'm finished on the squad," he answered matter-of-factly. "In the meantime, Tom and I are off the case."

His words knocked her back a step. Claire ran a hand through her hair and shook her head, distraught by the news. She stared at the floor, weighing things, then pronounced a verdict. "Then we have to end this."

"Not a chance, Claire," Dylan refused, shaking his head.

"But you love working Homicide," she implored. "You love being a cop. I can't let you jeopardize that. If you love somebody you don't ask them to sacrifice something they love for you. It's not right."

Dylan breached the distance between them and looked down at Claire with a sly twinkle in his eye. "So you love me, then?"

Claire's eyes flashed with surprise. She stepped away but found her back against the wall. "I didn't say that."

Dylan took a step forward. "Yes you did," he insisted with a self-satisfied smile.

"I, I meant it in the general sense, not sp-specifically," Claire stammered unconvincingly.

Dylan leaned in closer and put one arm on the wall behind Claire, enclosing her. "Okay then, coward, I'll say it. I love you. You're the one. Don't ask me how I know that because I couldn't articulate it even if I had the dictionary memorized. I just know. So there will be no more talk of quitting us. Are we clear?"

Claire nodded compliantly. Dylan pulled her to him and gave her a penetrating kiss that weakened her knees and filled her with anticipation. She kissed him urgently, hungry and oblivious to the sirens approaching. Dylan pulled back. "Company's coming. Do as you're told, don't go upstairs until Forensics are finished, and I'll be back later to finish this." He kissed her on the forehead then went outside to greet Farak and Bennett.

Claire watched through the window as the four detectives huddled together. A few minutes later Forensics knocked and she led them upstairs, then watched through the window again as Dylan and Tom left in their vehicle and the Sex Crimes detectives entered the house, their footsteps on the stairs.

∞

Dylan and Tom waited in the parking lot of Westview Elder Centre, the air impatient. "This was our arrest," Tom sulked. "Reassigned. What bullshit."

"At least we get to watch."

"That sounds sadly pornographic."

"Everything sounds pornographic to you. Maybe *you* should be working Sex Crimes. Or Vice."

Tom laughed. "Speaking of which, what do you think Doolie's doing over there with his hand in his lap?"

"Waiting for Farak and Bennett so he can get the money shot."

"He's such a wanker."

"They're all wankers, but today that wanker's our friend."

Dylan sat at attention when he saw the special transport van pull up, followed by the unmarked cruiser and the paramedics. "They're here." He signalled to Doolie, who returned the nod but stayed in his vehicle. Dylan and Tom alighted from their cruiser and walked over to the entrance.

Farak briefed the paramedics on the situation, then turned to Dylan and Tom. "Remember, we have an agreement."

The four officers marched into Westview liked they owned the place and headed straight for Armin Keller's room. As they passed the nurses' station Barbra looked up, first in shock then amusement when Tom flashed her a grin and a surreptitious thumbs up. She followed them to Keller's room where the detectives found Armin finishing his midmorning snack. He looked confused at first, not recognizing Farak and Bennett, but Armin's face went white when he saw Dylan and Tom and the paramedics follow into the room. "What the hell is this?" Armin demanded angrily.

"Armin Keller," declared Farak, "I'm arresting you for incest and aggravated sexual assault commencing in or around 1969 in the city of Vancouver. It is my duty to inform you that you have the right to retain and instruct counsel in private, without delay. You may call any lawyer you want. There is a 24-hour telephone service available which provides a legal aid duty lawyer who can give you legal advice in private. This advice is given without charge and the lawyer can explain the legal aid plan to you. If you wish to contact a legal aid duty lawyer, I can provide you with the telephone number. Do you understand?"

"Nonsense!" squeaked Armin. "I've done nothing wrong!"

"I'll take that as a yes. Do you want to call a lawyer?"

"Of course I do, you imbecile!"

"Fair enough. Armin Keller, you are not obliged to say anything but anything you do say may be given in evidence."

Bennett turned to the paramedics. "Okay, boys, check him out."

Armin simmered with contempt as the paramedics checked his vitals and ruled him fit for transport to lock-up. "Blood pressure's a bit high at the moment," the lead paramedic said with a hint of sarcasm, "but other than that he's fine. You'll need to take his meds with you, though."

"We keep them locked at the station," Barbra offered without waiting to be asked.

"Lead the way, luv," Tom chirped unprofessionally and had almost reached the door when Farak pulled him back with one hand. "Sorry."

Bennett walked Barbra back to the nurses' station where she unlocked the cabinet and took out one of the many red baskets that lined the shelves. "Should I just put them in a bag?" she asked, gesturing to the array of bottles.

"Please. And we'll need a copy of his schedule and dosages."

Barbra did as requested, and as she handed the bag and paperwork over she whispered with unmitigated spite, "I hope he dies in prison."

"You and me both."

A paramedic wheeled Armin out of his room and down the hall, then through the double entrance doors where Doolie was waiting to ambush Keller. Armin's expression when the camera turned on him and a microphone was shoved into his face was, Dylan thought to himself, priceless for the mixture of fear and contempt. "Armin Keller," Doolie shouted at the old man, "do you have anything to say to the charges against you?" Armin slumped down in his wheelchair and tried to shield his eyes with his one good hand, a particularly satisfying shot that would later make the cut. Farak and Bennett stepped between Keller and the camera on the pretext they were protecting Keller's privacy, even as they left sufficient space between them to allow the cameraman a close-up of Keller's stricken face.

Keller was loaded into the special transport van and the doors slammed shut behind him and locked. "Is he travelling first or cattle class?" the officer asked Farak.

"First," Dylan replied for Farak. "I'd like him to survive at least long enough to suffer the humiliation of a strip search."

"First it is then," the officer confirmed and set off slowly, sparing Armin the rough ride he was due. Bennett called ahead to notify the jail a special needs prisoner was en route, then she and Farak headed there to process Armin. Dylan and Tom jumped into their vehicle and sped off after their colleagues, who had promised them a front row seat at Armin's interview. As they drove off they witnessed Doolie interviewing Barbra, and through the open cruiser window she could be heard saying, "He spit at me. *Spit* at me. Says no Jew lady is allowed to touch him."

଼

Frau Müller watched from her living room window as the forensics team loaded up their van and left Claire's house. The plum cake and banana bread were cooling on the kitchen counter, and now that it seemed the coast was clear Frau Müller put the kettle on and called Claire. Claire knew immediately the invitation was a pretext to chat about the police that had just left, but she welcomed the visit anyway, if only to take her mind off those horrific photographs.

"Just a small piece, please," Claire requested as she sat down at Frau Müller's table. "I missed half my breakfast." Frau Müller took the hint and moments later a tuna sandwich and glass of apple juice was set before Claire.

"All this excitement's not good for you, Claire. You're getting too thin."

"I know. And it certainly isn't what I signed up for when I bought the house. Still, my suffering is miniscule compared to others. I guess I should count my blessings."

Frau Müller saw the dark behind Claire's eyes. "I saw the police here again. Did—"

"I can't tell you anything this time," Claire interjected. "Dylan would have my head."

"Hmmm, Dylan, huh?" Frau Müller lightly pried. "And which would he be, the Latino man or the detective?"

Claire laughed and accepted the bait. "The detective."

"Oh, I'm so glad. I saw the news the other night. I was worried you might be getting yourself into a spot of trouble. When I saw the police I was afraid they were here to arrest *you*."

"Heaven's no. It's Armin Keller that's being arrested."

Frau Müller gasped. "Oh, I knew it! He murdered that poor baby, didn't he?"

"I'm sure he did, but unfortunately there's insufficient evidence to prove it. He's been arrested for assaulting his daughter."

"*Sexually*?!" asked Frau Müller, clutching her chest. Claire didn't answer but her silence spoke volumes. Frau Müller sat back in her chair, her eyes downcast. "That poor, poor girl." Frau Müller wrung a dishtowel in her hands then absentmindedly swept the crumbs from the table onto a plate. "Ever since the baby was found I can't help but feel guilty. If only I'd been a nosier neighbour maybe someone would have intervened sooner."

As if that's possible, Claire thought, but what came out was, "I don't think you should blame yourself."

"But—" Frau Müller was interrupted by the doorbell. "Well, now, who could that be?" she said, rising. She disappeared into the front of the house and Claire heard a raised, excited male voice. Curious, Claire went to the front door to find a flustered Frau Müller on the front step with a microphone in her face and Chris Doolie's cameraman pushing his way forward.

"Please leave us alone," Claire demanded as she pulled Frau Müller back inside and closed the door. "I'm sorry," Claire apologized as the reporter banged on the door, "I forgot to warn you the police decided to talk to the media about the case."

"Oh," Frau Müller replied, straightening her hair in the hall mirror. "I don't mind if he asks questions. Just caught me by surprise, that's all. Do you think I need lipstick?"

Of course, because lipstick is just what the situation calls for. "You look fine," Claire assured her, "but I can't talk to them so I'll just make my way out the back. Thank you for lunch." Claire made a hasty departure as Frau Müller opened the door, smiled for the camera, then happily began recounting everything she knew about her former Nazi neighbours.

TWENTY-SEVEN

Claire snuck through the backyard and made her way down the alley. She thought at first just to hang around Commercial Drive until sufficient time had passed and that reporter was likely gone, but realized with regret she didn't have her purse with her, only her house keys. So instead Claire found herself headed for Maria's with the intention of killing two birds with one stone.

She found Maria in the yard minding her two older children as they splashed about a small blow-up swimming pool. "Claire!" Maria called out cheerfully when Claire opened the gate. "I'm so glad you're here." Maria rose to kiss Claire hello. "I've been so worried. Come, sit, I have lemonade." Maria disappeared inside the house to get another glass while Claire settled down in a lawn chair. Minutes later Maria was handing a tall, cold glass to Claire and plying her favour with spicy chicken pastries. "I'm so sorry about Rafael, Claire. I really had no idea."

"I know," Claire reassured Maria. "I'm not angry with you at all. But how are you taking the news?"

"I'm shocked, of course, but not surprised. Corruption is so common in Mexico that sometimes even good people don't think what they're doing is bad."

"And Carlos?"

"Carlos insists Rafael is innocent. I think Carlos can't accept his judgment was wrong. He's a very proud man. Rafael's arrest embarrasses him." She paused and looked anxiously over at her children. "I'm worried, Claire. What if the cartel wants Carlos to launder their money now that

Rafael has been arrested? They are powerful, dangerous men. It can be risky to say no. Maybe that's what happened to Rafael."

Claire placed a comforting hand on Maria's arm. "Perhaps." Truth be told Claire didn't think Rafael was a frightened man who had been coerced but an arrogant one who thought himself too smart to get caught. She recalled the brutality of his disbelief when she had refused to see him again, and shuddered.

"Are you cold?" asked Maria. "I can get you a shawl."

"No," Claire recovered quickly. "The lemonade just hit my spine, that's all." She then deftly changed the subject, commenting on how tall Maria's eldest was growing. The diversion worked: Maria forgot about Rafael as she waxed on at length about the children, about Juan's excellence in school and Bonita's role as flower girl for a friend's upcoming wedding. To Claire's surprise she discovered this time she didn't mind talk of children, a change in attitude she attributed to Dylan and his easy love, his unconditional acceptance and willingness to explore other parenting options. She thought of Carlos' words to Maria, about God wanting them to look outside their own hearts, and decided the same held true for her. It was a decision based more on expedience than real belief, an uncomfortable fact she acknowledged only inwardly and for which she felt a twinge of guilt. At some point she would have to accept her fate without strings attached, without hidden contrary thoughts and silent prayers. Anything less only invited a lifetime of disappointment and regret.

The women talked for a few hours more and then Claire, declining Maria's invitation to stay for dinner, made her way back home. As expected the reporter was gone now, having rushed back to his stations to edit a story for the evening's news. Baby Jane would likely lead, Claire thought, maybe even for a whole day or two before the public's attention deficit disorder kicked in and they looked to sate their appetite elsewhere. It appalled her that a murdered child could so easily be forgotten but at least, Claire thought selfishly next, the press wouldn't be knocking on her door much longer.

She turned her attention to the dinner she'd promised Dylan, opened the fridge in search of ideas, and came up empty. So she grabbed her purse and headed back out to Commercial Drive, intent on coming up with suitable meal ideas by the time she reached her favourite Italian grocery.

Dylan and Tom took their positions on the other side of the one-way glass, still grumbling about the consideration shown to Armin for no other reason than his age and failing health: he had been brought into the jail through a special entrance and his processing expedited, sparing him the discomfort of waiting with other prisoners in the pre-hold cell; and he was searched more gently than was warranted. Such luxuries no one deemed deserved but protocol demanded otherwise, and everyone was determined that Armin Keller would not slip through their fingers on a technicality.

He showed no emotion when Farak relayed the discovery of the photographs, and refused to be interviewed without counsel. The interview was terminated and Armin led away to a special cell where, under the watchful eye of the duty nurse, he could wait for whomever it was he called.

Dylan and Tom lumbered back to their desks to find Sergeant McTavish waiting for them, his arms folded across his broad chest. "Gentlemen, my office," he bristled.

Shit.

"Which part of 'this case has been reassigned' didn't you two understand?" snapped a surly McTavish when the door closed behind his officers.

"We only observed, sir," Dylan argued. "It was a Sex Crimes arrest."

"A Sex Crimes arrest related to *your* homicide, related to *your* contaminated complainant. Are you *trying* to work for the defence?"

"In all fairness, sir," Tom chimed in, "we couldn't help that photos were found in Claire Dawson's home. And we didn't know what she'd found until we got there, after which we made certain that we remained at arm's length."

"And of course you didn't think to ask in advance of attending, did you?" McTavish asked, glaring at Dylan.

"I—"

"Enough excuses!" McTavish barked. "Consider this your final warning. Stay away from this case or you're done. Now get out of my office, both of you."

"Sorry, Tom," Dylan said quietly as he and his partner shuffled back to their desks. "I never expected this to go quite so pear-shaped."

"No apology necessary, mate. I counselled you to go after the twelve."

"True. And I guess you can always return to the Motherland."

"Fuck that," Tom snorted. "There's always Australia."

ભ્

Benjamin Keller entered the police station and asked for Dylan and Tom. When the elevator doors opened, Keller rose to greet the detectives only to find himself surprised by the arrival of Rebecca. She was just starting shift after a workout in the department's gym, and her face was still flush and dewy from a shower. She looked beautiful, and for a moment Benjamin forgot why he was there. He called out, but when she looked over at the sound of her name her cheeks burned. She tucked her head down and tried to walk briskly by, but Benjamin was determined not to let her get away so easily. "Rebecca," he said again, jumping in between her and the door. "I'm so glad to see you."

"Why?" she replied angrily, and her anger caught Ben off guard.

"Because, well, because I just am."

"I know what they found. And you're here to do what now, defend your uncle? When you should be defending *her*. But then again, why doesn't that surprise me?" Her last words Rebecca practically spit at Ben, and he found himself paralyzed by regret, unable to stop her as she stomped off through the station doors.

Moments later Tom and Dylan alighted from the elevator and Benjamin quickly gathered himself back into form. "Detectives," Benjamin greeted them politely.

"What can we do for you, Ben?" asked Dylan.

"I understand you've arrested my uncle for incest and rape."

"Not us. Sex Crimes," Dylan said with a shake of his head.

"And don't tell me you're here to represent him," Tom added snidely.

Benjamin shot Tom a look of mild exasperation: Becky's reaction Ben understood, but this Tom was clearly just thick. "Detective, I have no idea how they do things on your side of the pond, but here that would be conflict of interest: I'm the legal guardian of the victim. Besides, the day I defend a pedophile is the day hell freezes over. Even I have a bottom line, gentleman." Benjamin paused, then softened his tone and added, "And you may be tickled to hear that my uncle is going to have some difficulties finding suitable counsel: I've made it clear to the community that if Armin is defended by anyone more experienced than an articling student, they're not welcome to ask me for future favours. No, I'm here in my capacity as Elisabeth's guardian. I understand you have evidence of the crimes against her."

Dylan nodded. "Photographs. They were hidden in the wall behind an access panel. A private album of sorts."

"I wish to see them."

Dylan shook his head. "No you don't, Ben. You really don't."

Benjamin understood. "I appreciate your concern, detective, but I'm preparing a civil action against my uncle on Elisabeth's behalf. I must insist."

Dylan shrugged. "Okay, but you need to talk to Jamal Farak or Gail Bennett up in Sex Crimes. They're in charge of the file."

"I'd prefer it were you," Benjamin replied, and the detectives saw in his eyes the shame behind the polished veneer.

Dylan glanced sideways at Tom. "Australia?"

Tom shrugged. "What the hell."

"Okay, Ben, but don't say we didn't warn you. Tom will escort you to an interview room; I'll be there shortly. I have to get permission from Farak then find out where the photos are, whether they've been logged into evidence already or still with Forensics."

Fifteen minutes later Dylan sat down across from Benjamin in the interview room and opened up an envelope containing the photographs, now individually wrapped in plastic and numbered. Dylan deliberately chose the earliest, most faded and benign of the images to show Benjamin, who studied it as if it were a riddle he couldn't solve, his hands shaking as he ran his forefinger down the leg that hung limply over the side of the bed. It was hard to contain his emotions, to contain the rage he could feel mixing with the bile that burned a hole in his stomach, to keep from breaking down. He imagined Armin would love to see that, would love to see the mighty Benjamin Keller weeping like a girl, reduced, exposed, inconsolable. He imagined Armin would rape him too if the old man could still get it up.

"And the others."

Dylan and Tom cast a wary glance at each other. "Are you sure about this, mate?" asked Tom. "They're not pretty."

Benjamin gestured with his hand: give them to me. Dylan shrugged in defeat and emptied the envelope onto the table, the horrific images fanned out like a deck of deviant playing cards. Ben took them all in, picking up one and then the other, his back rigid, his face hard. The only sign of the turmoil within was the bobbing of his Adam's apple as he fought the dryness that plagued his throat. "I'll need copies," he said dispassionately, his voice hoarse.

"Once you've filed the writ against Armin, file a motion and we'll comply," replied Dylan. "I'm sure the department will assist in any way it can."

"Thank you," Ben whispered.

"I'll see you out," offered Tom, and led a subdued Ben out of the interview room. Dylan put the photographs back in the envelope without looking at them again. He'd had enough for one day.

He made his way back to Forensics to return the photographs. The package weighed barely a few ounces yet Dylan felt as if he were carrying a load of bricks. Armin Keller was in jail but the case was still far from over. There was still the murder to prove, and there was still a middle-aged woman whose soul was imprisoned. It was unlikely Elisabeth would even understand her father had been arrested and charged for his crimes against her, and unlikelier still it would make a difference. Elisabeth didn't need a conviction, she needed a miracle, and Dylan wasn't in the business of miracles. Far from it, he thought as he handed his heavy cargo back over to Ident.

Dylan slowly made his way back to the squad room, painfully aware of the limitations of his office and the system he had chosen to be a part of. What he wasn't aware of was that one hour earlier Rafael Morales had made bail and was sulking in his luxury condo, determined not to return to prison.

CR

Jackal crawled down the embankment toward Coyote, curled up in a ball and licking his wounds. The sight disgusted Jackal: what had possessed him to put any faith in such a contemptible creature? "Coyote," Jackal called out, "will you lie down and sulk like a dog? There is one who deserves your wrath yet you allow her to remain oblivious to her crimes against you."

Coyote looked up at Jackal. His emaciation was starting to show, his flesh so thin Coyote could count the old animal's ribs. "You are dying, my friend. Soon *you* will lie down like a dog. Why should I give credence to your counsel?"

"Because if you don't you are staring at your future. You, the son of esteemed hunters, sires of greatness and privilege, will you die contrary to your clan or live up to its dignity? Do you not possess the fight of your father? Was he foolish to invest his hope in such a son?"

Coyote sprang to his feet, the fire of righteous indignation buring in his eyes. Jackal watched until the animal's flanks disappeared into the brush, then smiled to himself and returned to his den in anticipation of a feast.

CB

Claire lifted her heavy grocery bags onto the kitchen counter and began emptying them. She had decided upon baked sole fillets with crusty sautéed sage butter and toasted almond dressing, a roasted vegetable medley, and then fresh local raspberries on ice cream for dessert. With the night promising to be warm and fragrant she decide upon dinner on the patio, so she unpacked a vintage oil lamp and set it aside for the moment on the pine table she'd moved from the living room to the kitchen.

She glanced up at the clock. It was almost five, time for the early news. She wanted to see what was said about Baby Jane, and since Dylan wouldn't be over until after six Claire could watch now and start the meal afterwards. She finished putting the food away then moved into the living room and turned on the television.

The story led as expected. There was a shot of Claire's house, followed by the arrest of Armin Keller on charges of sexual assault, his body contorted as he tried to shield his face from the camera's incriminating eye. Then there was a lengthy sound bite from Frau Müller and speculation on a possible connection between Armin's alleged crimes and his Nazi affiliations, followed by an evasive if diplomatic quote from Constable Brown on behalf of the police department. But what Claire didn't expect was Doolie's closing remarks: "We learned as well that Armin Keller is also the key suspect in the death of an infant forty years ago whose remains were found in his former home; and the home's new owner, Claire Dawson, is in a relationship with the lead detective on the infant homicide, but whether the relationship led to the discovery of the remains or arose from them is uncertain. It's also uncertain whether this will adversely affect the case against the accused. This after an accusation of witness tampering made against Vancouver Police in the Conford affair last April resulted in that case being thrown out of court. The department has thus far refused to comment on the relationship, stating only that they do not discuss the private lives of their officers. This is Chris Doolie, CKRW, Vancouver."

Claire slunk down on the couch. "Oh, God," she moaned, "what was I thinking saying anything to Frau Müller? Dylan's going to kill me."

Claire wasn't the only one troubled by the news. Rafael was also watching the report, his fifth shot of whisky dulling his senses but not his distress. He had just called his father, expecting support and money for a lawyer, but was met instead with a cascade of expletive-laden castigations for shaming the family. The news of Rafael's arrest had aired on Mexican television, and the Morales name was now sullied and linked inexorably with the Baja Cartel. His father was being accused of using his grocery chain as a means of laundering money, and the lack of any evidence to support this wasn't stopping the tax department or the Agencia Federal de Investigación from descending upon him like a hurricane. "Look what you've done to this family?" his father had screamed in rapid Spanish. "We cannot show our faces in public. You have destroyed everything I built. Did you think of anyone but yourself when you took their money, you stupid fuck? You lie down with pigs, you wake up in shit! Our name is now shit! *You* are shit!" Rafael had tried to explain but his father wouldn't listen, instead throwing the phone onto the floor and hollering at the walls. There was a scraping sound as Rafael's mother picked the phone up off the floor, but all she managed to say through her stream of tears was, "I have no son. My son is dead to me," then put the phone down in its cradle.

And now this! Claire Dawson was fucking a detective! What role had she played in the arrest? Had she been wearing a wire on their dates? Rafael had been so careful not to reveal anything of use, had deliberately kept her preoccupied with lavish compliments and perfectly timed caresses. But then he remembered the black Crown Victoria parked down the street when they had left Pierre's and Claire's startled look of recognition. "*Puta!*" he spit as he bolted from the couch. He grabbed a thousand-dollar lamp off an end table and smashed it against the wall. "Fucking *puta!*" he screamed again as he grabbed a heavy statue and used it to smash his antique Mexican sofa table into a heap of splintered painted wood. "Fucking *puta*, fucking bitch," he yelled over and over and over again as he trashed the room piece by piece by expensive piece.

The room in shambles, his fury spent, Rafael fell back on the couch and took another shot of whiskey. Then, with quiet, concrete resolve, Rafael picked up the gun lying on the coffee table and loaded it.

TWENTY-EIGHT

No one saw Rafael Morales park his car in an alley a block from Claire's house and make his way to her backyard. He slipped in between the cedars that lined the rear of the property then ducked behind a giant rhododendron. From there he could see Claire at the stove, her back to the window. Rafael glanced over at each neighbour's house and saw no sign of anyone watching. Confident he could move, he stepped out from behind the bush and walked briskly along the fence then onto Claire's porch and the invitation that was the open patio door.

It took her only a second to register his presence but that was more time than Rafael needed to step inside and raise his gun. Claire froze and opened her mouth to scream but nothing came out but a breathless "Rafael!" He closed the patio door and locked it, then took a menacing step toward Claire. "Bitch!" he sneered at her. "You set up me!"

"No, Rafael, no," Claire implored, reaching out the palm of her hand in a gesture intended to calm him. "I didn't. I didn't know anything about the police watching you, I swear. Please put down the gun. I know you don't want to hurt anybody."

"You know nothing!" he yelled at her, waving the gun erratically, his words slurred. "You think you so smart. Your cop boyfriend, he tell you spy on me? He tell you trick me?"

"No, Rafael, I swear. Please."

"You ruined my family! My father—" Rafael chocked on the word, unable to finish. His head was pounding fiercely, his father's words ricocheting around Rafael's brain: *Our name is shit! You are shit!*

"Rafael, please put down the gun. We can talk."

"No talk, *puta!*" he ordered her with a menacing rise of his gun. "I no criminal! I not go to jail!" He raised his chin and looked down his nose at Claire. "I am Rafael Morales, son of Antonio Morales, son of Ernesto Morales. My family is proud. My family has honour. And you, *puta*, you spit on our honour."

"Rafael—"

"Down!" he ordered, pointing with the gun to the floor in front of the stove. "On your knees, *puta!*"

"Rafael—"

"Get on knees you belong!"

Reclaim your power.

"No!" Claire growled defiantly as she grabbed the hot fry pan off the stove and swung it at Rafael. She hit him square across his jaw; the gun flew from his hand and slid across the linoleum, and Rafael fell back into the pine table, knocking the oil lamp onto the floor. The antique glass shattered, spraying kerosene across the linoleum. Rafael recovered his footing and came hard at her; Claire swung the pan at his head again but this time he was ready for it, ducking the blow and landing a heavy punch into her solar plexus. She felt a crushing pain in her chest as a rib fractured and punctured her right lung. She collapsed against the fridge then slid down to the floor, fighting to stay conscious as she fell.

Becky Wilson sat in her cruiser in front of Claire's house, oblivious to what was going on inside. Her head hurt from the public revelation of Dylan and Claire's involvement, and the loser Rebecca had picked up at the Cop Shop was sending her annoying text messages, asking for more. She ignored the messages: she didn't want him. The one she wanted would be here tonight, would be with *her*, the perfect one, the one who wasn't damaged goods. All of Becky's hopes had been lost to that woman, had evaporated when Becky first saw Dylan smile at Claire Dawson despite the dire circumstances and the cloak of dust.

When they found her, Becky wondered as she fingered the service revolver cradled in her lap, would he understand? Would he know the location of her death was no accident. Would he miss her? Would he realise what he'd lost and blame himself? Would he regret not having loved her when he'd had the chance? She imagined him on top of Claire, his dark chest pressed against her milk white breasts, her legs wrapped around his buttocks ... The image cut through Becky like a knife, the blade slicing

246

through her heart so swiftly she felt only the excruciating aftershock. She clenched her jaw against the unbearable pain. She had to stop it. She curled her hand around the grip of the gun, lifted it to her temple ...

Claire pushed through the pain and lunged at Rafael, pulling him to the ground. They struggled in the mess of glass and kerosene, the pungent liquid soaking into their clothes and the small cuts inflicted by the glass. Claire's hand fell upon a large shard and she slashed Rafael deep across his cheek. He grabbed his face and fell back, stunned, but then the sight of his blood on his hands infuriated him and he flew into an even greater rage. He leapt to his feet and came after her again, but in that second that Rafael lost his dominance Claire scrambled toward the wall, grabbed the gun and fired.

The sound of a gunshot reverberated through the air. Becky startled, her gun falling onto the center console with a clang before sliding to the floor on the passenger side. She looked toward Claire's house, then heard the second shot. Becky went into automatic pilot. She radioed for assistance then grabbed her gun and raced toward the house.

The bullets stopped Rafael cold. He looked down, dazed, at the bullet holes in his chest and abdomen, then his eyes glazed over and he collapsed against the stove. His kerosene soaked sleeve fell into the open flame and ignited but he didn't feel the searing of his flesh, falling dead in a blazing heap on the floor.

Claire screamed as the room erupted in fire. She scrambled into the dining room, away from the flames, terrified of her own kerosene permeated clothing. The fire spread in the blink of an eye, fuelled first by the accelerant and then by the linseed oil and cork dust of the linoleum floors, and within seconds the thick smoke forced Claire down to the floor for air.

Miles away on the other side of Burrard Inlet, Ta'ah was jolted awake from her peaceful nap on the porch. She closed her eyes again and saw Coyote dead on the forest floor and Claire lying near him, struggling to breathe as flames and dark, heavy smoke billowed around her. Ta'ah rose from her chair as quickly as her old bones would allow her and called out to the two adolescent boys playing one-on-one behind the house. "John Joseph, fetch your grandfather! Tell him to bring his drum! And tell him to call the others!" John Joseph heard the alarm in Ta'ah's voice and ran off toward his grandfather's house. Then turning to her great-grandson Ta'ah said, "Jeremiah, come, you must drum for me."

The teenager's eyes bulged with apprehension. "But Ta'ah, I've just started drumming. I'm not ready. Please, wait for the elders."

"There's no time! The Creator decides when a warrior is ready and you are being called." Ta'ah entered the house, Jeremiah in step behind her, compliant if still apprehensive. "Bring me the phone," she beckoned, gesturing to the cordless phone across the kitchen. Jeremiah did as he was told, fidgeting quietly as Ta'ah called Dylan.

Dylan's cellphone rang. He looked up from his computer where he was typing in his report and checked the call display. It was Ta'ah. Odd, she rarely called him at work. He answered, perplexed. "Ta'ah?"

"Dylan," Ta'ah urged. "Go to Claire. She's in danger. Coyote is dead."

"Ta'ah, what are you talking about? Morales is in jail," Dylan answered as he motioned for Tom to call the jail. Tom mouthed "I'm on it" and grabbed his desk phone.

"Dylan, just go!"

"Ta'ah, what's this about?"

"There's no time. Just go!"

"Okay, okay, I'm going." He rose from his chair just as Tom hung up the phone.

"Morales made bail two hours ago," he said, also rising.

"Damn it!" Dylan cursed as he reached for the keys to their squad car. Tom grabbed a radio and pressed the earpiece into his ear as the two raced out of the squad room and down to their car.

They were just approaching their cruiser when over the radio Tom heard the chatter. "Dylan! Shots fired! 1834 Lakewood." Tom saw Dylan's knees buckle. "I'll drive."

Officer Wilson crept up the front steps of the house, her weapon drawn. She peered in through the front window and saw fire in the back of the house. She tried the door but it was locked so she went around back, creeping along the edge of the house. She checked the back door: locked. She moved up onto the deck, peered in through the patio window and saw a body on the floor, engulfed in flames. Wilson holstered her gun, grabbed a patio chair and smashed it through the window, but the sudden influx of air ignited the fire, the explosion so violent it threw Wilson back toward the patio edge. Her ankle twisted and she lost her footing, falling down the short flight of stairs before landing hard against the concrete walkway, her head cracking against a large landscaping stone.

Claire screamed as a ball of fire exploded in the kitchen. The fire gathered speed, filling the house with a thick black smoke that coated

Claire's lungs and stung her face. "Dylan!" she screamed, her voice hoarse from the heat. "Somebody! Help me!" Claire began to cough, a dry rasp that felt like sandpaper against her throat and the delicate tissue of her esophagus. She cried and coughed and heaved in the smoke until at last she fell unconscious, the fight in her gone.

Ta'ah took her drum from its place in the closet and handed it to Jeremiah. She took out her medicine bag and, moving over to sit on the living room couch, took out a jar and purified herself with its contents. As Ta'ah whispered a powerful prayer she rubbed the medicine onto her forehead and, reaching beneath her cardigan, over her heart. Then she nodded to Jeremiah. "Begin."

Jeremiah began to drum, nervously at first, the rhythm unsteady, but with each beat his confidence grew until the sound of the drum filled the room and sent Ta'ah deep within herself. She entered the spirit world and found Coyote dead as she had seen, and Claire unconscious as the forest burned around her. In the near distance Ta'ah saw Jackal emerge from his den, his eyes flashing with fear, the dry brush around him catching fire from embers carried by the wind. He reached inside his den and dragged out his captive, a young girl Ta'ah guessed to be about thirteen years old. She had chestnut hair and vacant eyes, and when she saw the fire she didn't run as one would expect but instead crouched on the ground beside Jackal, watching dispassionately as the flames descended upon them. Jackal let out a fierce howl and nipped at the girl to run but she didn't move. Her eyes remained fixed on a point behind Jackal, and before he could turn to see what she was looking at, an old cedar tree, weakened by the flames, came crashing down onto Jackal, pinning him against the rocks and singeing his fur. He yelped in pain and called out to the girl to help him but it sounded more an order than a plea, his arrogance so pervasive he assumed she would instinctively obey. The girl watched a moment as Jackal writhed beneath the weight of the burning tree, stinging from the flames as they licked along the trunk, then simply turned her back on him and walked away, headed for the safety of the river below.

In his cell at the remand centre, Armin Keller began convulsing and gasping for air. The duty nurse sprung to her feet and hit the alarm. She restrained Armin so he wouldn't fall out of his wheelchair onto the floor, then called out to the officer who arrived to assist her. "Help me get him onto the floor! And hand me that pillow!"

"What the hell's happening?!"

"He's stroking. Call the paramedics."

Jacob Joseph arrived at Ta'ah's, followed shortly by John George and Pete Williams. As each man entered the living room he said nothing, simply put the beater to his drum and fell into rhythm beside Jeremiah. The drums' heavy, powerful sound soon filled the whole house and could be heard all the way down the street. Members of the reserve began to gather in the yard, curious to know what emergency had called the drummers to Ta'ah's side, and some of the women and elders began to pray that whatever it was it might end satisfactorily.

Ta'ah summoned the wind spirits for help. A strong current blew in from behind her, pushing the flames and smoke away from her and Claire. Ta'ah struggled to pull Claire to safety but the dead weight of the younger woman's body was too heavy. Ta'ah called out for her guardians but the roar of the fire drowned out her voice. She saw Bear trying to push through to reach them but in the next moment Bear disappeared behind a wall of flame and Ta'ah feared Bear had perished.

Dylan and Tom arrived at Claire's to find the house engulfed in flames. Two patrol units had already arrived but were waiting for the fire department and tending only to Wilson, semi-conscious and bleeding from her head. Her colleagues had pulled her to safety at the back of the yard and were awaiting the paramedics.

"Is anyone inside?" Dylan yelled above the roar.

"Two," one officer confirmed. "But there's nothing we can do." In the distance sirens could be heard approaching but Dylan was deaf to everything but the screaming in his own head. He fought off Tom's efforts to hold him back and raced onto the patio, disappearing through the broken glass and into the flames. He saw Claire lying lifeless on the dining room floor, a wall of flame between them.

Dylan moved deeper into the fire, desperately searching about for a path to Claire. The heat was unbearable, the room impassable, the smoke overpowering. But then Dylan felt a spray of water hit his back and he turned to see Tom with the garden hose, spraying a path back to the patio door and gesturing urgently for Dylan to get out. Dylan raced back to the door but, instead of abandoning Claire, he grabbed the hose from Tom's hands and pulled it inside the house. Dylan could hear Tom yelling at him but it was as if through a fog; the only sound that was real to Dylan was the hiss of steam as he beat a path to Claire. He picked her up in his arms and ran for their lives.

Ta'ah's grasp weakened and she fell back on her bottom with a thud. She tried to get up but her hip hurt fiercely. And then she heard it: the cry of Eagle as he emerged from beyond the burning forest, his mighty wings beating rapidly as he swept down from the sky and grabbed Claire in his talons. "To the river, Ta'ah!" he called out as he lifted Claire's limp body into the air and raced to the water below.

Dylan carried Claire to the safety of the back lawn as the fire trucks pulled up behind the house and firefighters scrambled to contain the inferno. A firefighter grabbed Claire as Dylan collapsed onto the grass, his lungs filled with acrid smoke. Two firefighters tended to Claire, calling over the radio for a second ambulance as they began performing CPR, while another pulled an oxygen mask over Dylan's face. He heaved in the pure air, his eyes unfocused yet never leaving Claire as he prayed for any sign of life.

Ta'ah kept her eyes on Eagle as she limped down and into the river. Eagle set Claire down in the water and Ta'ah rolled Claire onto her back, keeping her afloat by pulling her arms back and linking her own arm through Claire's. With her free hand Ta'ah washed water over Claire's face and tried to coax her back to consciousness. Ta'ah looked up at Eagle, anxiously racing back and forth in the red sky, the span of his wings casting a moving shadow across the women below. And then, from the other side of the river, came the unmistakable sound of dolphins singing.

Ta'ah looked over and saw three Pacific white-sided dolphins poking their heads above the current and singing to Claire, beckoning her with their dulcet tones. They sang of love and future promises, of adventures that awaited and discoveries to be made. Their voices never wavered, each note as clear and bright as the last. The dolphins sang and sang and sang until, finally, Claire stirred and opened her eyes.

She woke up wheezing into her oxygen mask. The firefighters stopped CPR and rolled Claire onto her side to clear her airways as Dylan burst into tears. He pulled off his oxygen mask and crawled to her side. He held her in his arms, stroking her face while she slowly regained consciousness. When her eyes finally focused again Claire saw Dylan, his tears juxtaposed against a smile that spread as wide as his shoulders. "I heard the dolphins singing," she whispered.

Dylan nodded his understanding. "I know, my love. I know." He kissed her several times again before reluctantly deferring to the paramedics who stepped in to take Claire to hospital.

Ta'ah collapsed against the back of the sofa and opened her eyes. The drummers slowly let their drums fall silent and waited for Ta'ah to speak. "Jackal is trapped," she reported after taking a moment to reorientate herself in this world. "His captive is free. Claire is alive. Scared and hurt, but otherwise alright." Murmurs of praise for the Great Spirit rippled through the room. Ta'ah thanked her drummers, paying special attention to Jeremiah who beamed with pride at the recognition and the encouraging pats on the back from the elders. Ta'ah then laid down on the couch to rest, her mind and body weakened by the ordeal, as the men made their way out of the house and back to their own homes. Those gathered on the lawn followed at a respectful distance, and within the hour news of Ta'ah's battle with the demon was on its way to becoming legend.

TWENTY-NINE

Dylan sat beside Claire's hospital bed stroking her arm while she slept. Upon arriving at hospital Tom had insisted Dylan let the doctors check him out too, and after a short argument Dylan had agreed to a chest X-ray and some more oxygen treatment; but as soon as he was given a clean bill of health he saddled Tom with the task of documenting the day's events and retired to Claire's side. A chest tube had been inserted to drain the air from her pleural cavity, her fractured rib was taped, the poison-inflamed cuts to her back and arms from the broken oil lamp had been cleaned and bandaged, and a nose tube carried a carefully monitored oxygen mix to her damaged lungs. She was lucky to be alive.

Claire stirred as the sedative began to wear off. Dylan smiled as she opened her eyes to find him there. Satisfied that he was near, she closed her eyes again and drifted in and out of sleep for another hour or so before finally waking up. "Where am I?" she asked groggily, her voice still hoarse from the smoke.

"You're in hospital. But don't worry, you're going to be okay."

Claire became aware of a terrible pain in her chest. "Are you sure?" she whispered.

"I'm sure."

She looked over and saw his reddened face. "What happened to your face?"

"Heat burn. It'll be okay," he shrugged. "No worse than a sunburn."

"The fire," she murmured as memories of her ordeal began to seep back into her consciousness. "But how?"

253

"I went in for you," Dylan said. "They said you were dead but I didn't believe it." His voice was short, angry, but she knew he wasn't angry so much as frightened, and she smiled despite the pain.

"You saved my life?"

"Me and a few others," he answered modestly. "It was a group effort."

"Thank you."

"Anytime."

"And the house?"

"It's gone, Claire. I'm sorry."

"I'm not."

They both looked over at the sound of a knock at the door. It was Tom. "Hey, buddy," Dylan said.

Tom approached and gave Claire a peck on the cheek. "Claire, luv, glad you're alright."

"Do I look as bad as I feel?"

"Worse," Tom quipped. "But Dylan's an ugly mutt so he'll still be happy to have you."

"Good thing you're not a doctor, Farrow," Dylan quipped back. "Your bedside manner alone would kill your patients."

Tom chuckled then turned serious. "Listen, Claire, I have to ask you something. Rafael Morales' car was found a block from your place and the charred remains of a man were found in the debris. Is it him?"

Claire nodded, her face twisting in pain. "It's okay, Claire," Tom said gently, "you don't have to talk about it. That's all we need to know for now. When you're up to it we can talk again, okay?" Claire nodded and her face slowly relaxed again. "Well, um, I'll leave you two alone. But, hey, when you get out of here what say we all get together at my place for a potluck and a pint. You can meet my better half. Though don't tell her I called her that or she'll use it against me."

"I'd like that."

"Okay, well, I should go. There's a queue outside." He turned to leave. "Oh," he stopped and spun back around on one foot, "almost forgot. You two might be pleased to know there won't be any trial against Armin Keller so you can pretty much carry on as you like."

Dylan's head shot up. "What the hell are you talking about?"

"Jail called. Keller had a massive stroke. Brain was oxygen deprived for several minutes. Major damage. He's in ICU in a vegetative state. Lights on"—Tom knocked on the door—"nobody home." And with that he left the room. "All yours," he was heard saying to someone in the hallway.

Moments later Ta'ah shuffled in on Stan's arm. He helped her to the bedside then stepped around and tightly embraced his nephew. Ta'ah took Claire's hand in her own and squeezed it. "You'll be fine, my child," said Ta'ah, beaming down at Claire. "You're a fighter."

"You were there," Claire whispered.

"What do you remember?"

"It was hot, so hot I could feel my skin burning from the heat. Everything went black. But then suddenly I felt a cool wind pushing the heat away. It was the strangest thing. Then I was flying, and then water. Cool water. I wanted to fall beneath the current and just drift away but something was holding me up. And then I heard dolphins singing, like on the tape I had when I was a kid. They coaxed me back. I opened my eyes and saw you, and then I saw Dylan." Claire squeezed Ta'ah's hand and began to cry. "Thank you. Thank you for coming to get me."

Ta'ah stroked Claire's face and patted her head. "Rest now, daughter. Tomorrow I will bring medicine for your wounds." She kissed Claire on the forehead, leaned over to kiss her grandson's cheek, then took the arm Stan offered her and shuffled out of the room.

A nurse came in and gave Claire another shot of morphine. As Claire slowly drifted off to sleep she whispered, "Dylan, there's something I need to tell you. This morning, when you asked me, I lied. I do love you."

Dylan kissed her as she closed her eyes. "I know." He settled back down in the chair, put his head on Claire's arm, and drifted off to sleep himself.

CR

Benjamin Keller walked Elisabeth to their favourite bench in the garden at Bellevue, *Pride and Prejudice* in his left hand. It was taking every ounce of self-control he had to appear normal, flashbacks of the photographs of her and Armin a constant agitation. Benjamin was terrified he might break down in front of Izzy and confuse or upset her with his anger, so he pressed his fingers into the book and fought to keep his voice steady.

He sat her down and read for an hour, and as he led her back toward the common room he asked, "Are you enjoying our book, Izzy? Or would you prefer a different one?"

"This one," she whispered.

Ben stopped dead in his tracks. "Izzy?"

Elisabeth kept her head down but lifted her eyes up to Ben's. "I like this one," she repeated.

Benjamin thought he was going to faint. "Izzy, don't move. I'm going to get someone, okay? Don't move." He ran into the common room and yelled over to the nurses' station, "Vicky, call Dr. Mitchell! It's Izzy! She's talking!" Ben ran back to Elisabeth's side, his heart singing. Elisabeth just stood there as Ben hugged her over and over again, unaware of the importance of her few words and perplexed by his excitement.

An hour later, after Elisabeth had been taken to her room to be bathed in preparation for bed, a still jubilant Benjamin was discussing her miraculous recovery with Dr. Mitchell, who upon receiving the call had left his dinner to return to the hospital. "This is indeed a significant event, Ben, but slowly, slowly. There's still a lot of work to do."

"I want to take her home with me," Ben pronounced from his seat across from Mitchell's desk. "I'll hire private care and she can receive treatment from you on an outpatient basis."

Mitchell raised his palms at Ben: *Slow down.* "Small steps, Ben. Small steps, okay? First we see if this change is permanent, then we see how she responds to treatment, and from there we can discuss her leaving the hospital." He rose from his desk and walked around to pat Ben's shoulder. "I know this is very exciting for you. It is for me, too. But let's give her time to adjust to this change before we subject her to anything as radical as a new environment. We don't want to shock her back into her former state."

Ben nodded reluctantly. "You're right. You're right. Small steps." He rose to leave. "I just never thought I would see this day. I feel like I did the day my kids were born."

Ben left the hospital and pulled out his cellphone. He wanted to celebrate with someone and he knew exactly whom.

Becky Wilson answered her phone with a curt "What do you want, Ben?"

"Come for a drink with me?"

"Piss off," she said.

"Don't hang"—he said as she cut him off—"up. Damn." He typed out a text message and tried that next: "PLS. I need 2 C U. 911."

A moment later she texted him back. "OK. Solarno's. Robson. 20 min."

She was waiting at the bar, already tucked into a gin and tonic despite the stitches in her head and a warning not to mix her painkillers with alcohol. "This better be good," she said without looking at him.

"It is. Elisabeth talked tonight for the first time in years."

"I'm happy for you, Ben," Rebecca said flatly, then felt like a bitch. "Sorry, that was nasty," she added, staring into her drink.

"Rebecca," Ben said, the regret in his voice surprisingly sincere. "I'm sorry. I was a prick. You trusted me. You told me about your dad and instead of helping you heal I threw salt in the wounds. I didn't understand and I didn't want to. I think it's because I always suspected my uncle and I couldn't face it. I couldn't face knowing I let Izzy down. Every time I looked at you I saw my failure. I saw her pain and her suffering in your eyes and I couldn't bear it. Please forgive me."

The ice in her glass tinkled erratically as Becky raised her drink to her lips and downed the last of it. She motioned for the bartender to bring her another but Ben countermanded the request with a wave of his hand. "You don't need another drink, Rebecca. What you need is a nice dinner and good company. And if you'll let me, I'm offering both." He held out his hand to her. She looked at his hand then his face, unsure of his motives. "No hidden agenda, I swear. Just dinner and ... and a second chance maybe?"

"Really?"

He nodded. "You're a good woman, Rebecca. Better than I deserve. Recent events, well let's just say they've been illuminating. And humbling."

"You?" she laughed incredulously. "Humbled?"

"Yeah me," he grinned back. "Now, are you coming to dinner?"

Becky considered his offer for a moment, weighing it against another gin and tonic, then decided to take a chance. She gave him her hand and let him lead her out of the bar. "Where to?" he asked.

"Doesn't matter," Rebecca replied, "just as long as it's forward."

Ben squeezed her hand and leaned down to kiss her. She pulled him to her and kissed him back, a familiar desire stirring again between them. "It'll be different this time, I promise," he whispered, then took Rebecca's hand again and walked her back into his life.

CR

Three days later, after her lung had re-inflated and her blood oxygen levels were deemed sufficient, Claire was released from hospital. Dylan had been given the day off to tend to her, arriving with cotton drawstring pants and a zippered hoodie he'd rushed out that morning to buy her. "I wasn't sure what your size is," he said awkwardly, "so I thought something loose would be the safest bet."

"Thank you. It's perfect. I guess I have a lot of shopping ahead of me, huh?"

"Can't imagine a woman would find that tortuous."

Claire laughed then winced and grabbed her side. "Ow! Damn it. No making me laugh for the next six weeks."

"Sorry."

He took the hoodie from her hands and helped her dress. "Listen, Claire, I've been thinking. While the insurance company is building you a new house you're going to need a place to live. I'd like you to move in with me."

"Under one condition," she agreed, smiling, "when the house is finished you have to move in with *me*."

"Okay," Dylan smiled back, "but *only* if you agree to build a basement 'cause otherwise there won't be anywhere to banish my comfy couch and big screen TV. And I'm afraid we three are a package deal."

"Deal."

"Well, if you'll agree to *that* then I suppose we'll also need to start discussing a more permanent arrangement."

"Is that a proposal?" Claire asked, unsure.

"Well, sort of. I guess. Yes."

"That is the *lamest* proposal I've ever heard."

"Yes, I think it was," Dylan laughed. "Okay, then while you're getting better I'll try to think up something more romantic, and you'll just have to agree to appear surprised."

"I'll do my best."

"By the way," Dylan said as they left the room and headed down the hallway, "I have some good news. Benjamin Keller called me this morning. Elisabeth has come out of her catatonic state."

Claire gasped with amazement. "She's talking?"

"Only a little. But it's a start."

Moments later they were headed home. "Can we stop by the house?" Claire asked as Dylan manoeuvred his jeep out of the parking lot and onto the road.

"Are you sure?"

"It's just a house, Dylan. I want to see if any of my papers can be salvaged. I don't even have a driver's license on me."

He drove her home as requested. When they pulled up to the curb Frau Müller came rushing out, her heavy bosom bobbing to and fro as she sprinted across the lawn. "Claire, oh Claire!" Frau Müller exclaimed. "I've been so worried. I didn't hear what happened until I arrived home that evening. It was Agnes' turn to host canasta."

Claire looked over at the scorched side of Frau Müller's house and frowned. "Your house, it's been damaged. I'm so sorry."

"Pah," Frau Müller said, waving away Claire's concern. "It's just cosmetic. The adjuster has already been and gone. Some new siding and paint and it'll be as good as new again. I was thinking of changing the colour anyway."

The three walked around Claire's house, surveying the destruction. The outer walls were still standing but charred trusses were the only evidence left that a roof had once existed. Several of the new vinyl window frames had melted, the glass blackened and shattered. Claire stepped under the police tape that hung limply around the smoke and water damaged patio, then walked through the doorframe, Dylan behind her, while Frau Müller waited anxiously in the yard, afraid someone might be hurt by falling wreckage.

Claire stepped over the pile of debris that had fallen through the ceiling from her office, the floor above partially collapsed, and began to sift through the wreckage. It was pointless: what hadn't burned had been destroyed by water. They moved into what remained of the living room, all Claire's efforts having been reduced to nothing. "Too bad he didn't burn the place down *before* I did all this work," she said ruefully. "Inconsiderate bastard." Claire sighed and returned to the charred remains of what had earlier been destined to become her fabulous dining room, and stared at the closet where Baby Jane had been found. The walls of the room were still standing, the faded wallpaper scorched and bubbled from the heat then soaked by the firefighters. The wallpaper was falling down in places, revealing large patches of old green paint behind it, and Claire remarked dryly that she wasn't sure which was uglier and more deserving of this fate. "I'm glad you can laugh about it," Dylan said as he put an arm around her shoulders. "I'm not sure I could."

"You didn't find a dead baby in your wall. It tends to colour your attachment to a place."

"What's that?" Dylan asked as he moved, curious, toward the wall beside the closet door. A piece of the wallpaper had fallen away, and if one had an eye for detail as Dylan had you could just make out letters scratched into the wall. Dylan pulled at the paper until he'd cleared a patch the size of a tombstone, then read the words etched into the plaster:

Here lies Uta Keller,
born of my daughter,
sired by my husband,
killed by his hand
and my cowardice.
May God and Elisabeth forgive me
for the crimes I witnessed and documented
but never revealed.

Therese Keller
July 16, 1971

"So he did kill her. Only it's too late now, isn't it?" Claire pondered as she ran her fingers over the epitaph. "What are you doing?" she asked next when she saw Dylan pull out his cellphone.

"I'm calling Forensics. This needs to be documented and removed."

"But what's the point? Keller's never going to trial. His victims are never going to get justice."

"That's not relevant, Claire. This is crucial evidence and it closes the case. And his victims don't need justice anymore: they've been freed. Ta'ah once told me that fire purifies everything. It has cleared this house of all the evil and negative energy that was within it and released any trapped souls. It's a clean slate, Claire, for you to build upon."

"For *us* to build upon," she corrected him, wrapping her arms around him and keeping him close as he called Ident with the news.

☙

Claire plopped down on the blanket she was sharing with Dylan's aunt

Sylvie and handed her one-half of a popsicle. Over the last six weeks Claire's wounds had healed nicely with the help of Ta'ah's medicine, and the lovers had settled into an easy co-existence that belied the cramped quarters of Dylan's apartment, though Claire joked it probably had more to do with the fact that she had arrived without any luggage. Their days were filled with practical matters, which for Claire meant dealing with the insurance company, shopping for essentials, and meeting with the builder of her new home, and which for Dylan meant his job: McTavish had forgiven his wayward officer after experiencing a peculiar dream in which an old Native woman had gently washed away his anger, a dream he'd found oddly erotic; and upon waking he had reached for his wife.

Evenings were filled with dinners out or a DVD and a home-cooked meal, leisurely bouts of lovemaking, and endless hours of talking. Claire insisted Dylan tell her about his work, which he did but leaving out the more gruesome details of the murders despite Claire's insistence that *hearing* about them was far removed from actually *seeing* them. So he capitulated, recounting the details of the prostitute whose body had been found in a flop house disembowelled, the insects in her belly determining how long she'd been there, whereupon Claire promptly threw up. When she threw up again the next morning Dylan pressed a cold washcloth to her face and said under no circumstances would he indulge her curiosity again.

The cost of rebuilding the house exceeded the limits of Claire's insurance by a small margin, but the adjuster allotted a credit for the new windows. The architect designed the kitchen to incorporate the cupboards already ordered and paid for, which was also credited toward the cost of rebuilding, and when all was done and dusted Claire was just about even. The additional cost of adding a basement she funded with her original renovation budget, refusing Dylan's offer to pay for that out of his savings and investments. "You saved my life," she had pronounced, putting the argument to rest, "the least you deserve is a basement."

They were at Ta'ah's today under a hot sun, Dylan playing three on three with a handful of cousins and nephews while Claire and Sylvie cheered and jeered from the sidelines. "You suck, Jason," Claire called out when Jeremiah scored a basket against Dylan.

"That's Jeremiah," Sylvie corrected Claire. "Jason's the shorter one."

Claire sighed. "How on earth am I ever going to remember everybody's names? There's so *many* of you."

"Just do what I do," Sylvie replied with a chuckle. "Point and say, 'Hey you. Yeah you. You know who I'm talking about.' And if they give you a smart reply, you clip them on the side of the head and say, 'Mind your elders.'"

Claire laughed. She was never happier than when she visited Ta'ah with Dylan. There was so much love and laughter here that anytime Claire felt burdened by past events she only had to come bake a pie with Ta'ah or help tend her herb garden and the tension melted away faster than the popsicle Claire was struggling to keep from dripping all over her T-shirt. "Did Dylan ever tell you the cock story?" Sylvie asked.

"No, what's the cock story?"

"Well," Sylvie said with a puckish grin on her face, "Dylan was six and had just started school with his best friend, Andy. One day they're eavesdropping on the older boys in the locker room after gym and they hear them all boasting, 'My cock's bigger than your cock.' Poor Dylan and Andy, they don't know what this is. So they ask Sister Henderson, 'Sister Henderson, what's a cock?' Sister Henderson, she turns all red then says, 'Why it's just a male chicken, a rooster. And don't you be using that word again.'

"So now it's the following Sunday and there's a potluck after church, and Ta'ah's made her famous fried chicken. Dylan and Andy are sitting across from Ta'ah, slowly eating the thighs, and Ta'ah's thinking they're behaving a little strangely because with each bite they're slowly chewing and looking up at the ceiling like they've never eaten chicken before and can't quite place the taste. Then Dylan turns to Ta'ah and in a voice as loud and clear as a bell says, 'Ta'ah, what does cock taste like? Is it the same as chicken?'" Claire roared with laughter and fell onto her back. "Ta'ah turns all red," Sylvie continued between fits of giggles, "and my father's laughing so hard he falls out of his chair and bruises his hip real bad. Bothered him every time it rained after that but he always said the pain was worth it for the memory."

At the sound of the women's laughter Ta'ah looked up from her garden where she was picking sage, and smiled. She adored Claire, and was happy for her grandson whose spirit had been soaring these past weeks. And then in her peripheral vision Ta'ah saw a spirit a few feet away, squatting down and exploring the herbs. The spirit was presented as a little girl, about four years old Ta'ah guessed, dark-haired and long-legged, and the fingers that patted the herbs were long and slender like a piano player's. "Hello, child," said Ta'ah. "What brings you to my garden?"

The little girl looked up, consternation in her bright emerald eyes. "Bear says it's time," she answered matter-of-factly, looking away toward the edge of the yard. "She says I'm ready now." Ta'ah followed the girl's gaze and saw Bear sitting on her haunches in front of the medicine hut, watching. "But I'm scared it will hurt again."

"You were very brave to give your life to save your mother's," Ta'ah said gently. "Very brave. But you don't have to be brave this time. This time you will be wanted and loved very much. Bear has chosen well for you."

The girl didn't reply but put her head down again and continued exploring the herbs. "These are pretty."

"I shall teach you all about them when you're old enough," Ta'ah promised.

"Okay," the girl replied, sighing.

"So tell me, child," Ta'ah asked in a soothing voice, "what shall we call you when you join us again in this world? I can't imagine you'll want to be called Baby Jane."

The girl pondered this a moment then replied, "I like your name. I want to be called Sarah, too."

"Then Sarah Two we shall call you," Ta'ah chuckled, tickled by her pun. "Now, Sarah Two, you had better get a move on before someone steals your place."

Sarah Two's head shot up, her eyes wide with surprise. "Someone can *do* that?" she asked.

"They can," said Ta'ah. "So you best decide quickly."

Sarah Two looked anxiously over at Bear, who motioned with her head toward Claire and let out a reassuring growl. Sarah Two looked back at Ta'ah, then at Bear again, trying to make up her mind. A moment passed and then, summoning her courage, Sarah Two picked herself up, took a deep, deep breath, cast one last fearful glance at Ta'ah, then ran toward the blanket—and disappeared into Claire.

CR

Claire sat at the river's edge and gazed out over the water. She was squatting on all fours, and when she looked down she saw not her hands but thick, furry paws. Curious, she peered into a shallow pool where the current didn't flow and saw in the watery reflection a lioness, majestic and proud, her peridot eyes sparkling in the sun. She raised a shapely, graceful limb and slapped the water with her paw and this time her reflection remained in the concentric ripples.

"We meet again, my Lady," said Bear in salutation as she ambled up beside Claire.

"Bear, what do you see, there, in the water?" asked Claire.

"I see a woman who knows she's a lioness," replied Bear.

"Hmmm, yes," murmured Claire with a wry smile. "Most curious, don't you think?"

M.A. Demers is a freelance writer and fine art photographer. She currently resides near Vancouver, British Columbia, Canada.
You can connect with her on:
her website, www.mademers.com
her blog, www.mademers.com/bad_egg
and on Facebook (tinyurl.com/4kckenf).

8172859R0

Made in the USA
Charleston, SC
15 May 2011